About

New York Times and *USA Today* ~~~
Barbara Dunlop has written more than fifty novels for
Mills & Boon, including the acclaimed Gambling Men
series for Mills & Boon Desire. Her sexy, light-hearted
stories regularly hit bestsellers lists. Barbara is a four-time
finalist for the Romance Writers of America's *RITA*® award.

Karen Booth is a Midwestern girl transplanted in the
South, raised on '80s music and way too many readings
of *Forever* by Judy Blume. Married to her real-life Jake
Ryan, she has two amazing kids with epic hair, a very
bratty cat, and loves getting up before dawn to write
romance. With plenty of sparks.

A typical Piscean, award-winning *USA Today* bestselling
author **Yvonne Lindsay** has always preferred the stories
in her head to the real world. Married to her blind-date
sweetheart and with two adult children, she spends her
days crafting the stories of her heart and loves to read
or travel when she's not working. Yvonne loves to hear
from readers, contact her via yvonnelindsay.com or
Facebook.com/YvonneLindsayAuthor

A Christmas Seduction

BARBARA DUNLOP

KAREN BOOTH

YVONNE LINDSAY

MILLS & BOON

First Published in Great Britain 2023
By Mills & Boon, an imprint of HarperCollins*Publishers* Ltd,
1 London Bridge Street, London, SE1 9GF

www.harpercollins.co.uk

HarperCollins*Publishers*
Macken House, 39/40 Mayor Street Upper,
Dublin 1, D01 C9W8, Ireland

ISBN: 978-0-263-32112-8

This book is produced from independently certified FSC™ paper
to ensure responsible forest management.

For more information visit: www.harpercollins.co.uk/green

Printed and Bound in the UK using 100% Renewable Electricity
at CPI Group (UK) Ltd, Croydon, CR0 4YY

TWELVE NIGHTS OF TEMPTATION

BARBARA DUNLOP

For Jane Porter

One

A banging on Tasha Lowell's bedroom door jarred her awake. It was midnight in the Whiskey Bay Marina staff quarters, and she'd been asleep for less than an hour.

"Tasha?" Marina owner Matt Emerson's voice was a further jolt to her system, since she'd been dreaming about him.

"What is it?" she called out, then realized he'd never hear her sleep-croaky voice. "What?" she called louder as she forced herself from beneath the covers.

It might be unseasonably warm on the Pacific Northwest coast, but it was still December, the holiday season, and the eight-unit staff quarters building had been around since the '70s.

"*Orca's Run* broke down off Tyree, Oregon."

"What happened?" she asked reflexively as she crossed the cold wooden floor on her bare feet. Even as she said the words, she knew it was a foolish question. Wealthy, urbane Matt Emerson wouldn't know an injector pump from an alternator.

She swung the door open, coming face-to-face with the object of what she suddenly remembered had been a very R-rated dream.

"The engine quit. Captain Johansson says they're anchored in the bay."

This was very bad news. Tasha had been chief mechanic at Whiskey Bay Marina for less than two weeks, and she knew Matt had hesitated in giving her the promotion. He'd be right to hold her responsible for not noticing a problem with *Orca's Run*'s engine or not anticipating some kind of wear and tear.

"I serviced it right before they left." She knew how important this particular charter was to the company.

Orca's Run was a ninety-foot yacht, the second largest in the fleet. It had been chartered by Hans Reinstead, an influential businessman out of Munich. Matt had recently spent considerable effort and money getting a toehold in the European market, and Hans was one of his first major clients. The last thing Whiskey Bay Marina needed was for the Reinstead family to have a disappointing trip.

Tasha grabbed the red plaid button-down shirt she'd discarded on a chair and put it on over her T-shirt. Then she stepped into a pair of heavy cargo pants, zipping them over her flannel shorts.

Matt watched her progress as she popped a cap on top of her braided hair. Socks and work boots took her about thirty seconds, and she was ready.

"That's it?" he asked.

"What?" She didn't understand the question.

"You're ready to go?"

She glanced down at herself, then looked back into the dim bedroom. "I'm ready." The necessities that most women carried in a purse were in the zipped pockets of her pants.

For some reason, he gave a crooked smile. "Then let's go."

"What's funny?" she asked as she fell into step beside him.

"Nothing."

They started down the wooden walkway that led to the Whiskey Bay Marina pier.

"You're laughing," she said.

"I'm not."

"You're laughing at me." Did she look that bad rolling straight out of bed? She rubbed her eyes, lifted her cap to smooth her hair and tried to shake some more sense into her brain.

"I'm smiling. It's not the same thing."

"I've amused you." Tasha hated to be amusing. She

wanted people, especially men, *especially* her employer, to take her seriously.

"You impressed me."

"By getting dressed?"

"By being efficient."

She didn't know what to say to that. It wasn't quite sexist…maybe…

She let it drop.

They went single file down the ramp with him in the lead.

"What are we taking?" she asked.

"Monty's Pride."

The answer surprised her. *Monty's Pride* was the biggest yacht in the fleet, a 115-footer, refurbished last year to an impeccably high standard. It was obvious what Matt intended to do.

"Do you think we'll need to replace *Orca's Run*?" She'd prefer to be optimistic and take the repair boat instead. *Monty's Pride* would burn an enormous amount of fuel getting to Tyree. "There's a good chance I can fix whatever's gone wrong."

"And if you can't?"

"What did the captain say happened?" She wasn't ready to admit defeat before they'd even left the marina.

"That it quit."

It was a pathetic amount of information.

"Did it stop all of a sudden?" she asked. "Did it slow? Was there any particular sound, a smell? Was there smoke?"

"I didn't ask."

"You should have asked."

Matt shot her a look of impatience, and she realized she'd stepped over the line. He was her boss after all.

"I'm just thinking that taking *Monty's Pride* is a whole lot of fuel to waste," she elaborated on her thinking. "We can save the money if I can do a quick repair."

"We're not even going to try a quick repair. I'll move the

passengers and crew over to *Monty's Pride* while you fix whatever's gone wrong."

Tasha hated that her possible negligence would cost the company so much money. "Maybe if I talk to the captain on the radio."

"I don't want to mess around, Tasha." Matt punched in the combination for the pier's chain-link gate and swung it open.

"I'm not asking you to mess around. I'm suggesting we explore our options. *Monty's Pride* burns a hundred gallons an hour."

"My priority is customer service."

"This is expensive customer service."

"Yes, it is."

His tone was flat, and she couldn't tell if he was angry or not.

She wished she was back in her dream. Matt had been so nice in her dream. They'd been warm, cocooned together, and he'd been joking, stroking her hair, kissing her mouth.

Wait. No. That was bad. That wasn't what she wanted at all.

"I want Hans Reinstead to go back to Germany a happy man," Matt continued. "I want him to rave to his friends and business associates about the over-the-top service he received, even when there was a problem. Whether we fix it in five minutes or five hours is irrelevant. They had a breakdown, and we upgraded them. People love an upgrade. So much so, that they're generally willing to gloss over the reason for getting it."

Tasha had to admit it was logical. It was expensive, but it was also logical.

Matt might be willing to take the financial hit in the name of customer service, but if it turned out to be something she'd missed, it would be a black mark against her.

They approached the slip where *Monty's Pride* was moored. A crew member was on deck while another was on the wharf, ready to cast off.

"Fuel?" Matt asked the young man on deck.

"Three thousand gallons."

"That'll do," Matt said as he crossed the gangway to the stern of the main deck.

Tasha followed. *Monty's Pride*'s twin diesel engines rumbled beneath them.

"Is my toolbox on board?" she asked.

"We put it in storage."

"Thanks." While they crossed the deck, she reviewed *Orca's Run*'s engine service in her mind. Had she missed something, a belt or a hose? She thought she'd checked them all. But nobody's memory was infallible.

"It could be as simple as a belt," she said to Matt.

"That will be good news." He made his way to the bridge, and she followed close behind.

She had to give it one last shot, so as soon as they were inside, she went for the radio, dialing in the company frequency. "*Orca's Run*, this is *Monty's Pride*. Captain, are you there?"

While she did that, he slid open the side window and called out to the hand to cast off.

She keyed the mike again. "Come in, *Orca's Run*."

Matt brought up the revs and pulled away from the pier.

Matt knew he had taken a gamble by using *Monty's Pride* instead of the repair boat, but so far it looked like it had been the right call. Two hours into the trip down the coast, even Tasha had been forced to admit a quick fix wasn't likely. She'd had Captain Johansson walk her through a second-by-second rehash of the engine failure over the radio, asking him about sounds, smells and warning lights. Then she had him send a deckhand back and forth from the engine room for a visual inspection and to relay details.

He'd been impressed by her thorough, methodical approach. But in the end, she concluded that she needed to check the engine herself. There was nothing to do for the next three hours but make their way to Tyree.

It was obvious she was ready to blame herself.

But even if the breakdown turned out to be her fault, it wasn't the end of the world. And they didn't even know what had happened. It was way too early to start pointing fingers.

"You should lie down for a while," he told her.

She looked tired, and there was no point in both of them staying up all night.

"I'm fine." She lifted her chin, gazing out the windshield into the starry night.

There were clusters of lights along the shore, only a few other ships in the distance, and his GPS and charts were top-notch. It was an easy chore to pilot the boat single-handed.

"You don't have to keep me company."

"And you don't have to coddle me."

"You have absolutely nothing to prove, Tasha." He knew she took pride in her work, and he knew she was determined to do a good job after her promotion. But sleep deprivation wasn't a job requirement.

"I'm not trying to prove anything. Did you get any sleep at all? Do you want to lie down?"

"I'm fine." He knew she was perfectly capable of piloting the boat, but he'd feel guilty leaving all the work to her.

"No need for us both to stay awake," she said.

"My date ended early. I slept a little."

Since his divorce had been finalized, Matt and his friend TJ Bauer had hit the Olympia social circuit. They were pushing each other to get out and meet new people. They met a few women, most were nice, but he hadn't felt a spark with any of them, including the one he'd taken out tonight. He'd come home early, done a little Christmas shopping online for his nieces and nephews and dozed off on the sofa.

"You don't need to tell me about your dates," Tasha said.

"There's nothing to tell."

"Well, that's too bad." Her tone was lighter. It sounded like she was joking. "It might help pass the time."

"Sorry," he said lightly in return. "I wish I could be more entertaining. What about you?" he asked.

As he voiced the question, he found himself curious about Tasha's love life. Did she have a boyfriend? Did she date? She was always such a no-nonsense fixture at the marina, he didn't think of her beyond being a valued employee.

"What about me?" she asked.

"Do you ever go out?"

"Out where?"

"Out, out. On-a-date out. Dinner, dancing…"

She scoffed out a laugh.

"Is that a no?"

"That's a no."

"Why not?" Now he was really curious. She might dress in plain T-shirts and cargo pants, but underneath what struck him now as a disguise, she was a lovely woman. "Don't you like to dress up? Do you ever dress up?"

He tried to remember if he'd ever seen her in anything stylish. He couldn't, and he was pretty sure he'd remember.

She shifted on the swivel chair, angling toward him. "Why the third degree?"

"Since stories of my dates won't distract us, I thought maybe yours could." He found himself scrutinizing her face from an objective point of view.

She had startling green eyes, the vivid color of emeralds or a glacial, deep-water pond. They were framed in thick lashes. Her cheekbones were high. Her chin was the perfect angle. Her nose was narrow, almost delicate. And her lips were deep coral, the bottom slightly fuller than the top.

He wanted to kiss them.

"Nothing to tell," she said. Her voice jolted him back to reality, and he turned to the windshield, rewinding the conversation.

"You must dress up sometimes."

"I prefer to focus on work."

"Why?"

"Because it's satisfying." Her answer didn't ring true.

He owned the company, and he still found time for a social life. "I dress up. I date. I still find time to work."

She made a motion with her hand, indicating up and down his body. "Of course you date. A guy like you is definitely going to date."

He had no idea what she meant. "A guy like me?"

"Good-looking. Rich. Eligible."

"Good-looking?" He was surprised that she thought so, even more surprised that she'd said so.

She rolled her eyes. "It's not me, Matt. The world thinks you're good-looking. Don't pretend you've never noticed."

He'd never given it much thought. Looks were so much a matter of taste. He was fairly average. He'd never thought there was anything wrong with being average.

"I'm eligible now," he said.

The rich part was also debatable. He hadn't had enough money to satisfy his ex-wife. And now that they'd divorced, he had even less. He'd borrowed money to pay her out, and he was going to have to work hard over the next year or two to get back to a comfortable financial position.

"And so are you," he said to Tasha. "You're intelligent, hardworking and pretty. You should definitely be out there dating."

He couldn't help but compare her with the women he'd met lately. The truth was, they couldn't hold a candle to her. There was so much about her that was compelling. Funny that he'd never noticed before.

"Dazzle them with your intelligence and hard work."

"Can we not do this?" she asked.

"Make conversation?"

"I'm a licensed marine mechanic. And I want people to take me seriously as that."

"You can't do both?"

"Not in my experience." She slipped down from the high white leather chair.

"What are you doing?" he asked. He didn't want her to leave.

"I'm going to take your advice."

"What advice is that?"

"I'm going to lie down and rest." She glanced at her watch. "You think two hours?"

"I didn't mean to chase you away."

"You didn't."

"We don't have to talk about dating." But then he took in her pursed lips and realized he still wanted to kiss them. Where was this impulse coming from?

"I have work to do when we get there."

He realized he'd be selfish to stop her. "You're right. You should get some sleep."

As she walked away, he considered the implications of being attracted to an employee. He couldn't act on it. He shouldn't act on it.

Then he laughed at himself. It wasn't like she'd given him any encouragement. Well, other than saying he was good-looking.

She thought he was good-looking.

As he piloted his way along the dark coastline, he couldn't help but smile.

Tasha's problem wasn't dating in general. Her problem was the thought of dating Matt. He wasn't her type. There was no way he was her type. She knew that for an absolute fact.

She'd dated guys like him before—capable, confident, secure in the knowledge that the world rolled itself out at their feet. She knew all that. Still, she couldn't seem to stop herself from dreaming about him.

They'd arrived off Tyree and boarded *Orca's Run* shortly

after dawn. Tall and confident, he'd greeted the clients like he owned the place—which he did, of course.

Tasha had kept to the background, making sure her tool-box was moved discreetly on board, while Matt had charmed the family, apologizing for the delay in the trip, offering *Monty's Pride* as a replacement, explaining that the larger, faster yacht would easily make up the time they'd lost overnight.

It was obvious the client was delighted with the solution, and Tasha had turned her attention to the diesel engine. It took her over an hour to discover the water separator was the problem. In an unlikely coincidence, the water-in-fuel indicator light bulb had also broken. Otherwise, it would have alerted her to the fact that the water separator was full, starving the engine of fuel.

The two things happening together were surprising. They were more than surprising. They were downright strange.

From their anchorage in Tyree, Matt had taken the launch and run for parts in the small town. And by noon, she'd replaced the water separator. While she'd worked, she'd cataloged who'd had access to *Orca's Run*. Virtually all the staff of Whiskey Bay Marina had access. But most of them didn't know anything about engines.

There were a couple of contract mechanics who did repairs from time to time. And there were countless customers who had been on the property. She found her brain going in fantastical directions, imagining someone might have purposely damaged the engine.

But who? And why? And was she being ridiculously paranoid?

She had no idea.

While she'd worked, diesel fuel had sprayed her clothes and soaked into her hair, so she'd used the staff shower to clean up and commandeered a steward's uniform from the supply closet.

After cleaning up, her mind still pinging from possibility to possibility, she made her way up the stairs to the main cabin. There she was surprised to realize the yacht wasn't yet under way.

"Did something else go wrong?" she asked Matt, immediately worried they had another problem.

He was in the galley instead of piloting the yacht. The deckhand had stayed with *Monty's Pride*, since the bigger ship needed an extra crew member. Matt and Tasha were fully capable of returning *Orca's Run* to Whiskey Bay.

"It's all good," Matt said.

"We're not under power?" Her hair was still damp, and she tucked it behind her ears as she approached the countertop that separated the galley from the main living area.

"Are you hungry?" he asked, placing a pan on the stove.

She was starving. "Sure. But I can eat something on the way."

"Coffee?"

"Sure."

He extracted two cups from a cupboard and poured. "*Monty's Pride* is headed south. Everyone seems happy."

"You were right," she admitted as she rounded the counter. "Bringing *Monty's Pride* was a good idea. I can cook if you want to get going."

He gave a thoughtful nod. "This charter matters."

"Because it's a German client?"

"It's the first significant booking out of the fall trade show. He's a prominent businessman with loads of connections."

"I'm sorry I argued with you." She realized her stance had been about her pride, not about the good of the company.

"You should always say what you think."

"I should listen, too."

"You don't listen?"

"Sometimes I get fixated on my own ideas." She couldn't help but revisit her theory about someone tampering with the engine.

Matt gave a smile. "You have conviction. That's not a bad thing. Besides, it keeps the conversation interesting."

He handed her a cup of coffee.

She took a sip, welcoming the hit of caffeine.

He seemed to ponder her for a moment. "You definitely keep things interesting."

She didn't know how to respond.

His blue eyes were dark but soft, and he had an incredibly handsome face. His chin was square, unshaven and slightly shadowed, but that only made him look more rugged. His nose was straight, his jaw angular and his lips were full, dark pink, completely kissable.

Warm waves of energy seemed to stream from him to cradle her. It was disconcerting, and she shifted to put some more space between them. "The engine was interesting."

Mug to his lips, he lifted his brow.

"The odds of the water separator filling and the indicator light going at the same time are very low."

His brow furrowed then, and he lowered the mug. "And?"

"Recognizing that this is my first idea, and that I can sometimes get fixated on those, it seems wrong to me. I mean, it seems odd to me."

"Are you saying someone broke something on purpose?"

"No, I'm not saying that." Out loud, it sounded even less plausible than it had inside her head. "I'm saying it was a bizarre coincidence, and I must be having a run of bad luck."

"You fixed it, so that's good luck."

"Glass half-full?"

"You did a good job, Tasha."

"It wasn't that complicated."

A teasing glint came into his eyes. "You mean, you're that skilled?"

"The cause was peculiar." She could have sworn she'd just serviced the water separator. "The repair was easy."

Their gazes held, and they fell silent again. Raindrops clattered against the window, while the temperature seemed to inch up around her. Her dream came back once again, Matt cradling her, kissing her. Heat rose in her cheeks.

She forced herself back to the present, trying to keep her mind on an even keel. "It could have been excess water in the fuel, maybe a loose cap. I did check it. At least I think I checked it. I always check it." She paused. "I hope I checked it."

He set down his mug. "Don't."

She didn't understand.

He took a step forward. "Don't second-guess yourself."

"Okay." It seemed like the easiest answer, since she was losing track of the conversation.

He took another step, and then another.

Inside her head, she shouted for him to stop. But she didn't make a sound.

She didn't want him to stop. She could almost feel his arms around her.

He was right there.

Thunder suddenly cracked through the sky above them. A wave surged beneath them, and she grabbed for the counter. She missed, stumbling into his chest.

In a split second, his arms were around her, steadying her.

She fought the desire that fogged her brain. "Sorry."

"Weather's coming up," he said, his deep voice rumbling in her ear and vibrating her chest, which was pressed tight against his.

"We won't be—" Words failed her as she looked into his blue eyes, so close, so compelling.

He stilled, the sapphire of his eyes softening to summer sky.

"Tasha." Her name was barely a breath on his lips.

She softened against him.

He lowered his lips, closer and closer. They brushed lightly against hers, then they firmed, then they parted, and the kiss sent bolts of pleasure ricocheting through her.

She gripped his shoulders to steady herself. A rational part of her brain told her to stop. But she was beyond stopping.

She was beyond caring about anything but the cataclysmic kiss between them.

It was Matt who finally pulled back.

He looked as dazed as she felt, and he blew out a breath. "I'm…" He gave his head a little shake. "I don't know what to say."

She forced herself to step back. "Don't." She had no idea what to say either. "Don't try. It was just…something…that happened."

"It was something," he said.

"It was a mistake."

He raked a hand through his short hair. "It sure wasn't on purpose."

"We should get going," she said, anxious to focus on something else.

The last thing she wanted to do was dissect their kiss. The last thing she wanted to do was admit how it impacted her. The last thing she wanted her boss to know was that she saw him as a man, more than a boss.

She couldn't do that. She had to stop doing it. In this relationship, she was a mechanic, not a woman.

"We're not going anywhere." He looked pointedly out the window where the rain was driving down.

Tasha took note of the pitching floor beneath her.

It was Matt who reached for the marine radio and turned the dial to get a weather report.

"We might as well grab something to eat," he said. "This could last awhile."

Two

Waiting out the storm, Matt had fallen asleep in the living area. He awoke four hours later to find Tasha gone, and he went looking.

The yacht was rocking up and down on six-foot swells, and rain clattered against the windows. He couldn't find her on the upper decks, so he took the narrow staircase, making his way to the engine and mechanical rooms. Sure enough, he found her there. She'd removed the front panel of the generator and was elbow deep in the mechanics.

"What are you doing?" he asked.

She tensed at the sound of his voice. She was obviously remembering their kiss. Well, he remembered it, too, and it sure made him tense up. Partly because he was her boss and he felt guilty for letting things get out of hand. But partly because it had been such an amazing kiss and he desperately wanted to do it again.

"Maintenance," she answered him without turning.

He settled his shoulder against the doorjamb. "Can you elaborate?"

"I inspected the electric and serviced the batteries. Some of the battery connections needed cleaning. Hoses and belts all look good in here. But it was worth changing the oil filter."

"I thought you would sleep."

This was above and beyond the call of duty for anyone. He'd known Tasha was a dedicated employee, but this trip was teaching him she was one in a million.

She finally turned to face him. "I did sleep. Then I woke up."

She'd found a pair of coveralls somewhere. They were miles too big, but she'd rolled up the sleeves and the pant legs. A woman shouldn't look sexy with a wrench in her hand, a smudge of oil on her cheek, swimming in a shapeless steel gray sack.

But this one did. And he wanted to do a whole lot more than kiss her. He mentally shook away the feelings.

"If it was me—" he tried to lighten the mood and put her at ease "—I think I might have inspected the liquor cabinet."

She smiled for the briefest of seconds. "Lucky your employees aren't like you."

The smile warmed him. It turned him on, but it also made him happy.

"True enough," he said. "But there is a nice cognac in there. Perfect to have on a rainy afternoon." He could picture them doing just that.

Instead of answering, she returned to work.

He watched for a few minutes, struggling with his feelings, knowing he had to put their relationship back on an even keel.

Work—he needed to say something about work instead of sharing a cozy drink.

"Are you trying to impress me?" he asked.

She didn't pause. "Yes."

"I'm impressed."

"Good."

"You should stop working."

"I'm not finished."

"You're making me feel guilty."

She looked his way and rolled her eyes. "I'm not trying to make you feel guilty."

"Then what?"

"The maintenance needed doing. I was here. There was an opportunity."

He fought an urge to close the space between them. "Are you always like this?"

"Like what?"

"I don't know, überindustrious?"

"You say that like it's a bad thing."

He did move closer. He shouldn't, couldn't, *wouldn't* bring up their kiss. But he desperately wanted to bring it up, discuss it, dissect it, relive it. How did she feel about it now? Was she angry? Was there a chance in the world she wanted to do it again?

"It's an unnerving thing," he said.

"Then, you're very easily unnerved."

He couldn't help but smile at her comeback. "I'm trying to figure you out."

"Well, that's a waste of time."

"I realize I don't know you well."

"You don't need to know me well. Just sign my paycheck."

Well, that was a crystal clear signal. He was her boss, nothing more. He swallowed his disappointment.

Then again, if he was her boss, he was her boss. He reached forward to take the wrench from her hand. "It's after five and it's a Saturday and you're done."

Their fingers touched. Stupid mistake. He felt a current run up the center of his arm.

Her grip tightened on the wrench as she tried to tug it from his grasp. "Let it go."

"It's time to clock out."

"Seriously, Matt. I'm not done yet."

His hand wrapped around hers, and his feet took him closer still.

"Matt." There was a warning in her voice, but then their gazes caught and held.

Her eyes turned moss green, deep and yielding. She was feeling something. She had to be feeling something.

She used her free hand to grasp his arm. Her grip was strong, stronger than he'd imagined. He liked that.

"We can't do this, Matt."

"I know."

She swallowed, and her voice seemed strained. "So let go."

"I want to kiss you again."

"It's a bad idea."

"You're right." His disappointment was acute. "It is."

She didn't step back, and her lips parted as she drew in a breath. "We need to keep it simple, straightforward."

"Why?"

"The signature on my paycheck."

"Is that the only reason?" It was valid. But he was curious. He was intensely curious.

"I'm not that kind of girl."

He knew she didn't mean to be funny, but he couldn't help but joke. "The kind that kisses men?"

"The kind that randomly kisses my boss—or any coworker for that matter—while I'm working, in an engine room, covered in grease."

"That's fair."

"You bet, it's fair. Not that I need your approval. Now, let go of my hand."

He glanced down, realizing they were still touching. The last thing he wanted to do was let her go. But he had no choice.

She set down the wrench, replacing it with a screwdriver. Then she lifted the generator panel and put it in place.

He moved away and braced a hand on a crossbeam above his head. "The storm's letting up."

"Good." The word sounded final. Matt didn't want it to be final.

He was her boss, sure. He understood that was a complication. But did it have to be a deal breaker? But he wanted to get to know her. He'd barely scratched the surface, and he liked her a lot.

They'd brought *Orca's Run* back to the marina, arriving late in the evening.

Tasha had spent the night and half of today attempting to purge Matt's kiss from her mind. It wasn't working. She kept reliving the pleasure, then asking herself what it all meant.

She didn't even know how she felt, never mind how Matt felt. He was a smooth-talking, great-looking man who, from everything she'd seen, could have any woman in the world. What could possibly be his interest in her?

Okay, maybe if she'd taken her mother's advice, maybe if she'd acted like a woman, dressed like a woman and got a different job, maybe then it would make sense for Matt to be interested. Matt reminded her so much of the guys she'd known in Boston, the ones who'd dated her sisters and attended all the parties.

They'd all wanted women who were super feminine. They'd been amused by Tasha. She wasn't a buddy and she wasn't, in their minds, a woman worth pursuing. She hadn't fit in anywhere. It was the reason she'd left. And now Matt was confusing her. She hated being confused.

So, right now, this afternoon, she had a new focus.

Since she'd been promoted, she had to replace herself. Matt employed several general dock laborers who also worked as mechanical assistants, and they pulled in mechanical specialists when necessary. But one staff mechanic couldn't keep up with the workload at Whiskey Bay. Matt owned twenty-four boats in all, ranging from *Monty's Pride* right down to a seventeen-foot runabout they used in the bay. Some were workboats, but most were pleasure craft available for rental.

Cash flow was a definite issue, especially after Matt's divorce. It was more important than ever that the yachts stay in good working order to maximize rentals.

Tasha was using a vacant office in the main marina building at the edge of the company pier. The place was a sprawling, utilitarian building, first constructed in 1970, with major additions built in 2000 and 2010. Its clay-colored steel siding protected against the wind and salt water.

Inside, the client area was nicely decorated, as were Matt's and the sales manager's offices. But down the hall, where the offices connected to the utility areas and eventually to the boat garage and the small dry dock, the finishing was more Spartan. Even still, she felt pretentious sitting behind a wooden desk with a guest chair in front.

She'd been through four applicants so far. One and two were nonstarters. They were handymen rather than certified marine mechanics. The third one had his certification, but something about him made Tasha cautious. He was a little too eager to list his accomplishments. He was beyond self-confident, bordering on arrogant. She didn't see him fitting in at Whiskey Bay.

The fourth applicant had been five minutes late. Not a promising start.

But then a woman appeared in the doorway. "My apologies," she said in a rush as she entered.

Tasha stood. "Alex Dumont?"

"Yes." The woman smiled broadly as she moved forward, holding out her hand.

Tasha shook it, laughing at herself for having made the assumption that Alex was a man.

"Alexandria," the woman elaborated, her eyes sparkling with humor.

"Of all people, I shouldn't make gender assumptions."

"It happens so often, I don't even think about it."

"I hear you," Tasha said. "Please, sit down."

"At least with the name Tasha nobody makes that mistake." Alex settled into the chair. "Though I have to imagine you've been written off a few times before they even met you."

"I'm not sure which is worse," Tasha said.

"I prefer the surprise value. That's why I shortened my name. I have to say this is the first time I've been interviewed by a woman."

Alex was tall, probably about five foot eight. She had wispy, wheat-blond hair, a few freckles and a pretty smile. If Tasha hadn't seen her résumé, she would have guessed she was younger than twenty-five.

"You're moving from Chicago?" Tasha asked, flipping through the three pages of Alex's résumé.

"I've already moved, three weeks ago."

"Any particular reason?" Tasha was hoping for someone who would stay in Whiskey Bay for the long term.

"I've always loved the West Coast. But mostly, it was time to make a break from the family."

Tasha could relate to that. "They didn't support your career choice?" she guessed.

"No." Alex gave a little laugh. "Quite the opposite. My father and two brothers are mechanics. They wouldn't leave me alone."

"Did you work with them?"

"At first. Then I got a job with another company. It didn't help. They still interrogated me every night and gave me advice on whatever repair I was undertaking."

"You lived with them?"

"Not anymore."

Tasha couldn't help contrasting their experiences. "I grew up in Boston. My parents wanted me to find a nice doctor or lawyer and become a wife instead of a mechanic. Though they probably would have settled for me being a landscape painter or a dancer."

"Any brothers and sisters?"

"Two sisters. Both married to lawyers." Tasha didn't like to dwell on her family. It had been a long time since she'd spoken to them. She stopped herself now, and went back to Alex's résumé. "At Schneider Marine, you worked on both gas and diesel engines?"

"Yes. Gas, anywhere from 120-horse outboards and up, and diesel, up to 550."

"Any experience on Broadmores?"

"Oh, yeah. Finicky buggers, those."

"We have two of them."

"Well, I've got their number."

Tasha couldn't help but smile. This was the kind of confidence she liked. "And you went to Riverside Tech?"

"I did. I finished my apprenticeship four years ago. I can get you a copy of my transcript if you need it."

Tasha shook her head. "I'm more interested in your recent experience. How much time on gasoline engines versus diesel?"

"More diesel, maybe seventy-five/twenty-five. Lots of service, plenty of rebuilds."

"Diagnostics?"

"I was their youngest mechanic, so I wasn't afraid of the new scan tools."

"You dive right in?" Tasha was liking Alex more and more as the interview went on.

"I dive right in."

"When can you start?"

Alex grinned. "Can you give me a few days to unpack?"

"Absolutely."

Both women came to their feet.

"Then, I'm in," Alex said.

Tasha shook her hand, excited at the prospect of another female mechanic in the company. "Welcome aboard."

Alex left, but a few minutes later, Tasha was still smiling when Matt came through the door.

"What?" he asked.

"What?" she returned, forcibly dampening her exhilaration at the sight of him.

She couldn't do this. She *wouldn't* do this. They had an employer-employee relationship, not a man-woman relationship.

"You're smiling," he said.

"I'm happy."

"About what?"

"I love my job."

"Is that all?"

"You don't think I love my job?" She did love it. And she had a feeling she'd love it even more with Alex around.

"I was hoping you were happy to see me."

"Matt." She put a warning in her voice.

"Are we going to just ignore it?"

She quickly closed the door to make sure nobody could overhear. "Yes, we're going to ignore it."

"By *it*, I mean our kiss."

She folded her arms over her chest and gave him a glare. "I know what you mean."

"Just checking," he said, looking dejected.

"Stop." She wasn't going to be emotionally manipulated.

"I'm not going to pretend. I miss you."

"There's nothing to miss. I'm right here."

"Prepared to talk work and only work."

"Yes."

He was silent for a moment. "Fine. Okay. I'll take it."

"Good." She knew with absolute certainty that it was for the best.

He squared his shoulders. "Who was that leaving?"

"That was Alex Dumont. She's our new mechanic."

Matt's brows went up. "We have a new mechanic?"

"You knew I was hiring one."

"But…"

Tasha couldn't help an inward sigh. She'd seen this reaction before. "But…she's a woman."

"That's not what I was going to say. I was surprised, is all."

"That she was light on testosterone?"

"You keep putting words in my mouth."

"Well, you keep putting expressions in your eyes."

He opened his mouth, but then he seemed to think better of whatever he'd planned to say.

"What?" she asked before she could stop herself.

"Nothing." He took a backward step. "I'm backing off. This is me backing off."

"From who I hire?"

Matt focused in on her eyes. His eyes smoldered, and she felt desire arc between them.

"I can feel it from here," he said, as if he was reading her mind.

Her brain stumbled. "There's…uh… I'm…"

"You can't quite spit out the lie, can you?"

She couldn't. Lying wouldn't help. "We have to ignore it."

"Why?"

"We do. We do, Matt."

There was a long beat of silence.

"I have a date Saturday night," he said.

A pain crossed her chest, but she steeled herself. "No kidding."

"I don't date that much."

"I don't pay any attention."

It was a lie. From the staff quarters, she'd seen him leave his house on the hill on many occasions, dressed to the nines. She'd often wondered where he'd gone, whom he'd been with, how late he'd come home.

And she'd watched him bring women to his house. They often dined on the deck. Caterers would set up candles and white linens, and then Matt and his date would chat and laugh the evening away.

She'd paid attention all right. But wild horses wouldn't drag the admission out of her.

So Saturday night, Matt had picked up the tall, willowy, expensively coiffed Emilie and brought her home for arctic char and risotto, catered by a local chef. They were dining in his glass-walled living room to candlelight and a full moon. The wine was from the Napa Valley, and the chocolate truffles were handcrafted with Belgian chocolate.

It should have been perfect. Emilie was a real estate company manager, intelligent, gracious, even a little bit funny. She was friendly and flirtatious, and made no secret of the fact that she expected a very romantic conclusion to the evening.

But Matt's gaze kept straying to the pier below, to the yachts, the office building and the repair shop. Finally, Tasha appeared. She strode briskly beneath the overhead lights, through the security gate and up the stairway that led to the staff quarters. Some of his staff members had families and houses in town. The younger, single crew members, especially those who had moved to Whiskey Bay to work at the marina, seemed to appreciate the free rent, even if the staff units were small and basic. He was happy at the moment that Tasha was one of them.

He reflexively glanced at his watch. It was nearly ten o'clock. Even for Tasha, this was late.

"Matt?" Emilie said.

"Yes?" He quickly returned his attention to her.

She gave a very pretty smile. "I asked if they were all yours?"

"All what?"

"The boats. Do you really own that many boats?"

"I do," he said. He'd told this story a hundred times. "I started with three about a decade ago. Business was good, so I gradually added to the fleet."

He glanced back to the pier, but Tasha had disappeared from view. He told himself not to be disappointed. He'd see her again soon. It had been a few days now since they'd run into each other. He'd tried not to miss her, but he did. He'd find a reason to talk to her tomorrow.

Emilie pointed toward the window. "That one is *huge*."

"*Monty's Pride* is our largest vessel."

"Could I see the inside?" she asked, eyes alight. "Would you give me a tour?"

Before Matt could answer, there was a pounding on his door.

"Expecting someone?" she asked, looking a little bit frustrated by the interruption.

His friends and neighbors, Caleb Watford and TJ Bauer, were the only people who routinely dropped by. But neither of them would knock. At most, they'd call out from the entryway if they thought they might walk in on something.

Matt rose. "I'll be right back."

"Sure." Emilie helped herself to another truffle. "I'll wait here."

The date had been going pretty well so far. But Matt couldn't say he was thrilled with the touch of sarcasm he'd just heard in Emilie's voice.

The knock came again as he got to the front entry. He swung open the door.

Tasha stood on his porch, her work jacket wrinkled, a blue baseball cap snug on her head and her work boots sturdy against the cool weather.

His immediate reaction was delight. He wanted to drag her inside and make her stay for a while.

"What's up?" he asked instead, remembering the promise he'd made, holding himself firmly at a respectful distance.

"Something's going on," she said.

"Between us?" he asked before he could stop himself, resisting the urge to glance back and be sure Emilie was still out of sight.

Tasha frowned. "*No*. With *Pacific Wind*." She named the single-engine twenty-eight-footer. "It's just a feeling. But I'm worried."

He stepped back and gestured for her to come inside.

She glanced down at her boots.

"Don't worry about it," he said. "I have a cleaning service."

"A cable broke on the steering system," she said.

"Is that a major problem?"

He didn't particularly care why she'd decided to come up and tell him in person. He was just glad she had.

It was the first time she'd been inside his house. He couldn't help but wonder if she liked the modern styling, the way it jutted out from the hillside, the clean lines, glass walls and unobstructed view. He really wanted to find out. He hadn't been interested in Emilie's opinion, but he was curious about Tasha's.

"It's not a big problem," she said. "I fixed it. It's fixed."

"That's good." He dared to hope all over again that this was a personal visit disguised as business.

"Matt?" came Emilie's voice.

He realized he'd forgotten all about her.

"I'll just be a minute," he called back to her.

"You're busy," Tasha said, looking instantly regretful. "Of course you're busy. I didn't think." She glanced at her watch. "This is Saturday, isn't it?"

"You forgot the day of the week?"

"Matt, honey." Emilie came up behind him.

Honey? Seriously? After a single date?

Not even a single date, really. The date hadn't concluded yet.

"Who's this?" Emilie asked.

There was a dismissive edge to her voice and judgment in her expression as she gave Tasha the once-over, clearly finding her lacking.

The superior attitude annoyed Matt. "This is Tasha."

"I'm the mechanic," Tasha said, not seeming remotely bothered by Emilie's condescension.

"Hmph," Emilie said, wrinkling her perfect nose. She wrapped her arm possessively through Matt's. "Is this an emergency?"

Tasha took a step back, opening her mouth to speak.

"Yes," Matt said. "It's an emergency. I'm afraid I'm going to have to cut our date short."

He wasn't sure who looked more surprised by his words, Emilie or Tasha.

"I'll call you a ride." He took out his phone.

It took Emilie a moment to find her voice. "What *kind* of emergency?"

"The mechanical kind," he said flatly, suddenly tired of her company.

He typed in the request. He definitely didn't want Tasha to leave.

"But—" Emilie began.

"The ride will be here in three minutes," he said. "I'll get your coat."

He did a quick check of Tasha's expression, steeling himself for the possibility that she'd speak up and out him as a liar.

She didn't.

He quickly retrieved Emilie's coat and purse.

"I don't mind waiting," Emilie said, a plaintive whine in her voice.

"I couldn't ask you to do that." He held up the coat.

"How long do you think—"

"Could be a long time. It could be a very long time. It's complicated."

"Matt, I can—" Tasha began.

"No. Nope." He gave a definitive shake to his head. "It's business. It's important." It might not be critical, but Tasha had never sought him out after hours before, so there had to be something going on.

"You're a *mechanic*?" Emilie asked Tasha.

"A marine mechanic."

"So you get all greasy and stuff?"

"Sometimes."

"That must be awful." Emilie gave a little shudder.

"Emilie." Matt put a warning tone in his voice.

She crooked her head back to look at him. "What? It's weird."

"It's not weird."

"It's unusual," Tasha said. "But women are up to nearly fifteen percent in the mechanical trades, higher when you look at statistics for those of us under thirty-five."

Emilie didn't seem to know what to say in response.

Matt's phone pinged.

"Your ride's here," he told Emilie, ushering her toward the door.

Tasha stood to one side, and he watched until Emilie got into the car.

"You didn't have to do that," Tasha said as he closed the door.

"It wasn't going well."

"In that case, I'm happy to be your wingman."

Matt zeroed in on her expression to see if she was joking. She looked serious, and he didn't like the sound of that.

"I don't need a wingman."

"Tell me what's going on." He gestured through the archway to the living room.

She crouched down to untie her boots.

"You don't have to—"

"Your carpet is white," she said.

"I suppose."

Most of the women he brought home wore delicate shoes, stiletto heels and such.

Tasha peeled off her boots, revealing thick wool socks. For some reason, the sight made him smile.

She rose, looking all business.

"Care for a drink?" he asked, gesturing her forward.

She moved, shooting him an expression of disbelief on the way past. "No, I don't want a drink."

"I opened a great bottle of pinot noir. I'm not going to finish it myself."

"This isn't a social visit," she said, glancing around the room at the pale white leather furniture and long, narrow gas fireplace.

She was obviously hesitant to sit down in her work clothes.

"Here," he suggested, pointing to the formal dining room. The chairs were dark oak, likely less intimidating if she was worried about leaving dirt on anything.

While she sat down, he retrieved the pinot from the glass porch and brought two fresh glasses.

He sat down cornerwise to her and set down the wine.

She gave him an exaggerated sigh. "I'm not drinking while I work."

"It's ten o'clock on a Saturday night."

"Your point?"

"My point is you're officially off the clock."

"So, you're not paying me?"

"I'll pay you anything you want." He poured them each some of the rich, dark wine. "Aren't you on salary?"

"I am."

"You work an awful lot of overtime."

"A good deal for you."

"I'm giving you a raise." He held one of the glasses out for her.

"Ha ha," she mocked.

"Take it," he said.

She did, but set it down on the table in front of her.

"Twenty percent," he told her.

"You can't do that."

"I absolutely can." He raised his glass. "Let's toast your raise."

"I came here to tell you I might have made a big mistake."

Three

Tasha reluctantly took a sip of the wine, noting right away that it was a fantastic vintage. She looked at the bottle, recognizing the Palmer Valley label as one of her parents' favorites, and the Crispin Pinot Noir as one of their higher-end brands.

"You have good taste in wine," she said.

"I'm glad you like it."

His smile was warm, and she felt an unwelcome glow in the pit of her stomach.

To distract herself, she tipped the bottle to check the year.

"You know the label?" he asked, sounding surprised.

"Mechanics can't appreciate fine wine?"

He paused to take in her expression. "Clearly, they can."

It was annoying how his deep voice strummed along her nervous system. She seemed to have no defenses against him.

She set down her glass and straightened in her chair, reminding herself this was business.

"What did I say?" he asked.

"I came here to tell you—"

"I just said something wrong," he persisted. "What was it?"

"You didn't say anything wrong." It was her problem, not his. "*Pacific Wind* broke down near Granite Point."

"Another breakdown?"

"Like I said, a cable was broken."

"But you fixed it." He slid the wineglass a little closer to her. "Good job. Well done, you."

"It shouldn't have happened. I serviced it just last week. I must have missed a weak point."

His lips tightened in what looked like frustration. "Why

are you so quick to blame yourself? It obviously broke *after* you did your work."

"The sequence of events isn't logical. It shouldn't have broken all of a sudden. Wear and tear should have been obvious when I was working on it." She'd been mulling over the possibilities for hours now. "It could have been a faulty part, weak material in the cable maybe, something that wasn't visible that would leave it prone to breaking."

"There you go."

"Or…" She hesitated to even voice her speculation.

"Or?" he prompted.

"Somebody wanted it to break. It's far-fetched. I get that. And on the surface, it seems like I'm making excuses for my own incompetence—coming up with some grand scheme of sabotage to explain it all away. But the thing is, I checked with the fuel supply company right after we got back from Tyree. We were the only customer that had a water problem. And none of our other yachts were affected, only *Orca's Run*. How does that work? How does water only get into one fuel system?" She gave in and took another drink of the wine.

"Tasha?" Matt asked.

"Yeah?" She set down her glass, oddly relieved at having said it out loud. Now they could discuss it and dismiss it.

"Can you parse that out a little more for me?"

She nodded, happy to delve into her theory and find the flaws. "It's far from definitive. It's only possible. It's possible that someone put water in the fuel and damaged the pump. And it's possible someone partially cut the cable."

"The question is, why?"

She agreed. "Do you have any enemies?"

"None that I know about."

"A competitor, maybe?"

He sat back in his chair. "Wow."

"*Wow* that somebody could be secretly working against you?"

"No. I was just thinking that after-dinner conversation with you is *so* much more interesting than with Emilie."

"So you think my theory is too far-fetched." She was inclined to agree.

"That's not what I said at all. I'm thinking you could be right. And we should investigate. And that's kind of exciting."

"You think it's exciting? That someone might be damaging your boats and undermining your company's reputation?"

He topped up both of their glasses. "I think it could be exciting to investigate. It's not like anything was seriously or permanently damaged. It seems like more mischief than anything. And haven't you ever wanted to be an amateur sleuth?"

"No." She could honestly say it had never crossed her mind.

"Come on. You investigate, diagnose and fix problems all the time."

"There are no bad guys lurking inside engines."

"The bad guy only adds a new dimension to the problem."

She couldn't understand his jovial attitude. There wasn't a positive side to this. "There's something wrong with you, Matt."

"Will you help me?" he asked, his eyes alight in a way that trapped and held her gaze. His eyes were vivid blue right now, the color of the bay at a summer sunrise.

"It's my job." She fought an inappropriate thrill at the prospect of working closely with him. She should be staying away from him. That's what she should be doing.

"We need to start with a list of suspects. Who has access to the engines and steering systems?"

"I do, and the contract mechanics from Dean's Repairs and Corner Service. And Alex now. But she wasn't even here when we had the *Orca's Run* problem."

"Was she in Whiskey Bay?"

"Yes but… You're not suggesting she's a mole."

"I'm not suggesting anything yet. I'm only laying out the facts."

Tasha didn't want to suspect Alex, but she couldn't disagree with Matt's approach. They had to start with everyone who had access, especially those with mechanical skills. Whoever did this understood boats and engines well enough to at least attempt to cover their tracks.

"At least we can rule you out," Matt said with a smirk.

"And you," she returned.

"And me. What about the rest of the staff? Who can we rule out?"

"Can we get a list of everyone's hours for the past couple of weeks?"

"Easily."

"What about your competitors?" It seemed to Tasha that Matt's competitors would have motive to see him fail.

"They'd have a financial motive, I suppose. But I know most of the ones in the area, and I can't imagine any of them doing something underhanded."

"Maybe they didn't," she said, realizing the enormity of her accusations. Never mind the enormity, what about the likelihood that somebody was out to harm Matt's business?

She was reevaluating this whole thing. "Maybe it was just my making a mistake."

He paused and seemed to consider. "Do you believe that's what happened?"

"Nobody's perfect." She knew her negligence could account for the cable.

Then again, the water in the fuel of *Orca's Run* was something else. It was a lot less likely she'd been responsible for that.

He watched her closely, his gaze penetrating. "Tasha, I can tell by your expression you know it wasn't you."

"I can't be one hundred percent certain."

He took her hand in both of his. "I am."

Their gazes met and held, and the air temperature in the room seemed to rise. Subtle sounds magnified: the wind, the surf, the hiss of the fireplace. Heat rushed up her arm, blooming into desire in her chest.

Like the first rumblings of an earthquake, she could feel it starting all over again.

"I have to go." She jumped to her feet.

He stood with her, still holding her hand. His gaze moved to her lips.

They tingled.

She knew she should move. She needed to move *right now*.

She did move. But it was to step forward, not backward.

She brought her free hand up to his. He interlaced their fingers.

"Tasha," he whispered.

She should run. Leave. But instead she let her eyes drift closed. She leaned in, crossing the last few inches between them. She tipped her chin, tilted her head. She might not have a lot of experience with romance, but she knew she was asking for his kiss.

He didn't disappoint.

With a swift, indrawn breath, he brought his lips to hers.

The kiss was tender, soft and tentative. But it sent waves through her body, heat and energy. It was she who pressed harder, she who parted her lips and she who disentangled her hands to wrap her arms around his neck.

He gave a small groan, and he embraced her, his solid forearms against her back, pressing her curves against the length of his body, thigh to thigh, chest to chest. Her nipples peaked at his touch, the heat of his skin. She desperately wanted to feel his skin against hers. But she'd retained just enough sanity to stop herself.

The kiss was as far as it could go.

She reluctantly drew back. She wished she could look away and pretend it hadn't happened. But she didn't. She wouldn't. She faced him head-on.

His eyes were opaque, and there was a ghost of a smile on his face.

"You're amazing," he said.

"We can't do that." Regret was pouring in, along with a healthy dose of self-recrimination.

"But, we do."

"You know what I mean."

"You mean *shouldn't*." His closeness was still clouding her mind.

"Yes, shouldn't. No, can't. You have to help me here, Matt." She stepped away, putting some space between them.

He gave an exaggerated sigh. "You're asking a lot."

She wanted to be honest, and she wanted both of them to be realistic. "I like it here."

He glanced around his living room that jutted out from the cliff, affording incredible views of the bay. He was clearly proud of the design, proud of his home. "I'm glad to hear that."

"Not the house," she quickly corrected him.

"You don't like my house?"

"That's not what I mean. I do like your house." The house was stunningly gorgeous; anyone would love it. "I mean I like working at Whiskey Bay. I don't want to have to quit."

His expression turned to incredulity. "You're making some pretty huge leaps in logic."

She knew that was true, and she backpedaled. "I'm not assuming you want a fling."

"That's not what I—"

"It's hard for a woman to be taken seriously as a mechanic."

"So you've said."

"I want to keep my personal life and my professional life separate."

"Everybody does. Until something happens that makes them want something else."

Now she just wanted out of this conversation. "I'm afraid I've given you the wrong idea."

"The only idea you've given me is that you're attracted to me."

She wanted to protest, but she wasn't going to lie.

He continued. "That and the fact that you believe my company is the target of sabotage."

She quickly latched onto the alternative subject. "I do. At least, it's a possibility that we should consider."

"And I trust your judgment, so we're going to investigate."

Tasha drew a breath of relief. They were back on solid ground. All work with Matt, no play. That was her mission going forward.

Matt couldn't concentrate on work. He kept reliving his kiss with Tasha over and over again.

He was with TJ and Caleb on the top deck of his marina building, standing around the propane fireplace as the sun sank into the Pacific. The other men's voices were more a drone of noise than a conversation.

"Why would anyone sabotage your engines?" TJ broke through Matt's daydreaming.

"What?" he asked, shaking himself back to the present.

"Why would they do it?"

"Competition is my guess." Matt hadn't been able to come up with another reason.

Caleb levered into one of the padded deck chairs. It was a cool evening, but the men still sipped on chilled beers.

"What about your surveillance cameras?" Caleb asked.

"Not enough of them to provide full coverage. They're pretty easy to avoid if that's your intention."

"You should get more."

"I've ordered more." It was one of the first moves Matt had made. He took a chair himself.

"Did you call the police?" TJ asked, sitting down.

"Not yet. I can't imagine it would be a priority for them. And I want to make sure we're right before I waste anybody's time."

"So, Tasha is wrong?"

Matt found himself bristling at what was only the slightest of criticisms of Tasha. "No, she's not wrong."

"I'm just asking," TJ said, obviously catching the tone in Matt's voice.

"And I'm just answering. She's not one hundred percent convinced yet either. So, we'll wait."

"Until it happens again?" Caleb asked. "What if it's more serious this time? What if whoever it is targets more than the marina?"

"Are you worried about the Crab Shack?" Matt hadn't thought about the other businesses in the area, including the Crab Shack restaurant run by Caleb's new wife, Jules, who was five months pregnant with twins.

"Not yet." Caleb seemed to further contemplate the question. "I might ask Noah to spend a little more time over there."

"Nobody's going to mess with Noah," TJ said.

"He's scrappy," Caleb agreed.

Caleb's sister-in-law's boyfriend had spent a short time in jail after a fistfight in self-defense. He was tough and no-nonsense, and he'd protect Jules and her sister, Melissa, against anything and anyone.

"What about your security cameras at the Crab Shack?" TJ asked Caleb. "Would any of them reach this far?"

"I'll check," Caleb said. "But I doubt the resolution is high enough to be of any help."

"I'd appreciate that," Matt said to Caleb.

It hadn't occurred to him to worry about Tasha's or anyone else's safety. But maybe Caleb was onto something. Maybe Matt should take a few precautions. So far, the incidents had been minor, and nobody had come close to being hurt. But that wasn't to say it couldn't happen. The incidents could escalate.

"Matt?" It was Tasha's voice coming from the pier below, and he felt the timbre radiate through his chest.

He swiftly rose and crossed to the rail, where he could see her. "Are you okay?"

She seemed puzzled by his concern. "I'm fine."

"Good."

"*Never Fear* and *Crystal Zone* are both ready to go in the morning. I'm heading into town for a few hours."

"What for?" The question was out of Matt's mouth before he realized it was none of his business. It was after five, and Tasha was free to do anything she wanted.

"Meeting some guys."

Guys? What did she mean *guys*? He wanted to ask if it was one particular guy, or if it was a group of guys. Were they all just friends?

"Hey, Tasha." TJ appeared at the rail beside him.

"Hi, TJ." Her greeting was casual, and her attention went back to Matt. "Alex will fill the fuel tanks first thing. The clients are expected at ten."

"Got it," Matt said, wishing he could ask more questions about her evening. Or better still, invite her to join them, where they could talk and laugh together.

Not that they were in the habit of friendly conversation. Mostly, they debated. But he'd be happy to engage her in a rollicking debate about pretty much any subject.

As she walked away, TJ spoke up. "I may just take another shot."

"Another shot at what?" Matt asked.

"At your mechanic."

"What?" Matt turned.

"I like her."

"What do you mean *another* shot?" Matt was surprised by the level of his anger. "You took a shot at her already?"

TJ was obviously taken aback by Matt's reaction. "I asked you back in the summer. You told me to go for it."

"That was months ago."

"That's when I asked her out. I suggested dinner and dancing. That might have been my mistake."

Matt took a drink of his beer to keep himself from saying anything more. He didn't like the thought of Tasha with any guy, never mind TJ. TJ was the epitome of rich, good-looking and eligible. Matt had seen the way a lot of women reacted to him. Not that Tasha was an ordinary woman. Still, she was a woman.

TJ kept talking, half to himself. "Maybe a monster truck rally? She is a mechanic."

Caleb joined them at the rail.

TJ tried again. "Maybe an auto show. There's one coming up in Seattle."

"You can't ask her out," Matt said.

The protest caught Caleb's attention. "Why can't he ask her out?"

"Because she's already turned him down."

"I could be persistent," TJ said.

"I really don't think dinner and dancing or persistence was the problem," Matt said.

"How would you know that?" TJ asked.

Caleb's expression took a speculative turn. "You have a problem with TJ asking Tasha out?"

"No," Matt responded to Caleb. Then he reconsidered his answer. "Yes."

TJ leaned an elbow on the rail, a grin forming on his face. "Oh, this is interesting."

"It's not interesting," Matt said.

"Is something going on between you two?" Caleb asked.

"No. Nothing is going on."

"But you like her." TJ's grin was full-on now.

"I kissed her. She kissed me. We kissed." Matt wasn't proud that it sounded like he was bragging. "She's a nice woman. And I like her. But nothing has happened."

"Are you telling me to back off?" TJ asked.

"That's pretty loud and clear," Caleb said.

TJ held up his hands in mock surrender. "Backing off."

"She said she was meeting a guy tonight?" Caleb raised a brow.

Matt narrowed his gaze. "She said *guys*, plural. They're probably just friends of hers."

"Probably," said TJ with exaggerated skepticism, still clearly amused at Matt's expense.

"It took you long enough," Caleb said.

"There is no *it*," Matt responded. It had taken him too long to notice her. He'd own that.

"Have you asked her out?"

"We're a little busy at the moment. You know, distracted by criminal activity."

"That's a no," TJ said. "At least I took the plunge."

"You got shot down," Caleb reminded TJ.

"No risk, no reward."

"She's gun-shy," Matt said. He didn't know what made her that way, but it was obvious she was wary of dating.

"So, what are you going to do?" Caleb asked.

"Nothing."

"That's a mistake."

"I'm not going to force anything." The last thing Matt wanted to do was make Tasha feel uncomfortable working at the marina.

He wanted her to stay. For all kinds of different reasons, both personal and professional, but he definitely wanted her to stay.

The Edge Bar and Grill in the town of Whiskey Bay was a popular hangout for the marina staff. It also drew in the working class from the local service and supply businesses. The artsy crowd preferred the Blue Badger on Third Avenue. While those who were looking for something high-end and refined could choose the Ocean View Lounge across the highway. While the Crab Shack was becoming popular, drawing people from the surrounding towns and even as far away as Olympia.

Tasha liked the Edge. The decor was particularly attractive tonight, decked out for the season with a tree, lights and miles of evergreen garlands. A huge wreath over the bar was covered in gold balls and poinsettia flowers.

As was usual, the music had a rock-and-country flare. The menu was unpretentious. They had good beer on tap, and soda refills were free. She was driving her and Alex home tonight, so she'd gone with cola.

"Have you heard of anybody having any unexpected engine problems lately?" she asked Henry Schneider, who was sitting across the table.

Henry was a marine mechanic at Shutters Corner ten miles down the highway near the public wharf.

"Unexpected how?" he asked.

"We had some water in the fuel with no apparent cause."

"Loose cap?"

"Checked that, along with the fuel source. The water separator was full."

"There's your problem."

"I swapped it out, but I couldn't figure out how it got that way."

Henry gave a shrug. "It happens."

Alex returned from the small dance floor with another mechanic, James Hamilton, in tow.

"So, no reports of anything strange?" Tasha asked Henry.

"Strange?" James asked, helping Alex onto the high stool.

"Unexplained mechanical failures in the area."

"There's always an explanation," James said. "Sometimes you just have to keep looking."

"You want to dance?" Alex asked Henry.

"Who says I was through dancing?" James asked her.

"Dance with Tasha." Alex motioned for Henry to come with her.

He swallowed the remainder of his beer and rose from his chair.

James held out his hand to Tasha.

She gave up talking shop and accepted the invitation.

James was younger than Henry, likely in his late twenties. He was from Idaho and had a fresh-faced openness about him that Tasha liked. He was tall and lanky. His hair was red, and his complexion was fair. She didn't think she'd ever seen him in a bad mood.

It wasn't the first time they'd ever danced together, and he was good at it. He'd once told her barn dancing was a popular pastime in the small town where he'd grown up. She knew he'd left his high school sweetheart behind, and she got the feeling he'd one day return to her, even if he did prefer the West Coast to rural Idaho.

As the song ended, a figure appeared behind James. It took only a split second for Tasha to recognize Matt.

"What are you doing here?" she asked him, her guard immediately going up. She assumed this was too simple, too low-key to be his kind of place. "Is something wrong?"

"Dance?" he asked instead of answering.

James backed away. "Catch you later."

Matt stepped in front of her as a Bruce Springsteen song came up.

He took her hand.

"Did something happen?" she asked. "Was there another breakdown?"

"Nothing happened. Can't a guy go out for the evening?"

She struggled to ignore his light touch on her back and the heat where his hand joined hers. It was a lost cause. "This isn't your typical hangout."

"Sure it is."

"I can tell when you're lying."

He hesitated. "I was worried about you."

"Why?"

"There's a criminal out there."

She almost laughed. "If there is, he's focused on your company. It has nothing to do with me."

"We don't know that."

"We do."

He drew her closer as they danced, even though she knew getting more intimate with Matt was a big mistake.

But the words didn't come. Instead of speaking, she followed his lead. It was the path of least resistance, since their bodies moved seamlessly together. He was tall and solid and a smooth, skilled dancer.

She told herself she could handle it. They were in public after all. It's not like they would get carried away.

"I know you like to be independent," he said.

"I am independent."

"The truth is, people are less likely to harass you if you're with me."

His words were confusing.

"Nobody's been harassing me. Nobody's going to harass me."

Matt glanced around the room with apparent skepticism, as if he was expecting a gang of criminals to be lurking next to the dance floor.

"See that guy in the red shirt?" She pointed. "He worked at Shutters Corner. And the guy talking to Alex? He's Henry's coworker. They're local guys, Matt. They're mechanics. There are a lot of local mechanics here. And I'm talking to them all."

Matt's hold on her tightened. "Are you dancing with them all?"

She tipped her chin to look up at him, seeing his lips were thin and his jaw was tight.

He looked jealous. The last thing she wanted him to be was jealous. But her heart involuntarily lifted at the idea.

"No." The sharp retort was as much for her as it was for him. "I'm here asking questions. I'm gathering evidence, if you must know."

"Oh," he drawled with immediate understanding.

"Yes, *oh*. If anybody's having the same problems as us, these guys are going to know about it."

"That's a really good idea."

She put a note of sarcasm into her tone. "Why, thank you."

"I'm not crazy about the dancing part."

"*You* asked *me*," she pointed out.

"What? No, not with me." He canted his head. "With them."

She wanted to point out that he was dating other women. But she quickly stopped herself. Matt's romantic life was none of her business. And hers was none of his. The more women he dated, the better.

His voice lowered. "You can dance with me all you want."

"We're not going there, Matt."

"Okay." His agreement was easy, but his hold still felt intimate.

"You say okay, but we're still dancing." She knew she could pull away herself. She knew she should do exactly that, but he felt so good in her arms, she wanted to hang on just a little bit longer.

"The song will be over soon." He went silent for a moment. "How are you getting home?"

"Driving."

"You came alone?"

"I drove with Alex. Matt, I've been going out at night on my own for the past six years."

"Not while my boats were being sabotaged all around you."

"We don't know that they are being sabotaged. Honestly, I'm beginning to regret sharing my suspicions with you." The last thing she'd expected was for him to go all bodyguard on her.

"We don't know that they're not. And don't you dare hold anything back."

She stopped dancing. "Matt."

His hand contracted around her shoulder. "I didn't mean for that to sound like an order."

"Is there something you're not telling me?"

Had there been some development? Was there a danger she didn't know about?

"I heard TJ ask you out."

The statement took her completely by surprise. "That was a long time ago. You can't possibly suspect TJ."

Sure, she'd turned TJ down. But he and Matt were good friends. He wouldn't take out his anger with her by harming Matt. Plus, he hadn't even seemed to care that much. He was still friendly to her.

"I *don't* suspect TJ."

The song changed to a Christmas tune. It wasn't the best dance music in the world, but Matt kept leading, so she followed.

"Then why are we talking about him?"

Matt seemed to be reviewing their conversation so far. "It was Caleb."

"You suspect Caleb?" That was even more outlandish than suspecting TJ.

"Caleb's the one who got me worried about the sabotage. He's worried about Jules, which got me to thinking about you. And then TJ mentioned that he'd asked you out."

"Caleb worries too much. And TJ was months ago."

"So, you're not interested in him?"

Tasha was more than confused here. "Did he ask you to ask me?"

One minute, she thought Matt was romancing her, and she braced herself to shut him down. And then he seemed to be TJ's wingman. Their kisses notwithstanding, maybe she was reading his interest all wrong.

Before Matt could respond, she jumped back in. "TJ's not my type."

Alex appeared beside Tasha on the dance floor.

She took Tasha's arm and leaned into her ear. "James offered me a ride home."

Tasha pulled back to look at her friend. "Is that a good thing?"

Alex's eyes were alight. "You bet."

Since Alex had a done a whole lot more dancing than drinking, Tasha wasn't worried about her. And Tasha had known James for months. He seemed like a very upstanding guy.

"Do you mind if I bail on you?" Alex asked.

"Not at all. I'll see you later."

Alex grinned. "Thanks." Her walk was light as she moved away.

"So, you're driving home alone," Matt said. "I'll follow you."

Tasha rolled her eyes at him.

"I'm serious."

"Thanks for the dance," she said and pulled back from his arms.

She was going to have another drink. She was going to chat with Henry and the other mechanics. She didn't need a bodyguard.

Four

Matt hung back as Tasha approached her compact car in the Edge's parking lot. It was in a dark corner, and he moved out of the building's lights so his eyes could adjust.

It was obvious she knew he was there, knew he'd waited for her to leave for home. She'd shot him a look of frustration as she'd headed for the front door and he'd risen from his seat at the bar.

Now, she shook her head with exaggerated resignation and gave him a mocking wave as she slipped into the driver's seat.

He didn't really care how she felt. Caleb had him worried about safety. He headed for his own car at the opposite side of the parking lot. The bar was only half-full at ten o'clock. But even on a weeknight, the crowd here would keep going until midnight, when the place shut down.

Tasha's engine cranked. Then it cranked again. But it didn't catch and start. A third crank was followed by silence.

Matt turned back.

She was out of the car and opening the hood.

"Need some help?" he asked as he approached.

She laughed. "You *have* read my résumé, right?"

"I'm not questioning your technical skills. And it's obviously a dead battery."

Her annoyance seemed to fade. "That's exactly what it is."

As they gazed at the cold engine, a thought struck him. "Could this be sabotage?"

"No." Her answer was definitive.

"How can you be sure?"

"Because it's related to my having an old battery. I've been limping it along for a while now. Do you have cables?"

"In my BMW?"

"BMWs run the same way as any other car."

"My battery's under warranty. And I have roadside assistance. You don't have cables?"

Tasha was a be-prepared kind of woman. Jumper cables seemed like the kind of thing she would carry.

She looked embarrassed. "I do. Usually. I took them out of my trunk to help Alex move her stuff."

"Come on," he said, motioning to his car.

"I'll call a tow truck and get a jump."

"There's no need." He wasn't about to leave her standing in a dark parking lot waiting for a tow truck. "I'll bring you back tomorrow with your jumper cables."

"I can take care of it."

His frustration mounted. "Why are you arguing?"

She squared her shoulders and lifted her chin but didn't answer.

"Well?" he prompted.

"I don't know."

He couldn't help but grin. "Pride?"

"Maybe. I don't like to be rescued."

"But you'll accept help from a random tow truck driver."

She dropped the hood down, and the sound echoed. "He's paid to help me. But you're right. I'm wrong. I'd appreciate the ride home."

"Did you just say I was right?"

She locked the driver's door and started walking. "I did."

He fell into step beside her. "It's fun being right."

"Calm down. It's not that exciting."

He hit the remote to unlock the doors. "You're positive somebody wasn't messing with your battery?"

"I'm positive. It's unrelated. And if we try to link it in, we'll set ourselves off in the wrong direction."

Matt thought about her logic for a moment. "Okay. Now you're the one who's right."

She cracked a smile. "Thank goodness I'm evening things up."

He opened the driver's door while she did the same on the passenger side.

"But I'm not wrong," he pointed out.

"Maybe a little bit."

"Maybe not at all. I just asked a question. Postulating something is not the same as being incorrect about it."

"You're right," she said and plunked into the seat.

He leaned down to look through his open door. "That's two for me."

She was smiling as she buckled her seat belt.

He started the engine, turned down the music and pulled out of the parking lot.

The temperature was in the fifties, but the interior heated up quickly, and Tasha unzipped her fitted gray leather jacket. She wore a purple tank top beneath it over a boxy pair of faded blue jeans and brown Western-style boots. Her hair was pulled into a high ponytail. It was mostly brunette, but it flashed with amber highlights as they drove.

She looked casual and comfortable, sexy at the same time. He liked it. He liked it a lot.

"Nobody I talked to knew anything," she said. "Nothing weird going on out there in the broader Whiskey Bay mechanical world."

"So the marina is the target."

"That would be my guess. Or it's a couple of coincidences. It could still be that."

He didn't disagree. He hoped it was a couple of coincidences. "I'm going to check out my competition."

"How?"

"'Tis the season. There are a lot of gatherings and parties coming up. The business community likes to celebrate together."

"I remember."

"Were you here last year?"

She'd been working at the marina only since March.

"I was talking about the business community anywhere. It was the same while I was growing up."

"You went to corporate Christmas parties?" He tried to picture it.

"I read about them," she continued, quickly. "They sounded...posh and snooty and boring."

He laughed at how she wrinkled her nose. "They're not bad. They are fancy. But some of the people are interesting."

She gave a derisive scoff.

"Hey, I'm one of those people. Am I that bad?"

"In some ways, yes."

"What ways?" He tried not to let her opinion get to him.

"The way you dress. The way you talk."

"What's wrong with the way I talk?"

She seemed to think about that. "It's clear and precise, with very little slang. You have a wide vocabulary."

"I'm not seeing the problem."

"It sounds posh."

"What about you?"

She was easily as articulate as him.

"I'm perfectly ordinary."

She wasn't. But he wasn't going to get into that argument right now.

"And so are the people at the corporate parties. You shouldn't be biased against them." He slowed the car and turned from the highway down his long driveway that wound through the woods.

"I can't stand those frilly, frothy dresses, those pretentious caviar and foie gras canapés, and the ceaseless conversation about who's making partner and the who's marrying who."

He wasn't about to admit she'd nailed it—at least when it came to some of the guests at those parties.

"You shouldn't knock it until you've tried it," he said instead.

"You're right."

He chuckled. "And I've hit the trifecta."

Then the headlights caught his house. He blinked to check his vision on what he thought he saw there. His stomach curled. It couldn't be.

"Who's that?" Tasha asked as the car came to a stop.

Matt shut off the engine. "My ex-wife."

Tasha gazed through the windshield. "So that's her."

"I take it you haven't met her?"

"I only saw her from a distance. She didn't seem to be around much."

Those last few months, his ex had used any excuse to travel.

"She liked France," he said. "She still likes France. There's a man there."

"Oh," Tasha said with obvious understanding.

"Yeah." Matt released his seat belt. "I can't even imagine what she's doing back here."

He and Tasha both stepped out of the car.

"Hello, Dianne," he said as he approached the lit porch.

Her dark hair was pulled back from her face with some kind of headband, the ends of her hair brushing her shoulders. She wore a black wool jacket with leather trim, a pair of black slacks and very high heels. Her makeup was perfect, as always. Her mouth was tight. Her eyes narrowed.

"Where have you been?" she asked. Then her gaze swept Tasha.

"This is Tasha." He didn't like the dismissive expression on Dianne's face. "She and I have been dancing."

He felt Tasha's look of surprise but ignored it.

"What are you doing here?" he asked Dianne.

"I need to speak with you."

Her nostrils flared with an indrawn breath. "It's a private matter."

"Well, I'm not about to end my evening early to listen to you."

Whatever Dianne had to say to him—and he couldn't imagine what that might be—it could wait until morning.

"You can call me tomorrow, Dianne." He started for the door, gesturing for Tasha to go ahead of him.

"It's about François," Dianne blurted out.

Matt kept walking.

Whatever was going on between Dianne and her new husband was completely their business. Matt couldn't stay far enough away.

"He left me."

Matt paused. "I'm sorry, Dianne. It's none of my business."

"He stole my money."

"Matt?" Tasha said with a little tug against his hand.

"*All* of my money," Dianne said.

"It'll still wait until morning." Matt punched in the key code to his front door. "Do you need me to call you a ride?"

"*Matt,*" Dianne practically wailed.

"We're divorced, Dianne. As I recall, your settlement was more than generous."

Matt had only wanted it to be over. Although his lawyer had argued with him, he'd given her everything she'd asked for. It had meant significant refinancing of the marina, but if he worked hard, he'd be back on solid footing within two or three years.

He retrieved his phone and pulled up his ride app, requesting a car. "Call me tomorrow. I assume you still have my number?"

"I'm in trouble, Matt," Dianne said. "Deep trouble."

"Then I suggest you call a lawyer."

Her voice rose. "I didn't commit a crime."

"I'm glad to hear that. Your car will be here in a couple of minutes."

He opened the door and Tasha went inside.

"How can you be so cruel?" Dianne called out from behind him.

He turned. "How can you have the nerve to ask me to drop everything and deal with your problems? You cheated

on me, left me and put my business at risk through your un-
bridled greed."

A pair of headlights flashed through the trees.

"Your ride is here, Dianne." He stepped through the open
door, closing it to then face Tasha.

Matt leaned back against his front door as if he expected
his ex-wife to try to break it down.

"Sorry about that," he said.

Tasha wasn't sure how she should feel about the exchange.
She knew divorces could be acrimonious, and Matt was
within his rights to stay at arm's length from his ex-wife,
but Dianne had seemed genuinely upset.

"It sounds like she could use a friend," Tasha said.

"Truthfully, it's hard to know for sure. She's a drama
queen. Her reaction to a fire or a flood is the same as her reaction to a broken fingernail."

Tasha tried not to smile. It didn't seem like there was anything funny in the situation.

Matt pushed away from the door. "She was supposed to
be in France. She was supposed to stay in France. I'd really
hoped she'd stay in France forever. I need a drink. Do you
want a drink?"

He started down the short staircase to the glass-walled
living room. On the way, he seemed to absently hit a wall
switch, and the long fireplace came to life. Fed by gas, it was
glassed in on all sides and stretched the length of the living
room, separating a kitchen area from a lounge area where
white leather armchairs faced a pair of matching sofas.

Tasha knew she should head home. But she found herself
curious about Matt, about Dianne, and she'd been sipping on
sodas all night long. A real drink sounded appealing.

"I'm thinking tequila," Matt said as he passed one end of
the fireplace into the kitchen.

Tasha threw caution to the wind. "I love margaritas."

"Margaritas it is." He opened a double-doored stainless steel refrigerator. "We have limes." He held them up. "Glasses are above the long counter. Pick whatever looks good."

Feeling happier than she had any right to feel about sharing a drink with Matt, Tasha moved to the opposite end of the kitchen. Near the glass wraparound wall, she opened an upper cupboard, finding a selection of crystal glasses. She chose a pair with deep bowls and sturdy-looking bases.

"Frozen or on the rocks?" he asked.

"Frozen."

He was cutting limes on an acrylic board. "There should be some coarse salt in the pantry. Through that door." He pointed with the tip of his knife.

Tasha crossed behind him to the back of the kitchen.

The walk-in pantry was impressive. It was large and lined with shelves of staples and exotic treats.

"Do you like to cook?" she called out to him.

"It's a hobby."

She located the coarse salt and reemerged. "I wouldn't have guessed that."

"Why?" He seemed puzzled.

"Good question."

"Thanks."

"You seem—" she struggled to put it into words "—like the kind of guy who would have a housekeeper."

"I do."

"Aha!"

"She's not a cook. I decided a long time ago that I couldn't do everything around here and run a business, too, so I chose to do the things I like the best and give up the things I didn't enjoy."

"What is it you like best?" Tasha helped herself to one of the limes. She'd spotted some small glass bowls in the cupboard and retrieved one for the salt.

"Cooking, working, the gym."

"Dating?" she asked.

"That's recent."

"But you like it. You do it quite a lot now."

"I do, and I do." He stilled then and seemed to think more about his answer.

"What?" she prompted.

"Nothing. That about sums it up."

"What about friends?"

"Caleb and TJ? Sure. I hang with them whenever I can. With them being so close, we don't really plan anything, we just drop by. It's kind of like background noise."

"Like family," Tasha mused as she cut the lime in half.

She'd observed the relationship between the three men. It was as if they were brothers. She'd like to have close relationships like that. But she had absolutely nothing in common with her two sisters.

"Like family," Matt agreed. "They're going to flip when they find out Dianne's back."

"Do you expect her to stick around?"

It was none of Tasha's business. And she wasn't entitled to have an opinion one way or the other. But she liked that Matt was single. After all, a fantasy was fun only if it had an outside chance of coming true.

The knife slipped, and she cut her finger.

"Ouch!"

"What happened?" He was by her side in an instant.

"I wasn't paying attention."

"Is it bad?" He gently took her hand. "You're bleeding."

"Just a little. Don't let me ruin the drinks."

He seemed amused by her priority as he reached for a tissue from a box on the counter. "Let's get you a bandage."

"I bet it'll stop on its own." She pressed the tissue against the cut.

"This way." He took her elbow. "We can't have you bleeding into the salt."

He led her up the steps toward the entry hall, but then veered right, taking her down a long hallway with plush silver-gray carpet. Some of the doors were open, and she saw an office and what looked like a comfortable sunroom.

"This is nice," she said.

They entered one room, and it took her only a second to realize it had to be the master bedroom. She hesitated and stumbled.

"Careful," he said.

"This is…"

He paused and glanced around at the king-size bed with taupe accents, two leather and polished metal easy chairs, twin white bedside tables and a polished oak floor with geometric-patterned throw rugs. Here, too, there were walls of windows looking across the bay and over the forest.

"What?" he prompted.

"Big." She settled on the word. She wanted to say *intimidating*, maybe even *arousing*. She was inside Matt's bedroom. How had that happened?

"I know there are bandages in here." He gestured toward the open door to an en suite.

She struggled to even her breathing as she entered the bathroom. "This is big, too."

"I like my space. And I didn't need too many bedrooms, so it was easy to go for something big for the master."

She moved with him to the sink.

"Do you want kids?" She had no idea where that question came from.

He shrugged. "Dianne didn't want them. I'm easy. I could go either way." Then he gave a chuckle as he opened the upper cabinet.

Tasha averted her eyes. Seeing what was in his medicine cabinet seemed far too personal.

"I figure once I meet Caleb's twins," Matt continued, "it'll either make me want some of my own, or cure me of that idea forever."

He set a small bandage on the counter, shut the cabinet and gently removed the tissue from her cut finger.

"I can do this myself," she said, feeling the effects of his closeness.

She liked his smell. She liked his voice. His touch was gentle.

"Two hands are better than one." He turned on the water, waited a moment then tested the temperature.

Tasha could feel her heart tap against her rib cage. Her gaze was caught on his face. He looked inordinately sexy, and amazingly handsome.

"What about you?" he asked, his attention on her finger as he held it under the warm flow of water.

"Huh?" She gave herself a mental shake and shifted her gaze.

"Do you want kids?"

"Sure. I suppose so. Maybe."

"You haven't thought about it?"

She really hadn't. Her focus had been on her career and making it to the top of her profession. "I guess I'm not in any rush."

"Fair enough." He wrapped the small bandage around the end of her finger and secured it in place. "Good as new."

"Thank you." She made the mistake of looking into his eyes.

His twinkled, and he smiled at her.

For a moment, she thought he was going to kiss her. But instead, he brushed a playful finger across the tip of her nose and stepped back.

"Our ice is melting," he said. "We better blend those drinks."

Sitting across from Dianne at a window table in the Crab Shack, Matt had asked for a water. Now he wished he'd ordered something stronger.

He hadn't wanted to meet her at his house. He was steadily working to move forward with his life; he didn't want to go backward.

"You gave him control of your *entire* portfolio?" Matt couldn't believe what he was hearing.

"He had a mansion," Dianne said, a whine in her tone. "He had a yacht and a jet and memberships at these exclusive clubs. He didn't even want a prenup. Why wouldn't I trust him?"

"Because he was a con artist?"

She gave a pout. "How was I supposed to know that?"

"You weren't," Matt acknowledged. "What you were supposed to do was keep control of your own assets." He was appalled that she would be so blindly trusting of anyone.

"It was all in French," she said. "I couldn't understand it. It only made sense for him to take over the details."

It sounded like the man had taken over a whole lot more than just the details of her assets. He'd obviously taken complete charge of her money. But Matt wasn't about to lengthen the debate. He'd agreed to meet Dianne today, but he had no intention of stepping back into her life, no matter what kind of mess she'd made of it. And by the sounds of it, she'd made a pretty big mess.

Her exotic French husband had taken her money and disappeared, leaving a trail of debts and charges of fraud behind him.

"So, what are you going to do?" he asked her.

She opened her eyes wide, and let her lower lip go soft. "I miss you, Matt."

"Oh, no you don't." He wasn't going there. He so wasn't going there. "What are you going to do, Dianne? *You*, not me. You alone."

Her eyes narrowed, and he stared straight back at her.

Then what looked like fear came over her expression. "I don't know *what* to do."

"Get a job?" he suggested.

The Crab Shack waitress arrived with their lunches, lobster salad for Dianne, a platter of hand-cut halibut and fries for Matt. He had developed a serious fondness for the Crab Shack's signature sauces.

Dianne waited for the waitress to leave. Then she leaned forward, her tone a hiss. "You want me to work? I don't know how to work."

"I don't *want* you to do anything."

"I can't do it, Matt," she said with conviction.

"I'm not going to solve this for you, Dianne." He popped a crispy fry into his mouth.

"You've got loads of money."

"No, I don't. I had to refinance everything to pay your settlement. And even if I did have money, you have no call on it."

"That's my home." She gazed out the window at the cliff side where his house jutted out over the ocean.

"It *was* your home. Temporarily. I paid for the house. Then I paid you half its value in the divorce. Then you sucked out every nickel of my business profits."

"But—"

"Enjoy your lunch, Dianne. Because it's the last thing I'll ever buy for you."

Her mouth worked, but no sounds came out.

"Matt?" Caleb's wife, Jules, arrived to greet him, her tone tentative. She'd obviously caught the expression on his face and Dianne's and knew something was wrong.

He neutralized his own expression. "Jules. How are you?"

Her stomach was well rounded from the twins she was carrying.

"Doing great." She rested a hand on her belly. Then she turned to Dianne, obviously waiting for an introduction.

"Jules, this is my ex-wife, Dianne."

Jules's eyes widened. "Oh."

"She's in town for a short visit."

"I see." It was pretty clear Jules didn't see. As far as Caleb or anybody else knew—including Matt—Dianne had planned to spend the rest of her life in France. "It's nice to meet you, Dianne. Welcome to the Crab Shack."

Dianne didn't respond, her face still tight with obvious anger.

"Are you coming to the chamber of commerce gala?" Matt asked Jules, ignoring Dianne's angry silence.

Jules was coming up on six months pregnant, and her doctor had advised her to keep her feet up as much as possible.

"I'll definitely be there. I'm good for a couple of hours between rests."

"You look fantastic."

Dianne shifted restlessly in her seat, drawing Jules's brief glance.

"You'll be there?" Jules asked Matt.

"I agreed to speak."

"Oh, good. You'll be so much more entertaining than the mayor, and that Neil Himmelsbach they had on Labor Day. I should let you two finish lunch."

Matt rose to give her a quick hug and a kiss on the cheek. "Nice to see you, Jules."

She patted his shoulder. "Better go." Her attention moved to the front entrance, where a customer had just entered the restaurant.

Matt did a double take when he saw it was Tasha. He paused, watching, wondering what she was doing at the Crab Shack.

"Sit *down*," Dianne said to him.

Matt didn't want to sit down. He was waiting to see if Tasha would notice him and react in some way, maybe a wave, maybe a hello, maybe to come over and talk to him.

But she didn't.

"I'll be right back," he said to Dianne, taking matters into his own hands.

"But you—"

He didn't hear the rest.

"Hey, Tasha," he said as he came up to her.

She looked at him in obvious surprise.

"Lunch break?" he asked.

He couldn't help but notice she was dressed in clean jeans and wearing a silky top and her leather jacket. She didn't dress like that for work.

"I started early this morning." It was obviously an explanation for her boss.

"You don't need to punch a time clock with me. Take as long a lunch as you want."

"I'm having lunch with Jules."

"Really?" The revelation surprised Matt. He hadn't realized she and Jules were getting to know each other.

"She invited me," Tasha said.

"That's nice. That's good."

Tasha's gaze strayed past him, and he could tell the moment she spotted Dianne.

"This is going to sound weird," he said, moving in closer and lowering his voice.

"That would be a first."

"Can I kiss you on the cheek? Maybe give you a hug? Just a little one."

Tasha stared up at him. "Are you drunk?"

"No. It's Dianne. It would help me if she thought you and I were… You know…"

"I take it she wants to rekindle something?"

"She wants money above anything else. If she believes I'm with you, it'll stop her from thinking romancing me to get it is an option."

Tasha glanced around the crowded restaurant. It was clear she was checking to see if they knew anyone else here.

"Jules will understand the score," he assured her, assuming she didn't want anyone to get the wrong impression. "I'm sure Caleb's told her all about Dianne."

"I'm not worried about Jules."

"Then what?"

Something was making her hesitate. He dared to hope she

was remembering those brief moments in his bathroom when he'd felt a connection to her. Could she be worried about developing feelings for him?

But then her answer was brisk. "Nothing. I'm not worried about anything. Kiss on the cheek. Quick hug. No problem."

Though he was disappointed, Matt smiled his appreciation. "You're the best."

"You gave me a twenty percent raise. It's the least I can do."

So much for his musings about her feelings for him.

"This is above and beyond," he whispered as he moved in for the cheek kiss.

She smelled amazing. She tasted fantastic. It was brutal for him to have to pull back.

"You know it is," she said with a thread of laughter.

He gave her an equally quick hug. "I owe you."

He squeezed her hands, wishing with all his heart the crowd would disappear from around them and he could be alone with her.

Then he turned away, heading back across the restaurant to where Dianne was glaring at him.

Five

As always, Tasha was impressed with the Crab Shack. During lunch, it was bright and airy, with wooden tables, a casual ambiance and sweeping views of the ocean and cliffs. Then for dinner, they set out white tablecloths, candles and linen, bringing up the outdoor lighting, making it both elegant and cozy. It was no surprise that its popularity was growing fast.

Back in Boston, expensive restaurants had been the norm for her on weekends. She'd been forced to stop whatever it was she was doing far too early in the afternoon, clean up, dress up and go on parade to impress her parents' associates with their three perfect daughters.

She had wasted so much valuable time primping and engaging in inconsequential conversation. To top it off, the food had been absurdly fancy, not at all filling. There were many nights that she'd gone home and made herself a sandwich after dining at a five-star restaurant.

But the Crab Shack wasn't like that. The food was good and the atmosphere comfortable. It was refreshing to be in a place that was high quality without the pretention.

"It's this way," Jules told her, leading a weaving pattern through the tables.

Tasha gave in to temptation and took a final glance at Matt's handsome profile before following.

Jules led her into an office next to the kitchen. "It's a bit crowded in here," she apologized.

"Not a problem."

The square room held a desk with a computer and stacks of papers, a small meeting table with three chairs, and a couple of filing cabinets. It wasn't as bright as the restaurant, but there was a window that faced toward the marina and Caleb's partially built Neo restaurant.

Jules gestured to the table. "I hope you don't mind, I ordered us a bunch of appetizers."

"That sounds great." Tasha wasn't fussy.

"I do better with small things." Jules gave a self-conscious laugh. "That sounds silly. What I mean, is I tend to graze my way through the day rather than attempting a big meal."

"I can imagine your stomach is a bit crowded in there."

Jules was glowing with pregnancy.

"Between the three of us, we do fight for space," Jules said.

Tasha smiled.

Jules opened a laptop on the table. "We have security video files going back three weeks."

"I really appreciate this," Tasha said.

"Caleb has ordered more security cameras, better security cameras with higher resolution. The ones we have now don't show a lot of detail at a distance."

"Anything will help."

Jules moved the mouse and opened the first file.

To say it was boring was an understatement. They set it on a fast speed and sat back to watch.

"Matt's not normally an affectionate guy," Jules mentioned in an overly casual tone.

The observation took Tasha by surprise. It also put her on edge.

"He hugged you," Jules continued, turning her attention from the screen to Tasha. "And he kissed you."

"On the cheek," Tasha said, keeping her own attention on the view of the marina.

The camera angle showed the gate, part of the path and the first thirty feet of the pier. The yachts rocked in fast motion, while people zipped back and forth along the pier and the sun moved toward the horizon.

"It's still odd for him."

"It was for Dianne's benefit," Tasha said. "He wants her to think we're dating."

"They're divorced."

Tasha gave a shrug. "It could be ego, I suppose."

"That doesn't sound like Matt."

Tasha agreed. "Dianne seems to need money. Matt's worried she'll try to latch back onto him."

"Now, *that* sounds like the Dianne I've heard about."

On the video, the lights came up as the sun sank away.

That had been Tasha's impression, as well. "I only met her briefly last night, but—"

"Last night?" The interest in Jules's tone perked up.

"We were coming back from the Edge, and she was waiting for him."

"A date?"

"No." Tasha was careful not to protest too strongly. "A coincidence. I was there talking to the mechanics in the area. I wanted to know if anyone else was having weird engine failures."

"That's a good idea."

"I thought so. Wait, what's that?" Tasha pointed at the screen. The picture was dark and shadowy, but it looked like someone was scaling the fence. She checked the date and time stamp. "That's the night before *Orca's Run* went out."

"So, it was sabotage."

"Maybe."

They watched the figure move along the pier. It went out of the frame before coming to the slip for *Orca's Run*.

"That has to be it," Jules said.

Tasha wasn't as ready to draw a concrete conclusion. "It didn't look like he was carrying anything, no fuel, no water."

"But he broke in. Whoever it was, was up to no good."

"It's evidence of that," Tasha agreed. She'd hate to assume something and potentially be led in the wrong direction. "We should watch the rest of the video. I can do it myself if you're busy."

"No way. This is the most interesting thing I've done lately. And I'm supposed to sit down every couple of hours." Jules made a show of putting her feet up on the third chair.

There was a light rap on the door, and a waitress pushed it open, arriving with a tray of appetizers and two icy soft drinks.

"I hope you're hungry," Jules said as the server set everything down on the table.

"I'm starving."

"Make sure you try the crab puffs. They're my secret recipe."

"I'm in." Tasha spread a napkin in her lap and helped herself to a crab puff.

"I've been going nuts over smoked salmon," Jules said, going for a decorative morsel on a flat pastry shell. "I don't know why, but my taste buds are big into salt."

Tasha took a bite of the crab puff. It was heavenly. "Mmm," she said around the bite.

Jules's eyes lit up. "See what I mean?"

"You're a genius."

"They're the most popular item on the menu. Caleb wants to steal them for Neo, but I won't let him."

"Stick to your guns," Tasha said before popping the second half of the crab puff into her mouth.

"Oh, I will. We're each half owner of the other's restaurant now, but it's still a competition."

"I hope you're winning. Wait. Take a look." Tasha drew Jules's attention to the laptop screen.

The figure returned to the gate and seemed to toss something over the fence beside it. The two women watched as he climbed the fence, then appeared to look for the object. But then something seemed to startle him, and he ducked away, out of camera range.

"He was up to something," Jules said.

"That was definitely odd," Tasha said. "It could have been tools. I wish we had a better view."

The video got boring again, nothing but yachts bobbing on the midnight tide. Jules took a drink and went for another crab puff.

The office door opened and Caleb appeared.

"How's it going in here?" he asked.

Jules stretched her back as she spoke. "We saw a guy climb over the fence onto the pier and sneak back out again."

Caleb moved past Tasha. He stood behind Jules's chair and began rubbing her shoulders.

"What did he do?" Caleb asked.

"He threw something over the fence," Jules said. "Tasha thinks it might have been tools."

"We couldn't tell for sure," Tasha put in, not wanting to jump to conclusions. "And the frame's not wide enough to see what he did while he was on the pier. It could have been nothing."

The door opened again, and Matt joined them.

"I'll bet it was something," Jules said.

"You'll bet what was something?" Matt asked, glancing around at all three of them.

Tasha couldn't stop herself from reacting to his presence. She imagined his hands on her shoulders, the way Caleb was rubbing Jules's.

"There was a guy," Jules said.

"It might have been something," Tasha jumped in, shaking off the fantasy. "A guy climbing the fence and leaving again. But we couldn't see enough to be sure. There's a lot more video to watch."

"Dianne gone?" Jules asked Matt.

"Hopefully."

"What happened?" Caleb asked. "I didn't expect to see her back in Whiskey Bay...well, ever."

"Neither did I," Matt said. "It turns out her French finance tycoon wasn't all he claimed to be."

"Uh-oh," Caleb said.

"All that money she got in the divorce..."

"No way," Caleb said.

Tasha kept her attention fixed on the screen and away from Matt.

"All gone," he said.

"How is that possible?" Jules asked. "You gave her a fortune."

"The court gave her a fortune," Matt said.

"You didn't fight it."

"I wanted my freedom."

"And she's back anyway," Caleb said. "That didn't work out so well."

"You're not giving her any more money," Jules said.

Tasha wanted to echo the advice, but she didn't feel that it was her business to jump in. Matt and Caleb had been good friends for years. She knew Matt thought of him as a brother.

"I told her to get a job."

"Good advice."

"Let's see if she takes it." Matt didn't sound convinced she would.

Then his hand did come down on Tasha's shoulder. The warmth of his palm surged into her, leaving a tingle behind.

"Anything else going on?"

It was daylight on the video now and people were moving back and forth along the pier: crew, customers, delivery companies and Matt. She watched Matt stride confidently through the frame, and her chest tightened.

She had to struggle to find her voice. "Nothing out of the ordinary. It would be nice to have a wider view."

"You've looked through your own footage?" Caleb asked Matt.

"We have," Matt answered. "But the camera showing the main part of the pier had malfunctioned."

"Malfunctioned?" The skepticism was clear in Caleb's tone.

"We had a technician look at it. The case was cracked.

Salt spray got in and caused corrosion. It might be wear and tear, but it could have been pried open on purpose."

"Who would do that?" Caleb asked. "Why would they do that?"

"I wish I knew," Matt said. "I hate to suspect staff, but there are a couple of new hires on the dock. We're checking into their histories."

"Why would staff have to climb the fence?" Caleb asked.

"Not everyone has the combination," Tasha answered. "Not everyone needs it."

"I don't hand it out to the new hires," Matt said.

Tasha knew the footage narrowed the list of suspects—at least of possible staff members as suspects.

"A little to the left," Jules said on a moan.

Caleb smiled down at his wife.

Matt's hand tightened around Tasha's shoulder.

Arousal washed through her with the force of a riptide.

She ordered herself to concentrate. She refocused on the screen, desperately hoping something would happen on the pier to distract her from his touch.

Matt was happy to speak at the chamber of commerce's annual Christmas gala. He knew the chamber did important work. He'd benefited from its programs in the past. Without its loan guarantees, he never could have purchased Whiskey Bay Marina, never mind grown it to the size it was today, or recovered from the financial hit of his divorce for that matter.

He'd started life out in South Boston. There, his father ran a small residential construction company, while his mother did home care for the elderly. His parents had raised six children. Matt was the youngest and easily the most ambitious. His older siblings all still lived in the South Boston area, most working for his father, all raising families of their own.

They seemed content with barbecues and baseball games. But Matt had wanted more. He'd always wanted more out of life. He'd worked construction long enough to put himself through college and set aside a nest egg. Then he'd bought a few fixer-upper houses, sold them for a profit and finally ended up on the West Coast taking what was probably a ridiculous risk on the Whiskey Bay Marina. But it had turned out well.

It seemed people found it an inspiring story.

Finished with his cuff links and his bow tie, he shrugged into his tux jacket. It was custom fitted and made him feel good, confident, like he'd arrived. It was a self-indulgent moment, dressing in an expensive suit for a fine dinner. And he'd admit to enjoying it.

Tonight he had an additional mission. The owners of the three other marinas in the area would be at the gala. A competitor would have a motive for sabotage. Matt had never trusted Stuart Moorlag. He seemed secretive, and Matt had heard stories of him cutting corners on maintenance and overbilling clients. He could have financial troubles.

There was a knock on the front door, and Matt made his way past the living room to the entry hall. He'd ordered a car for the evening to keep from having to drive home after the party.

But it wasn't the driver standing on his porch. It was Tasha.

"We have a problem," she said without preamble, walking into the entry hall.

"Okay."

Then she stopped and looked him up and down. "Wow."

"It's the gala tonight," he said.

"Still. Wow."

"Is *wow* a good thing?"

"You look pretentious."

"So, not good." He told himself he wasn't disappointed.

He'd have been surprised if she had liked him in a tux. He wished she did. But wishing didn't seem to help him when it came to Tasha.

"Good if pretentious was your goal."

"Well, that was a dig."

"I'm sorry. I didn't mean it to sound like that. What I meant was, you'll impress all the people at what I'm guessing is a very fancy event tonight."

"Thanks. I think." It wasn't quite an insult anymore, but it wasn't quite a compliment either. He decided to move on.

He gave a glance to his watch. He had a few minutes, but not long. "What's the problem?"

"The sabotage is escalating."

That got his instant and full attention. Tasha definitely wasn't one to exaggerate.

"How?" he asked.

"I found a peeled wire in the electric system of *Salty Sea*. It seemed suspicious, so I checked further and found a fuel leak."

He didn't understand the significance. "And?"

"Together, they would likely have started a fire."

"Are you *kidding* me?" He couldn't believe what he was hearing.

"I wish I was."

"People could have been *hurt*?"

A fire on a boat was incredibly serious, especially in December. If they had to jump into the water, hypothermia was the likely result.

"Badly," she said.

He didn't want to leave her to attend the gala. He wanted to explore what she'd found, talk this out. He wanted to plan their next move.

"I have to go to the gala," he said, thinking maybe they could meet later. "I'm speaking at it. And the other marina owners will be there. I was going to use it as an excuse to feel them out."

She didn't hesitate. "I want to come."

The statement took him completely by surprise. He couldn't help but take in her outfit of cargo pants, jersey top and a work jacket.

"Not like this," she said, frowning at him.

"Do you have something to wear?"

Her hands went to her hips, shoulders squaring. "You don't think I can clean up, right?"

Registering the determination in her expression—although he had his doubts—he wasn't about to argue that particular point. He looked at his watch again. "I don't have a lot of time. My car will be here in a few minutes."

Her lips pursed in obvious thought. "I don't have a ball gown in my room. But did Dianne leave anything behind? A dress or something?"

"You want to wear my ex-wife's clothes?" Matt was no expert, but that didn't sound like something an ordinary woman would volunteer to do.

"What've you got?"

"You're serious?"

"You don't think I look serious?" she asked.

"You look very serious."

"So?"

He gave up, even though he had major reservations about how this was going to turn out. "There are some things left in the basement. This way." He led her around the corner to the basement stairs.

He flipped the switch as they started down. "She was a shopaholic. Didn't even bother to take all of it with her. Some of the stuff has probably never been worn."

They went past the pool table and entered a cluttered storage room. The dresses were in plastic film, hanging on a rack, jackets and slacks beside them, shoes in boxes beneath. "I hadn't had the time to get rid of it yet."

"I'll be quick," Tasha said, marching up to the rack and searching her way through.

After a few minutes, she chose something red with sparkles.

"Wow," he said.

"You don't think I can pull off red?"

"It's very bold."

"Trust me. I want them to notice." She hunted through the shoe boxes. "I don't suppose you know what size shoe your ex wore?"

"I have no idea."

Tasha held up a black pump, turning it to various angles. Then she straightened, stripped off her boot and fuzzy sock and wiggled her foot into it.

"It'll do," she said.

"Seriously? Just like that?" He'd seen Dianne spend two hours choosing an outfit.

"You said you were in a hurry." Tasha brushed by him.

"Yes, but…"

"Then, let's do this."

He followed behind, shutting off the lights as they went. "You're a strange woman."

"If by *strange*, you mean *efficient*, then thank you."

By *strange*, he meant *unique*. She was like nobody he'd ever met. Not that it was a bad thing. It was a good thing. At the very least, it was an entertaining thing.

"Yes," he said. "I meant efficient."

"Can I borrow your bathroom?"

"Be my guest."

There was another knock on the front door. This time it was sure to be the driver.

"I have to speak at eight," he called to Tasha's back as she scooted down the hall, clothes bundled in her arms, wearing one work boot and one bare foot.

She waved away his warning, and he turned to answer the door.

Ten minutes later, or maybe it was only five, she emerged from the hallway looking ravishing.

Matt blinked, thinking it had to be an optical illusion. No woman could go from regular Tasha to this screaming ten of a bombshell in five minutes. It wasn't possible.

Her hair was swooped in a wispy updo. The straps of the

dress clung to her slim, creamy shoulders. It sparkled with rhinestones as she walked, the full red skirt swishing above her knees. Her green eyes sparkled, the dark lashes framing their beauty. Her lips were deep red, her cheeks flushed, and her limbs were long, toned and graceful.

He couldn't speak.

"Will I do?" she asked, giving him a graceful twirl. Her tone was softer than normal, her words slower and more measured.

He opened his mouth. "Uh…"

"Don't get all fussy on me, Matt. It was a rush job."

"You look terrific."

She glanced down at herself. "Good enough."

"No, not just good enough. Jaw dropping. How did you do that?" How had this gorgeous, feminine creature stayed hidden beneath the baggy clothes and grease all this time?

"I took off my other clothes and put these ones on."

There was more to it than that. "Your hair?"

"Takes about thirty seconds. Are you ready?"

"I'm ready." He was more than ready. He was *so* ready to go on a date with Tasha.

Okay, so they were investigating more than they were dating. And the new information she'd just brought him was unsettling. They'd have to talk more about that in the car.

But she was more ravishingly beautiful than he could have possibly imagined, and she was his partner for the gala. He felt fantastic, far better than he had merely putting on the fine tux, maybe better than he'd felt in his whole life.

At the ballroom in downtown Olympia, Tasha felt like she was stepping into her own past. She'd been to this party dozens of times, the chamber orchestra, the high-end hors d'oeuvres, the glittering women and stiffly dressed men. And, in this case, the rich Christmas decorations, floral arrangements, garlands of holly and evergreen, thousands of white lights, swirls of spun-glass snow and a huge Christmas tree on the back wall, covered in oversize blue and white ornaments and twinkling lights.

"You going to be okay in all this?" Matt asked as they walked through the grand entry.

"I'll be fine." She could do this in her sleep.

"We'll have to sit down near the front. They want me close by for my presentation."

"No problem." She was used to her parents being VIPs at events in Boston. From the time she was seven or eight, she'd learned to sit still through interminable speeches and to respond politely to small talk from her parents' friends and business connections. "Shall we mingle our way down?"

He looked surprised by the suggestion. "Sure."

"Can you point out the other marina owners?"

They began walking as Matt gazed around the room.

"Hello there, Matt." A fiftysomething man approached, clasping Matt's hand in a hearty shake.

"Hugh," Matt responded. "Good to see you again." He immediately turned to Tasha. "This is Tasha Lowell. Tasha, Hugh Mercer owns Mercer Manufacturing, headquartered here in Olympia."

Tasha offered her hand and gave Hugh Mercer a warm smile. "It's a pleasure to meet you, sir." She quickly moved her attention on to the woman standing next to Hugh.

Hugh cleared his throat. "This is my wife, Rebecca."

"Hello, Rebecca," Tasha said, moving close to the woman, half turning away from Hugh and Matt. If she'd learned anything over the years, it was to keep her attention firmly off any man, no matter his age, who had a date by his side. "I *love* that necklace," she said to Rebecca. "A Nischelle?"

Rebecca returned Tasha's smile. "Why, yes. A gift from Hugh for our anniversary."

"How many years?" Tasha asked.

"Twenty-five."

"Congratulations on that. Was it a winter wedding?"

"Spring," Rebecca said. "We were married in New York. My parents lived there at the time."

"I love New York in the spring." Tasha put some enthusiasm in her voice. "Tell me it was a grand affair."

"We held it at Blair Club in the Hamptons."

"Were the cherry blossoms out?" Tasha had been to the Blair Club on a number of occasions. Their gardens were legendary.

"They were."

"It sounds like a dream." Tasha looped her arm through Matt's, taking advantage of a brief lull in the men's conversation. "Darling, I'm really looking forward to some champagne."

He covered her hand. "Of course. Nice to see you, Hugh. Rebecca, you look fantastic."

"Enjoy the party," Hugh said.

Tasha gave a cheery little wave as they moved away.

"*What* was that?" Matt whispered in her ear. "Cherry blossoms? You made it sound like you'd been there."

She didn't want to reveal her past to Matt. She wanted it kept firmly there—in the past.

"Cherry blossoms seemed like a safe bet in the spring. You don't mind my pulling us away from the Mercers, do you? They're not our target."

Too late, it occurred to her that Matt might have some kind of reason for chatting Hugh up. She hoped she hadn't spoiled his plans.

"You were right. They're not our targets." He put a hand on the small of her back. "There. Two o'clock. The man with the burgundy patterned tie."

Ignoring the distraction of Matt's touch, Tasha looked in that direction. "Tall, short brown hair, long nose?"

"Yes. That's Ralph Moretti. He owns Waterside Charters. They're smaller than Whiskey Bay, but they're closest to us geographically."

"Is he married?"

Matt's hand flexed against her waist. "Why?"

"So I know how to play this."

"Play this?"

"If he's up to something, he'll be a lot more likely to give information away based on my giggling, ingenuous questions than if you start grilling him. But if he has a wife who's likely to show up halfway through the conversation, it going to throw us off the game."

"You're going to flirt with him?" Matt did not sound pleased.

"I wouldn't call it flirting."

"What would you call it?"

"Disarming." She sized up Ralph Moretti as they drew closer.

"There's a distinction?" Matt asked.

"Absolutely."

They'd run out of room. Ralph was right there in front of them.

"Moretti," Matt greeted with a handshake.

"Emerson," Ralph responded.

Ralph's guarded tone immediately piqued Tasha's interest.

It took about half a second for his gaze to move to her and stop.

"Tasha Lowell." She offered him her hand.

"Call me Ralph," he told her, lightly shaking. He was gentlemanly enough not to squeeze.

"Ralph," she said with a bright smile. "Matt tells me you have a marina."

"I do indeed."

"I have a thing for boats."

The pressure of Matt's hand increased against her back.

"Really?" Ralph asked, with the barest of gazes at Matt. "What do you like about them?"

"Everything," she said. "The lines of the craft, the motion of the waves, the way they can take you on adventures."

"A woman of good taste," he said.

"How far do you go?" she asked.

Matt coughed.

"Excuse me?" Ralph asked.

Tasha leaned in just a little bit. "Your charters. Oregon? California? Do you go up to Canada?"

"Washington and Oregon mostly," he said.

"Are you looking to expand?"

Ralph's gaze flicked to Matt. Was it a look of guilt?

"Maybe in the future," Ralph said, bringing his attention back to Tasha.

"What about markets?" she asked.

His expression turned confused, maybe slightly suspicious.

"Do you get a lot of women clients?" She breezed past the topic she'd intended to broach. "Party boats. Me and my friends like to have fun."

"Ah," he said, obviously relaxing again. "Yes. Waterside can party it up with the best of them."

"Whiskey Bay—" she touched Matt lightly on the arm "—seems to go for an older crowd."

He stiffened beside her.

She ignored the reaction and carried on. "I don't know if I've seen your advertising. Do you have a website?"

"We're upgrading it," Ralph said.

"Expanding your reach? There is a Midwest full of clients right next door. Spring break would be an awesome time to get their attention."

"Do you have a job?" Ralph asked her.

She laughed. "Are you offering?"

"You'd make one heck of an ambassador."

She held up her palms. "*That's* what I keep telling Matt."

"You're missing the boat on this, Matt." There was an edge of humor to Ralph's tone, but he kept his gaze on Tasha this time.

Matt spoke up. "She can have any job she wants at Whiskey Bay for as long as she wants it."

Ralph quickly glanced up. Whatever he saw on Matt's expression caused him to take a step back.

"It was nice to meet you, Tasha," Ralph said.

"Moretti," Matt said by way of goodbye. Then he steered Tasha away.

"Well, that was interesting," Tasha said.

"Is *that* what you call it?"

"Yes. He wants to expand his business. And something about you put him on edge."

"Because he was trying to steal my date."

"Nah." She didn't buy that. "He reacted when I asked if he was expanding. And he's revamping his website. He's looking to make a move on your customers."

"He's looking to make a move on you."

"Don't be so paranoid."

A wave of mottled mauve silk moved in front of them.

"Hello, Matt."

Tasha was astonished to come face-to-face with Dianne.

"Dianne," Matt said evenly. "What are you doing here?"

"Enjoying the season." She eyed Tasha up and down, a delicate sneer coming over her face as she looked down her nose.

Tasha had seen that expression a thousand times, from women and girls who were certain they were a cut above a plain-looking mechanic and not the least bit hesitant to try to put Tasha in her place.

Still, Tasha felt like she should muster up some sympathy. Dianne was in a tough spot.

"Merry Christmas," she said to Dianne in her most polite voice.

"I see you got out of those oily rags," Dianne returned. "Is that last year's frock?"

"I like to think Bareese is timeless," Tasha said with an air of indifference.

Dianne wrinkled her nose.

Tasha took in Dianne's opulent gown. "Your Moreau must

be worth a fortune." She blinked her eyes in mock innocence. "You could auction it after the party. For the funds, I mean."

Matt stifled a laugh.

Dianne's complexion went a shade darker. "Why, you little—"

"Time for us to take our seats," Matt said, taking Tasha's hand. "What is up with you?" he asked as they moved away.

Tasha winced. "I'm sorry. I shouldn't have said that."

"That's not what I meant."

"It was really rude."

The lights blinked, and the MC made his way onto the stage.

"Dianne was the one who was rude. And I'm grateful," Matt continued, picking up the pace. "You keep it up, and she's going to leave town in a hurry. Besides, she deserves a little of her own medicine for once."

Matt's odd compliment warmed Tasha. She wasn't particularly proud of going mean-girl debutante on Dianne. But Matt's life would be better if Dianne left. And Tasha found she wanted that, too.

Six

Matt's speech had gone well. People had laughed in the right spots and clapped in the right spots. He was happy to have been entertaining. But he was happier still to watch Tasha's face in the front row. Every time she'd smiled, he'd felt a physical jolt.

He couldn't believe how feminine, how beautiful, how downright elegant she'd looked surrounded by the splendor of the ballroom. And now, swaying in his arms, she was graceful and light. The transformation was astonishing. Cinderella had nothing on Tasha.

"You've done this before," he guessed as he guided her into a slow spin.

"Danced? Yes, I have."

"Been the belle of a ball."

She smiled at that as she came back into his arms. "I'm far from the belle of any ball."

The dance floor was nicely filled. The music was superb, and beautiful women floated past on the arms of their partners. None could hold a candle to Tasha.

"You are to me," he said.

"You're flirting?"

"No. I'm disarming."

She gave a short laugh. "It's not going to work."

He supposed not. "You have definitely done this before."

"I've been to a few balls in my time."

"I never would have guessed. I mean before tonight I never would have guessed. You sure don't let on that there's an elegant lifestyle in your past."

"I don't spend much time dwelling on it."

"You're very good at this." He'd been stunned at her abil-

ity to make small talk, to get the other marina owners to relax
and be chatty. They hadn't come up with any solid leads or
suspects, but they'd learned Waterside Charters was expanding and Rose and Company was taking delivery of a new
seventy-five-foot yacht in the spring. Both would be com-
peting head-to-head with Whiskey Bay Marina.

"You don't have to like something to be good at it."

"Do you like dancing?" he asked, wanting to hear that she
did, hoping to hear that she liked dancing with him.

"Yes. But not necessarily in these shoes."

He glanced down. "Do they hurt?"

"You've never worn high heels before, have you?"

"That would be a no."

"Yes, they hurt. They don't fit all that well."

"Should we stop?"

"I'll survive."

He debated finding them a place to sit down. But he liked
having her in his arms. So he settled for slowing the pace,
inching even closer to her. It was a good decision.

"So where did you attend these formative balls?"

"Boston, mostly. Some in New York. Once in DC when
I was around seventeen."

"You're a fellow Bostonian?" He was surprised by the
idea.

She drew back to look at him. "You, too?"

"Southie."

"And you left?" She seemed to be the one surprised now.

"I did. The rest of my family stayed in the neighborhood,
though."

The song ended, and another started. He danced them
right through the change.

"Brothers and sisters?" she asked.

"Three brothers, two sisters. I'm the youngest. What about
you?"

"Wow. Six kids?"

"Yep."

"Your parents must have been busy."

"It was busy and crowded. I had absolutely no desire to live like that. Where did you grow up?"

Since she'd talked about balls and flying off to New York and Washington for parties, he was guessing she wasn't a Southie.

It took her a minute to answer. "Beacon Hill."

So, she had lived posh.

"It's nice up there," he said.

"It's snooty up there. At least the people I knew, and especially my parents' friends and associates. I couldn't wait to get away from their judgment."

"Spread your wings?" he asked.

"Something like that. Yes, very much like that."

He found the insight quite fascinating. "Does your family still live there?" For some reason, learning she was from Boston made their connection seem stronger.

"Absolutely."

"Brothers and sisters?" he asked when she didn't offer details.

"Two sisters. Youngest here, too," she said with an almost guilty smile.

"Makes it easy to get away with things," he said.

"Made it easy to slip town."

"Are you close to them?"

He'd never heard her talk about her family. Then again, they hadn't had a whole lot of in-depth conversations about either of their backgrounds. Mostly he liked to leave his alone.

"We don't have a lot in common." There was something in her tone, not regret exactly, but acceptance of some kind.

"I hear you," he said, recognizing the emotion.

He and his family seemed to operate in different dimensions. He saw value in financial success. He'd worked hard to get here, and he had no problem enjoying it. The rest of his family held financial success in suspicion. He'd tried to get his mind around it, but at the end of the day he just couldn't agree.

Dianne had understood. It was one of the things that first drew him to her. She liked the finer things, and was unapologetic about her ambition. That trait might have turned on her now. But the theory was still sound. He was still going after success.

"My family…" he began, wondering how to frame it. "They're content to pay the bills, throw potlucks on Sundays, take their kids to community center dance lessons and cheer for the Red Sox at tailgate parties."

"Oh, the horror," she mocked.

"I want more," he said.

"Why?"

"Why not?" He looked around the ballroom. "This is nice. This is great. And who wouldn't want the freedom to take any trip, eat at any restaurant, accept any party invitation."

"Are you free, Matt? Really?"

"I'm pretty damn free."

His choice of lifestyle had allowed him to work hard, to focus on his business, to succeed in a way that was satisfying to him. If he'd strapped on a tool belt in Southie, met a nice woman and had a few kids, it would have meant being dishonest about himself.

It was Tasha's turn to look around the room. "This all doesn't feel like a straitjacket to you?"

"Not at all." He didn't understand her attitude. She seemed to be having a good time. "And I'm here by choice."

"These people don't seem disingenuous to you?"

"Maybe the ones that are sabotaging my boats. But we're not even sure they're here. It's just as likely they're at the Edge."

"What's wrong with the Edge?"

"Nothing. Did I say there was something wrong with the Edge?"

"You used it as a negative comparator to this party."

"It's a whole lot different than this party. Like Beacon Hill and Southie. Do you honestly think people prefer Southie?"

"They might."

Matt wasn't buying the argument. "Sure. People from Southie are proud. I get that. Believe me, I've lived that. But you give them a real and serious choice, they'd be in Beacon Hill in a heartbeat."

Tasha's steps slowed. "It's kind of sad that you believe that."

"It's not sad. And I don't just believe that. It's true."

She stopped. "Thanks for the dance, Matt."

"You can't honestly be annoyed with me." It wasn't reasonable.

"I'm going to rest my feet."

"I'll take you—"

"No." She put her hand on his chest and moved back. "Go mingle. I'll see you later on."

"Tasha." He couldn't believe she was walking away.

Tasha wasn't angry with Matt. She felt more sad than anything.

Sure, he'd made some money in his life. But up to now he'd struck her as being mostly down-to-earth. She'd thought the money was incidental to him, running a business that he loved. It was disappointing to discover that his goal had been wealth.

Seeing him tonight, she realized her initial instincts were right. He was exactly the kind of man she'd left behind. Ironically, he was the kind of man her parents would love.

If this were a Boston party, her parents would be throwing her into his arms. The Lowells were an old Bostonian family, but her parents wouldn't hold Matt's Southie roots against him, not like her grandparents or great-grandparents would have.

In this day and age, money was money. Her father in particular respected men who pulled themselves up from nothing. It was a darn good thing they weren't back in Boston right now.

She crossed the relative quiet of the foyer, following the signs to the ladies' room. She needed to freshen up. Then she really was going to find a place to sit down and rest her feet. The shoes might be slightly large, but they were also slightly narrow for her feet, and she had developed stinging blisters on both of her baby toes.

As she passed an alcove, she caught sight of Dianne's unmistakable mauve dress. Dianne was sitting on a small bench, gazing out a bay window at the city lights. Her shoulders were hunched, and they were shaking.

Tasha felt like a heel. One of the reasons she avoided these upper-crust events was that they brought out the worst in her. She seemed too easily influenced by the snobbery and spitefulness.

The last thing in the world she wanted to do was comfort Matt's ex-wife. But it was partly her fault that Dianne was upset. She'd been insufferably rude in suggesting she auction off her dress.

Tasha took a turn and crossed the alcove, coming up beside Dianne.

Dianne looked up in what appeared to be horror. She quickly swiped her hand beneath her eyes. But the action did nothing to hide the red puffiness.

"Are you okay?" Tasha asked.

"I'm fine." Dianne gave a jerky nod. "Fine."

It was patently obvious it was a lie.

Tasha gave an inward sigh and sat down on the other end of the padded French provincial bench. "You don't look fine."

"I got something in my eyes. Or maybe it was the perfume. Allergies, you know."

Tasha told herself to accept the explanation and walk away. She didn't know Dianne. Given the circumstances, fake though her relationship with Matt was, she was likely the last person Dianne wanted to talk to. But it would be heartless to simply leave her there.

"You're obviously upset," Tasha said.

"Aren't *you* the observant one."

"Don't."

"Why? What do you want? To rub my nose in it? Again?"

"No. I want to apologize. I was nasty to you earlier. I'm really sorry about that. I thought you were…" Tasha struggled for the right words. "Stronger. I thought you were tough. I didn't mean to upset you."

Dianne's tone changed. "It's not you. It's…" She closed her eyes for a long second. A couple of more tears leaked out. "I can't," she said.

Tasha moved closer. She put a hand on Dianne's arm. "Will talking to me make it any worse?"

Dianne drew in a shuddering breath. She opened her eyes and gazed at Tasha for a long time.

"I've made such a mess of it," she finally said.

"You mean losing the money?"

Dianne nodded. "François was charming, attentive, affectionate. Matt was working all the time. He never wanted to travel with me. I thought… I thought our life together would be different. But it wasn't any fun. It was all work, work, work. And then I met François. It wasn't on purpose. I'm not a bad person."

"I don't think you're a bad person." Tasha was being honest about that.

Dianne might not be the right person for Matt, and maybe she had a selfish streak, but right now she just seemed sad and defeated. Tasha would have to be made of stone not to feel sympathy.

Dianne gave a brittle laugh. "I thought François not wanting a prenup was the perfect sign, the proof that he loved me for me. He seemed to have so much more money than I did. And he'd invested so successfully, that I thought I couldn't lose…but I did lose. And I'd hoped Matt…"

"What exactly do you want from Matt?" Tasha might be sympathetic, but she knew sympathy alone wouldn't help Dianne.

Dianne shrugged. "At first… At first I thought there might still be a chance for us. I was the one who left him, not the other way around. I thought he might still…" She shook her head. "But then I met you, and I realized he'd moved on."

A part of Tasha wanted to confess. But she knew Matt wouldn't consider a reconciliation with Dianne. And telling Dianne she and Matt weren't dating would be a betrayal of him. She couldn't do it.

"So, now what?" Tasha asked.

"I don't know." Dianne's tears welled up again. "I honestly don't know."

"You need to know," Tasha said as gently as she could. "You need a plan. You need to take care of yourself."

"I can't."

"You can. Everyone can. It's a matter of finding your strengths."

"My strength is marrying rich men."

"That's not true. It's not your only strength. And even if it was your only strength, it's a bad strength, not one you want to depend on. Look what happened last time."

"I have no money," Dianne said, looking truly terrified. "I've nearly maxed out my credit cards. I've missed payments. They're going to cancel them. I really will be selling my clothes on the street corner."

"Okay, now you're being melodramatic."

"I'm not," she moaned.

"What about your family? Could you stay with family?"

Dianne gave a choppy shake of her head. "There's no one."

"No one at all?"

"My dad died. My stepmother sent me to boarding school. She couldn't wait to get me out of the house."

"Are they in Washington State?"

"Boston."

Tasha was surprised. "You, too?"

Dianne stilled. "You're from Boston?"

"I am."

Dianne searched Tasha's face. "You're a Lowell. *The* Lowells?"

Tasha was embarrassed. "I don't know if there are any 'the' Lowells."

"The Vincent Lowell Library?"

"My grandfather," Tasha admitted.

"Does Matt know?" Before Tasha could respond, Dianne continued on a slightly shrill laugh. "Of course he knows. Why didn't I see that before? You're his dream match."

Tasha was confident Matt didn't know. And there wasn't much to know anyway. The Lowells might be an old Boston family. But there were plenty of those around. It wasn't all that noteworthy.

"Do you want to go back to Boston?" Tasha asked, turning the subject back to Dianne.

"No. Never. That's not in the cards."

"Do you want to stay here?" Tasha was trying to find a starting point, any starting point for Dianne.

Dianne lifted her head and looked around. "There's nothing left for me here either." Her voice cracked again. "Not without Matt."

"You really need to think about a job. You're young. Get started on a career. Did you go to college?"

"Only for a year. I took fine arts. I didn't pass much."

"What would you like to do? What are you good at?"

Dianne looked Tasha in the eyes. "Why are you doing this?"

"I want to help," Tasha answered honestly.

"Why? I'm nothing to you."

"You're a fellow human being, a fellow Bostonian, part of the sisterhood."

Dianne gave a hollow laugh. "There's no sisterhood. Are you a do-gooder? Am I a charitable thing for you?"

"No." Tasha gave it some thought. "I don't know, really." It was as honest as she could be.

"I gave parties," Dianne said in a tired, self-mocking voice. "I can make small talk and order hors d'oeuvres."

The germ of an idea came to Tasha.

Caleb had fancy restaurants all over the country. Perhaps Jules, Tasha knew her better than she did Caleb, might be willing to help Dianne.

"I'm going to ask around," Tasha said.

"Matt won't like that."

"Doesn't matter." Tasha wasn't sure if Matt would care or not. But surely he'd be in favor of anything that put Dianne back on her feet, helped her to take care of herself.

She didn't have to make a big deal with Jules. And if Matt did find out, he'd see the logic and reason, she assured herself. He was a very reasonable man.

On the drive home, Tasha seemed lost in thought. Either that, or she was still annoyed with Matt for appreciating financial security. He'd wanted to talk about it some more, maybe help her understand his motivations. But he didn't want to rekindle their argument. He liked it better when they were on the same side of something.

"Could we really have had a fire?" he asked her.

She turned from where she'd been gazing out the window into the darkness. "What?"

"On *Salty Sea*. Would there have been a fire?"

"Yes. Almost certainly. The fuel from the fuel line leak would have sprayed across the spark from the electric short, and *bam*, it would have ignited."

"It looks odd," he said. "You talking about the inner workings of an engine while you're dressed like that."

"That's why I don't dress like this."

"You look terrific."

"I feel like a fraud. I can't wait to get out of this getup." She reached down and peeled off the black pumps.

The action was sexy, very sexy. He immediately imagined her shrugging down the straps of the dress. He shifted in his seat.

"Feet sore?" he asked.

"And how. Steel-toed boots might be clunky, but they're built for wearing, not for show."

"They wouldn't go with the dress."

"Ha ha."

"And it would be hard to dance in them."

Tasha curled her legs up on the seat, a hand going to one foot to rub it. "I'd be willing to give it a shot."

Matt curled his hands to keep them still. "The new cameras are being installed tomorrow."

"We need them. I'm doubling up on my inspections. Alex and I are going to check every boat the morning before it leaves port."

"Won't that be a lot of work?"

"I couldn't do everything I'd like, not without hiring three more mechanics. But we can cover the basics."

"Do you need to hire someone else?"

She switched her self-massage to the other foot. "I'll call in all the contract mechanics. But I have to believe this is temporary. The next time that guy tries something, we're going to catch him on camera and have him arrested."

Matt gave in to temptation and reached across the back seat for one of her feet.

"Don't." She jumped at his touch.

He looked meaningfully at the driver. "It's just a foot."

"That's not a good idea."

He ignored her, settling her foot in his lap and pressing his thumb into the arch.

She gave a small moan.

"Those blisters look awful," he said.

Her baby toes and the backs of her heels were swollen and red.

"They'll heal."

"Why didn't you say something?"

"I did."

"You didn't tell me how bad it was." He massaged carefully around the swollen skin.

"That feels good," she said.

"Do you need to take the day off tomorrow?"

"You're funny."

"I'm serious. It's Sunday. Don't work."

"And let Alex do it all?"

He didn't have a comeback for that. He had to admire Tasha's work ethic. Still, he couldn't let her burn herself out. And her feet were going to be painful tomorrow.

"As long as I don't put on the same shoes," she said. "I'll use bandages and wear thick socks. I'll be fine."

"You're a trouper," he said with honest admiration.

The driver slowed as Matt's driveway came up on the right.

"You're easily impressed," she said.

"Not really."

They were silent as the car cruised through the trees to the house. While they did, Matt continued his massage. His image of her strong and sturdy on the job faded to how she was now...soft, smooth, almost delicate.

When the car came to a stop, he reached to the floor and collected her shoes.

"What are you doing?" she asked.

"Wait right there." He exited from his side and tipped the driver.

Then he went around to her, opening the door and reaching in to lift her from the seat.

"Oh, no you don't," she protested.

"Oh, yes I do. You can't put these shoes back on. You'll burst the blisters and bleed all over the place."

"Then I'll walk barefoot."

"Over the rocks and through the mud? Hang on."

"Put me down."

But even as she protested, he hoisted her easily into the air, and her arms went around his shoulders. He pushed the sedan door shut with his shoulder and started to the stairs that led to the staff quarters.

"This is ridiculous," she said. "Nobody better see us."

"It's dark."

"There are lights on the porch."

"It's after midnight. Everyone will be asleep."

"They better be."

He couldn't help but smile to himself. He'd learned by now that Tasha hated anything that made her look remotely weak.

"Blisters are nothing to be ashamed of," he said.

"I'm not ashamed of having blisters." She paused. "I'm ashamed of having some Neanderthal carry my apparently feeble self to my room."

"I'm wearing a tux."

"So?"

"I'm just saying, your average Neanderthal probably didn't wear a tux."

The joke got him a bop in the shoulder.

"Not much of a comeback," he said.

"We're here. You can put me down now."

"Not yet." He mounted the stairs for the second floor.

She squirmed in his arms. "I can walk on wooden stairs in my bare feet."

"Splinters."

"I'm not going to get splinters."

"We're here. Where's your key?"

"You can put me down on the mat."

"I like holding you." He did. He was in absolutely no hurry to put her down. "You're light. You're soft. Your hair smells like vanilla."

"It's not locked," she said.

"Are you kidding me?" he barked. "With all that's been going on?" He couldn't believe she would be so cavalier about her own safety.

He reached for the doorknob and opened the door. He set her down on the floor inside and immediately turned on the light switch, checking all the corners of the room, the small sitting area, the kitchenette, the double bed. Then he crossed to the bathroom and opened up the door.

"Matt, this is silly."

He was annoyed with her. No, he was downright angry. Somebody was targeting them for unknown reasons, and so far it had more to do with her than with anybody else at Whiskey Bay, and she was leaving her door unlocked?

He turned back. "Please tell me you lock it at night."

She looked decidedly guilty. "I can start."

He took the paces that brought him in front of her. "You bet your life you're going to start. You're going to start tonight, now, right away."

"You don't need to get upset," she said.

"You're scaring me." His gaze fell on her gorgeous green eyes. "I'm afraid for you." He took in her flushed cheeks. "I want to protect you. I…"

Their gazes meshed, and the sound of the surf filled the silence. She just stood there in the shadows looking like his fondest dream come true.

She looked delicate and enticing. Her hair was mussed. One strap had fallen down, leaving her shoulder bare. He wanted to kiss her shoulder. He wanted to taste that shoulder more than he'd ever wanted anything in his life.

He gave in.

He leaned forward, gently wrapping his hands around her upper arms. He placed a light kiss on her shoulder. Then he tasted her skin with the tip of his tongue. He kissed her again, made his way to her neck.

She tipped her head sideways, giving him better access.

He brushed her hair back, kissing his way to her ear, her temple, her closed eyes and finally her mouth.

She kissed him back, and he spread his fingers into her hair.

She stepped into his arms, an enchanting, elegant, utterly feminine woman pressing against his hard, heated body.

He reached out and pushed the door shut behind her.

He deepened their kiss.

He began to unzip her dress, paused, running his hands over the smooth skin of her back.

"Don't stop," she gasped. "Don't, don't stop."

Seven

Everything flooded from Tasha's mind, everything except the taste of Matt's lips, the feel of his hands and the sound of his voice. His heart beat against her chest where they pressed together. She wanted this. No, she needed this. Whatever it was that had been building between them for days on end was bursting out, and there was no stopping it.

She pushed off his tux jacket, and he tossed it on the chair. She tugged his bow tie loose, and it dangled around his neck. She kissed his square chin, struggled with the buttons of his shirt, while his hands roamed her back.

His hands were warm, the fingertips calloused. As she peeled away his tuxedo, the urbane facade seemed to melt away along with it. He was tough underneath, muscular and masculine. A small scar marred his chest, another across his shoulder.

She kissed the shoulder and traced a fingertip along his chest. "What happened?"

"Working," he answered, his breathing deep. "Winch handle and a rogue wave."

"You should be more careful."

"I will."

She couldn't help but smile at his easy capitulation.

His hands went to her dress straps. He eased them down, baring her breasts in the cool air.

"Gorgeous," he said stopping to stare.

It had been a long time since a man had seen her naked, never if you didn't count an eighteen-year-old freshman. She was glad it was Matt, glad he seemed pleased, happy to bask in the heat of his gaze.

He slowly reached out, brushing his thumb across her

nipple. She sucked in a breath, a shudder running through to her core. She closed her eyes, waiting for him to do it again.

"Oh, Tasha," he whispered, his hand closing over her breasts.

She tipped her head for his kiss, and her dress slithered to the floor.

His palms slipped to her rear, covering her satin panties. His lips found hers again, his kiss deep and delicious. His shirt separated, and they were skin to skin.

"You're so soft." His hand continued its exploration of her breast.

Rockets of sensation streamed from her hard nipples to the apex of her thighs.

Impatient, she reached for his belt, looping it free, popping the button of his pants and dragging down the zipper.

He groaned as her knuckles grazed him.

Then he scooped her back into his arms and carried her to the double bed, stripping back the blankets to lay her on the cool sheets. He was beside her in a moment, shucking his pants.

He came to his knees, hooking his thumbs in the waist of her panties, drawing them slowly down, to her thighs, to her knees and over her ankles.

He kissed her ankle, then her knee, then her thigh and her hip bone, making his way to her breasts, kissing them both, making her heartbeat echo all through her.

She raked her fingers into his hair. A buzzing started within her, making her twitch with need.

"You have a condom?" she asked breathlessly. She was woefully unprepared.

"I've got it," he said. "Don't worry."

He rose up and kissed her mouth. Then his hands went on a glorious exploration, touching her everywhere, discovering secrets, making her writhe with impatience and need.

"Please, Matt," she finally whimpered.

"Oh, yes," he said, levering above her, stroking her thighs. She watched him closely as he pressed slowly, steadily inside.

She rocked her hips upward, closing her legs around him.

He moved, pulling out, pushing in, grasping her to him as he kissed her deeper and deeper. She met his tongue thrust for thrust, and her hands gripped his back. She needed an anchor as gravity gave way.

The room grew hotter. The waves sounded louder on the rocks below. Matt's body moved faster, and she arched to meet him, the rhythm increasing.

Fulfillment started as a deep glow, burning hotter, moving outward, taking over her belly, then her breasts, then her legs and her arms. It tingled in her toes and in the roots of her hair. She cried out as sensation lifted her. Then she flew and then floated.

"Tasha," Matt cried, his body shuddering against her.

She absorbed every tremor, his body slick, his heartbeat steady. Her waves of pleasure were unending, until she finally fell still, exhausted, unable to move beneath his comfortable weight on top of her.

She didn't know what she'd done.

Okay, she knew what she'd done. She knew exactly what she'd done. She also knew she shouldn't have done it.

"Stop," he muttered in her ear.

"Stop what?"

He rose up on an elbow. "I can feel you second-guessing yourself."

"We can't undo that," she said.

"Who wants to undo it?"

"We do. We should. That wasn't part of the plan."

"There was a plan?"

"Quit laughing at me."

He enveloped her in a warm hug.

It shouldn't have felt so great. It couldn't feel this great.

"Oh, Tasha. We made love. People do it all the time. The world will keep spinning, I promise."

"Maybe *you* do it all the time."

"I didn't mean that the way it sounded." He eased back to look at her again. He smoothed the hair from her eyes. "I don't do it all the time. My marriage was on the rocks for quite a while. And since then... Well, I've only just started dating again."

Tasha shouldn't have cared whom Matt had been with before her. But she found herself glad that he hadn't had an active sex life. She didn't want it to matter, but it did.

"I'm—" She stopped short, realizing she was going to sound hopelessly unsophisticated.

His eyes widened, and he drew sharply back. "You weren't..."

"A virgin? No. I would have said something."

"Thank goodness."

"I did have a boyfriend," she said. "Right after high school."

"One?" Matt asked. "Singular?"

"I couldn't date anyone in trade school. There were three women in a class of thirty-six. We were way too smart to get involved with anyone. It could have killed our chances of being treated as peers."

"I suppose," Matt said. Then he touched a finger to the bottom of her chin. "So, you're saying one then? Just the one guy?"

"Just the one," she admitted, feeling a bit foolish. She should have kept her mouth shut.

"Tasha Lowell." His kissed her tenderly on the mouth. "I am honored."

"Oh, that didn't sound outmoded at all."

He grinned. "You could be honored back at me."

"Okay," she said, fighting a smile. "Matt Emerson, I am honored. And I'm embarrassed. And I'm certainly soon to be regretful."

"But not yet?" he asked on an exaggerated note of hopefulness.

"I can feel it coming."

"You have nothing to regret."

She wriggled to relieve the pressure on her hip, and he eased off to one side.

"You said that about our kiss," she said, sitting up and pulling a sheet over her breasts.

"Did you?" He traced a line along her knuckles.

"I don't know." Things had changed so fundamentally between them. Was that single kiss to blame?

She didn't want to talk about it right now. She didn't want to dissect this.

"I could stay," he offered in a soft voice.

She jumped an inch off the bed and her voice rose an octave. "What?"

"I don't have to rush off."

"Yes, you do." She looked around for her clothes, realizing she needed to get out of the bed right now. "You can't stay here. It's the staff quarters. You need to get out while it's still dark, before anybody starts work."

He didn't look happy. But he also seemed to understand. "I know. This isn't exactly discreet. But I don't want to leave you." He reached for her.

She evaded his grasp. "If you don't. If somebody sees you, then it's trade school all over again. Only this time I had a one-night stand with the teacher."

His brow went up. "How am I the teacher?"

"You know what I mean. You're in a position of authority. It's worse than sleeping with a peer. I lose any and all credibility. Everybody's reminded that I'm not one of the guys."

"They respect you, Tasha. And who says this is a one-night stand?"

"Who says it's not? So far that's exactly what it is."

"But—"

"But nothing, Matt. The mathematical odds that this leads to something, I mean something besides a fling based on chemistry alone, are, I don't know, maybe five, six percent.

The mathematical odds of this leading to the dismantling of my credibility and reputation are around ninety. What would you do if you were me?"

"Where did you come up with five or six percent?"

"I did a quick calculation in my head."

"That's insane." He reached for her again, and she backed to an ever safer distance.

She didn't want him to leave. But he had to leave. He had to leave now before she weakened.

"Please, Matt," she said.

He hardened his jaw. "Of course." He threw back the covers and came to his feet.

She didn't want to watch him walk naked across the room. But she couldn't help herself. He was magnificent, and the sight of him brought back instant memories of their lovemaking.

Her skin flushed. Then goose bumps formed. But she had to be strong. She would force herself to let him leave.

With Noah Glover's electric expertise to guide them, Matt, Caleb and TJ had spent the day installing the new security cameras. Now as a thank-you, Matt was hosting dinner for Caleb and Jules, TJ and Jules's sister, Melissa, along with Noah.

Watching Caleb with Jules, and Noah with Melissa, Matt couldn't help thinking about Tasha. She'd made herself scarce all day, while he'd spent most of it watching for her. He couldn't stop thinking about her. He'd lain awake half the night thinking about her, wishing he could have slept with her. After their mind-blowing lovemaking, his arms felt completely empty without her.

"I hope the extra cameras do the trick," TJ said as he joined Matt by the dining table.

Matt was setting out plates and glasses, since Jules had all but kicked him out of the kitchen.

"I don't care what it takes," Matt responded. "I'm catching this guy and throwing him in jail. His last stunt could have caused a fire. People could have been seriously hurt, or worse."

"Your competition?" TJ asked, gazing through the glass wall to the marina below.

"I talked to all of them at the gala last night. Waterside Charters is expanding, and Rose and Company bought a new seventy-five-footer. Both would be happy to steal business from me. But I don't see them doing it this way."

"Then what?" TJ asked.

"If I have my way, we'll find out soon." Matt took in the overview of the marina, his gaze settling on the staff quarters. Tasha was there.

Giving up fighting with himself, he extracted his cell phone. "I'll just be a minute," he said to TJ, then moved down the hall.

He typed into his phone: Dinner with Caleb and Jules at my place. Talking about the new cameras. Can you come?

He hit Send and waited. It was a stretch of an excuse, but he didn't care. He wanted her here with him.

Jules and Melissa were laughing in the kitchen. TJ's voice blended with Caleb's and Noah's. Everybody sounded happy. It had been a good day's work. It was a good night with friends. Matt should have felt terrific.

His phone pinged with Tasha's response. Just leaving. Meeting some people for drinks.

Disappointment thudded hard in his stomach. He wanted to ask who. He wanted to ask where. Mostly, he wanted to ask why she'd choose them over him.

"Hey, Matt?" Noah appeared and moved down the hall toward him.

"Hi. Thanks again for your help today."

"Sure." Noah looked nervous.

"What's up?" Matt asked.

Noah glanced down the hall behind him. "You mind if I hijack dessert tonight?"

"You brought dessert?"

"No, no. I brought a bottle of champagne."

Matt waited for the explanation.

"And this," Noah said, producing a small velvet box.

There was no mistaking the shape of the box.

"Are you serious?" Matt asked, surprised.

Noah flipped it open to reveal a diamond solitaire. "Dead serious."

"Are you sure?" Matt lowered his voice. "I mean, not are you sure you want to propose, Melissa is amazing. Are you sure you want to do it in front of us?"

Noah gave a self-conscious grin. "You've all been fantastic. You're all family. I really think she'd want to share the moment."

"That's a bold move. But you know her better than the rest of us. Well, maybe not better than Jules. Does Jules know?"

"Nobody knows."

"Okay." Matt couldn't help but grin. He had to admire Noah for this one. "Dessert's all yours."

Noah snapped the ring box shut and tucked it back in his pocket.

Matt slapped him on the shoulder as they turned for the living room. "I thought you looked a little overdressed tonight."

It was rare for Noah to wear a pressed shirt, jacket and slacks. He was more a blue jeans kind of guy.

"Everything's ready," Jules called out from the kitchen.

"Let's get this show on the road," Melissa added.

Matt and TJ took the ends of the rectangular table, with Caleb and Jules along the glass wall, and Noah and Melissa facing the view.

Matt lit the candles and Caleb poured the wine. Caleb had the best-stocked cellar, and he always brought along a few bottles. Matt had long since given up trying to compete.

"Why haven't you decorated for the holidays?" Jules asked Matt, gazing around the room. "No tinsel? No tree?"

Caleb gave a grin as he held the baked salmon platter for Jules. "Our place looks like Rockefeller Square attacked the North Pole."

"You don't even have a string of lights," Melissa said, helping herself to a roll.

"There's not a lot of point." Matt wasn't about to put up the decorations he'd shared with Dianne. And he didn't care enough to go shopping for more.

"Is it depressing?" Jules asked him, looking worried. "Being here on your own for Christmas?"

Depressed was the last thing Matt was feeling. Relieved was more like it. The last Christmas with Dianne had been painful.

"I'm fine," he told Jules. "I'm just not feeling it this year."

"Well, I can't stand it," Melissa said. "We need to do something. You do have decorations, right?"

"Whoa," Noah said. "That's up to Matt."

"No big deal," Matt was quick to put in. The last thing he wanted was for Noah and Melissa to get into an argument tonight.

"He needs new stuff," TJ said. "That's what I did. Well, I waited one Christmas." He sobered as he added some salad to his plate.

The table went silent, remembering the loss of TJ's wife.

He looked up at the quiet table. "Oh, no you don't. It's been two years. I'm all right, and I'm looking forward to Christmas this year."

"You'll come to our place," Jules said. "You'll *all* come to our place."

"We can figure it out closer to the day." Matt didn't want to hold her to the impulsive invitation.

It was her first Christmas with Caleb. And Noah and

Melissa would be engaged. The two sisters were working through a rocky, although improving, relationship with their father. They might not need a big crowd around them.

Matt's thoughts went back to Tasha. He wondered to what she'd done last year for Christmas. Had she gone home for a few days? Had she celebrated here with friends? He didn't know. He was definitely going to ask.

Conversation went on, and it was easy for him to coast. He laughed in the right places, made the odd comment, but his mind wasn't there. It was with Tasha, where she'd gone, what she was doing, whom she was doing it with.

As they finished eating, Matt cleared away the plates while Jules cut into the chocolate hazelnut layer cake. He couldn't take any credit for it. A local bakery, Persichetti, had delivered it earlier in the day.

"I love Persichetti cake," Melissa said with a grin. "Do you have whipped cream?" she asked Matt.

"Coming up." He had it ready.

"A man after my own heart."

Matt couldn't help but glance at Noah. But Noah just grinned and rolled his eyes. He was clearly confident in his relationship. Matt couldn't help but feel a stab of jealousy. He couldn't remember ever being that content.

When Matt sat down, Noah rose.

"Before we start," Noah said.

"No." Melissa gave a mock whine.

"Hold tight," he said to her, giving her a squeeze on the shoulder.

Then he went to the refrigerator and produced the bottle of champagne he'd squirreled away.

"We need the right beverage for this." Noah presented the bottle.

"Oh, my favorite," Melissa said, clearly mollified by the offer of champagne.

Matt quickly moved to get six flutes from his cupboard.

"Nice," Caleb said. "What's the occasion?"

"Good friends," Noah said as he popped the cork. "Good family." He filled the flutes and Matt passed them around.

Then Matt sat down again.

Noah took Melissa's hand. He raised it and gave it a gentle kiss.

Something in his expression made her go still, and everyone went quiet along with her.

"You accepted me from minute one," he said to her. "All of you." He looked around at the group. "Every one of you welcomed me in, without judging, without suspicion."

"I judged a little," Caleb said.

Jules reached out to squeeze her husband's hand.

"You were protecting Jules," Noah said. "And you were protecting Melissa. And you were smart to do that with my history."

"You proved me wrong," Caleb said.

"I did. And now, I think, I hope…" Noah drew a deep breath. "Melissa, darling." His hand went to his pocket and extracted the ring box.

When she saw it, Melissa's eyes went round, and a flush came up on her cheeks.

Matt quickly reached for his phone, hitting the camera button.

Noah popped open the box. "Marry me?"

Melissa gasped. Jules squealed. And Matt got a fantastic picture of the moment.

Melissa's gaze went to the ring, and she leaned closer in. "It is absolutely gorgeous."

"Not as gorgeous as you."

She looked back to Noah. "Yes," she said. "Yes, yes, yes!"

His grin nearly split his face. Everyone cheered.

Her hand trembled as he slipped the ring on her finger. Then he drew her to her feet and kissed her, enveloping her in a sheltering hug. He looked like he'd never let her go.

Matt took one more shot, finding his chest tight, his

thoughts going back to Tasha. He'd held her that tight and more last night. And, in the moment, he'd never wanted to let her go.

Tasha had to get away from Matt for a while. She needed to do something ordinary and find some perspective. Their lovemaking last night had tilted her universe, and she was desperate to get it back on an even keel.

She and Alex had taken a cab to the Edge tonight. They'd started with a couple of tequila shots and danced with a bunch of different guys. Then James Hamilton showed up and commandeered Alex for several dances in a row.

Tasha moved from partner to partner, and by the time she and Alex reconnected at the table, she was sweaty and on a second margarita. The drinks were bringing back memories of Matt, but she'd stopped caring.

James was talking to a couple of his friends across the room, leaving Alex alone with Tasha.

"So, are the two of you an item?" she asked Alex.

Alex shrugged. "I don't know. I like him. He seems to want to hang out a lot. Why?"

"Does it worry you?" Tasha asked. "Dating a mechanic. Do you think you'll lose your credibility? I always worried about dating someone in the business."

"It's a risk," Alex agreed, sipping some ice water through a straw. "But so far all we're doing is dancing."

"Oh." Tasha was surprised by that.

"You thought I was sleeping with James?"

"You left together the other night."

Alex laughed. "I wonder if that's what everybody thinks. And if it is…" She waggled her brows. "What's holding me back?"

Tasha felt terrible for making the assumption, worse for saying it out loud. "I didn't mean to judge, or to push you in any particular direction."

"You're not. You won't. You need to stop worrying so much. We're here to have fun."

"That's right. We are." Tasha lifted her drink in a toast.

As she clinked glasses with Alex, a man at the front door caught her attention. It was Matt. He walked in, and his gaze zeroed in on her with laser precision.

"No," she whispered under her breath.

"What?" Alex asked, leaning in to scrutinize her expression.

"Nothing. Do you mind if I dance with James?"

"Why would I mind? Go for it. I can use the rest."

Tasha slipped from the high stool at their compact round table. As Matt made his way toward her, she went off on an opposite tangent, heading straight for James.

"Dance?" she asked him brightly.

He looked a little surprised, but recovered quickly. "You bet." He took her hand.

The dance floor was crowded and vibrating, and she quickly lost sight of Matt, throwing herself into the beat of the music.

The song ended too soon, and Matt cut in. James happily gave way.

"No," Tasha said to Matt as he tried to take her hand.

"No, what?"

"No, I don't want to do this."

The music was coming up, and she had to dance or look conspicuous out on the floor. She started to move, but kept a distance between them.

He closed the gap, enunciating above the music. "We're going to have to talk sometime."

She raised her voice to be heard. "What's the rush?"

"You'd rather let things build?"

"I was hoping they'd fade."

"My feelings aren't fading."

She glanced around, worried that people might overhear. The crowd was close, so she headed for the edge of the floor.

Matt followed.

When they got to a quieter corner, she spoke again. "Give it some time. We both need some space."

"Can you honestly say your feelings are fading?"

Her feelings weren't fading. They were intensifying.

"If nothing else, we work together," he said. "We have to interact to get our jobs done. And besides, beyond anything else, I'm worried about you."

"There's nothing to worry about." She paused. "Okay, but that thing is *you*."

"Very funny. I'm watching for anything unusual."

"So am I." She'd been working on the sabotage problem all night.

"What I'm seeing is a guy."

Her interest perked up. "At the pier?"

"Not there. Don't look right away, but he's over by the bar. He's been staring at you. And it looks odd. I mean, suspicious."

"What's that got to do with your yachts?"

"I don't know. Maybe nothing."

"Probably nothing. Almost certainly nothing."

"Turn slowly, pretend you're looking at the bottle display behind the bar, maybe picking out a brand. Then glance at the guy in the blue shirt with the black baseball cap. He's slouched at the second seat from the end."

"That sounds needlessly elaborate." She felt like she was in a spy movie.

"I want you to know what he looks like. In case he shows up somewhere else."

"This is silly."

"Humor me."

"Fine." She did as Matt suggested, focusing on the bottles, then doing a quick sweep of the guy Matt had described.

He looked like a perfectly normal fiftysomething, probably a little shy and nerdy sitting alone having a drink. He wasn't staring. He was likely people watching and just happened on Tasha when Matt walked in.

She turned back to Matt. "Okay, I saw him."

"Good. You need a drink?"

"I have a drink."

Matt looked at her hands.

The truth was Tasha didn't normally leave her drinks alone. She'd done it now because Matt had thrown her when he walked in. She hadn't been expecting him, and she'd taken the first opportunity to get out of his way. She might be in a low-risk environment, but it wasn't a risk she normally took.

"I'll get myself a new drink." She started for the bar, hoping he'd stay behind. She'd come here to clear her head, avoid the memories of Matt's lovemaking. She had to focus, wanting to figure out whether the marina was in trouble...or maybe Matt was? The last thing she needed was to be distracted by his quick smile, broad chest and shoulders, his handsome face...

A tune blasted from the turntable, while voices of the crowd ebbed and flowed, laughter all around them under the festive lights. He fell into step beside her.

"I thought you were having dinner with Caleb and Jules," she said.

"Dinner ended early. Noah and Melissa got engaged."

Tasha was getting to know Melissa, and she'd met Noah a few times. "Noah proposed in front of everyone?"

"It was a daring move on Noah's part." Matt's gaze swept the room, obviously checking on the guy at the end of the bar. "I expect it left everybody feeling romantic, so they wanted to head home. Bit of a bummer for TJ. He fights it, but he's lonely. He liked being married."

"How did his wife die?" Tasha liked TJ. Her heart went out to him over the loss.

"Breast cancer."

"That's really sad."

"Yeah." Matt's voice was gruff. "It's been a tough haul. Let me get you that drink."

"I'm going to take off." She wanted to stay, but she needed to go. Clearing her head with Matt in front of her was impossible.

"We need to talk eventually."

"Later."

"I don't want you to be upset."

"I'm not. Actually, I'm not sure what I am."

He hesitated. "Okay. Fine. I don't want to push."

Relieved, she texted for a cab and let Alex know she was leaving. She knew it was the right thing to do, but she couldn't shake a hollow feeling as she headed for the parking lot.

Eight

When Tasha left the bar, the stranger left, too.

Matt followed him as far as the door, watching to be sure he didn't harass her in the parking lot. But she got immediately into a cab and left.

The stranger drove off a few minutes later in the opposite direction.

Back inside, Matt returned to the table to where Alex was now sitting.

"Hey, boss," she greeted with a smile.

"Having a good time?" he asked.

"You bet. Have you met James Hamilton?"

Matt shook the man's hand. "Good to meet you, James."

James nodded. "You, too."

Matt returned his attention to Alex. "Did you happen to notice if anyone was paying particular attention to Tasha tonight?"

Alex looked puzzled, but then shook her head. "She was dancing with lots of guys, but nobody in particular. A lot of them she knows from the area."

"Do you mean the old dude in the black cap?" James asked.

"Yes," Matt answered. "He was watching her the whole time I was here."

"Yeah. I noticed it most of the night. I don't know what his deal was. He never talked to her."

Alex looked to James. "Somebody was watching Tasha?"

"She's pretty hot," James said. "I just thought it was a bit of a creep factor. You know, because the guy was old. But he seemed harmless enough."

"He left when she left," Matt said.

James's gaze flicked to the door. "Did he give her any trouble?"

"No. I watched her get into a cab."

James gave a thoughtful nod.

"With everything that's going on at the marina…" Matt ventured.

"I know what you mean," Alex said. "It's happening more and more."

"What do you mean more and more?" Matt asked.

"Little things," Alex said. "Stupid things."

"Was there something besides the fuel leak and the electric short?"

"None worth getting excited about on their own. And we've checked the cameras. Nobody climbed the fence again."

"So a staff member? While you were open during the day?"

"It's possible. But I hear you've done at least ten background checks and didn't find anything."

Matt knew that was true.

"What's weird to me," Alex continued, "is that they're always on jobs done by Tasha."

Matt felt a prickle along his spine. "Are you sure about that?"

"Positive. We fix them. It doesn't take long."

"Why hasn't she said anything to me?" He'd hate to think the change in their personal relationship had made her reluctant to share information.

"She's starting to question her own memory. Any of them could have been mistakes. But any of them could have been on purpose, too."

"There's nothing wrong with her memory."

Tasha was smart, capable and thorough.

"I'm still wondering if it could be an inside job. I don't want to think that about any of my employees, but… As you're new to the team, has anyone struck you as suspicious?" A hand clapped down on Matt's shoulder.

He turned quickly, ready for anything. But it was TJ.

"Didn't know you were headed out, too," TJ said.

"I didn't know you hung out here," Matt responded, surprised to see his friend.

"I spotted your car in the lot. I was too restless to sleep. Hey, Alex." Then TJ turned his attention to James, holding out a hand. "TJ Bauer."

"I know who you are," James said.

"Really?"

"My mom's on the hospital auxiliary. I hear all about your generous donations."

Matt looked to TJ. He knew TJ's financial company made a number of charitable contributions. He hadn't realized they were noteworthy.

TJ waved the statement away. "It's a corporate thing. Most companies have a charitable arm."

"They were very excited to get the new CT scanner. So on behalf of my mom and the hospital, thank you."

"I better buy you a drink," Matt said to TJ.

"You'd better," TJ returned. "So, what's going on?"

"Some guy was watching Tasha all night long."

"Tasha's here?" TJ gazed around.

Matt couldn't seem to forget that TJ had been attracted to Tasha. Sure, it was mostly from afar, and sure, he'd promised to back off. Still, Matt couldn't help but be jealous.

"She left," he said.

"Too bad." Then TJ gave an unabashed grin and jostled Matt with his elbow.

Alex watched the exchange with obvious interest.

Matt braced himself, wishing he could shut TJ up.

But TJ was done. He drummed his hands against the wooden tabletop. "Is there a waiter or waitress around here?"

"I can go to the bar," James quickly offered.

"I'll come with," Alex said, sliding off the high stool.

"Whatever they have on tap," TJ said.

"Same for me," Matt said, sliding James a fifty. "Get yourselves something, too."

"Best boss in the world." Alex grinned.

"You know how to keep employees happy," TJ said as the pair walked away.

"I wish I knew how to keep one particular employee safe."

"You've got the new cameras now."

"Alex just told me there've been a couple of other minor incidents that looked like tampering. Tasha didn't say anything to me about them." Matt was definitely going to bring that up with her. He wished he could do it now. He didn't want to wait until morning.

"She probably didn't want you going all white knight on her."

"I don't do that."

"You like her, bro."

Matt wasn't about to deny it.

"And you worry about her. And she strikes me as the self-sufficient type."

"She is that," Matt agreed. "But she knows we're all looking to find this guy. Why would she withhold information?"

"Ask her."

"I will. The other thing Alex said was the weird things only happened after Tasha had done a repair, not when it was Alex or anyone else. And this guy watching her tonight? That makes me even more curious." Matt hated to think Tasha might be some kind of target in all this.

"It seems unlikely tonight's guy is related to the sabotage," TJ said.

"He followed her out."

"Probably working up his nerve to ask her on a date."

Matt scoffed at that. "He was twice her age."

"Some guys still think they have a shot. And he doesn't know he'd have to go through you to get to her."

Matt didn't respond. He didn't usually keep things from

his friend, but he had no intention of telling TJ how far things had gone with Tasha. "I'm worried about her."

"Worry away. Just don't do anything outrageous."

Like sleeping with her? "Like what?"

"Like locking her up in a tower."

Despite his worry, Matt couldn't help but smile at that. "My place does have a great security system."

TJ chuckled. "Now *that* would be an example of what not to do."

"I won't." But there were a dozen reasons why Matt would love to lock her away in his house and keep her all to himself.

As the sun rose in the early morning, Tasha made her way up from the compact engine room into the bridge and living quarters of the yacht *Crystal Zone*. Between reliving her lovemaking with Matt and worrying about the sabotage, she'd barely been able to sleep. After tossing and turning most of the night, an early start had seemed like the most productive solution.

Now, she came to the top of the stairs in the yacht's main living area, and a sixth sense made her scalp tingle. She froze. She looked around, but nothing seemed out of place. She listened, hearing only the lapping of the waves and the creak of the ship against the pier.

Still, she couldn't shake the unsettling feeling. She wrinkled her nose and realized it was a scent. There was an odd scent in the room. It seemed familiar, yet out of place. She tried to make herself move, but she couldn't get her legs to cooperate.

She ordered herself to quit freaking out. Everything was fine with the engine. It was in better shape than ever, since she kept fussing with it. The door to the rear deck was closed. Dawn had broken, and she could see through the window that nobody was outside.

Nobody was watching her.

She forced herself to take a step forward, walking on the

cardboard stripping that covered the polished floor to protect it from grease and oil. *Crystal Zone* was going out today on a six-day run.

Then she heard a sound.

She stopped dead.

It came again.

Somebody was on the forward deck. The outer door creaked open. She grabbed for the biggest wrench in her tool belt, sliding it out. If this was someone up to no good, they were going to have a fight on their hands.

She gripped the wrench tightly, moving stealthily forward.

"Matt?" a man's voice called out.

It was Caleb.

Her knees nearly gave way with relief. Nobody had broken in. Caleb had the gate code and was obviously looking for Matt.

She swallowed, reclaiming her voice. "It's Tasha. I'm in here."

"Tasha?" Caleb appeared on the bridge. "Is Matt with you?"

"He's not here."

"I saw the light was on. Why are you starting so early?" Caleb glanced at his watch.

"Couldn't sleep," she said, her stomach relaxing. She slid the wrench back into the loop.

"Way too much going on," he said with understanding.

"I heard Melissa and Noah got engaged."

"They did. It was pretty great." Caleb moved farther into the living area. "Did Matt tell you Melissa and Jules are determined to decorate his place for the holidays?"

"I'm sure he appreciates it."

Caleb chuckled. "I'm sure he doesn't. Dianne was big on decorating."

"Oh."

"I heard you met her." Caleb seemed to be fishing for something.

"I did."

"How did it go?"

Tasha couldn't help remembering her last conversation with Dianne. "I'm not sure. She seems...sad."

The answer obviously surprised Caleb. "Sad? Dianne?"

Tasha weighed the wisdom of taking this chance to ask Caleb directly about a job. She didn't want to put him on the spot.

Then again, she didn't know him very well, so he could easily turn her down without hurting her feelings.

"Can I ask you something?" she asked.

He looked curious. "Fire away."

"I know you have Neo restaurant locations all over the country."

"We have a few."

"Dianne is in pretty dire straits. She's lost everything."

Caleb's expression hardened a shade, but Tasha forced herself to go on.

"She has no money. And she needs a job. I think she's pretty desperate."

"She snowed you," Caleb said, tone flat.

"That doesn't seem true. She didn't know I was there. And she was pretty obviously distraught. Also, she doesn't strike me as somebody whose first plan of attack would be to seek employment."

"You've got that right. She likely hasn't worked a day in her life."

"She admits she doesn't have a lot of marketable skills. But she said she can host parties. She's attractive, articulate, refined."

"What are you getting at?"

"Maybe a hostess position or special events planner somewhere...not here, maybe on the eastern seaboard?"

"Ah." A look of comprehension came over Caleb's face. "Get her out of Matt's hair."

"Well, that, and give her a chance at building a life. If she's telling the truth, and she definitely seemed sincere, she has absolutely nothing left and nowhere to turn."

"It's her own fault," Caleb said.

"No argument from me. But everybody makes mistakes."

He paused, seeming to consider the point. "I know I've made enough of them." He seemed to be speaking half to himself.

"Will you think about it?" Tasha dared to press.

"I'll see what I can do. I suppose it's the season to do the right thing."

"It is."

Light rain drizzled down from the gray clouds above, the temperature hovering in the fifties. It hadn't snowed this year. Snow was always a rare event in this pocket of the coast, and the last white Christmas had been ten years back.

"If you come across Matt, will you tell him I'm looking for him?" Caleb was probably regretting his decision to check inside *Crystal Zone*.

"Anything I can help you with?" she asked.

"Nope. I just want to warn him that Jules and Melissa are going shopping today for holiday decorations. He better brace himself to look festive."

Tasha couldn't stop a smile. "I'll tell him."

"Thanks."

"No, thank you. Seriously, Caleb, thank you for helping Dianne."

"I haven't done anything yet."

"But you're going to try."

He turned to leave, but then braced a hand on the stairway, turning back. "You do know this isn't your problem."

"I know. But it's hard when you don't have a family. People to support you."

He hesitated. "You don't have a family?"

"Estranged. It's lonely at times."

"Same with me," he said. "But my wife, Jules, Melissa,

Noah, TJ, they're good people, I've found a family here. I bet you have, too."

"Soon you'll have two more members in your new family."

Caleb broke into a wide smile. "You got that right. See you, Tasha."

"Goodbye, Caleb."

The sun was now up, and Tasha's feeling of uneasiness had completely faded. She was glad she'd asked Caleb about the job directly. It was better than dragging Jules into the middle of it.

Tasha gathered up the rest of her tools, turned off the lights and secured the doors. She'd head to the main building and get cleaned up before she started on the next job. Alex would probably be in by now, and they could plan the details of their day.

Out on the pier, she shifted the toolbox to her right hand and started to make her way to shore. Almost immediately she saw Matt coming the other way.

His shoulders were square, his stride determined and his chin was held high. She wondered if he'd found some information on the saboteur.

"Morning," she called out as she grew closer.

He didn't smile.

"Did something happen?" She reflexively checked out the remaining row of yachts. She didn't see anything out of place.

"I just talked to Caleb."

"Oh, good. He was looking for you." She struggled to figure out why Matt was frowning.

"You asked him about Dianne." The anger in Matt's tone was clear.

"I…" She'd known it was a risk. She shouldn't be surprised by his anger. "I only asked if he could help."

"Without even *telling* me, you asked my best friend to give my ex-wife a job?"

When he put it that way, it didn't sound very good.

"Only if he didn't mind," she said.

"You don't think that was unfair to him? What if he doesn't want to hire her? Heck, I'm not sure I'd want to hire her."

"Then he can say no. It was a question. He has a choice."

"You put him in an impossible situation."

"Matt, I know it was a bad divorce. Dianne might not be the greatest person in the world. But she is a person. And she is in trouble."

"She got herself into it."

"She made a mistake. She knows that."

Tasha set down the toolbox. It was growing heavy. "You can give her a break, Matt. Everybody deserves a break at some point."

"There's such a thing as justice."

"It seems she's experienced justice and then some."

"You don't know her."

"She can't be all bad. You married her. You must have loved her at some point, right?"

The question seemed to give him pause. The wind whipped his short hair, and the salt spray misted over them.

"I'm not sure I ever did," he finally said.

"What?" Tasha couldn't imagine marrying anyone she didn't love. She would never marry someone she didn't love.

"I didn't see her clearly at first. It seemed like we wanted the same things out of life."

The admission shouldn't have taken her by surprise. Matt had never made a secret of the fact that he wanted wealth, status and luxury.

"Don't be like them," she said.

He looked confused. "Like Dianne? I'm not like Dianne. I've worked hard for everything I've earned, and I appreciate it and don't take it for granted."

"I know." She did. "What I mean is, don't turn into one of those callous elites, forgetting about the day-to-day struggles of ordinary people."

"Except that Dianne is calculating."

"She needs a job."

"She does. But all she's ever aspired to is a free ride."

"Desperation is a powerful motivator. And Caleb can always fire her."

Matt clamped his jaw. "You shouldn't have interfered."

"Maybe not." She couldn't entirely disagree. "I felt sorry for her."

"Because you're too trusting."

Tasha didn't think that was true, but she wasn't going to argue anymore. She'd done what she'd done, and he had every right to be upset. "I have to meet Alex now."

"Right." He looked like he wanted to say more. "I'll catch you later."

"Sure." At this point, she had her doubts that he'd try.

Matt entered the Crab Shack after the lunch rush to find Caleb at the bar talking with his sister-in-law, Melissa.

He knew he couldn't let this morning's argument sit. He had to address it right away.

He stopped in front of Caleb, bracing himself. "I didn't mean to jump down your throat this morning."

"Not a problem," Caleb easily replied.

From behind the bar, Melissa poured them each an ice water and excused herself.

"I was shocked is all," Matt said. "Tasha put you in an awkward situation. I should have made it clear right then that I didn't want you to do it."

"It's already done."

"What?"

Caleb stirred the ice water with the straw. "Dianne has a job at the Phoenix Neo and a plane ticket to get there."

"You didn't. Why would you do that? We didn't even finish our conversation."

"I didn't do it for you, Matt. I did it for Dianne. I did it for everyone."

"She probably won't work out."

"Maybe, maybe not."

"She needs to face the results of her own actions. It's not up to you to rescue her."

"I didn't rescue her. I gave her a shot. She's lost her fortune. She's lost you. She's lost that guy she thought was going to be her Prince Charming. It's not up to me, you're right. It's up to her. She'll make it at Neo or she won't, just like any other employee we've ever hired."

Matt hated to admit it, but Caleb was making good points. Dianne was on her own now. And she'd have to work if she wanted to succeed. There was justice in that.

"And she's in Phoenix," Caleb finished. "She's not here."

"I suppose I should thank you for that," Matt said. He took a big swallow of the water. Not having to see Dianne, frankly, was a huge relief.

"You bet you should thank me for that. And that's what friends do, by the way."

"There's a fire!" Melissa suddenly cried from the opposite side of the restaurant. "Oh, Matt, it looks like one of your boats!"

Matt dropped his glass on the bar and rushed across the room. Smoke billowed up from the far end of the pier. He couldn't tell which yacht was on fire, but all he could think of was Tasha. Where was Tasha?

"Call 911," he yelled to Melissa as he sprinted for the door.

He jumped into his car. Caleb clambered in beside him. Caleb barely got the door shut, and Matt was peeling from the parking lot.

"Can you tell what's on fire?" he asked Caleb as they sped along the spit of land that housed the Crab Shack.

"It has to be a boat. *Orca's Run* is blocking the view. But I don't think it's the one on fire."

"How the hell did he do it?" Matt gripped the steering wheel, sliding around the corner at the shoreline, heading for the pier. "If it's a stranger, how did he get to another one? Everyone's been on the lookout."

"I can see flames," Caleb said. "It's bad."

"Can you see people? Tasha?"

"There are people running down the pier. I can't tell who is who."

It felt like an eternity before Matt hit the parking lot. He slammed on the brakes, but it was still a run to get to the pier. The gate was open, and he sprinted through. "Grab the hoses," he called to the deckhands and maintenance crews. Could it be one of them? Was it possible that someone on the inside had actually set a boat on fire? "Start the pumps!"

The staff drilled for fires. At full deployment, their equipment could pump over a hundred gallons a minute from the ocean.

It was the fifty-foot *Crystal Zone* that was on fire. The entire cabin was engulfed in flames, and they were threatening the smaller craft, *Never Fear*, that was moored directly behind on a floater jutting out from the pier.

He looked behind him to see three crew members lugging lengths of fire hose. Caleb was helping them. But Matt didn't see Tasha. Where was Tasha?

And then he saw her. She was climbing onto the deck of *Salty Sea*, which was in the berth next to *Crystal Zone*. It was barely ten feet away from the flames. There were clients on that boat, two families due to leave port in a couple of hours. The smoke was thick, and she quickly disappeared into it.

Matt increased his speed, running up the gangway to the deck of *Salty Sea*.

"Tasha!" His lungs filled with smoke, and he quickly ducked to breathe cleaner air.

And then he saw her. She was shepherding a mother and two children toward the gangway.

"Five more," she called out harshly as she passed him.

He wanted to grab her. He wanted to hug her. He wanted to reassure himself that she was okay. But he knew it would have to wait. The passengers needed his help.

Eyes watering, he pressed on toward the cabin.

There he met one of the dads, the other mother and the remaining two children.

"Follow me," he rasped, picking up the smallest child.

They made it quickly to the gangway, where the air was clear.

"We're missing one," Tasha said, starting back.

"Stay here!" he told her.

She ignored him, pushing back into the smoke.

Together, they found the last man. He was on the top deck, and Matt guided him to a ladder. They quickly got him to the gangway, and he made his way down.

Matt took a second to survey the disastrous scene.

Neither he nor Tasha said a word.

Caleb and the workers were connecting the lengths of hose.

Alex was preparing the pump.

His gaze went to *Crystal Zone*. She was a complete loss, and *Never Fear* was next. It was too far away from the pier. The spray wouldn't reach it.

Then Matt heard it or smelled it or felt it.

"Get down!" he shouted, grabbing Tasha and throwing her to the deck, covering her body with his and closing his eyes tight.

Never Fear's gasoline tanks exploded. The boom echoing in his ears, the shock wave and heat rushed over him. People on the dock roared in fear.

While debris rained down on him and Tasha, and his ears rang from the boom, Matt gave a frantic look to the people on the pier.

Some had been knocked down, but *Crystal Zone* had blocked most of the blast. He and Tasha had taken the brunt.

"We're good," Caleb called out to him, rushing from person to person. "We're all good."

Matt watched a moment longer before looking to Tasha beneath him.

"Are you hurt?" he asked her.

She shook her head. Then she coughed. When she spoke, her voice was strangled. "I'm fine." She paused. "Oh, Matt."

"I know," he said.

"I don't understand. Who would do this? People could have been killed."

"Yeah," he agreed, coughing himself. He eased off her. "Can you move?"

"Yes." She came to her knees.

He did the same.

She looked around. "You've lost two boats."

"Maybe three." *Salty Sea* was also damaged, its windows blown out from the blast.

Sirens sounded in the distance as the fire department made its way down the cliff road.

Matt took Tasha's hand. "We need to get off here. It's going to catch, too."

She came shakily to her feet.

Caleb met them at the bottom of the gangway.

Alex had the pumps running, and the crew was spraying water on the flames.

The fire engine stopped in the parking lot, and the firefighters geared up, heading down the pier on foot.

Matt turned Tasha to face him, taking in every inch of her. "Are you sure you're all right?"

"You're hurt," she said, pointing to his shoulder.

"You're bleeding," Caleb told him.

"It feels fine." Matt didn't feel a thing.

"You'll need stitches," she said.

"There'll be a medic here in a few minutes. They can bandage me up."

Looking around, it seemed Matt's was the only injury. He'd have plenty of attention. And his shoulder didn't hurt yet.

"Thank you." Tasha's low voice was shaking.

He wrapped an arm around her shoulders. "You probably

saved their lives." If she hadn't got everyone out of the cabin, they would have been caught in the blast.

"You, too."

He drew a deep breath and coughed some more.

"The media is here," Caleb said.

Matt realized publicity was inevitable. "I'll talk to them in a minute."

"Are you going to tell them about the sabotage?" Tasha asked.

"No. It's better that we keep that quiet for now."

"I checked *Crystal Zone* this morning. There was no reason in the world for it to catch fire." A funny expression came over her face.

"What is it?"

Her eyes narrowed.

"Tasha?"

"You're going to think I'm nuts."

"Whatever it is, tell me."

"When I came up from the engine room, I got this creepy feeling, a sixth-sense thing. It felt like somebody was watching me. But then Caleb showed up, and I thought he was the reason."

Fear flashed through Matt. "Somebody else was on the boat with you? Did you see who?"

"I didn't. I mean, besides Caleb. But now…"

"Mr. Emerson?" A reporter shoved a microphone in front of him.

Someone else snapped a picture.

He nudged Tasha to leave. She didn't need to face this.

He'd get it over with, answer their questions, get the fire out and then sit down and figure out what on earth was going on.

Nine

For the first time, Tasha wished her room in the staff quarters had a bathtub. She was usually content with a quick shower. Getting clean was her objective, not soaking in foamy or scented water.

But tonight, she'd have given a lot for the huge soaker tub from her old bathroom in Boston. She shampooed her hair a second time, trying to remove the smoke smell. She scrubbed her skin, finding bumps and bruises. And when she started to shake, she reminded herself that she was fine, Matt was fine, everybody was thankfully fine.

The police were getting involved now, so surely they'd get to the bottom of the inexplicable sabotage. Matt had said, and she agreed, this went far beyond what any of his competitors would do to gain a business advantage. So unless something had gone catastrophically wrong in an unplanned way today, they were looking for a much more sinister motive.

The firefighters had said the blaze had started in the engine room, identifying it as the source of the fire. They expected to know more specifics in the next few days.

She shut off the taps, wrapped a towel around her hair, dried her skin and shrugged into her terry-cloth robe. It was only eight in the evening, but she was going to bed. Maybe she'd read a while to calm her mind. But she was exhausted. And tomorrow was going to be another overwhelming day.

A knock sounded on her door, startling her. Adrenaline rushed her system, and her heart thudded in her chest. It was silly to be frightened. She was not going to be frightened.

"Tasha?" It was Matt.

"Yes?"

He waited a moment. "Can you open the door?"

She almost said she wasn't dressed. But the man had already seen her naked. The bathrobe, by comparison, was overdressed. She tightened the sash and unlocked the door, pulling it open.

"Hey," he said, his blue eyes gentle.

She fought an urge to walk into his arms. "Hi."

"How are you feeling?"

"I'll be fine."

"I didn't ask what you'd be. I asked how you are." He looked solid and strong, like a hug from him would be exactly the reassurance she needed right now.

But she had to be strong herself. "Sore." It was a truthful answer without going into her state of mind. "You?"

"Yeah. Pretty sore." He gestured into the room.

She stepped aside. It felt reassuring to have him here. It was good to have his company.

He closed the door and leaned back against it. "I don't think you're safe."

She was jumpy. But she knew it was a natural reaction to being so close to an explosion. She'd be fine after a good night's sleep.

"I'm okay," she said.

He eased a little closer. "We agree this wasn't a competitor. And if it's not Whiskey Bay Marina—and it's likely *not* Whiskey Bay Marina—then the next logical guess is you."

"That doesn't make sense." She couldn't wrap her mind around someone, *anyone*, targeting her.

"I'm afraid for you, Tasha."

"We don't know—"

He moved closer still. "I don't care what we know and don't know."

"Matt."

He took her hands in his. "Listen to me."

"This is wild speculation."

She tried to ignore his touch. But it felt good. It felt right. It felt more comforting than made sense. She prided herself on her independence, and here she was wishing she could lean on Matt.

"Somebody's targeted you," he said. "Somebody who's willing to commit arson and harm people."

"Why would they do that to me? Who would do that to me?"

"I don't know. All I do know is that it's happening, and you need protection. I want to do that, Tasha. I want to protect you." He squeezed her hands. "I couldn't live with myself if anything happened to you."

"You're blowing this out of proportion, Matt."

He crossed the last inches between them, and his arms brushed hers. "They set a boat on fire."

She didn't have a response for that.

"I want you to stay at the main house."

"You mean your house." That was a dangerous idea. It was a frightening idea. Just standing so close to him now, her emotions were swinging off-kilter.

"I have an alarm system. I have good locks on my doors. And I'm there. I'm *there* if anything goes wrong."

"It's nice of you to offer," she said, her logical self at odds with the roller coaster of her emotions.

She couldn't stay under the same roof as Matt, not with her feelings about him so confused, not with her attraction to him so strong, and certainly not right out there in front of the entire staff and crew of the marina.

"I am your boss, and as a condition of your employment, you need to stay safe, Tasha."

"You *know* what people will think." She grasped at a perfectly logical argument. No way, no how was she going to admit she didn't trust herself with him.

"I couldn't care less what people will think."

"I do. I care."

"Do you want a chaperone? Should we ask someone to come stay there with us?"

"That would make it look even worse."

He drew back a little and gently let her hands go, seeming to give her some space.

"I have a guest room. This is about security and nothing more. Everybody here knows you. If you don't make a big deal about the arrangement, neither will they. The police are involved. There's a serious criminal out there, and it has something to do with you."

She closed her eyes for a long second, steeling herself, telling herself she could handle it. She had control of her emotions.

He was right, and she needed to make the best of it. She'd go stay behind his locks and his alarm system. She'd be practical. She could keep her distance. And she'd keep it light.

"Do you have a soaker tub?" she joked, wincing at her sore muscles.

He gave a ghost of a smile. "Yes, I do. Get your things."

She moved to the closet where she had a gym bag, feeling every muscle involved. "I feel like I've been in a bar fight."

"Have you been in many bar fights?"

"Have you?" she countered.

"A couple. And, yeah, this is pretty much what it feels like."

Having accepted the inevitable, Tasha tossed some necessities into her gym bag, changed in the bathroom and was ready in a few minutes.

"You're frighteningly fast at that," Matt noted as they stepped onto the porch.

"I'm leaving my ball gowns behind."

"Are you going to lock it?" he asked, looking pointedly at the door.

"There's not much inside."

"With all that's going on?" He raised his brow.

"Fine. You're right. It's the smart thing to do." She dug into the pocket of her pants, found the key and turned it in the lock.

He lifted her bag from her hand. She would have protested, but it seemed like too much trouble. It was only a five-minute climb to the front door of his house. She couldn't bring herself to worry about which one of them carried her bag.

Inside Matt's house, boxes and bags littered the entryway. There were more of them in the living room, stacked on the coffee table and on the sofa and chairs.

"You did a little shopping?" she asked, relieved to have something to be amused about.

"Jules and Melissa. They were going to decorate tonight. But, well…maybe tomorrow."

"Maybe," Tasha echoed.

It was less than two weeks until Christmas, but she couldn't imagine Matt was feeling very much like celebrating the season.

He set her bag down at the end of the hall. "Thirsty?"

"Yes." She found a vacant spot on the sofa and sat down.

If Matt wanted to bring her a drink, she wasn't about to argue. He went into the kitchen, opening cupboards and sliding drawers.

Curious, she leaned forward to look inside one of the shopping bags. Wrapped in tissue paper were three porcelain snowmen with smiling faces, checkerboard scarves and top hats. They were adorable.

She spied a long, narrow white shelf suspended above the fireplace. It was sparsely decorated, so she set the snowmen up at one end.

"There's no way to stop this, is there?" Matt gazed in resignation at the snowmen.

"You don't like them?" She was disappointed.

"No. They're cute. They're different. Different is good." He had a glass of amber liquid in each hand. It was obvious from their balloon shape that he'd poured some kind of brandy.

"This is your first Christmas since the divorce." It wasn't a question. It was an observation.

"It is." He handed her one of the glasses. "Caleb gave Dianne a job in Phoenix thanks to you."

Tasha wasn't sure how to respond. She couldn't tell from Matt's tone if he was still angry. "We aren't going to fight again, are we?"

"No. I hope not. Too much else has happened."

She returned to the sofa and took a sip of the brandy.

"This is delicious," she said.

He took the only vacant armchair. "A gift from Caleb. He's more of a connoisseur than I am."

"He has good taste."

Matt raised his glass. "To Caleb's good taste."

She lifted her own. "Thank you, Caleb."

Matt sighed, leaned back in the soft chair and closed his eyes.

Tasha felt self-conscious, as if she'd intruded on his life.

She gazed at his handsome face for a few more minutes. Then her attention drifted to the glass walls, to the extraordinary view of the bay and the marina. The Neo restaurant was well under way. The job site was lit at night, a few people still working. She could see the flash of a welder and the outline of a crane against the steel frame of the building.

The yachts bobbed on the tides, a gaping black hole where the fire had burned. *Crystal Zone* hadn't been the finest in the fleet, but it was a favorite of Tasha's. She was going to miss working on it.

"You're going to have to help me," Matt said.

"Help you with what?"

He opened his eyes. "Buy a new boat. Make that two new boats."

"You'll be able to repair *Salty Sea*?"

"I think so. We'll have to strip it down, but it's not a total write-off. *Never Fear* is mostly debris at the bottom of the bay."

"Ironic that," she said.

"In what way?"

"We should have feared her."

Matt smiled. Then he took another sip of his brandy.

She set down her glass and looked into another of the shopping bags. This one contained cylindrical glass containers, stubby candles, glass beads and a bag of cranberries.

"I know exactly what to do with these," she said.

"Here we go." He sat up straighter.

She opened the bag of glass beads, slowly pouring a layer into each of the two containers. "Do you mind if I put this together?"

"Please do."

She set the candles inside, positioning them straight. Then she poured a layer of cranberries around them, finishing off with more glass beads.

While she worked, Matt rose and removed the bags from the coffee table, the sofa and elsewhere, and gathered them off to the side of the room. He positioned her finished creations in the center of the table and retrieved a long butane lighter from above the fireplace.

"You're not going to save them for Christmas?"

"I'm sure we can get more candles." He touched the lighter's flame to each wick. Lastly, he dimmed the lights. "This is nice."

When he moved past her, his shoulder touching hers, her nerve endings came to attention. He paused, and the warmth of his body seemed to permeate her skin.

She drew a deep breath, inhaling his scent. A part of her acknowledged that this was exactly what she'd feared and reminded herself she needed to fight it. Another part of her wanted the moment to go on forever.

"I'm glad you're here," he said in a soft tone.

It took a second to find her voice. She forced herself to keep it light. "Because you need help decorating?"

He didn't answer right away. When he did, he sounded disappointed. "Right. That's the reason."

She gave herself an extra couple of seconds, and then she eased away.

He seemed to take the hint and moved back to his chair.

She shook her emotions back to some semblance of normal. "So that's it?" She looked pointedly at the rest of the bags. "We're giving up on the decorating?"

"We're resting." He sounded normal again. "It's been a long day."

"Well, I'm curious now." It felt like there were unopened presents just waiting for her to dig in.

He gave a helpless shrug and a smile. "Go for it."

Tasha dug into a few more bags. She put silver stylized trees on the end tables, a basket of pinecones and red balls next to the candles. She hung two silver and snowflake-printed stockings above the fire, and wrestled a bent willow reindeer out of its box to set it up on the floor beside the fireplace.

When she discovered the components of an artificial tree, Matt gave up watching and rose to help.

"I knew you'd cave," she told him with a teasing smile.

"It says on the box that it's ten feet high. You'll never get it up by yourself."

"Oh, ye of little faith."

"Oh, ye of little height."

She laughed, amazed that she could do that at the end of such a trying day.

Together, they read the directions and fit the various pieces together, eventually ending up with a ten-foot balsam fir standing majestically in the center of the front window.

They both stood back to admire their work.

"Is that enough for tonight?" he asked.

"It's enough for tonight."

She felt an overwhelming urge to hug him. She wanted to thank him for helping with the tree. She wanted to thank him for saving her from the explosion.

More than that, she wanted to kiss him and make love to

him and spend the night in his arms. Her feelings were dangerous. She had to control them.

Steeling herself, she stepped away. "Okay to finish my brandy in the tub?"

His gaze sizzled on her for a moment.

"Alone," she said.

"I know."

She forced her feet to move.

Matt shouldn't have been surprised to find Tasha gone when he went into the kitchen for breakfast. She'd probably left early, hoping nobody would notice she hadn't slept in the staff quarters.

He wanted to text her to make sure she was all right. But he settled for staring out the window as he sipped his coffee, waiting until he spotted her on the pier with Alex. Only then did he pop a bagel in the toaster and check the news.

As expected, the fire was front and center in the local and state news. But he was surprised to see the article displayed prominently on a national site. He supposed the combination of fire, high-end yachts and an explosion, especially when there were pictures, was pretty hard to resist. They showed a shot of him and Tasha coming off *Salty Sea* after the explosion, side by side with a still photo of the crews fighting the flames.

He had planned to work at home this morning, as he normally did. But he was going down to the office instead. He wanted to be close to Tasha in case anything more happened.

Before he could leave, Jules and Melissa came by, calling out from the entryway.

"In the kitchen," he called back.

Jules spoke up. "We came to see how you were doing." She paused before coming down the four steps into the main living area. "And to see how you liked the decorations." She continued into the living room and gestured around. "Hey, you really got into the spirit."

"I did."

"Nice work." Melissa gazed around approvingly.

He knew he should credit Tasha. And he knew it wouldn't stay secret that she was sleeping here. But he wasn't in a rush to share the information. There was enough going on today.

"The insurance adjustors will be here at noon," he said instead.

"That's fast."

"I need to get things under way." If he was going to replace the boats before the spring season, he had no time to lose.

"Good thing it's the off-season," Melissa said, obviously following his train of thought.

"If there's anything to be grateful for, that's it. And that nobody got hurt." He was grateful for both things, but he wasn't going to relax until the perpetrator was caught and put in jail.

TJ was next through the door.

"How're you doing?" he asked Matt, giving Jules and Melissa each a nod.

"Fine." Matt thought about his conversation with Tasha last night, and he couldn't help but smile. "A bit like I've been in a bar fight."

TJ grinned back. "My guess is that two of the yachts are write-offs?"

"I'll confirm that today. But, I can't see how we save either of them."

"If you need interim financing, just let me know."

It was on the tip of Matt's tongue to refuse. He hated to take advantage of his friends. And he was already one favor down because of Caleb hiring Dianne.

But he had to be practical. TJ had access to almost unlimited funds. Matt would cover any interest payments. And having TJ write a check, instead of explaining the situation to a banker, would definitely speed things up.

"I might," he said to TJ. "I'm going to track down replacements just as soon as I can make some appointments."

"New yachts," Melissa said with a grin. "Now, *that's* what I call a Christmas gift."

"You can help me test them out," Matt offered.

"I'm your girl," she said.

Matt retrieved his cup and took the final swallow of his coffee. "Thanks for checking on me, guys. But I have to get to work."

"We'll get out of your way," Jules said.

"Nice job with the decorating," Melissa said as they turned to leave.

"I thought we were going to have to do it all," Jules said to her sister as they headed through the foyer.

As the door closed behind Jules and Melissa, TJ looked pointedly around the room. "What is with all this?"

"Tasha helped," Matt said.

"Last night?" TJ asked, his interest obviously perking up.

"I wanted her safely surrounded by an alarm system."

"So, it wasn't…"

"She slept in the guest room."

"Too bad."

"Seriously? She was nearly blown up yesterday. So were we."

"And you couldn't find it in your heart to comfort her?"

Matt knew it was a joke. TJ was absolutely not the kind of guy who would take advantage of a woman's emotional state.

"Is she staying again tonight?" TJ asked.

"Until we catch the jerk that did this. Yes, she's staying right here. I wish I hadn't committed to the mayor's party this evening."

"I could hang out with her."

Since TJ had once asked Tasha on a date, Matt wasn't crazy about that idea.

TJ put on an affronted expression. "You honestly think I'd make a move on her?"

"Of course not."

"Take her with you," TJ suggested.

"She hates those kinds of parties." It was too bad. Matt would happily keep her by his side.

"Everybody hates those kinds of parties."

"I don't."

"Then there's something wrong with you."

Matt didn't think there was anything wrong with him. There were a lot of positives to his hard work, and socializing was one of them. He employed nearly fifty people. He brought economic activity to Whiskey Bay, a town he loved.

And he liked the people of Whiskey Bay. He liked discussing issues with them. He liked strategizing with the other business owners, and he sure didn't mind doing it in a gracious setting.

"The food's good. The drinks are good. I like the music, and the company is usually pleasant. Plus tonight. Tonight everyone will want to talk about the fire. And I can use that as a way to pump them all for information. You never know what people might have seen or heard around town."

"Tell that to Tasha," TJ said.

Matt paused to think about that. He had to admit it was a good idea. "She was willing to come along last time when it was part of the investigation."

"Keeps her with you."

"She's a pretty skilled interrogator. You know, for somebody who hates those kinds of parties, she handles them beautifully. Did you know she grew up in Boston? Beacon Hill. She can hobnob with the best of them. And she's totally disarming. She's pretty, smart and funny. Easy to talk to. Trustworthy. People will tell her anything. It's perfect."

Matt stopped talking to find TJ staring quizzically at him.

"You do get what's going on here, right?" TJ asked.

"No." Did TJ know something about the saboteur? "Did you hear something? Did you see something? Why didn't you *say* something?"

"You're falling in love with Tasha."

Matt shook his head to get the astonishment out. "I thought you were talking about the fire."

"Mark my words."

"You're about a thousand steps ahead of yourself."

Being attracted to a woman didn't equate to happily-ever-after. Sure, he was incredibly attracted to Tasha. And he'd admit to himself that it wasn't simply physical. Although mostly what they did was argue. And they'd slept together exactly *one* time. TJ didn't even know about that.

Matt was miles away from thinking about love.

"I can read the signs," TJ said.

"Well, you're getting a false reading. And I'm going to work now." Matt started for his front door.

TJ trailed behind. "Better brace yourself, buddy. Because I *can* read the signs."

Officially, Tasha agreed to attend the mayor's party because she could talk to people, see if anybody knew anything. If the price for that was dancing with Matt, so be it.

Anticipation brought a smile to her face as she got ready for the evening.

Tasha quickly found a dress she liked in Matt's basement. Sleeveless, with a short, full skirt, it was made of shimmering champagne tulle. The outer dress was trimmed and decorated with hand-stitched lace, and the underdress was soft satin. Altogether, it was made for dancing.

A pair of shoes and the small clutch purse in a box below had obviously been bought to match the dress. The shoes were definitely not made for dancing, but Tasha was going to wear them anyway. Her more practical side protested the frivolous decision. But she wanted to look beautiful tonight.

She wanted to look beautiful for Matt.

She paused for a moment to let the thought sink in.

She had at first chosen a basic black dress from the rack. There was nothing wrong with it. It was understated but perfectly acceptable. Black wasn't exactly her color. But it was a safe choice.

"Tasha?" Matt called from the hallway.

"Yes?" she called back.

"We've got about twenty minutes, and then we should get going."

"No problem." But then she'd spotted a champagne-colored gown and it had held her attention. She'd left with both dresses, and she glanced from one to the other now. Letting out a deep breath, she plucked the champagne-colored one from the hanger. She couldn't help feeling like one of her sisters, primping for a fancy party in the hopes of impressing a rich man.

She'd never understood it before, and she didn't want to understand it now. But she did. She couldn't help herself. She wanted Matt to see her as beautiful.

She set the dress on the bed and shoes on the floor. The guest bathroom was spacious and opulent. Her few toiletries took up only a tiny corner of the vanity.

She stripped off her clothes, noting small bruises on her elbow and her shoulder. She was feeling a lot better than yesterday, but she was still sore. Her gaze strayed to the huge soaker tub next to the walk-in shower. She promised herself she'd take advantage of it later.

For now, she twisted her hair into a braided updo, brushed her teeth, put on some makeup and shimmied into the dress. She didn't have much in the way of jewelry, but she did have a little pair of emerald-and-diamond studs that her parents had given her for her eighteenth birthday.

The last thing she put on was the shoes. They weren't a perfect fit, but they did look terrific. She popped her phone and a credit card into the purse, and headed out to meet Matt.

His bedroom door was open, and the room was empty, as was the living room. Then she heard movement at the front door. Feeling guilty for having kept him waiting, she headed that way.

When she rounded the corner, he stopped still and his eyes went wide.

"What?" She glanced down at herself. Had she missed removing a tag?

"You look fantastic."

She relaxed and couldn't help but smile. The compliment warmed her straight through.

He moved closer. "I shouldn't be so shocked when you dress up like this."

He took her hands. "Seriously, Tasha. You're a knockout. It's a crying shame that you hide under baseball caps and boxy clothes."

His compliment warmed her, and she didn't know how to respond. She knew how she should respond—with annoyance at him for being shallow and disappointment in herself for succumbing to vanity. But that wasn't what she was feeling. She was feeling happy, excited, aroused. She'd dressed up for him, and he liked it.

"You're not so bad yourself," she said, her voice coming out husky.

He wore a tux better than anyone in the world.

"I don't want to share you," he said, drawing her closer.

"You think I'm yours to share?" She put a teasing lilt in her voice.

"You should be. You should be mine. Why aren't you mine, Tasha?" He searched her expression for a split second, and then his mouth came down on hers.

She knew there were all kinds of reasons that this was a bad idea. But she didn't have it in her. She wanted it as much as he did, maybe more. She wrapped her arms around his neck and returned his kiss.

She pressed her body against his. The arm at her waist held her tight. His free hand moved across her cheek, into her hair, cradling her face as he deepened the kiss. His leg nudged between hers, sending tendrils of desire along her inner thighs. Her nipples hardened against him, and a small pulse throbbed at her core.

He kissed her neck, nibbled her ear, his palm stroked up her spine, coming to the bare skin at the top of her back, slipping under the dress to caress her shoulder.

"Forget this," he muttered.

Then he scooped her into his arms and carried her farther into the house, down the hallway to his bedroom.

He dropped to the bed, bringing her with him, stretching her out in his arms, never stopping the path of his kisses.

"Matt?" she gasped, even as she inhaled his scent, gripped tight to his strong shoulders and marveled at how the world was spinning in a whole new direction. "The party."

Her body was on fire. Her skin craved his touch. Her lips couldn't get enough of his taste.

"Forget the party," he growled. "I need you, Tasha. I've imagined you in my bed so many, many times."

"I need you, too," she answered honestly.

It might have been the emotion of the past two days. Maybe it was the way he'd saved her. Maybe it was the intimacy of decorating for Christmas. Or maybe it was just hormones, chemistry. Matt wasn't like anyone she'd ever met.

He stripped off her dress and tossed his tux aside piece by piece.

When they were naked, they rolled together, wrapped in each other's arms.

She ended up on top. And she sat up, straddling him, smiling down.

"I have dreamed of this," he whispered, stroking his hands up her sides, moving to settle on her breasts.

"This might be a dream." She'd dreamed of him too, too many times to count. If this was another, she didn't want to wake up.

"You might be a dream," he said. "But this isn't a dream. This is so real."

"It feels real to me." Unwilling to wait, she guided him

inside, gasping as sensations threatened to overwhelm her. "Very, very, very real."

"Oh, Tasha," he groaned and pulled her close to kiss her.

She moved her hips, pleasure spiraling through her.

"Don't stop," he said, matching her motion.

"No way," she answered against his mouth.

She wanted to say more, but words failed her. Her brain had shut down. All she could do was kiss and caress him, drink in every touch and motion he made.

The world contracted to his room, to his bed, to Matt, beautiful, wonderful Matt.

She sat up to gaze at his gorgeous face. His eyes were opaque. His lips were dark red. His jaw was clenched tight. She captured his hand, lifted it to her face and drew one of his fingers into her mouth. Even his hands tasted amazing.

His other hand clasped her hips. He thrust harder, arching off the bed, creating sparks that turned to colors that turned to sounds. Lights flashed in her brain and a roar came up in her ears. Matt called her name over and over as she catapulted into an abyss.

Then she melted forward, and his strong arms went around her, holding her close, rocking her in his arms.

"That was…" he whispered in her ear.

"Unbelievable," she finished on a gasping voice.

"How did we do that? What's your magic?"

She smiled. "I thought it was yours."

"It's ours," he said.

Moments slipped by while they both caught their breaths.

"Are we still going to the party?" she asked.

"I'm not willing to share." He trailed his fingertips along her bare back.

She knew she should call him out for those words. But she was too happy, too content. She wasn't going to do anything to break the spell.

Ten

Matt resented real life. He wanted to lock himself away with Tasha and never come out. He'd held her in his arms all night long, waking to her smile, laughing with her over breakfast.

But she had insisted on going to work, and now he had a fire investigator sitting across from him in his office.

"Who was the last person to work on the engine before the fire?" Clayton Ludlow asked.

"My chief mechanic, Tasha Lowell. She's on her way here, but I can guarantee you she didn't make a mistake."

"I'm not suggesting she did. But I need to establish who had access to the engine room."

"After Tasha, I have no idea."

"You have security cameras?"

"I do."

"You reviewed the footage?" Clayton made some notes on a small pad of paper.

"Of course."

"Did anyone else board *Crystal Zone* the rest of the day?"

"Not that we could see. But Tasha thought…" Matt hesitated.

"Thought what?"

"She had a feeling someone was on board at the same time as her."

"Did she see someone?"

"No. It was just a feeling." And at this point, it was worrying Matt more than ever.

"There's nothing I can do with the *feeling* of another potential suspect."

"Tasha's not a suspect." Matt wanted the investigator to be clear on that.

Clayton's tone became brisk. "Are there blind spots left by the security cameras?"

"No."

Clayton's arched expression told Matt he was jumping to conclusions about Tasha.

"You know we've suspected sabotage," Matt said.

"I know. And we also know what started the fire."

Matt's interest ramped up. "How did he do it?"

"He *or she* left some oily rags in a pile. They ignited."

There was a knock on the door and Tasha pushed it open.

Matt waved her inside, and she took the vinyl guest chair next to Clayton.

Matt got straight to the point. "There were some oily rags left in the engine room. Any chance they were yours?"

He didn't believe for a minute they were, but he didn't want Clayton to think he was covering for Tasha. Not that he would need to. There was absolutely no way she was the saboteur.

"No," she said. "Never. Not a chance."

Matt looked to Clayton.

"How many boats do you work on in an average day?"

"One to six."

"So, you're busy."

"I'm busy," she said. "But I didn't forget something like that."

"How many boats did you work on the day of the fire?"

"Three." She paused. "No, four."

"This is a waste of time," Matt said.

Clayton ignored him. "The other problems Whiskey Bay has been having. I understand you were the last person to work on each of the engines."

"I was also the one to discover the wire short and the fuel leak that prevented the last fire." She slid a glance to Matt. It was obvious her patience was wearing.

Clayton made some more notes.

"Are you planning to charge me with something?" Tasha asked.

Her voice had gone higher, and her posture had grown stiff in the chair. Matt would have given anything to spirit her back to his house.

"Are you expecting to be charged with something?"

"No." She was emphatic.

Clayton didn't answer. He just nodded.

"We're wasting time," Matt said. "The real criminal is out there, and we're wasting time."

"Let me do my job," Clayton said.

"That's all we want." Matt nodded.

"It wasn't me," Tasha said.

"Noted. And now I have to finish my report." Clayton came to his feet.

Tasha stood, as well. "And I have engines to inspect. Think what you want about me," she said to Clayton. "But whoever is trying to hurt Matt's business is still trying to hurt Matt's business. If you don't want another disaster on your hands, help us find them."

She turned and left the office.

"Is she always so emotional?" Clayton asked.

"She's never emotional. And she's not emotional now. But I'm getting there." Matt rose. "Fill out your report. But if you pursue Tasha as a suspect or accomplice, you'll only be wasting valuable time."

Tasha paced her way down the pier, past the burned boats to *Monty's Pride*, which, thankfully, hadn't been damaged at all. She knew the inspector was only doing his job. But it was frustrating to have them spend so much time on her instead of looking for the real culprit. She had no doubt she'd be exonerated, no matter what people might believe right now. But she hated to think about the damage that could potentially be done in the meantime.

She heard the echoing sound of an open boat moving toward her. From the sound, she figured it was a small cartopper with a 150-horse outboard. Alex had chased a couple of reporters and a dozen lookie-loos away from the docks already this morning.

The red open boat was piloted by a man in a steel gray hoodie. He wasn't even wearing a life jacket.

"Jerk," she muttered under her breath, climbing down to the floater where it was obvious he was planning to dock.

"This is private property," she called out to him, waving him away.

He kept coming.

He didn't have a camera out yet; at least that was something.

She moved to the edge of the floater. "I said, this is private property."

He put a hand up to cup his ear.

He looked to be in his late fifties. He could be hard of hearing. Or it could simply be the noise of the outboard motor.

It was odd that he was wearing a hoodie. She associated them with teenagers, not older adults.

The boat touched broadside on the tire bumpers.

Tasha crouched to grasp the gunwale. "Is there something I can help you with?"

The man seemed oddly familiar.

"Have we met?" she asked, puzzled.

Maybe she'd been too quick to try to send him away. His business could be legitimate.

He shifted in his seat, coming closer to her.

And then she smelled it, the cologne or aftershave that she'd smelled the morning of the *Crystal Zone* fire.

"Only once," he said, raising an arm.

She jerked back, but she was too late.

Her world went dark.

* * *

It could have been minutes or hours later when she pushed her way to consciousness. She felt disoriented, and pain pulsed at her temples. Her first thought was to reach for Matt. She'd fallen asleep in his arms last night, and she wanted to wake up the same way.

She reached out, but instead of finding Matt, her hand hit a wall. No, it wasn't a wall. It was fabric. It was springy. It felt like the back of a sofa, and it had a musty smell.

She forced her eyes open, blinking in dim light.

The light was from a window up high in the room.

Her head throbbed harder, and she reached up to find a lump at her temple.

Then it all came back to her, the boat, the man, the smell. He'd hit her on the head. He'd knocked her out.

She sat up straight, pain ricocheting through her skull.

"You should have come home, Tasha." The voice was low and gravelly.

She looked rapidly around, trying to locate the source.

"Your mother misses you," he said.

She squinted at a shadowy figure in a kitchen chair across the room. "Who are you? Where am I? What do you want?"

"You're safe," he said.

She gave a hollow laugh. "I have a hard time believing that."

She gazed around the big room. It was more like a shed or a garage. She could make out a workbench of some kind. There were yard tools stacked against one wall, some sheers and a weed trimmer hanging on hooks.

"Where am I?" She put her feet on the floor, finding it was concrete.

The garage wasn't heated, and she was chilly.

"It's not important." He waved a dismissive hand. "We won't be here long."

"Where are we going?" Her mind was scrambling.

He'd pulled down his hoodie, but her vision was poor in

the dim light. She'd thought she recognized him, but she couldn't place him. And she found herself wondering if she'd been mistaken.

But the cologne smell was familiar. It was… It was…
Her father's!

"Where's my dad?" she asked, sitting forward, debating her odds of overpowering the man.

He was older, but she was woozy, and her pounding headache was making her dizzy.

"He's in Boston. As always. Why would he be anywhere else?"

She wasn't going to give away that she'd made the cologne connection. It might give her some kind of advantage.

"No reason."

The man rose to his feet. "Tasha, Tasha, Tasha. You have proved so difficult."

She wished she knew how long she'd been here. Would Matt have noticed her missing yet? There'd be no tracks, nothing on the security cameras. The man had used a boat. That's how he'd got onto *Crystal Zone* without being seen yesterday morning. He'd come by water.

"You were the one who lit the oily rags," she said.

She couldn't tell for sure, but it looked as if he'd smiled.

"Used a candle as a wick," he said with a certain amount of pride in his voice, taking a few paces in front of her. "The wax just disappears." He fluttered his fingers. "For all anyone knows, they spontaneously combusted. Didn't anyone teach you the dangers of oily rags?"

"Of course they did. Nobody's going to believe I'd make a mistake like that."

"Well, it wouldn't have come to that—" now he sounded angry "—if you hadn't spent so much time cozying up to Matt Emerson. Otherwise you would have been fired days ago. I didn't see that one coming."

Tasha was speechless. Who was this man? How long had he been watching her? And what had he seen between her and Matt? As quickly as the thought formed, she realized that some stranger knowing she'd slept with Matt was the least of her worries.

She was in serious trouble here. She had no idea what this man intended to do with her.

Cold fear gripped the pit of her stomach.

"Have you seen Tasha?" Matt had found Alex on the pier next to *Orca's Run*, moving a wheeled toolbox.

"Not since this morning. Didn't she talk to the investigator?"

"That was three hours ago." Matt was starting to worry.

"Maybe she took a long lunch."

"Without saying anything?"

Alex gave him an odd look, and he realized his relationship with Tasha was far different from what everyone believed.

"Have you tried the Crab Shack?" Alex asked.

"That's a good idea."

Tasha had been getting to know Jules and Melissa recently. Matt liked that. He liked that she fit in with his circle of friends.

"Thanks," he said to Alex, waving as he strode down the pier. At the same time, he called Jules's cell phone, too impatient to wait until he got there.

"I don't know," Jules said when he asked the question. "I'm at home, feet up. They're really swollen today."

"Sorry to hear that."

"It's the price you pay." She sounded cheerful.

"Is Melissa at the restaurant?"

"I expect so. Is something wrong, Matt? You sound worried."

"I'm looking for Tasha."

Jules's tone changed. "Did something happen?"

"I don't know. She's not around. I can't find her on the

pier or in the main building. I checked the staff quarters and nothing."

"Maybe she went into town?"

"Not without telling me."

There was a silent pause. "Because of the fire?"

It was on the tip of his tongue to tell Jules he thought Tasha was the target. He might not have any proof, but his instincts were telling him somebody was out to discredit her. Heck, they already had the fire department thinking she was the culprit. But he didn't want to upset Jules. Her focus needed to be on her and the babies. She needed to stay relaxed.

"It's probably nothing." He forced a note of cheer into his voice. "I'll walk over to the Crab Shack myself. Or maybe she did go into town. She might have needed parts."

"I'll let you know if I hear from her," Jules said.

"Thanks. You relax. Take care of those babies."

Matt signed off.

He'd been walking fast, and he headed down the stairs to the parking lot.

"Matt!" It was Caleb, exiting his own car.

Matt trotted the rest of the way, hoping Caleb had news about Tasha.

Caleb was accompanied by an older woman.

"What is it?" he asked Caleb between deep breaths.

Caleb gestured to the fiftysomething woman. "This is Annette Lowell. She came to the Crab Shack looking for Tasha. She says she's her mother."

Matt didn't know how to react. Could Annette's appearance have something to do with Tasha being gone? "Hello."

The woman flashed a friendly smile. "You must be Matt Emerson."

"I am." Matt glanced at Caleb. He was beyond confused.

"Annette came to visit Tasha," Caleb said, his subtle shrug and the twist to his expression telling Matt he had no more information than that.

"Was Tasha expecting you?" Matt asked, still trying to pull the two events together. Was Tasha avoiding her mother? Matt knew they were estranged.

"No. I haven't spoken to Tasha in over a year."

"Not at all?"

"No."

Matt didn't really want to tell the woman her daughter was missing. He wasn't even sure if Tasha was missing. There could still be a logical explanation of why he couldn't find her.

"I saw the coverage of that terrible fire," Annette said to Matt. "I hope you'll be able to replace the yachts."

"We will."

"Good, good. I'm *so* looking forward to getting to know you." Her smile was expectant now. "I had no idea my daughter was dating such an accomplished man."

Dating? Where had Annette got the idea they were dating?

Then he remembered the picture in the national news, his arm around Tasha's shoulder, the expression of concern captured by the camera. Annette must have seen it and concluded that he and Tasha were together. It was clear she was happy about it.

"I'm a little busy right now." He looked to Caleb for assistance.

It wasn't fair to dump this on Caleb, but Matt had to concentrate on Tasha. He had to find her and assure himself she was safe. He was trying his house next. There was an outside chance she'd gone up there for a rest and turned off her phone. It was a long shot. But he didn't know what else to do.

Caleb stepped up. "Would you like to meet my wife?" he asked Annette. "She's pregnant and resting at the house right now, just up there on the hill. We're having twins."

Annette looked uncertain. It was clear she'd rather stay with Matt.

"Great idea," Matt chimed in. "I'll finish up here, and maybe we can talk later."

"With Tasha?" she asked.

"Of course."

The answer seemed to appease her, and she went willingly with Caleb.

Once again, Matt owed his friend big-time.

Without wasting another second, he called Melissa and discovered Tasha hadn't been to the Crab Shack in a couple of days. He checked his house but found nothing. So he asked the crew and dockworkers to check every inch of every boat.

They came up empty, and Matt called the police.

They told him he couldn't file a missing persons report for twenty-four hours. Then they had the gall to suggest Tasha might have disappeared of her own accord—because she knew she'd been caught committing arson.

It took every ounce of self-control he had not to ream the officer out over the phone.

His next stop was the security tapes from this morning. While he was reviewing them in the office, Caleb came back.

"What was *that* all about?" Caleb asked Matt without preamble.

"I have no idea. But I have bigger problems."

Caleb sobered. "What's going on?"

"It's Tasha. I can't find her."

"Was she supposed to be somewhere?"

"Here. She's supposed to be here!"

Caleb drew back.

"Sorry," Matt said. "I'm on edge. She's been missing for hours. The police won't listen."

"The *police*?"

"The fire department thinks she's an arsonist."

"Wait. Slow down."

"She was the last person known to be on board *Crystal Zone*. They concluded some oily rags combusted in the engine room, and they blame her for leaving them there—possibly on purpose."

"That's ridiculous," Caleb said.

"It's something else. It's someone else." Matt kept his attention on the security footage. "There she is."

Caleb came around the desk to watch with him.

Tasha walked down the pier. By the time clock, he knew it was right after she'd talked to the fire investigator. She'd disappeared behind *Monty's Pride*.

Matt waited. He watched and he waited.

"Where did she go?" Caleb asked.

"There's nothing back there." Matt clicked Fast-Forward, and they continued to watch.

"That's an hour," Caleb said. "Would she be working on *Monty's Pride*?"

"We checked. She's not there. And she couldn't have boarded from the far side."

"I hate to say it," Caleb ventured. "Is there any chance she fell in?"

Matt shot him a look of disbelief. "Really? Plus the tide's incoming." He had to steel himself to even say it out loud. "She wouldn't have washed out to sea."

"I'm stretching," Caleb said.

"Wait a minute." The answer came to Matt in a lightning bolt. "A boat. If she left the pier without coming back around, it had to have been in a boat."

"The Crab Shack camera has a different angle."

Matt grabbed his coat. "Let's go."

Tasha's head was still throbbing, but at least her dizziness had subsided. She was thirsty, but she didn't want to say or do anything that might upset the man who held her captive. When he turned, she could see a bulge in the waistband of his pants.

It could be a gun. It was probably a gun. But at least he wasn't pointing it at her.

If she could get back to full strength, and if he came close enough, she might be able to overpower him. She knew instinctively that she'd get only one chance. If she tried and failed, he might go for the gun or knock her out again or tie her hands.

He'd been pacing the far side of the garage for a long time.

"You need something else to wear," he said. His tone was matter-of-fact. He didn't seem angry.

"Why?" she dared ask.

"Because you look terrible, all tatty and ratty. Your mother wouldn't like that at all."

"You know my mother?"

His grin was somewhat sickly. "Do I know your mother? I know her better than she knows herself."

Struggling to keep her growing fear at bay, Tasha racked her brain trying to place the man. Had they met back in Boston? Why was he wearing her father's favorite cologne?

"Why did you want me to get fired?" she dared to ask.

"Isn't it obvious? Your mother misses you. You need to come home."

Come home. It sounded like home for him, too. *He must live in Boston.*

"You thought if Matt fired me, I'd move back to Boston?"

"Ah, Matt. The handsome Matt. You wore a nice dress that night."

Tasha turned cold again.

"You must have liked it. You looked like you liked it, all red and sparkly. You looked like your sister Madison."

"Where's Madison?" Tasha's voice came out on a rasp. Had this man done something to the rest of her family?

"What's with all the questions?" he chided. "If you want to see Madison, simply come home."

"Okay," she agreed, trying another tactic. "I'll come home. How soon can we leave?"

He stared at her with open suspicion. "I'm not falling for that."

"Falling for what? I miss Madison. And I miss Shelby. I'd like to see them. A visit would be nice."

"No, no, no." He shook his head. "That was too quick. I'm not stupid."

"I simply hadn't thought about it for a while," she tried.

"You're trying to trick me. Well, it won't work."

"I don't want to trick you." She gave up. "I honestly want to give you what you want. You've gone to a lot of trouble here. You must want it very badly."

"First, you need to change."

Her heart leaped in anticipation. Maybe he'd leave the garage. Maybe he'd go shopping for some clothes. If he left her alone, especially if he didn't tie her hands, she could escape. There had to be a way out of this place.

"It's in the car."

"What's in the car?"

"The red dress."

She was back to being frightened again. "How did you get the red dress?"

He looked at her like she was being dense. "It was in your room. I took it from your room. I'm disappointed you didn't notice. You should take more care with such an expensive gown. I had it cleaned."

Tasha's creep factor jumped right back up again. At the same time, she realized she hadn't even noticed the dress was gone. When she'd thought back on that night, making love with Matt had been foremost on her mind. The dress had faded to insignificance.

The security cameras covered the marina but the staff quarters were farther back, out of range. He'd obviously slipped in at some point.

"I'll get it," the man said, heading for the door.

"I'm not changing in front of you," she shouted out.

He stopped and pivoted. "I wouldn't expect you to, dear. Whatever you think of me, I am a gentleman."

"What's your name?" She braved the question, then held her breath while she waited for him to answer or get angry.

"Giles."

"And you're from Boston?"

"The West End, born and raised." He seemed to expect her to be impressed.

"That's very nice."

"I'll get your dress. We need to go now."

"Where are we going?"

He turned again, this time his eyes narrowed in annoyance, and she braced herself. "Pay attention, Tasha. We're going to Boston."

She shuddered at his icy expression. He couldn't get her all the way to Boston as his prisoner. He'd have to drive. They couldn't board a plane.

It would be all but impossible to watch her every second. She'd escape. She'd definitely find a way to escape.

But what if he caught her? What would he do then?

Eleven

The Crab Shack security footage confirmed Matt's worst fears. The picture was grainy, but it showed Tasha being hauled into a boat and taken away.

"It's red," Caleb said, "but that's about as much detail as I'm getting."

"Probably a twenty-footer," Matt said. "There's no way they're leaving the inlet. That's something at least."

TJ arrived at the Crab Shack's office. "What's going on? Melissa said you were looking for Tasha."

"Somebody grabbed her," Matt said.

His instinct was to rush to his car and drive, but he didn't know where he was going. He should call the police, but he feared that would slow him down. He had to find her. He absolutely had to find her.

"What do you mean grabbed her?" TJ asked, his expression equal parts confusion and concern.

When Matt didn't answer, TJ looked to Caleb.

"Show him the clip," Caleb said.

Matt replayed it.

TJ swore under his breath.

"Matt thinks they won't leave the inlet," Caleb said. "It's a red twenty-footer. He might have pulled it onto a trailer, but maybe not. Maybe it's still tied up somewhere on the inlet."

"There are a lot of red cartoppers out there," TJ said, but he was taking out his phone as he said it.

Matt came to his feet. "We should start with the public dock." He was glad to have a course of action.

"What about the police?" Caleb asked.

"Herb?" TJ said into the phone. "Can you get me a helicopter?"

Matt turned to TJ in surprise.

"Now," TJ said and paused. "That'll do." He ended the call and pointed to the screen. "Can someone copy that for me?"

"Melissa?" Caleb called out.

She immediately popped her head through the doorway. "Can you help TJ print out what's on the screen?"

"I'm going to the public dock," Matt said. "You'll call me?" he asked TJ.

"With anything we find," TJ said.

Under normal circumstances, Matt would have protested TJ's actions. But these weren't normal circumstances. He didn't care what resources it took. He was finding Tasha.

"I'll talk to the police," Caleb said. "What about Tasha's mother?"

Both TJ and Melissa stared at Caleb in surprise. "She's up with Jules. She suddenly dropped by for a visit."

"Yes," Matt said. "Talk to her. It's really strange that she's here. She might know something."

Matt sprinted to his car and roared out of the parking lot, zooming up the hill to the highway and turning right for the public dock. He dropped his phone on the seat beside him, ready to grab it if anyone called.

The sun was setting, and it was going to be dark soon. He could only imagine how terrified Tasha must be feeling. She had to be okay. She *had* to be okay.

It took him thirty minutes to get to the public dock. He leaped over the turnstile, not caring who might come after him.

He scanned the extensive docking system, row upon row of boats. He counted ten, no, twelve small red boats.

"Sir?" The attendant came up behind him. "If you don't have a pass card, I'll have to charge you five dollars."

Matt handed the kid a twenty. "Keep the change."

"Sure. Okay. Thanks, man."

Matt jogged to the dock with the biggest concentration of red twenty-footers.

He marched out on the dock, stopping to stare down at the first one. He realized he didn't know what he was looking for. Blood on the seat? He raked a hand through his hair. *Please, no, not that.*

Even if he found the boat, what would that tell him? He wouldn't know which way they went. Did the kidnapper have a car? Maybe the attendant was his best bet. Maybe the kid had seen something.

His phone rang. It was TJ, and Matt put it to his ear. "Yeah?"

"We see a red boat. It's a possible match."

"Where?"

"Ten minutes south of you. Take Ring Loop Road, third right you come to."

"TJ." Matt wanted him to be right. He so wanted him to be right. "I'm looking at a dozen red twenty-footers here."

"He hit her on the head," TJ reminded him. "I don't think he'd risk carrying her unconscious through the public dock. And if she was awake, she might call out. This place is secluded. And the boat is only tied off at the bow. The stern line is trailing in the water, like somebody was in a hurry."

"Yeah. Okay." Matt bought into TJ's logic. "It's worth a shot."

"We'll keep going farther."

"Thanks." Matt headed back to his car.

He impatiently followed TJ's directions, finally arriving at the turnoff. He followed the narrow road toward the beach, shutting off his engine to silently coast down the final hill.

He could see a red boat at the dock. The tide was high, pushing it up against the rocky shore. There was an old building visible through the trees.

He crept around to the front of the building and saw a car with the trunk standing open. He moved closer, silent on his feet, listening carefully.

The building door swung open, and he ducked behind a tree.

Tasha appeared. Her mouth was taped. Her hands were behind her back. And she was wearing the red party dress. A man had her grasped tight by one arm.

She spotted the open trunk. Her eyes went wide with fear, as she tried to wrench herself away.

"Let her go!" Matt surged forward.

The man turned. He pulled a gun and pointed it at Matt. Matt froze.

Tasha's eyes were wide with fear.

"You don't want to do this," Matt said, regretting his impulsive actions. How could he have been so stupid as to barge up on the kidnapper with no plan?

"I know exactly what I want to do," the man returned in a cold voice.

"Let her go," Matt said.

"How about *you* get out of my way."

"You're not going to shoot her," Matt said, operating in desperation and on the fly. He could not let the guy leave with Tasha. "You went to too much trouble to get her here."

"Who said anything about shooting *her*?" The man sneered.

Matt heard sirens in the distance, and he nearly staggered with relief. "The police are on their way."

"Move!" the man yelled to Matt.

"No. You're not taking her anywhere."

The man fired off a round. It went wide.

"Every neighbor for ten miles heard that," Matt said. "You'll never get away. If you kill me, that's cold-blooded murder. If you let her go, maybe it was a misunderstanding. Maybe you drive away. Maybe, you let her go, and I step aside, and you drive off anywhere you want."

To Matt's surprise, the man seemed to consider the offer.

Matt took a step forward. "The one thing that's not happening here is you leaving with Tasha."

The sirens grew louder.

"Last chance," Matt said, taking another step.

The man's eyes grew wild, darting around in obvious indecision.

Then he shoved Tasha to the side.

She fell, and Matt rushed toward her and covered her with his body.

The kidnapper jumped into the car and zoomed off, spraying them with dust and stones.

As the debris settled, Matt pressed the number for TJ. Then he gently peeled the tape from Tasha's mouth. "Are you hurt?"

"He's getting away," she gasped.

"He won't." Matt put the phone to his ear.

TJ had a bird's-eye view, and he was obviously in touch with both Caleb and the police.

The call connected.

"Yeah?" TJ said.

"He's running, red car," Matt said to TJ. "I've got Tasha."

"We see him."

The helicopter whirled overhead.

"There's only one road out," Matt said to Tasha. "And TJ can see him from the air. There's no way for him to escape. Now, please tell me you're all right."

"I'm fine. Frightened. I think that man is crazy."

"Did he tell you what he wanted? Why are you dressed up? Never mind. Don't say anything. Just..." Matt removed his jacket and wrapped it around her shoulders. "Rest. Just rest."

He wrapped his arms around her, cradling her against his chest. All he wanted to do was hold her. Everything else could wait.

The small police station was a hive of activity. Matt hadn't left Tasha's side since he'd found her, and everything beyond him and the detective interviewing her was a blur of motion, muted colors and indistinct sounds.

"You said you might have recognized Giles Malahide?" the detective asked her for what she thought was about the tenth time.

"Why do you keep asking?" Matt interjected.

The detective gave him a sharp look. "I'm trying to get a full picture." He turned his attention to Tasha again. "You said he seemed familiar."

"His smell seemed familiar. He was wearing the same brand of cologne as my father. And he talked about my mother."

"What did he say about your mother?"

"That she missed me."

"Tasha, darling." It was her mother's voice.

Tasha gave her head a swift shake. She was in worse shape than she'd thought. She tightened her grip on Matt's hands, waiting for the auditory hallucination to subside.

"I *need* to see her." Her mother's voice came again. "I'm her *mother*."

Tasha's eyes focused on a figure across the room. It was her mother and she was attempting to get past two female officers.

"Matt?" Tasha managed in a shaky voice.

She looked to him. He didn't seem surprised. Her mother was here? Her mother was actually in the room?

"You called my mother?" she asked. "Why would you call my mother?"

"I didn't call her. She showed up asking for you."

"You said Giles Malahide talked about your mother?" the detective asked.

"Is that his full name?" Tasha asked. Not that it mattered. She really didn't care who he was, as long as he stayed in jail and got some help.

"What is *he* doing here?" Tasha's mother demanded.

Tasha looked up to see Giles Malahide being marched past in handcuffs.

Matt quickly put his arms around Tasha and pulled her against his shoulder.

"Annette," Giles called out. "Annette, I found her. I found her."

"Bring that woman here," the detective barked.

"Can we go somewhere private?" Matt asked the detective.

"Yes," he said. "This way."

They rose, and Matt steered Tasha away from the commotion, down a short hallway to an interview room, helping her sit in a molded plastic chair.

"What is going on?" Tasha managed.

"We're going to find out," the detective said. Then his tone became less brisk, more soothing. "I know you've gone through this already. But can you start from the beginning? From the first instance of what you believed to be sabotage?"

Tasha was tired.

"Is that necessary?" Matt asked. His tone hadn't moderated at all.

She put a hand on his forearm. "I can do it."

"Are you sure?"

"I'm sure."

She reiterated the entire story, from the water found in the fuel in *Orca's Run*, to her eerie feeling on board *Crystal Zone* before the fire, to her terror at the prospect of being thrown in the trunk of Giles's car.

As she came to the end, there was a soft knock on the door. It opened, and a patrolwoman leaned her head into the room. "Detective?" she asked.

"Come in, Elliott."

"We have a statement from Giles Malahide. It's delusional, but it corroborates everything Annette Lowell is saying."

"My *mother* knew about this?" Tasha couldn't accept that.

"No, no," Officer Elliott was quick to say. "Malahide acted on his own." She glanced to the detective, obviously unsure of how much to reveal.

"Go on," he said.

"Giles worked on the Lowell estate as a handyman."

"Estate?" the detective asked and looked to Tasha.

Officer Elliott continued, "They're the Vincent Lowell family, libraries, university buildings, the charity."

"Giles claims he's in love with Annette," Officer Elliott said. "And he believed her fondest wish was to have her daughter Tasha back in Boston in the family fold. He tracked Tasha down. He thought if she got fired from the Whiskey Bay Marina, she'd come home. When that didn't work, he took a more direct approach."

Tasha felt like she'd fallen through the looking glass. The officer's summary was entirely plausible, but it didn't explain how her mother had turned up in the middle of it all.

"Why is my mother here?" she asked.

"She saw your photo in the newspaper. The one taken at the fire. The story talked about Matt Emerson and his business and, well…" Officer Elliott looked almost apologetic. "She said she wanted to meet your boyfriend."

Tasha nearly laughed. She quickly covered her mouth and tipped her head forward to stifle the inappropriate emotion.

"Are you all right?" Matt's tone was worried.

"I'm fine. I'm…" She looked back up, shaking her head and heaving a sigh. "It's my mother." She looked at Matt. "She thinks you're a catch. She thinks I've found myself a worthy mate who will turn me into a responsible married woman." Tasha looked to Officer Elliott. "Her fondest wish isn't to have me back in Boston. Her fondest wish is to see me settled down, not rattling around engine parts and boat motors."

"Do we have a full confession?" the detective asked Officer Elliott.

"He's denied nothing. We have plenty to hold him on."

The detective closed his notebook. "Then we're done here. You're free to go, Ms. Lowell."

"Are you ready to see your mother?" Matt asked as they rose.

With all that had happened today, facing her mother seemed like the easiest thing she'd ever been asked to do. "As ready as I'll ever be."

"You're sure?"

"It's fine." Tasha had been standing up to her mother for years. She could do it again.

They made their way back to the crowded waiting room. Melissa, Noah, Jules, Caleb and Alex were all there. Tasha found herself glad to see them. It felt like she had a family after all, especially with Matt by her side.

Jules gave her a hug. "Anything you need," she said. "All you have to do is ask."

"I'm just glad it's over," Tasha said. "It would have been nice to have a less dramatic ending."

The people within hearing distance laughed.

"But at least we know what was going on," Jules said. "Everything can get back to normal now."

"Tasha." Her mother made her way through the small cluster of people. She pulled Tasha into a hug. "I was so worried about you."

"Hello, Mom."

Tasha swiftly ended the hug. They weren't a hugging family. She could only assume her mother had been inspired by Jules to offer that kind of affection.

"You look lovely," her mother said, taking in the dress.

"Thank you."

"Are you all right? I had no idea Giles would do something like that. Your father fired him months ago."

"It wasn't your fault," Tasha said.

Matt stepped in. "It's time to take Tasha home."

"Of course. Of course," Annette said. "We can talk later, darling."

If her mother had truly come looking for a reformed daughter with an urbane, wealthy boyfriend, she was going to be sadly disappointed.

While Tasha slept, Matt had installed Annette in another of his guest rooms. Then Caleb, the best friend a man could ever ask for, invited Annette to join him and Jules for dinner at the Crab Shack. Matt was now staring at the clutter of Christmas decorations, wondering if Tasha would feel up to finishing the job in the next few days, or if he should simply cart them all down to the basement for next year.

He heard a noise, and looked to find her standing at the end of the hall.

"You're up," he said, coming to his feet. Then he noticed she was carrying her gym bag. "What are you doing?"

"Back to the staff quarters," she said.

"Why?" He knew she had to go eventually. But it didn't have to be right away.

"Thanks for letting me stay here," she said, walking toward the front door.

"Wait. Whoa. You don't have to rush off. You're fine here. It's good."

The last thing he wanted was for her to leave. He'd hoped... Okay, so he wasn't exactly sure what he'd hoped. But he knew for certain this wasn't it.

"No, it's not good. The danger has passed, and things can go back to normal."

"Just like that?" He snapped his fingers.

"Just like nothing. Matt, what's got into you?"

He followed her to the entry hall. "Your mother's here, for one thing."

Tasha dropped the bag at her feet. "I know she's here. And I'll call her tomorrow. We can do lunch at her hotel or something. I'll explain everything. She'll be disappointed.

But I'm used to that. She'll get over it. She has two other perfectly good daughters."

"I mean she's here, here," Matt said, pointing to the floor. "I invited her to stay in my other guest room."

Tasha's expression turned to utter astonishment. "Why would you do that?"

"Because she's your mother. And I thought you were staying here. It seemed to make sense." He knew they weren't on the best of terms, but Annette had come all the way across the country to see Tasha. Surely, they could be civil for a couple of days.

"That was a bad idea," Tasha said.

"She told me you hadn't seen her in years."

"It's not a secret."

"Don't you think this is a good chance?"

Tasha crossed her arms over her chest. "You know why she's here, right?"

"To see you."

"To see *you*. She thinks I found a good man. She thinks I've come to my senses, and I'm going to start planning my wedding to you any minute now."

"I think she misses you," Matt said honestly. He hadn't spent a lot of time with Annette, but her concern for Tasha seemed genuine.

"She came out here because of the picture in the paper."

"The picture that told her where to find you," he argued.

"The picture that she thought told her a wealthy man was in my life."

"Stay and talk to her." What Matt really meant was stay and talk with him. But he couldn't say that out loud. He hated the thought of her going back to that dim little room where she'd be alone, and then he'd be alone, too.

"I'll see her tomorrow," Tasha said.

He couldn't let her slip away like this. "What about us?"

She looked tired, and a little sad. "There isn't an us."

"There was last night."

"Last night was…last night. Our emotions were high."

He didn't buy it. "Our emotions are still high."

"The danger is over. I don't need to be here. And I don't need you taking my mother's side."

"I'm not taking her side."

She put her hand on the doorknob. "I appreciate your hospitality, and what you've done for my mom. But my life is my own. I can't let her change it, and I can't let you change it either."

"Staying in my guest room isn't changing your life."

"No? I already miss your bathtub."

He couldn't tell if she was joking. "That's another reason to stay."

"No, that's another reason to go. I'm tough, Matt. I'm sturdy and hardworking. I don't need bubbles and bath salts and endless gallons of hot water."

"There's no shame in liking bath salts."

"This Cinderella is leaving the castle and going back home."

"That's not how the story ends."

"It's how this story ends, Matt."

"Give us a chance."

"I have to be strong."

"Why does being strong mean walking away?"

"Not tonight, Matt. Please, not tonight."

And then she was gone. And he was alone. He wanted to go after her, but it was obvious she needed some time.

Through the night, Tasha's mind had whirled a million miles an hour. It had pinged from the kidnapping to her mother to Matt and back again. She'd been tempted to stay and spend the night with him, and the feeling scared her.

She'd been tempted by Matt, by everything about his lifestyle, the soaker tub the pillow-top bed. She'd even wanted to decorate his Christmas tree.

She was attracted to his strength, his support and intelligence, his concern and kindness. She'd wanted to throw every scrap of her hard-won independence out the window and jump headlong into the opulent life he'd built.

She couldn't let herself do that.

"Tasha?" Her mother interrupted her thoughts from across the table at the Crab Shack.

"Yes?" Tasha brought herself back to the present.

"I said you've changed."

"I'm older." Her mother looked older, too. Tasha hadn't expected that.

"You're calm, more serene. And that was a lovely dress you had on yesterday."

Tasha tried not to sigh. "It was borrowed."

"That's too bad. You should buy some nice things for yourself. Just because you have a dirty day job, doesn't mean you can't dress up and look pretty."

"I don't want to dress up and look pretty." Even as she said the words, she acknowledged they were a lie. She'd wanted to dress up for Matt. She still wanted to look nice for him. As hard as she tried, she couldn't banish the feeling.

"I don't want to argue, honey."

"Neither do I." Tasha realized she didn't. "But I'm a mechanic, Mom. And it's not just a day job that I leave behind. I like being strong, independent, relaxed and casual."

"I can accept that."

The answer surprised Tasha. "You can?"

Her mother reached out and covered her hand. "I'm not trying to change you."

Tasha blinked.

"But how does Matt feel about that?"

"Everything's not about a man, Mom."

"I know. But there's nothing like a good man to focus a woman's priorities."

Tasha was nervous enough about Matt's impact on her priorities. "You mean mess with a woman's priorities."

"What a thing to say. When I met your father, I was planning to move to New York City. Well, he changed that plan right away."

"You exchanged a mansion in the Hamptons for a mansion in Beacon Hill?"

"What do you have against big houses?" Annette asked.

"It's not the house. It's the lifestyle. Would you have married a mechanic and moved to the suburbs?"

The question seemed to stump her mother.

"I'd do that in a heartbeat. It would suit me just fine. But I can't be someone's wife who spends all her time dressing up, attending parties, buying new yachts and decorating Christmas trees."

"It's not the same thing. I'd be moving down the ladder. You'd be moving up."

Tasha retrieved her hand. "I'm on a different ladder."

Her mother's eyes narrowed in puzzlement. "Not needing to work is a blessing. When you don't need to work, you can do whatever you want."

"I do need to work."

"Not if you and Matt—"

"Mom, there is no me and Matt. He's my boss, full stop."

Her mother gave a knowing smile. "I've seen the way he looks at you. And I can't help but hear wedding bells. And it has nothing to do with wishful thinking."

"Oh, Mom. Matt doesn't want to marry me."

Matt wanted to sleep with her, sure. And she wanted to sleep with him. But he was her boss not her boyfriend.

"Well, not yet," Annette said. "That's not the way it works, darling. If only you hadn't left home so soon. There's so much I could have taught you."

"Mom, I left home because I didn't want to play those games."

"They're the only games worth playing."

"Oh, Mom."

It was an argument they'd had dozens of times. But

strangely, it didn't upset Tasha as much as it normally did. She realized, deep down, her mother meant well.

"I want you to keep in touch, honey. Okay?" Annette said.

"Okay." Tasha agreed with a nod, knowing it was time to move to a different relationship with her family. She wasn't caving to their wishes by any stretch, but her mother seemed a lot more willing to see her side of things. "I will."

Her mother's expression brightened. "Maybe even come for Christmas? You could bring Matt with you. He can meet your father and, well, you can see what happens from there."

Baby steps, Tasha told herself. "You're getting way ahead of yourself, Mom."

"Perhaps. But a mother can hope."

Twelve

Matt sat sprawled on a deck chair in front of his open fire-place. He normally loved the view from the marina building's rooftop deck. Tonight, the ocean looked bland. The sky was a weak pink as the sun disappeared, and dark clouds were moving in from the west. They'd hit the Coast Mountains soon and rain all over him.

He should care. He should go inside. He couldn't bring himself to do either.

Tasha had asked him to back off, and he'd backed off. And it was killing him to stay away from her.

Footsteps sounded on the outdoor staircase a few seconds before Caleb appeared.

"What's going on?" he asked Matt.

"Nothin'." Matt took another half-hearted drink of his beer.

Caleb helped himself to a bottle of beer from the compact fridge. "Where's Tasha?"

Matt shrugged. "I dunno."

Caleb twisted off his cap and took a chair. "I thought you two were a thing."

"We're not a thing." Matt wanted to be a thing. But what Matt wanted and what he got seemed to be completely different.

"I thought she stayed with you last night."

"That was the night before. When she was in danger. Last night, she went home."

"Oh."

"Yeah. Oh."

Caleb fell silent, and the fire hissed against the backdrop of the lackluster tide.

"You practically saved her life," he said.

"I guess that wasn't enough."

"What the heck happened?"

TJ appeared at the top of the stairs. "What happened to who?"

"To Matt," Caleb said. "He's all lonesome and pitiful."

"Where's Tasha?" TJ asked. Like Caleb, he helped himself to a beer.

"I'm not doing that all over again," Matt said.

"What?" TJ asked, looking from Matt to Caleb and back again.

"Trouble in paradise," Caleb said.

"It wasn't paradise," Matt said. Okay, maybe it had been paradise. But only for a fleeting moment in time, and now he felt awful.

"You were her white knight," TJ said as he sat down. "I saw it from the air."

Matt raised his bottle to punctuate TJ's very valid point. "That jerk shot at me. There was actual gunfire involved."

"So what went wrong?" TJ asked.

"That's what I asked," Caleb said.

"I asked her to say. She wanted to leave."

"Her mom really likes you," Caleb said.

"That's half the problem."

"Did you tell her how you feel?" TJ asked.

"Yes," Matt answered.

"You told her you were in love with her?"

"Wait, what?" Caleb asked. "Did I miss something?"

"That's your wild theory," Matt told TJ.

He didn't even know why TJ was so convinced it was true.

Sure, okay, maybe someday. If he was honest, Matt could see it happening. He could picture Tasha in his life for the long term.

"You moved heaven and earth to rescue her," Caleb said.

"She was my responsibility. She's my employee. She was kidnapped while she was at work."

"I've never seen you panic like that," TJ said.

He pulled his chair a little closer to the fire. The world was disappearing into darkness around them, and a chill was coming up in the air.

"A crazed maniac hit Tasha over the head and dragged her off in a boat." How exactly was Matt supposed to have reacted? "You were the one who hired a chopper," he said to TJ.

"It seemed like the most expeditious way to cover a lot of ground."

"That doesn't make you in love with Tasha." Matt frowned. He didn't even like saying the words that connected Tasha with TJ.

"What would you do if I asked her out again?" TJ asked.

Matt didn't hesitate. "I'd respectfully ask you not to do that."

Caleb snorted.

"See what I mean?" TJ said to Caleb.

"That doesn't prove anything." Although Matt had to admit he was exaggerating only a little bit.

And it went for any other guy, as well. He didn't know what he might do if he saw her with someone else. She was *his*. She had to be his.

"I can see the light coming on." Caleb was watching Matt but speaking to TJ.

"Any minute now…" TJ said. "Picture her in a wedding dress."

An image immediately popped up in Matt's mind. She looked beautiful, truly gorgeous. She was smiling, surrounded by flowers and sunshine. And he knew in that instant he'd do anything to keep her.

"And how do you feel?" Caleb asked. The laughter was gone from his voice.

"Like the luckiest guy on the planet."

"Bingo," TJ said, raising his beer in a toast.

"You need to tell her," Caleb said.

"Oh, no." Matt wasn't ready to go that far.

"She needs to know how you feel," TJ said.

"So she can turn me down again? She doesn't want a romance. She wants her career and her independence. She wants everyone to think of her as one of the guys."

"She told you that?" Caleb asked.

"She did."

"Exactly that?" TJ asked.

"She said her life was her own, and I wasn't going to change it. She said this was how our story ended."

Caleb and TJ exchanged a look.

"Yeah," Matt said. "Not going to be a happily-ever-after." He downed the rest of his beer.

"Wuss," TJ said.

"Coward," Caleb said.

Matt was insulted. "A guy shot at me."

"Didn't even wing you," TJ said.

"That's nothing," Caleb said.

"It was something," Matt said.

TJ leaned forward, bracing his hands on his knees. "You still have to tell her how you feel."

"I don't *have* to do anything."

"Haven't we always had your back?" Caleb asked.

"I asked her to stay," Matt repeated. "She decided to go."

"You asked her to stay the night." TJ's tone made the words an accusation.

"I meant more than that."

"Then tell her more than that."

Caleb came to his feet. "Ask her to stay for the rest of your life."

"That's…" Matt could picture it. He could honestly picture it.

"Exactly what you want to do," TJ said.

Matt stared at his friends.

TJ was right. They were both right. He was in love with Tasha, and he had to tell her. Maybe she'd reject him, maybe she wouldn't. But he wasn't going down without one heck of a fight.

"You'll want to get a ring," TJ said.

"It always works better with a ring," Caleb said.

"It worked for Noah," Matt agreed. "Do you think I should ask her in front of everyone?"

"No!" TJ and Caleb barked out in unison.

"Noah was sure of the answer," TJ said.

"You guys think she's going to turn me down." That was depressing.

"We don't," Caleb said.

"Maybe," TJ said. "It would probably help to get a really great ring. You need a loan?"

"I don't need a loan."

Matt might not be able to purchase two new yachts on short notice. But he could afford an engagement ring. He could afford a dazzling engagement ring—the kind of ring no woman, not even Tasha, would turn down.

Tasha had found the solution to her problem. She hated it, but she knew it was right. What she needed to do was glaringly obvious. She wrote Matt's name on the envelope and propped her resignation letter against the empty brown teapot on the round kitchen table in her staff quarters unit.

Somebody would find it there tomorrow.

She shrugged into her warmest jacket, pulling up the zipper. Her big suitcase was packed and standing in the middle of the room. She'd stuffed as much as she could into her gym bag. Everything else was in the three cardboard boxes she'd found in the marina's small warehouse.

She should hand him the letter herself. She knew that. A better woman would say goodbye and explain her decision. But she was afraid of what would happen if she confronted him, afraid she might cry. Or worse, afraid she'd change her mind.

She'd dreamed of Matt for the past three nights, spectacular, sexy dreams where he held her tight and made her feel cherished and safe. She loved them while she slept, but it was excruciatingly painful to wake up. She'd spent the days working hard, focusing on the challenges in front of her, trying desperately to wear out both her body and her mind.

It hadn't worked. And it wasn't going to work.

She gazed around the empty room, steeling herself. Maybe she'd go to Oregon, perhaps as far as California. It was warm there. Even in December, it was warm in California.

She looped her gym bag over her shoulder and extended the handle on her wheeled suitcase. But before she could move, there was a soft knock on her door.

Her stomach tightened with anxiety.

Her first thought was Matt. But it didn't sound like his knock. He wasn't tentative.

It came again.

"Hello?" she called out.

"It's Jules," came the reply.

Tasha hesitated. But she set down the gym bag and made her way to the door. She opened it partway, mustering up a smile. "Hi."

"How are you doing?"

"I'm fine."

"I thought you might come to the Crab Shack to talk."

"I've been busy." Tasha realized she was going to miss Jules, as well. And she'd miss Melissa. Not to mention Caleb and TJ. She barely knew Noah, but what she knew of him she liked. It would have been nice to get to know him better.

"Are you sure everything's okay?" Jules asked, the concern in her eyes reflected in her tone.

"Good. It's all good." Tasha gave a rapid nod.

"Yeah? Because I thought you might…" Jules cocked her head. "Do you mind if I come in?"

Tasha glanced back at her suitcase. It wasn't going to stay a secret for long. But she wasn't proud of the fact that she was sneaking off in the dark.

Jules waited, and Tasha couldn't think of a plausible excuse to refuse.

"Sure," she said, stepping back out of the way.

Jules entered. She glanced around the room and frowned. "What are you doing?"

"Leaving," Tasha said.

"Are you going home for Christmas?"

"No."

Jules was clearly astonished. "You're *leaving*, leaving?"

"Yes."

"You quit your job?"

Tasha's gaze flicked to the letter sitting on the table. "Yes."

Jules seemed to be at a loss for words. "I don't get it. What happened?"

"Nothing happened." Tasha picked up her gym bag again. "I really need to get going."

"Matt knows?" Jules asked.

Tasha wished she could lie. "He will."

Jules spotted the letter. "You wrote him a Dear John?"

"It's a letter of resignation." Tasha made a move for the door.

"You can't," Jules said, standing in her way.

"Jules, don't do this."

"You're making a mistake."

Jules took out her phone.

"What are you—"

Jules raised the phone to her ear. A second passed, maybe two, before she said, "She's leaving."

Tasha grabbed her suitcase, making to go around Jules.

But Jules backed into the door, leaning against it. "Tasha, that's who."

"Don't be ridiculous," Tasha said to Jules.

"Right *now*," Jules said. "Her suitcase is packed and everything."

"Seriously?" Tasha shook her head. This was getting out of hand.

Jules's eyes narrowed on Tasha. "I don't know how long I can do that."

"Jules, *please*." Tasha was growing desperate. She didn't trust herself with Matt. There was a reason she'd quit by letter.

"Hurry," Jules said into the phone. Then she ended the call and flattened herself against the door.

Tasha glanced around for an escape. She could jump out the window, but it was quite a drop on that side. And her big suitcase wouldn't fit through. She'd probably sprain an ankle, and Matt would find her in a heap on the pathway.

"What have you done?"

"You'll thank me," Jules said, but she didn't look completely confident.

"This is a disaster. We made *love*."

"You did?"

Tasha gave a jerky nod. "Do you know how embarrassing this is going to be?"

"I promise it won't be."

"It will." Tasha was growing frantic. "We have chemistry. We have *so* much chemistry. He practically saved my life. Do you know what that does to a woman's hormones? I'll never be able to resist him."

Now Jules looked baffled.

"Why resist him?"

"Because I'm not going to be *that* woman."

"What woman is that?"

"The woman who had a fling with her boss, who lost all credibility. I'd have to quit eventually. I might as well do it now while I still have my dignity. It's important to me."

"But at what cost to your future? Don't you want to be happy, Tasha?"

Someone banged on the door.

"Open up," Matt shouted from the other side.

Tasha took a step backward, nearly tripping on the suitcase. The gym bag slipped from her shoulder.

Jules moved to the side, and Matt pushed open the door.

He took in the suitcase and the empty room, and then ze-roed in on Tasha.

"*What* are you doing?" His expression was part worry, part confusion.

"I'm resigning."

"Why?"

"You know why."

His eyes flashed with what looked like desperation. "I have no idea why."

"We can't go on like this, Matt."

"On like what? I did what you asked. I backed off."

"Yes, well…" She knew that was true, and she didn't dare admit that it hadn't helped. She still wanted him. She missed him. She…

Oh, no.

Not that.

She would *not* love Matt.

His expression turned to concern. "Tasha?" He closed the space between them. "You just turned white as a sheet."

"Go away," she rasped.

"I'm not going away." His hands closed gently around her arms.

Caleb appeared in the open doorway. "What's going on?"

"Shh," Jules hissed at him.

"Tasha." Matt's voice softened, and he stroked his palms along her arms. "Do you need to sit down?"

"No." She needed to leave, that's what she needed.

But she didn't want to leave. She wanted to fall into his arms. She wanted him to hold her tight. But she couldn't do it. It would only make things worse.

She loved him, and her heart was breaking in two.

He took her hands. "Tasha."

She gazed at their joined hands, feeling tears gather be-hind her eyes. Her throat went raw and her voice broke. "Please let me go."

"I can't do that."

TJ's voice sounded. "What did I—"

"Shh," Jules and Caleb said in unison.

Matt glanced over his shoulder. Then he looked into Tasha's eyes.

"They told me not to do it like this," he said. He lifted her hands, kissing her knuckles. "I'm not sure of your answer, and it would definitely work better with a ring."

Tasha squinted at him, trying to make sense of his words.

"But I love you, Tasha. I want you forever. I want you to marry me."

A roaring came up so fast in her ears, she was sure she couldn't have heard right.

She glanced past Matt to find Jules, Caleb and TJ all grinning.

"Wh-what?" she asked Matt.

"I love you," he repeated.

"I hate dresses." She found herself saying the first thing that came to her mind.

"Marry me in cargo pants," he said. "I don't care."

But she knew there was more to it than that. "You want someone to go yacht shopping with you, to take to fancy balls, to decorate your stupid Christmas tree."

He laughed softly and drew her into his arms.

"I'll go yacht shopping with him," Caleb offered.

"I'll go, too," TJ said. "After all, I'm the guy fronting the money."

"Let her speak," Jules said to both of them.

"You haven't thought this through," Tasha said.

"This is why you don't do it in front of people," Caleb whispered.

Jules elbowed him in the ribs.

"I've thought it through completely," Matt said.

She could see he was serious, and hope rose in her heart. She wanted to dream. She wanted to believe. Her voice went softer. "What if you change your mind?"

He arched a skeptical brow. "Change my mind about loving you?"

"About marrying a woman in cargo pants."

He drew back and cradled her face between his palms. "Tasha, I love you *exactly* the way you are."

Her heart thudded hard and deep inside her chest. She loved him, and she felt sunshine light up her world.

"I can't imagine my life without you and your cargo pants," he said.

Her heart lifted and lightened, and her lips curved into a gratified smile. "I suppose I could wear one more dress." She paused. "For the wedding."

His grin widened. "Is that a yes?"

She nodded, and he instantly wrapped her in a tight hug.

A cheer went up behind him.

"Yes," she whispered in his ear.

He kissed her then, deeply and passionately.

"Congratulations," TJ called out.

Matt laughed in clear delight as he broke the kiss. He kept one arm around Tasha, turning to his friends. "You could have given me some privacy."

"Are you kidding?" Caleb asked. "We were dying to see how this turned out."

"It turned out great," Matt said, giving Tasha a squeeze.

Jules moved forward. "Congratulations." She commandeered Tasha for a hug.

"You were right," Tasha said to her.

"Right about what?"

"I do thank you."

Jules smiled. "I knew it! I'm so happy for you, for both of you."

"I can't believe this has happened," Tasha managed, still feeling awestruck.

"I can't believe she didn't say it," Caleb put in.

"She did," Matt said. He pointed to his friends. "You all saw her nod. That's good enough for me. I have witnesses."

"The I-love-you part," Caleb said.

Matt looked to Tasha, showing surprise on his face. "You did. Didn't you?"

"I don't remember." She made a show of stalling.

"You don't remember if you love me?"

She teased. "I don't remember if I said it." She felt it with all her heart, and she couldn't wait to say it out loud. "I do love you, Matt. I love you so very much."

He scooped her up into his arms. "Good thing you're already packed." He started for the door.

"I've got the bags," TJ said.

Tasha couldn't help but laugh. She wrapped her arms around Matt's neck and rested her head against his shoulder. She was done fighting. They were going home.

It was late Christmas Eve, and Tasha stepped back to admire her handiwork on the tree.

Returning from the kitchen, two mugs of peppermint hot chocolate in his hands, Matt paused. He'd never seen a more amazing sight—his beloved fiancée making his house feel like the perfect home.

"We finally got it decorated," she said, turning her head to smile at him. "Yum. Whipped cream."

"Only the best," he said.

She was dressed in low-waisted black sweatpants, a bulky purple sweater and a pair of gray knit socks. Her hair was up in a ponytail, and she couldn't have looked more beautiful.

He moved forward, handing her one of the mugs. "It tastes fantastic."

"Thanks." She took a sip through the froth of whipped cream.

"And so do you." He kissed her sweet mouth.

"And not a ball gown in sight."

"This is better than any old ball."

"Music to my ears." She moved around the coffee table to sit on the sofa.

It was the moment he'd been waiting for. "Look at the time."

She glanced to the wall clock. "It's midnight."

"Christmas Day," he said.

She smiled serenely up at him. "Merry Christmas."

He set his mug down on the table and reached under the tree. "That means you can open a present."

Her smile faded. "We're not going to wait until morning?"

"Just one," he said, retrieving it.

He moved to sit beside her, handing over a small mint-green satin pouch. It was embossed in gold and tied with a matching gold ribbon.

"This is beautiful." She admired the package for a moment. Then she grinned like a little kid, untying the ribbon and pulling open the pouch.

His chest tightened with joy and anticipation.

She peeked inside. "What?" Then she held out her palm and turned the little bag over.

A ring dropped out—a two-carat diamond surrounded by tiny deep green emeralds that matched her irises.

"Oh, Matt." Her eyes shimmered as she stared at it. "It's incredible."

He lifted it from her palm. "You're what's incredible."

He took her left hand. "Tasha Lowell. I love you so much." He slipped the ring onto her finger. "I cannot wait to marry you."

"Neither can I." She held out her hand, admiring the sparkle. "This is perfect."

"You're perfect."

"Stop doing that."

"What?"

"One-upping my ring compliments."

"The ring can't hold a candle to you." He drew her into his arms and gave her a long, satisfying kiss.

By the time they drew apart, they were both breathless.

"So, what now?" she asked, gazing again at the glittery ring.

"Now we plan a wedding. You want big and showy? Or small with just our friends? We can elope if you want." Matt didn't care how it got done, just so long as it got done.

"My mom would die for a big wedding."

He smoothed her hair from her forehead. "You called her back, didn't you?" He hadn't wanted to ask, not knowing how Tasha was feeling about her mother's renewed interest in her life.

"This afternoon."

"Did it go okay?"

Tasha shrugged. "She hasn't changed. But I get it, and I can cope. She's completely thrilled about you, remember? I imagine she'll be taking out an ad in the *Boston Globe* in time for New Year's."

"Do you mind?"

He'd support whatever Tasha wanted to do about her relationship with her mother.

"It feels good to make peace." She paused. "I suppose it wouldn't hurt to make them happy."

He searched her expression. "Are you actually talking about a formal wedding?"

A mischievous smile came across her face. "We could let Mom go to town."

Matt put a hand on Tasha's forehead, pretending to check for a fever.

"I could dress up," she said. "I could do the glitz-and-glamour thing for one night. As long as I end up married to you when it's over."

"You would look stupendous." He couldn't help but picture her in a fitted white gown, lots of lace, shimmering silk or satin.

"You'd like it, wouldn't you?"

"I would not complain."

"Then let's do it."

He wrapped her in another tight hug. "When I picture our future, it just gets better and better."

"Next thing you know, we'll be having babies."

"With you," he said. "I definitely want babies." He pictured a little girl in front of the Christmas tree looking just like Tasha.

Maybe it was Jules's being pregnant, but he suddenly found himself impatient. He put a gentle hand on Tasha's stomach, loving the soft warmth. "How soon do you think we might have them?"

"I don't know." She reached out and popped the top button on his shirt. Then she opened another and another. "Let's go find out."

* * * * *

A CHRISTMAS RENDEZVOUS

KAREN BOOTH

For Val Skorup. You are the best cheerleader a person could ever want, a great friend and a total rock star.

One

Isabel Blackwell's head had hardly hit the pillow when the hotel alarm went off. The fire alarm.

Frustrated and annoyed, she sat up in bed and shoved back her sleep mask while the siren droned on out in the hall. This was getting old. The luxury Bacharach New York hotel had been her home for nearly two weeks and this was the fourth time the fire alarm had sounded. She'd intentionally gone to bed early to try to sleep away her difficult day. Her brother, Sam, had convinced her to take on a legal case she did not want—saving Eden's Department Store from a man with a vendetta and a decades-old promissory note. So much for the escape of a good night's rest.

"Attention, guests," the prerecorded message sounded over the hallway PA system. "Please proceed to the nearest fire exit in an orderly manner. Do not use the elevators. I repeat, do not use the elevators. Thank you."

"Do *not* use the elevators," Isabel mumbled to herself in a robotic voice. She tossed back the comforter, grabbed her robe, shoved her feet into a pair of ballet flats and dutifully shuffled down the hallway with the other guests. It was not quite 10:00 p.m., so she was the only one in her pajamas, but she refused to be embarrassed by it. Hers were pale pink silk charmeuse and she'd spent a fortune on them. Plus, if anyone should be feeling self-conscious, it was the hotel management. They needed to get their property under control.

She followed along down the stairs, through the lobby past the befuddled and apologetic bell captain, and out onto the street. Early December was not an ideal time to be parading around a Manhattan sidewalk in silk pj's, but she hoped that by now, the hotel staff had finely honed their skills of determining whether there was an actual fire.

The manager shot out of the revolving door, frantic. "Folks, I am so sorry. We're working as fast as we can to get you back inside and to your rooms." He fished a stack of cards from his suit pocket and began doling them out. "Please. Everyone. Enjoy a complimentary cocktail at the bar as our way of apologizing."

Isabel took his offering. She wasn't about to pass up a free drink.

"What if you already have one waiting for you?" a low rumble of a voice behind her muttered.

Isabel turned and her jaw went slack. Standing before her was a vision so handsome she found herself wondering if she had actually fallen asleep upstairs and was now in the middle of a splendidly hot dream. Tall and trim, the voice had a strong square jaw covered in neatly trimmed scruff, steely gray eyes and extremely enticing bedhead hair. It had even gone a very sexy salt-

and-pepper at the temples, pure kryptonite for Isabel. She had a real weakness for a distinguished man. "You had to leave a drink behind?" she had the presence of mind to ask. "That's a very sad story."

The voice crossed his arms and looked off through the hotel's glass doors, longingly. "The bartender had just poured the best Manhattan I've ever had. And it's wasting away in there." He then returned his sights to her, his vision drifting down to her feet, then lazily winding its way back up. As he took in every inch of her, it warmed her from head to toe. "Aren't you freezing?"

"No." She shook her head. "I run hot."

A corner of his mouth curled in amusement, and that was when she noticed exactly how scrumptious his lips were. He offered his hand. "Jeremy."

"Isabel." She wrapped her fingers around his, and found herself frozen in place. He wasn't moving, either. No, they were both holding on, heat and a steady current coursing between them. It had been too long since she'd shared even an instant of flirtation with a man, let alone a chemistry-laden minute or two. Her job was always getting in the way, a big reason she disliked it so much.

"You weren't kidding," he said. "How are you so warm?"

How are you so hot? "Lucky, I guess."

"Ladies and gentlemen," the hotel manager announced, poking his head out of the door. "Turns out it was a false alarm. You may go back inside."

"Looks like you can go rescue your Manhattan," Isabel said to Jeremy.

"Join me? I hate to drink alone." He cocked his head to one side and both eyebrows popped up in invitation.

Isabel had been fully prepared to go back upstairs

and simply take a few thoughts of dreamy Jeremy for a spin as she drifted off to sleep. "I'm in my pajamas."

"Don't forget the sleep mask." He reached up and plucked it from her hair. "Do these things really work?"

She smoothed back her hair, deciding this was only a good sign—he'd invited her to have a drink with him when she looked far less than her best. "They do work. Once you get used to it."

"I've never tried one. Maybe I should. I don't sleep that well."

Isabel fought back what she really wanted to say— that she wouldn't mind having the chance to make him slumber like a baby. Instead, she took the mask from his hand and tucked it into the pocket of her robe. "If you can stand to be seen with me, I'd love a drink."

"You could be wearing a potato sack and I'd still invite you for a drink." He stepped aside and with a flourish of his hand, invited her to lead the way.

Oh, Jeremy was smooth. For a moment she wondered if he was too much so. In her experience, men like that were only interested in fun. She'd moved to New York for a fresh start, so she could pursue a less unsavory line of legal work—adoption law, to be specific—and finally get serious about love. At thirty-eight, she was eager to get on with her life. Still, it was silly to judge yummy Jeremy by a few words in their first conversation. "Good to know your standards." Isabel marched inside and crossed the lobby, stopping at the bar entrance. Despite the generous disbursement of drink coupons from the manager, the room was sparsely occupied, with only a few people seated at the long mahogany bar. It was an elegant space, albeit a bit stuck in time, with black-and-white-checkerboard floors and crystal chandeliers dripping from the barrel ceiling.

"You'll have to let me know where you left your drink behind."

"Over here." Jeremy strolled ahead and Isabel took her chance to watch him from behind. The view was stunning—a sharp shoulder line atop a towering lean frame. His midnight-blue suit jacket obscured his backside, but she could imagine how spectacular it must be. He arrived at a corner table, and sure enough, there was his drink, along with a stack of papers, which he quickly shuffled into a briefcase.

"You really did leave in a hurry," she said. "Is this your first night staying here? I don't take the fire alarm all that seriously anymore. Most of the time it's nothing."

"I'm not a guest. I just had a meeting. I actually live in Brooklyn, but I thought I'd grab a drink before I headed home." He slid her a sly look. "Now I'm glad I did."

Isabel knew she should ask what he did for a living, but that would only lead to discussion of her own occupation. The last thing she wanted to do was talk about being a lawyer, a career she'd once dreamed of but that had since turned into a bit of a nightmare, another reason for moving away from Washington, DC. She'd somehow gone from earnest attorney to a political "fixer," cleaning up the personal messes of the powerful. She was good at it. Very good, actually. But she'd grown weary of that particular rat race. And in Washington, everyone was a rodent of one form or another.

"What would you like to drink?" Jeremy asked, pulling out a chair for her.

Isabel eased into the seat, which was sumptuously upholstered in white velvet with black trim. "I'll have a gin and tonic, two limes." She reached into her robe and pulled out the drink coupon, holding it out for Jeremy.

"Save that for a rainy day. It was my invitation. I intend to buy you a drink."

Isabel had to smile. It'd been a long time since a man had treated her nicely and actually made an effort. She'd been starting to wonder if gentlemanly behavior was a lost art. "Thank you."

Jeremy flagged down the bartender and was back with her drink in a few minutes. He sat next to her, his warm scent settling over her. It was both woodsy and citrusy, conjuring visions of a romantic fire crackling away. "So, tell me about yourself. What do you do?"

She had to make a choice right then and there as to how this night was going to go. Either they would do the same old getting-to-know-you routine that every man and woman who have just met must seemingly pursue, or they would head in a different direction. Coming to New York was supposed to be a fresh start for Isabel and she intended to follow through on that. She would not cling to old habits. She would try something new.

She reached out and set her hand on Jeremy's, which was resting on the tabletop. "I vote that we don't talk about work. At all. I don't think we should talk about where we went to school or who we used to date or how many important people we know."

Jeremy's eyes darkened, but there was a spark behind them—a mischievous glint. He was, at the very least, intrigued. "Okay, then. What do you want to talk about?"

She stirred her drink, not letting go of his hand. She loved that they already had this unspoken familiarity. Like they understood each other, and so soon after meeting each other. "I don't know. A little brutal honesty between strangers?"

He laughed and turned his hand until their palms were flat against each other. He clasped his fingers around hers. How that one touch could convey so much, she wasn't sure, but excitement bubbled up inside her so fast she thought she might pop like a cork from a champagne bottle. It was as if she'd been in a deep sleep and her entire body had rattled back to life. She wasn't the sort of woman who pinned a lot of hope on a man, but she found herself wondering where this might go.

"Like truth or dare, but just the truth part?" he asked.

Isabel swallowed hard, but did her best to convey cool. "Oh, no. I never said I wasn't up for a dare."

Jeremy was so tempted to dare Isabel to kiss him, he had to issue himself a mental warning: *Slow down, buddy*. He was essentially fearless, but he wasn't the guy to make leaps with a woman. Not anymore. He greatly enjoyed their company, but he'd been burned badly by a toxic marriage and the hellish divorce that followed. Since then, he'd learned to employ caution, but he did occasionally need to remind himself.

Still, he didn't want to waste his evening ruminating on his past mistakes. Not now. Not when he was sitting with Isabel, a woman who made him want to employ zero restraint. She was not only a captivating beauty, with sleek black hair framing a flawless complexion and warm brown eyes; she had a demeanor unlike any he'd ever encountered, from anyone—man or woman. What person goes to a bar in pale pink silk pajamas and matching robe and seems wholly comfortable? And the bit about not trying to impress each other? That was like a breath of fresh air. If he had to start talking about his job, he'd just get stressed. Especially after the meeting he'd had in this very bar an hour ago.

"I'm afraid I haven't played truth or dare since I was a teenager," he admitted.

"Me, neither. And almost all of the dares seemed to involve kissing."

It was as if she'd read his mind.

"But we aren't teenagers anymore, are we?" she added.

"Not me. I turned forty this year." Jeremy cleared his throat, struggling to keep up with her. He was usually laser-focused on a retort. As a lawyer, he got plenty of practice. "Okay, then. Tell me something almost nobody knows about you."

She smiled cleverly, stirring her drink. "That could take all night. I have lots of secrets." She bent her neck to one side and absentmindedly traced her delicate fingers along her collarbone.

The first secret Jeremy wanted to know was what was under those pajamas. He wanted to know *who* was under there—what Isabel would kiss like. What her touch would be like, what it would be like to have her naked form pressed against his. "How about three things I need to know about you? As a person. Three things you believe in."

She twisted up her beautiful lips, seeming deep in thought. "Okay. I believe that there is no good reason to lie, but that doesn't mean you have to confess everything. I believe that a good nap will cure most problems. And I believe that love is ultimately the only thing that ever saves anyone."

"Really?" Jeremy found that last part a bit too sunny and optimistic, but then again, he had his reasons for rolling his eyes at love.

"Like I said, a little brutal honesty between strangers. I have no reason to be anything less than ridiculously open and bare my soul."

"You're a therapist, aren't you? One of those people you pay hundreds of dollars an hour to, just so you can reveal the most humiliating things you've ever done."

She shook her head. "Hey. That's against the rules. We said we weren't going to talk about work."

"So I'm right. You *are* a therapist."

"No, you aren't right." She flashed her wide, warm eyes at him. "You aren't wrong, either."

Jeremy had to laugh while he marveled at the puzzle of Isabel. He wanted to peel back her layers, one by one… He suspected there were a lot of surprises to be found. "I suppose you want me to tell you my three truths now, huh?"

"It's only fair."

He had to think for a moment, knowing he had to match the clever balance she'd struck between revealing all and piquing his interest. He would not allow himself to be completely outdone by Isabel. "I believe that taking yourself too seriously is a trap. I believe that apologizing for making a lot of money is stupid. And I believe that there's nothing wrong with having fun."

She nodded, seemingly digesting his words. "Those are all very interesting."

"You're definitely a therapist."

"And you are definitely not good at following rules."

He shrugged. "Most rules are arbitrary."

"Like what?"

"Like the one that says you shouldn't invite a woman wearing her pajamas on a New York City sidewalk out for a drink."

She pointed her finger at him. "Yes. You're so right. That is a stupid rule."

He downed the last of his drink, sensing this was the moment when he had to decide whether he wanted to angle for an invitation upstairs. Fear was a big factor. He didn't want to endure a rejection from Isabel. Something told him she could deliver one in a particularly devastating way. "And yet I went there, didn't I? I took the chance."

"Yes, you did, didn't you? Which makes me wonder what you're after, Jeremy. A drink? Conversation? Or something more?" Isabel sat forward and drew her finger around the rim of her glass, looking at him, unafraid to confront him with her gaze.

He had to break the spell she had him under, but when he let his sights wander, it only got worse. The front of her robe had gaped open, revealing the gentle curve of the top of one breast. Jeremy felt the heat rising in his body, starting in his belly and radiating outward, up to his chest and down to his thighs. It would be so easy to blame it on the drink, but that heat was all created by Isabel. She pulled it out of thin air with her pouty lips, with her dark and sultry eyes, and with her sharp conversational skills. He was not the type to ask for more. Asking for anything only made things messy. It put you at a disadvantage, and he hated not feeling as though he had every weapon imaginable at his disposal. What was it about Isabel that made him want to lie down and give her everything?

"I want whatever you might be willing to give me," he admitted.

She smiled and the faintest blush crossed her cheeks. Good God, she was so beautiful he had to wonder if all of this was really happening. "So I'm in the driver's seat. That's what you're telling me."

"Of course. As it should be, right?"

She nodded, arching her eyebrows in a way that suggested she hadn't quite been prepared for the way their conversation had turned. He loved feeling like he could surprise her, even if the boost to his ego might be completely unwarranted. "So, Jeremy. Since I'm in charge, let me just share one more thing about myself. I don't know how you feel about good views, but I have a spectacular one of the city. Upstairs in my room."

Jeremy felt as though Isabel had just rolled Christmas, his birthday and Super Bowl Sunday into one day. "Funny you should ask, because I am a huge fan of views." He leaned closer and lowered his head, his heart thundering away in his chest like a summer storm.

Isabel drifted closer to him until their noses were almost touching. The rest of the room had faded away. Other people and their surroundings were a distant thought. It was just the two of them, their breaths in sync and their intentions apparently aligned, as well. "Truth or dare," she whispered.

"Dare," he answered without hesitation.

"Good answer." Her lips met his in the slightest of kisses. Her mouth only teased him, softer and more supple than he'd dared to imagine. She angled her head and took the kiss deeper, grasping his shoulder and digging her nails into his jacket. Her lips parted and her tongue skated along his lower lip, making every testosterone-driven part of him switch into high gear. The blood was pumping so fast it was hard to know which way was up.

He reached for her hip, the silk of her robe impossibly cool and soft against his skin. He pulled her closer, clawing at the tie at her waist, needing her. Wanting her.

Like he needed to breathe or eat or drink water. This whole business of not knowing much about each other was so hot. It left him wondering what the night had in store, when he hadn't been willing to gamble on the unknown in a long time.

"You never gave me my dare," he said, coming up for air.

"I dare you to come upstairs and take off your suit, Jeremy. I dare you to rock my world."

Two

It took every ounce of self-control Jeremy had to discreetly walk across that hotel lobby with Isabel. His gut was telling him to take her hand and run as fast as he could, jab the elevator button and get things going between them the instant they were inside. As long as they were alone.

Unfortunately, the elevator was not cooperating. "This thing is so slow," Isabel said, jamming the button a second time. She subtly leaned against him and rubbed the side of his thigh with her hand.

Everything in his body went so tight it felt as though he was strapped to a piece of wood. Blood drained from his hands and feet and rushed straight to the center of his body. He swallowed back a groan and strategically held his briefcase to obscure anyone's view of his crotch. His erection felt like it had its own pulse. He needed Isabel, now.

Finally the elevator dinged and they rushed on board as soon as the other passengers were off. He'd hoped they'd be able to ride alone, but at the last minute, someone shoved their hand between the doors.

It was an older gray-haired woman. "I'm sorry. Thought I'd catch it while I could. Otherwise you end up waiting forever."

"So true," Isabel said. She leaned against the back wall, standing right next to Jeremy. She looked over at him as her hand again caressed his thigh. She bit her lower lip and he thought he might faint. She was too hot for words.

Mercifully, the woman got off the elevator at the fifth floor, but being alone with Isabel only opened the floodgates. He dropped his briefcase as they smashed into each other, kissing hard, tongues and wet lips, insistent hands everywhere. He yanked at the tie on her robe, then fumbled with the buttons on her pajama top. Hers were inside his suit jacket, tugging his shirt out from the waist of his pants. By the time the elevator dinged on the eighteenth floor, they were both in a disheveled state of near-undress.

Isabel picked up his briefcase, handed it to him and dashed down the hall, with Jeremy in close pursuit. She pulled her key card from her robe pocket and Jeremy stole a look down the front of her pajama top, which was already half-unbuttoned. Her breasts were full, her skin creamy and he couldn't wait to have his hands all over them.

Isabel flung open the door and Jeremy again dropped his briefcase, relieved he didn't need to keep track of it anymore. Isabel took off her robe and undid the last two buttons on her pajama top, tossing it to the floor. He cupped her breasts in both hands, her skin even softer and more velvety smooth than he'd imagined. Her nipples tightened beneath his touch. He loved seeing and feeling how responsive she was to him. Her pajama pants hung loosely below her belly button, clinging to her curvy hips. He wanted to see every inch of her and with a single tug of the drawstring at her waist, they slumped to the floor. She had no panties on underneath and that view of everything to come made everything beneath his waist grow even tighter, even hotter.

"You have on way too many clothes," she said as she flew through the buttons on his shirt and he got rid of his jacket. She then seemed to notice exactly how fierce his erection was. "Very nice." She flattened her hand against the front of his pants and pressed hard, rubbing up and down firmly.

He wavered between full sight and blindness. It felt so impossibly good. He only wanted more. This time, Jeremy didn't have to disguise his reaction, and he let out a groan at full roar. Isabel responded by unzipping his pants while he toed off his shoes. A few seconds later, she had the rest of his clothes in a puddle on the floor. She wrapped her hand around his length and took careful strokes while he kissed her. It had been so long since he'd wanted a woman like he wanted her. Something about her left him letting down his guard.

"Do you have a condom?" he asked, realizing that he did not. This was not good planning on his part, but he did not make a regular habit of meeting women after work and going up to their hotel rooms.

"I do. In the bathroom. One minute." Isabel traipsed off and he watched her full bottom and long legs in graceful motion. He couldn't wait to be inside her.

She returned seconds later with a box, which she set on the bedside table after taking out a packet. She tore open the foil and closed in on him, a bit like a tiger stalks its prey. Jeremy liked feeling so wanted. It felt good to know that he still had the power to do this to a woman.

Isabel took the condom and gently placed it on the tip of his erection, then rolled it down his length, all while their gazes connected. She owned every touch, every action of her beautiful body, and Jeremy wanted to drown in her self-confidence. He wanted to live in the world she did—where there seemed to be zero reason to question oneself.

Across the room sat that big beautiful bed, with a crisp white comforter and countless pillows. But Jeremy wanted to make love to Isabel in every corner of this room, and the chair that was right next to him seemed like the perfect place to start. He took her hand and he sat down, easing his hips to the edge of the seat. Isabel didn't miss a beat, straddling his legs and placing her knees on the chair next to his hips. Jeremy reached between them and positioned himself, then Isabel lowered her body onto his. He kept both his hands on her hips while his sights were set solely on her stunning face. Her mouth went slack and she closed her eyes as she let him slide inside. She was a perfect fit. And Jeremy was nothing if not thankful to whatever forces in the universe had brought him to this moment.

Isabel dictated the pace, which was perfect for him. He wanted to know what she liked. Despite the fact that he had so much pent-up need inside him, this was all about her. He would not leave until she was fully satisfied. He eased one hand to her lower back and urged her to lean into him so he could kiss her. Fully and deeply. Meanwhile, Isabel rode his length up and down and

Jeremy struggled to keep up, to keep from reaching his destination too soon. He did not want to disappoint her.

Their kisses were soft and wet, tongues sensuously twisting together. Jeremy caressed her breast with one hand while the other cupped her backside, his fingers curled into the soft and tender flesh. Isabel raked her hands through his hair over and over again, telling him with soft moans and subtle gasps that she was happy. He felt her tightening around him, and that matched her breaths, which had become ragged and torn.

"I'm close," she muttered into his ear, then kissed his neck.

He'd passed close several minutes ago and had since been skirting the edge, trying to ward off his climax. "Come for me."

Isabel planted her forehead against his and went for it, riding his length faster, sinking as far down as she could with every pass. Jeremy was fairly sure he had no blood flow to the rest of his body as he steeled himself. As soon as she let go and called out, he did the same, following behind her. Her muscles gathered around him tightly, over and over again, and the relief that washed over him was immense.

All he could think as the orgasm faded and Isabel collapsed against his chest was that he had to have her one more time. And quite possibly one more time after that.

"I need you again, Isabel." Jeremy smoothed his hand over her naked back and kissed her shoulder, bringing everything in her post-bliss body back to a quick simmer.

"Already?" she asked, slowly easing herself off his lap. She stepped over to the bed, where a mere hour or so ago she'd been attempting to sleep, and pulled back the comforter. She certainly hadn't thought at that time that she'd end up with a man in her room later.

"I'm going to need a minute or two, but I swear that's all." Jeremy padded off to the bathroom.

Isabel climbed into bed and immediately rested her head back on the pillow, staring up at the ceiling. *Wow.* She was glad Jeremy wanted more. That first time had been so hurried. She wanted the opportunity to savor him.

Moments later, he joined her, climbing in next to her and pressing his long body against hers. "You're incredible. Once was not enough."

She could already feel his erection against her leg. She was nothing if not impressed. Jeremy with the salt-and-pepper hair had a very quick recovery time. Of course she was on board. Considering that they hardly knew each other, he had an uncanny ability to hit all of her most sensitive spots. She really appreciated a man who picked up on her cues and followed suit.

"We need another condom," she said, kissing him deeply.

He rolled over and sat on the edge of the bed, took one from the box on the nightstand. Isabel turned to her side and swished her hand across the silky sheets, feeling his body heat still there. She admired his muscled back in the soft light from the window. He was in unbelievable shape and she was happy to reap the rewards.

When he turned back to her, he smiled. "You are so beautiful. I'm still trying to figure out how I managed to talk you into taking me upstairs."

She swatted his arm, then pulled him closer as he reclined next to her. "You're no slouch. Believe me."

He kissed her sweetly, then his approach turned more

seductive, as he opened his mouth and their tongues found each other, swirling and swooping. He was an amazing kisser, there was no doubt about that. Isabel could have kissed him forever; they were in perfect sync. He rolled her to her back and hovered above her, holding his body weight with his firm arms. Isabel ran her hands from his wrists to his shoulders, her eyes closing and opening as he lowered his mouth to her neck, then her breast, taking her nipple between his lips. He was unhurried now, a stark contrast to the frenzied first time.

He positioned himself at her entrance and drove inside slowly, pushing her patience, letting her feel every inch as he filled her perfectly. Isabel rolled her head from side to side, feeling the cool pillow on her cheeks as Jeremy made the rest of her body red hot. She raised her knees to let him in deeper, and he was taking mind-bending strokes just like he had the first time. This was the advantage of a man later in life. He knew what he was doing.

He slipped his hand between their bodies and pressed his thumb against her apex, rolling in firm circles as he kept his even pace. She was surprised how quickly the tension wrapped itself around her, the way he drove her toward the edge of the cliff so perfectly. Right there. The climax was toying with her now, ebbing closer, then pulling away. Each pass brought it nearer and she could feel ahead of time just how intense it was going to be. She heard her own hums and moans, but her consciousness was so deep inside her own body that it came out muffled and fuzzy. Meanwhile, she became fitful and greedy, needing him closer. Needing more. She dug her heels into his backside, pulling him into her, and that was when the orgasm slammed into her, even harder and more intense than last time. This was an order of magnitude she hadn't been prepared for—sheer gratification awash in beautiful colors and hazy, unworried thoughts.

As she became more aware of the here and now, Isabel could tell that Jeremy was also near his peak. His breaths were labored, but light, just like they had been the first time. Puffs of air that seemed to go in one direction. Just in. And further in. In one sudden movement, he jerked, then his torso froze in place, his hips flush against her bottom. She wrapped her legs around him tightly and raked her fingers up and down his strong back, feeling every defined muscle. As her own pleasure continued to swirl around her, she blazed a trail of hot kisses against his neck, wanting to show her appreciation. Jeremy was magnificent. Absolutely perfect.

"Oh, no," he groaned. "The condom. It broke."

Just like that, the spell was broken. "Did you?" she asked. Had she really just been thinking that this was perfect? She should have known better. That did not exist. Not for her, at least.

"Did I come? Yes." He rolled off of her and jumped up from the bed, rushing off to the bathroom.

Isabel closed her eyes and pinched her nose. *Great.* So much for her fun with handsome Jeremy. So much for the idea of a third time. Or a fourth. This was about to come to a quick end, she guessed, at least judging by how quickly he had retreated to the bathroom.

He returned a few seconds later with a towel wrapped around his waist. He paced, running his hands through his hair. "I don't know what to say, other than I'm sorry."

Her instinct was to make him feel better, even when she was feeling worse by the second. "Not your fault. It happens."

Awkward silence followed, and she knew that Jeremy was planning his escape. He had his lips pressed tightly together like he couldn't figure out what to do next. Part of her was tempted to point to the door and save them both the embarrassment. Part of her wanted to put on her sleep mask and convince herself this part wasn't happening. They'd had such an amazing night together. It didn't seem fair that it should end like this. But that was life. Nothing to do about it but move on.

He sat on the edge of the bed, but it was about as far away from her as possible. The divide between them now felt like it was a mile wide. In some ways, she felt like she knew him even less now than she had when they'd first met downstairs. "I don't even know your last name. What if I just got you pregnant?"

Isabel knew that uncertain edge in his voice. She'd heard it before. One time in particular had been so painful she thought she might never recover. That had been over an actual pregnancy, not merely a fear of obligation. Her initial impression of Jeremy had been correct. He came off as smooth for a reason—he was all about the pursuit, not about sticking around. And that was fine. No harm, no foul. They hardly knew each other. It was understandable that he might feel trapped. It was now her job to let him off the hook, if only to allow herself to get on with her life.

"If it makes you feel any better, my name is Isabel Blackwell."

He glanced over at her. "Oh. Okay. My last name is Sharp."

Isabel grabbed the sheet and pulled it up over herself. Exchanging last names had done nothing to make this situation more comfortable. If anything, it made it so much more obvious that she wasn't built for one-night stands.

Isabel scooted up in bed until her back was against the headboard. "Look. Don't worry about it. It's okay. I keep track of my cycle pretty closely. I don't think there's any chance we're in trouble." She'd undersold that part by quite a bit. She'd been methodically tracking her periods for the last several years. If she managed to meet Mr. Right, she wanted to be able to try for a baby as soon as possible. Isabel prepared for everything in life. It was the best way to avoid surprises and the perfect distraction when you felt like the things you wanted weren't happening fast enough.

"Okay. Well, I wasn't sure if you wanted me to stay…" His voice trailed off, leaving Isabel to make the final declaration.

"No, Jeremy. It's okay. I think it's probably best at this point if you head home. I have a big meeting tomorrow and I'm sure you have things you need to do tomorrow. We probably both need a good night's sleep."

He nodded. "Sure. Yes. Of course." He got up from the bed and began collecting his clothes from their various locales across the room. He let go of the towel so he could step into his boxers, giving Isabel one last parting glance at perfect Jeremy. *Damn.* If only this hadn't started so absurdly. If only it hadn't ended so uncomfortably. He might have been a guy she would have wanted around for a while.

Wrapped up in the sheet, she climbed out of bed and padded past him to the bathroom. She quietly closed the door behind her and sucked in several deep breaths. *You're okay.* Moving to New York was supposed to be her new beginning, especially with men and the notion of having a personal life. So she'd had a false start. Jeremy was ultimately a nice guy. He was handsome, sexy and kind. They'd had some rotten luck, but that happened every day. Isabel needed to get past the idea that her fresh start was ruined by one mishap.

She stepped to the sink, took a sip of water from the glass on the vanity and prepared herself to walk back out into the room. "Worse things have happened." When she opened the bathroom door, Jeremy was standing right outside, suit on but no tie. His briefcase was in his hand. For a moment, she wondered what he did for work. Probably a Wall Street guy. He seemed the type— cocky, good-looking, sure of himself. She wouldn't ask him now.

"Okay, then. You off?" she asked.

He nodded. "Yes. Thank you for tonight. It was really nice. I swear."

She had to laugh at what a sad and funny situation she'd gotten herself into. She stepped closer to him and stole one last kiss. "Jeremy. You were amazing. And I hope you have a lifetime of making money and finding fun wherever you go."

He smiled, but it wasn't a full-throttle grin, not the smile that had first sparked her curiosity or the chemistry between them. "I hope you find everything you're looking for, Isabel Blackwell."

With that, she opened the door and watched as he walked down the hall to the elevator. She hoped Jeremy was right. She didn't want to go too much longer waiting.

Three

Jeremy finally gave in at 4:37 a.m. His night's sleep was a lost cause. He climbed out from under his down comforter and sat on the edge of his bed, elbows on his knees, and ran a hand through his hair. A deep sigh escaped his lips, but he could have sworn he heard a word in it. A name. Isabel. *What the hell was that? What the hell happened?*

He'd never had a woman work her way into his psyche in such a short amount of time—mere hours. Sure, part of it was the fact that he was still stinging from the way he'd had to exit her room, and her life. When they'd been down at the bar flirting and she offered the invitation to come upstairs, his plan had been to leave her happy and exhausted, positively aglow from sex. Instead, he'd departed while she was bundled up in a sheet like a hastily wrapped gift, granting him a dispassionate kiss goodbye and leaving him with the crushing sense that they would always have unfinished business.

Another sigh came. He was going to have to stop letting this get to him.

With a long day of client meetings ahead, he decided to get in a workout. He sometimes managed to sneak away at lunch and go to the Sharp and Sharp gym, but that likely wouldn't happen today. He flipped on the light in his master bedroom, grabbed a pair of shorts, a T-shirt and running shoes, then made his way up one set of stairs to the fourth floor of this renovated brownstone. He had a small theater and gym up there, additions he made after his ex-wife moved out. Kelsey never saw the point in watching movies and didn't want the "smell" of a workout space. But now that he was all on his own, Jeremy could do as he liked.

It wasn't much of a consolation.

Forty-five minutes on the treadmill and a half hour of free weights was enough to work up a sufficient sweat and shake off some of the lingering thoughts of Isabel. He hustled down to the second floor and the gourmet kitchen, where he prepared entirely too many meals for one. Coffee was dripping into the carafe when he heard a familiar sound coming from the patio off the back of the house.

Meow.

It was December 9. It was entirely too cold for an animal to be outside. Jeremy padded over to the glass door, and as had happened many times before, a large orange tabby cat was winding his way back and forth in front of the window. The cat had been to the house many times, and Jeremy had even taken him in once before, over a year ago when it was unbearably hot. The cat's visit had lasted less than a day. He slipped out the front door when Jeremy came home from work that night. Jeremy wasn't a cat person at all—he didn't really see the point of a pet that didn't do anything other than lounge around all day. He'd called Animal Control to see if they could catch him, but they'd seemed unconcerned. He'd even had his assistant call the veterinarian in his neighborhood of Park Slope, but they couldn't do much until someone caught the cat and brought him in. Jeremy kept hoping someone else would take on the burden, but apparently not. At least not today.

Meow. The cat reared up on its hind legs and pressed a single paw to the glass, peering up at Jeremy with eyes that were entirely too plaintive.

Jeremy crouched down and looked into his little cat face. "Buddy. What are you doing out there? It's six in the morning and it's freezing."

Meow. The cat pawed at the glass.

Jeremy straightened. This was the last thing he had time for, but temperatures weren't expected to get above freezing today. He couldn't let the poor thing suffer. Resigned, he flipped the dead bolt, turned the knob and tugged on it. Bitter cold rushed in, but not as fast as the cat. Jeremy closed the door, realizing he now had a big task ahead of him—he had to feed the cat and figure out where to put him all day while he was at work.

He went to the pantry to look for a can of tuna, but that was a bust. Then he remembered that he had some lox in the refrigerator from the bagel shop down the street.

"I guess we're going to find out if you like smoked salmon." He placed a slice of the fish on a plate and broke it into smaller pieces with his fingers. Jeremy had a feeling this was going to be a big hit. The cat was now rubbing against his ankles.

Jeremy put the plate on the floor and the cat began to scarf down the food. Mission one, accomplished. He filled a cereal bowl with water for the cat, then went about making his own breakfast of eggs and a bagel. As he sat at the kitchen island, the cat wound its way around the legs of his barstool, purring loudly enough for Jeremy to hear. He had to get to the office, so he sent a text to his housekeeper, who would be arriving around eight. There's a cat in the house. Don't ask. Can you bring a litter box and show it to him?

Margaret replied quickly. You got a cat?

Jeremy laughed. Not on purpose.

After getting cleaned up and dressed, Jeremy left for the office, arriving promptly at seven thirty, just like every other day. Not only was the weather unbearably cold, it was gray and dreary, somewhat typical for early December, although Jeremy couldn't help but feel like it was somehow sunnier outside than it was inside the Sharp and Sharp offices.

The other partners typically arrived at eight, but Jeremy had learned long ago that his boss, who was also his dad, demanded that his own son deliver more than everyone else. Jeremy had worked twice as hard to make partner. He brought in nearly twice as much billing. He worked like a dog for two reasons. First, he hoped that he would eventually make his father happy enough to loosen his iron grip on the firm and afford Jeremy some autonomy. The second reason fed into the first. When Jeremy had been in the middle of his divorce, he bungled a big case. The Patterson case, a multimillion-dollar wrongful termination suit. It should have been a slam dunk and instead, Jeremy dropped the ball, mostly because his personal life was falling apart. His dad might never forgive him for that grave error, but Jeremy had to keep trying. He had to live the life of a workaholic for the foreseeable future.

In recent months, his father had been pressuring him to bring on a very specific sort of big-fish client, someone with a case that could attract media attention, even of the tabloid variety. In the internet age, one juicy headline brought a lot of free exposure. And although his dad was a traditional and upstanding guy, he loved the spotlight. He basked in it. He loved knowing the firm's coffers were piled to the ceiling with cash.

"Morning, son," his dad said, poking his head into Jeremy's office. He truly was the spitting image of Jeremy, only twenty-three years older. A bit more gray. A few more deep creases. The uncanny similarities in their appearance made the problems in their relationship that much more difficult—on the outside they were nearly identical. On the inside, they couldn't have been more different. "Are we a go with the Summers case?"

"We are. I'm just waiting for the signed agreement to come in this morning and then we'll be in contact with the legal department at Eden's."

His dad glanced at the chair opposite Jeremy's desk. "May I?"

"Of course." Jeremy took a deep breath and prepared himself for what might come—there was no telling with his dad. Some days, he was calm and reasonable. Other times, he hit the roof over the smallest detail. It had been like that since Jeremy was a kid, and he still wasn't used to it.

"What do you think is the real reason Mr. Summers fired Mulvaney and Moore?"

"Honestly? I met with Mr. Summers last night and he's a little off his rocker. He's dead set on getting revenge against the Eden family. This is about far more than money. I'm sure that scared off the senior partners at M and M. They're an incredibly conservative firm." Jeremy leaned back in his chair. "Why? Are you worried about it? There's still time to call it off if you want."

His dad shook his head, pulling at his chin with his fingers. "No. No. I think it's a good thing. Summers is desperate and he's willing to pay for it. I don't have a problem with getting our hands dirty. Your grandfather always avoided it."

Jeremy's grandfather had been the first Sharp in Sharp and Sharp. In fact, Jeremy's dad had declined to add an extra Sharp to the firm's name when Jeremy made partner. He'd simply waited for his own father to pass away. Jeremy missed his grandfather. He was the real reason he'd become an attorney, and things had been much different around the office when he was still alive. His grandfather had a love for the law and the myriad ways it could be interpreted. He loved the arguments and the strategy. His dad had a love of money and winning. He refused to lose, something that had been hammered into Jeremy's head count-less times.

"I think it'll be just fine. I have it all under control." Jeremy knew nothing of the sort, but he had to lie. The truth was that the meeting with Benjamin Summers at the Bacharach had been chaotic. Thus the reason for the Manhattan. Thus the reason for perhaps not exercising the best judgment with Isabel.

"Don't let this one get away from you. If he's fired one firm, he'll fire another, and I don't think I need to tell you that it would be a real shame for our bottom line if we lost this billing. It'll be a scramble for you if you have to make up for it."

It was just like his dad to make not-so-thinly-veiled threats. "He's not going to fire us."

"At least you're only going up against the Eden's corporate lawyers. Those guys are so far out of their depth with a case like this. It should be a walk in the park if you do it right."

There went another insult wrapped up as praise. Jeremy wasn't about to point it out. It never did any good. "I'm not worried about it. I've got it all under control."

"Good." His dad rose from his seat and knocked his knuckle against Jeremy's desk, then made his departure. "Have a good day."

"You, too." Jeremy grumbled under his breath and got back to work, writing up the details for his assistant so she could set up the meeting with the Eden's legal team, which he hoped could happen tomorrow. It was the only thing he could do—try to move ahead. Try to make Dad happy. And after that, he'd need to dig into the mountain of work on his desk. Anything to take his mind off Isabel Blackwell and their amazing night that went horribly wrong.

Isabel arrived at Eden's Department Store shortly before 10:00 a.m. the morning after her rendezvous with Jeremy. Her lawyerly instincts normally had her keyed up and wide-awake before a client meeting, but she was so tired she could hardly drag herself out of the taxi.

She hadn't managed more than a few minutes of sleep. After his departure, Jeremy's warm smell lingered on the sheets, meaning the memory of his touch followed her with every toss and turn. If the condom hadn't broken, their night might have gone on to be nothing less than perfect. He might have asked to see her again, an invitation she would have eagerly accepted. She might have started her new life in New

York on a positive note. But the moment they had their mishap and Isabel witnessed firsthand how anxious he was to get out of her room and away from her, she knew he wasn't the right guy. It didn't matter that he was charming, sexy and one of the most handsome men she'd ever had the good fortune to meet. She needed more. She needed a man who would stick around, not run for the exits the instant things got serious.

Per her brother Sam's directions, Isabel took the elevator up to the top floor where the Eden's executive offices were. Sam was sitting in reception when she got there.

"Hey, handsome," she said as Sam got up out of his seat.

He was dressed in all black—suit, shirt and tie, just as most days. He placed a kiss on her forehead. "I'm so glad you're here."

Isabel wasn't quite so happy about it, but she was hopelessly devoted to her brother and that meant she was going to take one last dubious legal assignment before turning her sights to less messy work. "I'm still not sure I'm the right person for this job."

"Are you kidding me? You're the exact right person for this job. You're an expert at making problems like this go away."

The subtext of Sam's words made Isabel's stomach sour. This wasn't the sort of case that got wrapped up by legal wrangling and negotiation. Whenever you had very wealthy, powerful people fighting over something valuable, it inevitably turned into a race to the bottom. Who could dig up the most dirt? Who could make the other side cry for mercy first? "Sam, you know I don't want to tackle this like a fix. I just don't want to work like that anymore."

Sam put his arm around Isabel and snugged her close. "You worry too much. It's just a wealthy guy trying to get his hands on the store. You can handle this in your sleep."

First, I'd have to get some sleep. "But your girlfriend's family legacy is on the line. We can't afford to be cavalier about it."

"You mean fiancée." Mindy Eden appeared on the far side of the reception area and approached them, a big smile on her face.

Isabel knew full well that Sam and Mindy had gotten engaged. She'd merely slipped. Perhaps it was her subconscious reminding her how bothered she was that her younger brother had found the sort of happiness she desperately wanted for herself. "I'm sorry. Fiancée."

Mindy gave Isabel a hug, then wagged her fingers, showing off the square-cut diamond-and-platinum engagement ring Sam had given her. The thing was so big it looked like Mindy was walking around with an ice cube on her hand. "I honestly never thought this would happen."

Isabel didn't believe that for a minute. Mindy was lovely, but she seemed like the sort of woman who was accustomed to nothing less than getting exactly what she wanted out of life. "Why's that? You had to know my brother was over the moon for you."

Mindy elbowed Sam in the ribs. "I was oblivious to that for a while. I spent so much time focused on my career that I forgot to open my eyes."

Isabel took a shred of comfort in that. She and Mindy might have butted heads when they first met, but that was only because of Isabel's protectiveness of Sam. Mindy had hurt him and Isabel wasn't going to be the one to forgive her for it. Now that Sam and Mindy had reconciled, and the two women had gotten to know each other a little better, Isabel knew that she and Mindy had some things in common. They were both driven, determined and not willing to take crap from anyone. "I'll try to remember that when I jump back into the dating pool."

"Any prospects?" Mindy asked.

"I'm out of here if you're going to talk about guys," Sam said, turning away. "I don't do well with this subject when it comes to my sister."

Isabel grabbed his arm. "Oh, stop. We're not going to talk about that because there's nothing to say. I need to get an apartment. There are a million other things for me to accomplish before I can seriously think about dating. I have to find an office and get my new practice up and running."

"Don't put it off too long," Mindy said. She then cast her sights at Sam. "Are there any cute, eligible guys working for you right now? Maybe you can set her up."

Sam shook his head. "Something tells me she doesn't want that."

In truth, Isabel might not mind it. If Sam picked out a man for her, she'd not only know that he had been fully vetted, she'd have the knowledge that Sam approved. That was no small matter. "We'll see how I do. For now, let's sit down and talk about the case." Isabel was resigned to moving forward with this, and the sooner she started, the sooner she'd be done. So she'd delay her fresh start a few weeks. It wasn't the end of the world.

"Come on," Mindy said. "We're going to meet in Emma's office. It's the biggest. It used to belong to my gram."

Gram, or Victoria Eden, was the founder of Eden's Department Store, which at its height had more than fifty stores worldwide. Unfortunately, the chain was now down to a single location, the original Manhattan store. Mrs. Eden had passed away unexpectedly a little more than a year ago, and left the business to Mindy, her sister, Sophie, and their half sister, Emma. It was a bit of a tawdry story—all three women had the same father, and their two mothers were also sisters. Victoria Eden had brought the affair to light via her will, where she told everyone of her son's dalliance in an attempt to give Emma some justice.

Inside the office, Emma and Sophie were waiting. Isabel had met them both at a fund-raiser a month and a half ago, which was also when Sam and Mindy had finally figured out that they were desperately in love. Mindy made reintroductions and they all sat in the seating area—Isabel and Sophie on the couch, Sam in one chair with Mindy perched on the arm, and Emma opposite them.

"I guess we need to walk you through as much of this as we know," Mindy said. "I wish we had more information, but until a few weeks ago, we had no idea who Benjamin Summers was."

"He claims that our grandmother had an affair with his father, which is utterly preposterous," Sophie said. "Gram was devoted to our grandfather for as long as he was alive."

"Please, Soph. Can you not do this right now? Let me finish," Mindy said, returning her sights to Isabel. "This would have been nearly forty years ago if it really happened. Early days for the store, but our grandmother was doing well and by all accounts, very eager to expand. That's when Mr. Summers, the father, comes into play. Supposedly he lent our grandmother a quarter of a million dollars so she could open additional locations."

"That was a lot of money at that time," Isabel said. "And this is a handwritten promissory note?"

"Yes," Mindy said. "We've been going back through the store's old financials and bank records, but we can't find any record of an influx of money. There are large chunks of cash flowing into the store at that time, but it could have just been sales. Unfortunately, the accounting from that time is nowhere near as exact as it is now. Most of it is on paper."

Isabel's gears were starting to turn. As much as she'd said she didn't want to do this sort of work anymore—untangling the pasts of wealthy people—she had to admit that she had a real knack for it, and that made her feel as though she was ready to tackle it. "The first thing we're going to need to do is get the promissory note authenticated. There's a good chance it's not real."

"Do you think it could be a fake?" Emma asked.

"You'd be surprised the lengths people will go to in order to cash in."

"But Mr. Summers is so wealthy," Mindy said. "Why would he do that?"

Isabel sat back and crossed her legs. "It might not be the cash. It might be the store he's after."

"No. We can't let that happen," Sophie blurted.

Isabel didn't want to be the bearer of bad tidings. Losing the store was a real possibility. For now, Isabel needed to get up to speed on the materials in the case and see where the Eden sisters stood. "Let's not get ahead of ourselves. Give me some time to look over everything. I have several different financial detectives I've worked with in the past. They're going to need access to your records to see if we can figure out if the money ever flowed into the store at all."

"How long is all of that going to take?" Mindy asked.

"A few days to a few weeks. It just depends."

Mindy cleared her throat and Isabel sensed something bad was about to come to light. "Yeah. About that. We don't have that kind of time. Mr. Summers's lawyer sent a letter to the Eden's in-house counsel today. He's threatening a lawsuit right away if we don't come to the negotiating table tomorrow."

Isabel blinked several times while trying to absorb what Mindy had just said. "Mr. Summers not only wants us to start negotiating tomorrow, his lawyer isn't even aware the store is employing outside counsel?"

"We thought a sneak attack was the best approach. They're expecting someone else. Not Isabel Blackwell, Washington, DC, fixer."

Isabel cringed at the words. She didn't want to be that person anymore.

Sam sat forward and placed his hand on his sister's knee. "I have to agree. The store is too important to the Eden family for us to be anything less than completely strategic about this. They'll prepare for a corporate negotiation, not having any idea who they're dealing with."

Isabel took a deep breath, trying to ignore the way her already soured stomach grew even more uneasy. "Can I see the letter they sent?"

"Yes. Of course." Mindy hopped up from her seat and grabbed a thin folder from Emma's desk, handing it to Isabel.

Inside was a single page—the letter inviting Eden's Department Store's legal representation to the negotiating table. All looked in order until Isabel saw the name on the signature line. Then the blood drained from her face.

Jeremy Sharp. Oh my God.

Her big meeting tomorrow with the lawyer representing the man who wanted to take down Eden's Department Store? It would be the second run-in with her one-night stand. And apparently, they were about to go from the bedroom to the war room.

Four

"I don't want you to worry," Jeremy said as he escorted Benjamin Summers into one of the meeting rooms at Sharp and Sharp. "We have everything well in hand."

Mr. Summers turned to Jeremy and narrowed his eyes until they were only small slits. "Why aren't we meeting in the main conference room? The one with the big windows. The one you can see from the waiting room."

Jeremy pulled back a chair and offered Mr. Summers a seat. "Because this is more discreet." In truth, Jeremy preferred it because it meant his father couldn't interfere unless he walked right in on them. Jeremy had been in many client meetings where his dad paced back and forth outside that main conference room. It was unnerving as hell.

Mr. Summers sat in a huff. Jeremy hadn't spent a lot of time with him, but he'd always been like this—gruff and impatient. "I'm not worried about discretion. If anything, I'd prefer not to have it. I'd like the whole world to know that I'm going after Eden's. Victoria Eden destroyed my parents' marriage and this is the only way I can seek retribution on behalf of my mother."

Jeremy poured Mr. Summers a glass of water, hoping that might help to cool his temper. "I don't think it's a great idea to bring that up in this meeting. I know it's difficult to curb your personal feelings about the matter, but we need to focus on the bottom line, which is a very large unpaid debt."

Mr. Summers cleared his throat and tapped his fingers on the table. "Fine. I'll take your advice."

"Thank you. I appreciate that."

"For now."

One of the admins in the office poked his head into the conference room. "Mr. Sharp, the Eden's representatives and legal team have arrived. Shall I show them in?"

Jeremy turned to Mr. Summers, hoping he could get him to remain calm and collected. "Are you ready, Mr. Summers?"

"More than I've ever been."

Jeremy stood and straightened his jacket, then made his way to the door. The in-house counsel for Eden's was a crew of white-haired older men, much like his dad and Mr. Summers. He knew he could handle this easily as long as everyone could set aside their egos. But when he glanced down the hall, a stunning vision came into view—a woman who was not easy to handle. *Isabel.*

What the hell? For an instant, Jeremy shrank back from the door, his mind whirring with thoughts, even when there was no time to think. Before he knew what was happening, Isabel, along with another woman and a very tall man, were being led into the room by Jeremy's admin. "Mr. Sharp, this is Mindy Eden, COO of Eden's Department Store."

Mindy, willowy and poised with flame-red hair, offered her hand. "Mr. Sharp."

"Special adviser to Eden's, Sam Blackwell," his admin continued.

Sam, towering and dressed in black, shook Jeremy's hand. "Hello."

"And lastly, Isabel Blackwell, special counsel for Eden's."

Isabel stepped forward, but her beguiling scent arrived a split second before her. It filled his nose, and that sent memories storming into his mind—their white-hot tryst in her hotel room was not anything he would forget anytime soon. Unfortunately, he couldn't afford to think about what her luscious naked body looked like under her trim gray suit. He was too busy trying to tamp down his inner confusion. Had she known who he was when she seduced him? Had she seen him in the bar with Mr. Summers a mere fifteen minutes before the fire alarm sounded?

"It's nice to meet you." Isabel offered her hand. He'd noticed that night that her skin was unusually warm, but right now he felt as though he'd been burned.

Jeremy cleared his throat. "Nice to meet *you*, as well." He gestured to the other side of the long mahogany table, more rattled than when he'd worked his very first case. He couldn't help but feel as though they were being ambushed. He'd been led to believe that Eden's in-house counsel would be handling this. Unless Isabel was a new addition to their team, she was a ringer. "Please have a seat."

Isabel sat directly opposite Jeremy. The look on her face was difficult to decipher, but he reminded himself that he hardly knew her. What were her motives? What sort of person was she? Most important, what was her endgame? For a man with countless trust issues when it came to women, this was not only bringing all that to the surface in an uncomfortable way, it felt as though Isabel had opened an entirely new area of mistrust to explore. He deeply disliked the revelation.

Jeremy drew in a calming breath. *Focus.* He looked Isabel square in the eye. She met his gaze with steely composure. On the surface, she was quite simply stunning. Easily the sexiest woman he'd ever met. But he sensed now that beneath that flawless exterior was a woman who was at the very least, trouble. He didn't want to regret the other night, but perhaps he should. Would he feel as though he was at less of a disadvantage right now if it hadn't happened? "Ms. Blackwell, your client's grandmother borrowed 250 million dollars from Mr. Summers's father in 1982. She offered the Manhattan location of Eden's Department Store, the building, inventory and the land it sits on as collateral. By our calculations, with standard interest adjusted for inflation and compounded monthly, that unpaid loan now sits at a balance of just over 842 million."

"You have got to be kidding," Mindy Eden scoffed. "Why not just round it up to an even billion?"

Isabel placed her hand on Mindy's forearm, then smiled at Jeremy, the picture of cool composure. "And what exactly would Mr. Summers like for us to do about that?"

Jeremy had no choice but to continue. "As it's been nearly forty years, Mr. Summers expects the loan to be repaid in cash within thirty days or we'll begin proceedings to claim the property."

Isabel nodded, then licked her lips, making Jeremy

clutch the arm of his chair. "Any talk of property sei-zure is premature, Mr. Sharp. Frankly, my client had never even heard of Mr. Summers prior to the letter your team sent to the Eden's offices, so I don't know how the Eden family should be expected to simply hand over the keys to a multibillion-dollar business and property without exploring this matter as thoroughly as possible."

Jeremy knew he should be feeling as though he'd been put on notice, but he only felt incredibly turned on. Blood was coursing through his body so fast it was making his head swim. Oh, Isabel was good.

"My first priority is to determine the authenticity of the promissory note," Isabel continued, her cheeks flushed with brilliant pink. "We can't be expected to proceed without an expert analysis of the document. I'm not convinced it's authentic or that it has Victoria Eden's true signature on it."

This was not good news. And yet Jeremy noticed a significant tightening in his pants.

"Are you calling me a liar?" Mr. Summers bellowed.

Jeremy turned to his client. "Please, Ben," he mut-tered. "I've got this."

"It's a handwritten note, Mr. Summers." Isabel's voice was direct and cutting, while her chest was heav-ing in a way that brought back entirely too many mem-ories of the night at the Bacharach—having Isabel at his mercy, in her bed. "Anyone could have produced it. You could have fabricated it last week for all we know."

"It's real. I have no reason to lie," Benjamin said.

Isabel's eyebrows shot up. "From where I'm sitting, you have 842 million reasons to lie. Do you have fi-nancial problems I should know about, Mr. Summers? Is that what I'm going to find when I start looking into your businesses?"

"Ms. Blackwell," Jeremy said as a warning, stopping himself from uttering what he really wanted to say— *Ms. Blackwell, you and I need to hash this out on our own. Alone. On this conference table.* But he had to get his act together. "Ms. Blackwell, I'll thank you not to speak to my client directly, especially when you're accusing him of things that have no basis in fact. Mr. Summers is not on trial here."

"If he's going to get ugly about the matter in front of my client, I'm afraid I have no other choice. This is not as cut-and-dried as you're trying to paint it."

Jeremy sensed this meeting was starting to go off the rails and he had to get it back on track. More than anything, he really needed to ask Isabel a few questions that were not appropriate in front of their respective clients. "Ms. Blackwell, would you mind asking your clients to wait out in the lobby? I'll ask Mr. Summers to adjourn to my office so that you and I can discuss the terms of determining the authenticity of the note."

Isabel lifted her chin and narrowed her sights on Jeremy, seeming suspicious. "I'll give you five minutes."

I'd rather have ten. "Certainly."

Isabel turned to Mindy and Sam, and they conferred with heads bowed. Jeremy took his chance to chat with Mr. Summers.

"I don't like being taken out of the negotiations," Mr. Summers said in response.

"I assure you, this will be nothing more than boring legalese. Plus, it'll give me a chance to find out more of what exactly their strategy is. This isn't the usual Eden's team."

"It isn't? I expect my lawyer to know details like that."

Jeremy looked over at Isabel as she got up from the

table and made way for Mindy and Sam to leave the conference room. "In my experience, these things rarely go the way you think they will."

Isabel accompanied Sam and Mindy out to the luxe Sharp and Sharp lobby. With dark wood, soft light and tufted navy leather settees, it spoke of old money and an organization steeped in tradition. Isabel could only imagine how her life would have been different if she'd come to New York instead of Washington, DC, and gotten her start at a firm like this, where business was done aboveboard. Sure, Mr. Summers had made a spectacle in the meeting, but it was nothing more than a man, accustomed to getting everything he wanted, kicking up dust because she and the Eden family were not going to go down without a fight. It wasn't a real roll in the mud, one where people make threats to destroy other people's lives.

"Is this normal?" Sam whispered at Isabel. His body language suggested pure agitation. His back was stiff as a board. "For the other lawyer to kick everybody out of the room?"

Isabel surveyed the lobby, which was unoccupied except for the receptionist, who was on the phone. If they were going to discuss this, they needed privacy. She placed her hand on Sam's arm. She wasn't entirely sure what Jeremy's motives were, but she was curious. Their short string of quipping back and forth had really gotten her running hot. And damn, the man could rock a suit unlike any other. "I think he was trying to get his client to cool down. Which I think is for the best. Plus, I didn't want him saying anything disparaging in front of Mindy."

"Why?" Mindy asked. "You know I can take it."

Isabel laughed quietly. "I know you can. It's more that we need to walk a fine line between being tough and not escalating anything. Summers and Sharp are going to be all about taking things up a notch. It's my job to walk everything back."

"But you were the one who threatened to look into his business," Mindy said.

"I know. He still needs to know we're serious. And I had to let him know that I won't hestiate to call his bluff." What Isabel really meant to say was that old habits died hard.

Sam turned to Mindy. "I thought that was a brilliant move, personally. We need to fight fire with fire. We need to dig up dirt on this Summers guy and it's not a bad idea to go after his lawyer, too. I don't like that guy. He's smug and arrogant, the exact kind of guy I'd love to take down a notch."

Mindy looked at Sam like he had a screw loose. "Do you seriously not know who that guy is? Jeremy Sharp? Ex-husband of Kelsey Kline? The socialite?"

"Shh, you two," Isabel snapped, eying the receptionist, who thankfully hadn't seemed to overhear their conversation. Still, Isabel's mind was reeling. Jeremy had been married? And to a socialite? Both details came as a big surprise, but Isabel had fought her urge to look into his personal life when she learned that he was handling the case for Mr. Summers. Only the old Isabel did that. Now she might have no choice but to do at least a minimum of digging. Otherwise, she'd die of curiosity. She glanced at her brother. How could she tell Sam that the man he found so unlikable was someone she'd fallen into bed with? Sam would never judge her for it, but he would be disappointed, and as far as Isabel was concerned, that was worse.

"Sorry." Sam shoved his hands into his pockets. "I'm stressed. I hate that Mindy has to go through this."

"It's okay," Isabel offered, loving that her brother was so focused on Mindy's well-being. "Look, let's focus on the merits of the case. We need to get an expert to analyze the promissory note and make sure it's legitimate. I've already hired the financial forensic experts. They're going through the old Eden's books to see if there's any evidence the money flowed through the store." She turned to Mindy. "And I was thinking, if this relationship between Mr. Summers's dad and your grandmother was this significant, don't you think there'd likely be some evidence of it somewhere in her personal effects? Maybe old papers? Letters of some sort?"

"I got Gram's apartment after she passed away, but I never moved in. I had planned to, but it's only been a year and, well…" Mindy looked at Sam with utter adoration. "Your brother came along and everything changed."

"Our offer was accepted on the house out in New Jersey," Sam said to Isabel.

"It's way too much room for two people," Mindy added with a smile that said it didn't bother her at all.

Sam shrugged it off, but his grin was also a mile wide. "I want us to start having kids as soon as possible. I've put my life on hold for too long. And I've always wanted a family."

Isabel understood exactly what Sam was saying. She wanted those things for herself. In many ways, she felt like she and Sam would never truly heal from the trauma of losing their parents until they were each able to start a family.

"I'd still like to get married first," Mindy offered.

If these two were going to continue to ruminate about

their shared future, Isabel would never get any work done today. "Mindy, if you and I could get together and go through your grandmother's apartment, that would be great. In the meantime, I need to go back in there and hash things out with Mr. Sharp."

"Unless you need us, I think we'll take off and grab lunch," Sam said.

Isabel nodded. "Excellent idea."

Mindy hooked her arm in Sam's. "Thank you, Isabel, for having our backs. My sisters and I appreciate it more than you will ever know. Something about having a woman in charge makes us all breathe a little easier."

Sam's forehead crinkled in confusion. "I realize she's an amazing lawyer, but what does being a woman have to do with it?"

It was apparent Mindy was doing her best not to roll her eyes. "I like to be in control, and your sister and I are a lot alike. I know that she won't allow herself to fail. She'll keep at it until we win. She won't try to settle."

Winning was Isabel's preferred result, but this case wasn't going to be that simple. And her brief history with Jeremy would certainly complicate it. "There will have to be some negotiation, Mindy. That's just the way it works," Isabel said. She didn't make a habit of lowering her own bar, but if the note was determined to be authentic, Eden's was in a very difficult situation, one that Isabel would have to work miracles to get them out of.

"*If* the note is real," Mindy said. "I think there's a good chance that this is all a hoax."

Isabel could only hope for that right now. "I'd better get back in there and get it settled." She straightened her jacket and strode back down the hall. Wanting to appear confident and strong, she marched right into the room. And right into Jeremy. She reflexively braced herself, planting her hands on his chest. He gripped her elbows. She gazed up into his soft gray eyes. He intently peered down into hers. Her lips twitched with electricity, their connection fiercely uncomfortable to endure. Of course she'd fallen into bed with him that first night. Of course they'd given in to this. It would be impossible not to.

But now they were standing in a law office with a messy case to unravel. This was no time for rubbing up against Jeremy.

However badly she wanted to do exactly that.

She dropped her hands, and he dropped his, creating distance by stepping away. Isabel stared at the carpet, a perfectly ordinary office gray, as she struggled to regain her composure. She wasn't regretting the fact that they'd slept together. She found herself again regretting that she'd ever taken on this case.

"Sorry," Isabel said. "I guess I was in a hurry for us to get back to work."

Jeremy cleared his throat. "As am I. Lord only knows what Mr. Summers might do if left to his own devices in my office for too long." He flashed a quick smile at her. "Kidding, of course. He's fine in there." He strode to the door and closed it.

Isabel swallowed hard. Something about the sight of his hand against the ebony wood made her pulse skip a beat. She needed to get a grip. She was in the throes of battle with this man. Constantly reminding herself how sexy he was would only put her at a disadvantage. It didn't matter that he smelled good enough to eat. It didn't matter how unbelievable he looked in that suit.

"So," he started. "I take it this is why you didn't want to discuss your career the other night? Very clever of you."

"That wasn't the reason. I truly didn't want to talk about work. Is that so odd?"

"For someone who seems so eager to embrace her role as attorney, I find that a little peculiar."

"Eager? I'm just doing my job." She sat down and crossed her legs, hyperaware of the way her skirt hitched up an inch too far. She tugged at the hem as inconspicuously as possible. She needed to wrestle her side of their sexual tension into submission. It wasn't good for her or her client.

"Well, I have to admit that you're good at it. Very good." Jeremy sat down and drew a circle on the table with his index finger, making eye contact with her the whole time. Her mind zipped back to the memory of his hands on her naked skin—her breasts, her butt, her most delicate places—the parts that made her want him just as bad now as she had the other night. If only things hadn't ended so disastrously. "I got a little worked up there. You're definitely the most interesting person I've had the chance to spar with in recent history."

Isabel had always been drawn to that side of the law, where you make an argument, the other side responds with their own, and it then becomes a battle of wills, each party strengthening their stance until someone has no choice but to beg for mercy. Of course, it only felt good to come out on top. It felt horrible to lose. "Hopefully there won't have to be too much of that. I'd like to come to an agreement, starting with getting that note authenticated."

Just then the door flew open and a handsome, well-dressed older man stormed in. The resemblance to Jeremy was striking. It was like someone had hit the fast-forward button twenty years.

"Excuse me." The man barely glanced at Isabel. "Jeremy, can I speak with you?"

Jeremy impatiently rose from his seat, so fast that the chair rolled and hit the table with a thud. "We're in the middle of something. Can't this wait?"

"Why is Mr. Summers in your office?"

"He can't keep himself in line, that's why," Jeremy whispered, but it was loud enough for Isabel to hear every word.

The man unsubtly eyed Isabel, then returned his sights to Jeremy. "I'll go have a chat with him."

"Please don't."

Jeremy's voice was exceptionally firm, sending a thrill through Isabel, one she tried to ignore. She pulled out a legal pad and made a few scribbles to distract herself.

"All right then," the man said. "Check in with me when you're finished."

Jeremy said nothing in response as the man exited the room, but he had that stressed look on his face—the same one he'd had when he left Isabel's hotel room. "I'm sorry about that. My dad. He's supposed to be in partial retirement, but it only means that he has fewer clients but spends just as much time in the office."

"Leaving him too much time to interfere with what you're doing?" Isabel asked.

"Yes. Precisely."

Isabel didn't know much about Jeremy other than the revelation from Mindy that he'd been married, and apparently to a woman of some social stature, but she did feel bad that his own father was causing him distress. "No worries. Let's get back to the authentication. I've only been in New York a few weeks, so I don't have an expert on hand in the city. I know several in DC. I'm happy to bring one up."

"DC, huh? Big Washington lawyer?"

"Not exactly." Isabel pressed her lips together tightly.

"Something tells me you're underselling yourself." Jeremy's phone beeped with a text. "I'm so sorry, but I've been waiting for a message. Do you mind?"

"No. Of course not."

Jeremy pulled his phone from his pocket, seeming concerned. "Do you think we could discuss the authentication of the letter over dinner? I actually have to run home right now."

Run home during the day? Did Jeremy have a family? A girlfriend? He was becoming more of a puzzle by the moment. "I hope everything's okay."

He sighed heavily. "I think so. I ended up taking in a stray cat. It's a long story."

"Sounds like a lot."

"It's like everything in my life right now. Just one more thing on an endless list of obligations."

Isabel nodded, a bit chagrined that she'd been so right about Jeremy—he was not the guy who liked to be tied down. "Okay, then. You can tell me over dinner. Eight o'clock? The Monaco?"

Jeremy looked surprised. "It's impossible to get a reservation."

Isabel shrugged. "I know a guy."

"But you've only been in the city for a few weeks."

"Trust me. I got this."

Five

Dinner with Jeremy—hot and absurdly handsome Jeremy—was not the best plan. To some, it might seem like a particularly poor one. Did Isabel have a choice? Of course she did. She never liked to think that she didn't. But wrapping up this case on Mr. Summers's proposed timeline would take some artful work on Isabel's part if she was going to come out on top. For herself, her brother and his new family, she wanted nothing less than a win.

She did not want to be quibbling with this in January or having it drag out into February or March. She wanted this done so she could move on to the next phase of her career, adoption law. It would be a lot easier to get something out of Jeremy if the two of them had a good rapport, and well, the way things had played out at the Bacharach the night they met had not been a great start. She wanted to put that behind them, and in her experience, nothing cured a few bruised feelings

faster than a glass of wine and some conversation over
a delicious meal. Plus, the pasta carbonara at the Monaco was to die for.

First, she needed to get back to the Bacharach from
the Sharp and Sharp offices. Wanting to clear her head,
she opted to walk, even if she had to do it in heels. A
crisp December wind whipped between the tall buildings of Midtown Manhattan, bringing Isabel the focus
she craved. All around her, the city was abuzz with
the holidays. She strode past storefronts with extrav-
agant window displays, hosting scenes of Santa and
snowy ski chalets, candy canes and snowflakes. Red-
cheeked shoppers bustled along the sidewalk, loaded
down with department store bags, including silver-
and-white bags from Eden's, which was only seven or
eight blocks away. Isabel hadn't celebrated Christmas
in years. Well, not for real, with a tree and gifts and the
Wham! song some people try to avoid hearing. She and
Sam typically got together on Christmas Eve and spent
a few quiet days together, cooking and talking, content
with each other's company. It had been like that since
their parents died, when Sam was in high school and
Isabel in college. The holiday simply didn't have the
same meaning without their entire family together. Losing both parents in a six-month period had left them no
time to adjust. So she and Sam slipped into a new tradition, made up of celebrating the one thing they still
had—each other.

Isabel wasn't sure what would happen this year. Sam
had Mindy now. With that big lovely ring on her finger, they were buying their big house and talking about
children. Of course, Isabel was over the moon about the
whole thing. Yes, she'd been reluctant to accept Mindy
after the heartbreak she'd caused Sam, but in the end,

she'd been won over by Mindy's magnetic personality and determination. Plus, Isabel had to be nothing but in awe of her future sister-in-law. She'd accomplished the impossible, something no one else had managed in his thirty-six years on this planet—Mindy had found a way to make Sam happy.

Isabel arrived back at the Bacharach and dashed in through the revolving door, crossed the lobby and pressed the button for the elevator. She couldn't help but notice the woman in the fire department uniform speaking to the man she knew to be the hotel manager.

"The entire system?" the manager asked.

"I'm afraid so, sir. One minute it passes the test, the next minute it fails."

The elevator dinged and Isabel didn't hang around to hear more about the hotel's faulty alarm system. Hopefully it would get fixed soon.

Upstairs, she keyed into her room, unwound herself from her black wool coat, which she tossed onto the bed. She kicked off her pumps, sat at the desk and opened her laptop. She probably should have just given in to the urge to look into Jeremy yesterday, when she first learned that her one-night stand was opposing counsel. Less than a second after hitting the return button on *Jeremy Sharp*, a flurry of tabloid articles appeared. The first headline suggested exactly what Mindy had: Kelsey Kline Leaves Husband, Says Marriage "Loveless."

Isabel wasn't much for pulp or gossip, and she'd never even heard of Kelsey Kline before that morning, but the story was fascinating. The only daughter of a shipping magnate, heiress to a vast fortune, Ms. Kline was well-known in NYC as a party girl turned fashion blogger turned wedding planner. She was flat-out gorgeous, fit yet curvy, with high cheekbones, full lips and a stunning head of chocolate-brown hair. Isabel didn't know Jeremy particularly well, but Kelsey seemed like the kind of woman he might choose—fun and carefree.

As Isabel read on, the story turned dark and sad. Kelsey claimed that Jeremy was inattentive and unaffectionate, not the marrying type or a guy who was meant to settle down. She said point-blank that he broke her heart, getting married to him was a mistake, and she might never recover. There were even a few hints that he might have been unfaithful, although it was a subject carefully tiptoed around. No matter whether that was true or not, this was all another sign that Isabel might have dodged a bullet.

Kelsey filed for divorce less than three years after she and Jeremy had tied the knot in a lavish ceremony at a historic cathedral in the city. Other than being blamed for the end of the marriage, Jeremy was hardly mentioned in the article at all. It said that he had declined to comment, which Isabel took as confirmation that everything Kelsey had said was true, at least on some level. Otherwise, why not stick up for yourself?

Isabel took in a deep breath through her nose and closed her laptop, not wanting to read any more. She felt that familiar crawl over her skin after having peered into someone else's life. She realized there were plenty of people who lived for such salacious details, but Isabel had seen too much of the personal toll. At least she was now certain that she had made the right call when she'd let Jeremy off the hook after their first night together. She would have dinner with him tonight, get this case worked out and move on. That would be the end of her chapter with Mr. Sharp. And from the sound of that article, that was the best case scenario.

* * *

A few minutes before eight, Isabel climbed out of a town car in front of the Monaco. From the outside, the restaurant was a mystery—a dark wood facade with a large arched center door, the name in gold above. No random passersby would ever bother to step inside unprompted, out of either ignorance or perhaps fear of the unknown. But it was one of Isabel's favorite spots in Manhattan, owned by a former client who had top-tier restaurants all over the world—London, Madrid, Los Angeles, DC. Isabel's last assignment for the restaurateur had been to get his college-age daughter out of jail when she was arrested in Belize on spring break. It had been Isabel's job to not only deal with the legal side of getting her out and back into the US, but to keep the story out of the papers and away from her university. Thus had been her life of a lawyer turned fixer.

Isabel ducked through the door and into a dimly lit vestibule with an ornate tile floor, coat check and host stand. The sounds of the restaurant, a steady hum of conversation and clinking glass, filtered into the small space, even through the heavy emerald-green velvet drape that obscured the entrance into the dining room. Isabel gave her name to the hostess just as a rush of cold came in behind her. She turned and there was Jeremy. He was clearly flustered, his cheeks full of color as he pushed his hair back from his face. Isabel endeavored to ignore the way her pulse raced when she saw him. He turned his shoulders out of a charcoal-gray wool coat, dressed in black trousers and suit jacket, with a midnight-blue dress shirt that turned his gray eyes an even darker and more intense shade. Isabel had to hope that at some point the zap of attraction would subside.

Hopefully it wouldn't always feel like this to be around him, as if her body was on perpetual high alert.

"Everything okay?" she asked.

He smiled thinly. "Basically, yes. Just a crazy afternoon."

"Crazy good or crazy bad?"

He blew out a breath. "The stray cat I told you about? I thought it was a male, but it's a female. And she's pregnant."

Isabel pressed her lips together tightly to stifle a laugh. For the guy who seemed to be bothered by responsibility, this was pretty funny. "What are you going to do?"

"I'm going to buy you a drink as soon as we're seated for dinner. That's what."

Isabel signaled the hostess with a nod and they were led into the restaurant, just as beautiful as she'd remembered it, with its signature emerald-green circular booths for two, soft lighting and glamorous clientele. Jeremy waited for Isabel to sit before he slid into the other side of the booth. It was a sexy and intimate setting, perfect if there had been the possibility of any romance between them at all. But the article she'd read a few hours ago had put that idea to rest. Instead, she hoped to lean on the privacy of their table to start cutting their deal. They each ordered a drink from their server—a gin and tonic for Isabel and a Manhattan for Jeremy.

"I haven't been here in years," Jeremy said, flipping through the menu. Isabel already knew what she was going to order: her favorite pasta. "It's pretty much a date-night spot."

Isabel hadn't considered the possibility that Jeremy might have memories of this place with his ex-wife. Or other women. Her mind then made the next leap—did he think she was trying to make a romantic overture? She deeply hoped that was not the case. She didn't want to embarrass herself. "I love the food, though. It's exceptional."

"Indeed."

Their drinks were quickly delivered and they placed their dinner orders. "I suppose a toast is in order," Jeremy said once the server had left. "To making a deal."

Isabel was happy to hear that Jeremy didn't have romance on the brain. It might make it easier for her to set aside the thoughts that kept creeping into her consciousness—sharing a drink brought back too many memories of their blazing-hot first kiss. "Yes." She took a sip and placed her glass back on the table. "So, the authentication of the promissory note. Do you have an expert we can call on? I'd like to speak to them, of course, and have a detailed outline of their process, their experience in the field, and have them sign an agreement of impartiality."

"I have one person we work with, but I can assure you that they'll do a great job and they'll get it done quickly."

"We wouldn't want to mess with Mr. Summers and his thirty-day timeline."

"We're already nearly a week in. The clock started the day we sent the first letter. And you can't blame the guy. The loan is long overdue."

"And my clients had no idea the loan ever existed. You can't pay off what you don't know about."

"They don't seem eager to repay it now."

Isabel stirred her drink. "It's not a simple matter to pull that kind of cash together at one time. Especially not with so little time."

Jeremy shrugged it off. "I don't want to sound like a jerk, but it's not my problem."

Isabel did not like the way this was going. She saw too little room for negotiation. This case might be even tougher than she'd thought. "I would never say you sound like a jerk. But you do sound like the lawyer of a jerk."

Despite being referred to as the lawyer of a jerk, being out with Isabel was far more enjoyable than the many work-related obligations Jeremy endured on any given week. "If that's what I am, at least it pays the bills."

"Good to know you have your priorities," she said, then took a long sip of her drink.

Jeremy had to hide his amusement as the waiter delivered their meals. Isabel was a far cry from the usual blowhard attorney. He genuinely enjoyed her company. She was more than simply beautiful and smart. The world seemed different around her, the air charged with mystery and excitement. Jeremy had learned a lot about her after she'd left his office that afternoon. While working in Washington, DC, she'd gathered a passel of high-powered clients—senators, billionaires and cabinet officials. Not a single controversy or scandal seemed to stick to any of them, even when lawsuits were filed and whistles were blown. Accusations and rumors all vanished into thin air, and Jeremy was smart enough to know that didn't happen on its own. Did Isabel's beautiful exterior and graceful facade make it easier for her to sweep things under the rug or keep secrets? If so, it made her even more dangerous than he'd thought that morning. "So, I have to ask, why didn't you call me as soon as you realized that I was the opposing counsel? That part of this whole thing seems especially sneaky."

Isabel dabbed at the corners of her stunning mouth with a napkin. He had an improper desire to kiss her until her lipstick was gone. Despite being on opposite sides of the negotiating table, that sexual energy between them wasn't going anywhere. "Honestly?"

"Please. I don't do well with anything less." Jeremy found himself cutting his steak a little more aggressively than was warranted. Even the manipulation of words bothered him, which made being a lawyer difficult. So much of the job was about the careful parsing of language.

"It was my brother Sam's idea. He thought it would give us an advantage if you didn't know who exactly you would be facing. I apologize if you felt ambushed, but it was just a tactic."

That morning in his office had likely only been Jeremy's first taste of the sorts of things to which Isabel might resort. "It made me look like an ass in front of my client. I certainly don't appreciate that."

Isabel nodded. "Fair enough. I guess it wasn't the kindest thing to do. Sam is just very protective of his fiancée, Mindy, and the entire Eden family for that matter. And since it's just Sam and me in our family, I guess that I'm part of that scenario, too."

Jeremy understood family loyalty, but only to a point. If his grandfather were still alive, he'd still have undying devotion to the Sharp name. But his parents certainly didn't inspire that sort of allegiance. They'd treated him horribly in the aftermath of his divorce, more preoccupied by the public embarrassment than the fact that their son had experienced a great personal betrayal. "Do you actually like working for the Eden family?"

Isabel shot him a quizzical look. "That's a loaded question."

"Why?"

"The tone of your voice for starters. You sound as though the Eden family disgusts you."

Jeremy was letting his personal bias get in the way, but he couldn't help it. The Eden family and his ex's family seemed to be very much the same—wealthy beyond measure, treating the world as their personal playground. "It's just the entitlement. It drives me crazy. The Eden sisters have been handed a vast fortune and now they're quibbling over this debt. I assure you that Mr. Summers would not dredge up this matter if he didn't desperately want it resolved. It's a very personal thing for him. The affair between Victoria Eden and his father destroyed his family. I don't think we can discount the personal component of the case."

Isabel set her fork down on her plate. "And surely you know it takes two people to tango. Mr. Summers seems to want to assign all blame to Victoria Eden. He wants to paint her as a home-wrecker, when the reality is that his own father was complicit as well if the affair happened as he says it did. For all we know, his father could have instigated the whole thing."

Jeremy felt his pulse pick up. His heart hammered. He did love it when Isabel delivered a smart jab, even if he was on the receiving end of it.

"*If* the affair actually happened," she continued. "We don't know that for sure."

She bit down on her lip, her dark eyes scanning his face. Damn, her skin was beautiful in this soft light and all he could think was how badly he wanted to touch it. To touch her. Every inch. He wasn't the type of guy to rest too much of his self-worth on how things went in the bedroom, but he was certain that he had rocked Isabel's world during their one evening together, and it was still aggravating him that it had ended on such an inelegant note.

She shook her head and looked down at the table, her dark hair falling across her face. "I'm sorry. I just get worked up. I don't like seeing a woman shouldering the blame for this. Men and women are equal and should be treated as such, good or bad."

"Don't apologize for your anger. I'd much rather go up against someone with some passion behind what they do than deal with a robot."

Her eyebrows bounced and one corner of her mouth popped up into a smile. "I run way too hot to be a robot."

An abrupt tightening of the muscles in Jeremy's hips made him shift in his seat. Isabel was going to make him crazy by the time this case was wrapped up. For once, Jeremy was glad for Mr. Summers's ridiculous timeline. The sooner this case was done, the sooner he could decide if he wanted to pursue anything with her. It seemed like he had to at least try one more time, leave her with a smile on her face rather than having her push him out the door. "I know that. Firsthand."

"I hope that doesn't make you uncomfortable. You know. That we slept together. I'm trying to look at it as an odd coincidence."

"So you definitely weren't spying on me and Mr. Summers in the bar at the Bacharach?"

Isabel's eyes went wide. "Is that who your meeting was with that night?" She clamped her hand over her mouth, much like she had when he'd mentioned that his new roommate, the stray cat with no name, was going to have kittens.

"It is. Summers loves the bar there."

Isabel reached out and clasped Jeremy's forearm. "I swear I wasn't spying. I would never do that. I was legitimately up in my room trying to get some sleep when the silly alarm went off. It had been a hell of a day trying to find an apartment and look for a new office space. It's a lot to deal with at one time, especially when you're starting on a case that could easily end up being all-consuming."

Jeremy couldn't help but look at her hand on his arm, her slender fingers on the dark wool of his coat, and quietly wish he wasn't wearing a suit. "I had to ask." He cleared his throat, knowing he'd never truly believed that Isabel had been up to something nefarious that night, but it did make him wonder whether she was someone he could trust. "You know, I looked you up on the internet this afternoon. Judging by the work you were doing in DC, I'm up against quite a formidable foe."

"Please don't judge me by that. As far as I'm concerned, that was a lifetime ago. I'm actually getting ready to go into a whole new area of practice. Adoption law."

Now Jeremy was even more fascinated. This was a full one-eighty. "There's not exactly a lot of money in that, is there?"

Isabel shrugged. "There isn't. I'm not worried about that. I just want to have a body of work that I can be proud of."

"I take it that doesn't include the things you did in DC?"

She shook her head. "Definitely not. But I'm putting all of that behind me. For good."

So maybe he'd read Isabel all wrong. He could hardly

fault a person for wanting to do some good with her career. "Sounds like you've got it all figured out."

"And speaking of getting things figured out, let's say we get the note authenticated. At that point, we'll need to set up a time for in-depth negotiations to hammer out the details. But I don't have an office right now."

Jeremy sucked in a deep breath. He had serious concerns that as soon as the note was deemed authentic, Mr. Summers would further dig in his heels. But it was part of Jeremy's job to at least move forward in good faith. "It's not easy for me to get much done at the Sharp and Sharp office. Too many interruptions." He cleared his throat, racking his brain for an idea. "Is meeting at Eden's an option?"

"They don't have the room. I asked about a work space there, but the building is old and they're bulging at the seams." She placed her napkin across her plate and sat back.

"I have a full office big enough for two people at my place in Brooklyn. In fact, I probably have too much space. I have meetings there all the time when I need quiet, or when a client wants more discretion than they'll get walking into the front door of a law firm. Would you be comfortable with that idea?"

"Hmm..." She squinted at him. "I don't know. Is this some sort of come-on?"

Jeremy could feel the heat rising in his cheeks. "Most women aren't seduced by the idea of negotiations."

"Ah, but I'm not most women."

Jeremy swallowed hard, finding it difficult to get past the lump in his throat. "I noticed."

Isabel granted him a small smile. "Would that mean I'd get to meet your cat?"

"She's not my cat."

"She's come up in conversation an awful lot for a cat that isn't yours."

"I'm not a cat person at all. I just took pity on her because she was outside in the cold. Ironically, the only reason I hadn't let her in before was because she was so fat. Now I know why."

"What are you going to do about the kittens?"

Jeremy kneaded his forehead. His meeting with his neighborhood veterinarian was still fresh in his mind. "For now? I'm fostering her. We had such a late summer that I guess there's a big surplus of cats and the shelters are full. The vet said the kittens should be ready for adoption by Valentine's Day." Jeremy could hardly believe the words out of his own mouth. Like he needed another complication in his life.

"Well, I can't wait to meet her. I love cats. We always had them when I was a kid. My mom was obsessed with them."

"You haven't had one since?"

Isabel's face reflected something Jeremy hadn't seen before—sadness. "No. Not one of my own."

"Well, good. Maybe you're the answer to my prayers. I'm a bit out of my depth." He glanced over at her, wondering why he was allowing himself to get further entwined with Isabel. He knew he shouldn't be, especially not now. He should be creating distance. That was how you won. "With the cat. Not the case."

Six

Isabel arranged to meet Mindy at her grandmother's penthouse apartment on Central Park West on Sunday morning. It was only eleven days until Christmas and the clock was ticking on Mr. Summers's timeline. The results of the promissory note authentication were due back tomorrow. Then Isabel would have to get back into it with Jeremy. She wasn't quite sure what to make of the invitation to meet at his house, but she knew from experience that there was no substitute for sitting down at the negotiating table and hammering out details. So she would risk having to endure the temptation of Jeremy, being alone and sequestered with him, just so she could move forward with her life—finish up the Eden's case and start the new year with a whole new direction.

"Hey there." Mindy answered the door, dressed in the sort of outfit Isabel had never seen her wear—jeans and a sweater. No designer dress or sky-high heels. It was nice to see her dressed down and relaxed. "Come on in."

"Thanks." Isabel stepped into a bright and elegant foyer with white marble floors and a crystal-and-chrome fixture overhead. She took off her coat, glad she'd also gone for pants and a sweater. Even hot-running Isabel found it too cold outside for a dress.

"Thank you for suggesting we do this. It was a really good idea. Sophie is convinced that this whole Summers case is bogus. But I'm not so sure, especially after your forensic accountants found the money yesterday. And discovered that it went into my grandmother's personal account, not the business."

"It's starting to make sense now, isn't it? No wonder we couldn't find any evidence of it in the Eden's books. It never touched Eden's. Or at least not directly." Isabel was struggling just like Mindy, wondering how this all went together. "But we still don't know for certain that the money came from Summers and we also don't know where it eventually went."

"Only that it existed."

"Right."

Mindy waved Isabel across the foyer. "Come on. Let me show you the place."

They progressed down a skinny hallway and then the apartment opened up, with an entire wall of windows overlooking Central Park. The vista ahead was frosted with snow, a lovely match for the mostly white furnishings.

"My grandmother was all about punches of color." Mindy picked up a magenta throw pillow from one of several plush sofas. Behind it was a sunny yellow cashmere throw. The walls were dotted with an eclectic mix of art, wildly varied stylistically, from impressionist to modern, featuring nearly every shade of the rainbow. It all looked to be original. The space as a whole spoke of a very chic woman with impossibly expensive taste. Of course Victoria Eden had lived in such a grand and unbelievable space.

"I've seen that same thing at Eden's, especially in her old office."

Mindy nodded. "Emma's been afraid to change a thing. Too much tradition. The specter of my grandmother always looms large."

Tradition. Another reason Isabel could not let Eden's fall apart on her watch.

"I can't believe you never moved in here," Isabel said. "It's incredible. Completely gorgeous." She wandered over to a set of French doors that led out to a stone balcony, admiring the wintry scene. Mother Nature had already gone big this December.

"I knew that no matter what I did, Sophie would criticize my choices unless I left everything exactly as it was. And I do not want to live in a museum."

"That's not really fair to you, is it? So you just leave this sitting here because of your sister?"

Mindy shrugged. "I have no business complaining. Emma never knew our grandmother very well, so she enjoys coming up here and poking around, looking at old photos. Sophie likes it for the same reason, and I'd be lying if I said that I didn't enjoy it, too. It's comforting to be here. I can feel our grandmother's presence when I'm here and we all miss it. I can't fault anyone for wanting to put the world on pause."

Isabel nodded, appreciating the whole sad story. She knew very well what it was like to miss someone so desperately. She still felt that same way about her parents, especially her mom. "If only we could do that. It would be nice every now and then."

Mindy gathered her glorious red tresses in her hands and draped them over one shoulder. "It's only been a year since Gram died, and so much has happened. Just when we thought we were getting the store back on a more profitable path, this happens. I'm honestly wondering if we're not better off just selling, paying off Mr. Summers and moving on. I know Sophie and Emma want to keep Eden's alive at any cost, but sometimes, things just don't work out."

Isabel carefully considered Mindy's words. She loved that her future sister-in-law was both savvy and sweet. She could make shrewd business moves and still take everyone's feelings into account. "Have I told you how happy I am that my brother found a woman who is not only smart, but also incredibly thoughtful?"

Mindy smiled. "That's not what you thought of me the first time we met."

"I know. And I fully admit that you changed my mind."

Mindy reached out and rubbed Isabel's arm. "I'm excited to have you for a sister-in-law. Although, honestly, I have a feeling that I should probably just call you my sister. You and I are a lot more alike than Sophie or Emma and I."

Isabel felt like her heart was growing to twice its normal size. She and Sam were impossibly close, but that was such a small circle of family. Here was Mindy, forging a connection of her own with Isabel. She was so thankful for it. "That sounds amazing. I've always wanted a sister."

"Consider it done." Mindy grinned and placed her

arm around Isabel's shoulders, pulling her close. "Come on. Let's go dig through my grandmother's office."

The pair trekked through the living room to what appeared to be Victoria Eden's private quarters, with a large master bedroom, elegant bathroom with its own view of the park, dressing room and, finally, a generous home office. Like the rest of the house, a neutral backdrop of white and cream made room for the more over-the-top elements, like a crimson velvet club chair. Mindy stepped behind her grandmother's grand desk and opened the closet to reveal six large filing cabinets.

"I'm guessing we start here?" Mindy asked.

Isabel didn't have a better suggestion. "It's as good a place as any."

They quickly set up a system, methodically going through one drawer at a time, file folder after file folder, page after page of surprisingly meaningless paperwork. For a woman who had been considered a business tycoon, Victoria Eden had been keenly focused on the smallest of things.

Mindy shook her head and closed one folder. "She kept nearly thirty years of electric bills. Who does that?"

"Someone who's watching every penny? Maybe that's part of why she was so successful."

Mindy's shoulders dropped in exasperation. "I hope this doesn't end up being a big waste of time."

"I don't know. Compared to most things I do, this is pretty fun. Plus, we get to spend time together."

"There you go. Good job looking on the bright side. I need to do more of that."

"Actually, if anything, I'd take all of this mundane stuff as a good sign. Anyone who kept electric bills likely also kept far more important things."

"Even superpersonal things?"

Isabel closed up the folder she'd been sifting through and handed it over to Mindy. "Especially that."

After two more hours of pulling apart the contents of the filing cabinets, they were down to the last drawer. Mindy pulled the handle, but it only opened partway. "Can you help me with this?" she asked, peering down inside.

Isabel rushed over and knelt down next to Mindy. Sure enough, there was a large wood box, turned on its side, preventing the drawer from being opened the whole way. Mindy and Isabel quickly pulled out the hanging files in front of it. Mindy grabbed a letter opener from her grandmother's desk drawer and slipped it under the bottom of the box, twisting and pulling until the box popped free with a clatter of wood against metal.

Mindy closed the drawer and sat spread-eagled on the floor with the box between her knees. She flipped the small brass latch on the front. She looked up at Isabel, her eyes wide with astonishment. "It's a bunch of letters." She examined the first envelope. "The return address says Bradley Summers."

Goose bumps popped up on Isabel's arms. She sensed that another piece of the puzzle was about to fall into place. "Bingo."

Isabel and Mindy spent the next several hours devouring the correspondence sent by Bradley Summers to Victoria Eden, which seemed to begin in the spring of 1979, years before the loan would have been made. They arranged the letters in chronological order, which helped them sort out how the affair began: after Bradley and Victoria had a chance meeting at a cocktail party in the Hamptons. Bradley made mention that he was glad their spouses had not been on hand—Bradley's wife because she'd had one of her "many migraines" and Victoria's husband because he couldn't be bothered to stay away from the racetrack. It was an epic love story that sprouted up between two people thrown together by chance, who just happened to fulfill what the other was so desperately looking for. For the senior Mr. Summers, it seemed to be the undivided attention of a woman. *My sweet Victoria*, he wrote, *When we're together, I feel like I'm the only man in the world. Every moment with you is priceless, worth framing and hanging in a museum.*

"Wow. This is so romantic. They were head over heels for each other," Isabel said, handing over the letter she was holding to Mindy. She couldn't help but be astonished by what had been between these two people, sentiments that served as a very plain reminder that Isabel hadn't come close to finding that kind of passion or affection with a man. She hoped she wasn't running out of time.

When Mindy finished reading the final letter in the box, she looked over at Isabel with a tear in her eye. It was a bit incongruous with Mindy's normally tough exterior. "Their love affair was real." Mindy's shoulders dropped. "I don't know what to think about this. Or how I'm supposed to feel. I really loved my grandfather, but it's pretty well known in our family that he was not a great husband. This is at least confirmation that my grandmother stayed in a loveless marriage for her entire life."

"That part is incredibly sad." Isabel glanced down at the pile of letters. "It was also pretty clear that your grandfather had a serious gambling problem. Bradley mentions several times that he hated your grandmother living with the burden of his many debts. Do you think that's where the money could have gone?"

Mindy shrugged. "I have no idea. I mean, going to the racetrack with our grandfather is one of the only things I ever remember doing with him, but we were kids and it was nothing but fun. We'd drink soda and eat junk food and he'd let us pick our favorite horses so he could place bets. Sophie always picked names like Fancy Frolic, and I always picked ones like Emperor King. My grandfather used to tease me, saying that I needed to learn to like 'girl things.'" Mindy made air quotes. "As far as I was concerned, I liked what I liked. No big surprise, but he handed those same ideas down to our dad. Even so, those days at the track are some of my fondest memories of my grandfather. He at least wanted to spend time with us, which is more than I can say for my dad."

Isabel was struck by how even a family with great wealth and power could have such a bittersweet legacy. "If the money went to gambling debts, it might be harder to track down, especially depending on who he owed money to. And it still doesn't change the fact that it appears that the loan was real."

Mindy again looked down at the letters in her hand, but it was for several moments this time. She brushed her fingers across the envelope at the top of the pile. "This means that the store is really on the line, doesn't it? We aren't talking hypotheticals anymore. I mean, chances are that the promissory note is real, and we're going to have to find a way to pay off the debt."

"No matter what I'm able to negotiate, chances are that it'll still be a huge chunk of money, and from everything I've seen of Mr. Summers, he's serious about wanting it in one lump sum, right away. Early January, right after New Year's."

"It's just hard to come up with that kind of cash without a loan. And the most valuable thing we have to use as collateral is Eden's. It's all Sophie has, aside from her apartment and Eden House, our family's vacation home, which she would never let go of in a million years."

"What about selling this apartment?"

Mindy nodded, looking around the room. "Yeah. I could definitely do that, but we're talking maybe fifty million, and that's if we get top dollar from the right buyer, which could easily take a year to happen. It's a drop in the bucket compared to what we have to come up with."

"Can Sam help?"

"He's looking into selling some bigger properties, but like I said, that all takes time, and it all costs money, too. Real estate agents need to get paid. It sort of feels like we're throwing money into a big black hole." Surprisingly, a smile crossed Mindy's face.

"And you're happy about that?"

"No. No. I was just thinking about Sam and his reaction to this whole situation. He wants to fix everything. He gets so worked up about it, wanting to hold everything together. It's just so damn sweet. Every time he gets upset about it, I fall a little more in love with him."

Now Isabel was the one having to fight back tears. The struggles she and Sam had been through when they were young had been much harder on him, and Isabel still had a good deal of guilt over having been away at college when it happened. "You really love him, don't you?"

"It might sound corny, and I'm not a super sentimental person, but he is my soul mate. We work together in every way. I can't imagine my life without him." Mindy gathered the letters in her hands and squared the edges on the floor. "And I nearly lost him. I pushed him away so many times."

Isabel had never pushed anyone away, but she'd had many men shutter her out of their lives. It hurt an unimaginable amount, which was a big part of the reason Isabel had not initially liked Mindy. She hated the thought of her brother having his heart broken. "I feel like everything happens for a reason. Maybe you had to go through those early tests to know for sure that you're right for each other."

"That sounds a lot nicer than my version, which is basically just me being an idiot." Mindy shifted to her knees and got up from the floor. "So what do you think is going to happen with Eden's?"

"I think we're going to have to count on Mr. Summers's good graces and hope that they'll agree to a reduced settlement and a payment plan."

"Do you think these letters might help?" Mindy asked. "What if we showed them to him? Showed him how much his father really loved my grandmother? It might make him see that the loan really was made out of love. It's not our fault his parents couldn't make their marriage work."

Isabel shook her head. "No. Absolutely not. I think you should put those letters back where you found them, and for the time being, I wouldn't tell anyone about them other than Sam and your sisters."

"Okay, then. What's next?"

"I'm guessing that I'm going to get a phone call from Jeremy Sharp tomorrow morning saying that the note was authenticated. And that's when we start negotiating from a disadvantage."

"You don't think you're better than him?"

Now it was Isabel's turn to smile at an inopportune time. "It's not a matter of better. Jeremy is plenty skilled. He's a shrewd attorney."

Mindy narrowed her sights, and Isabel immediately worried that her future sister-in-law was onto something. "Is it just me or is he superhot, too? I mean, I know Sam thinks he's a weasel, but there's no accounting for his taste. Especially not when it comes to hotness."

Isabel's cheeks flushed with warmth. There had been many times at dinner the other night when she'd caught herself holding her breath in awe of Jeremy's appeal. "He's extremely handsome. There's no doubt about that."

"It was sexy the way you two were arguing at that first meeting. It felt like there were sparks flying. Or is that stupid of me to say?"

Isabel already felt bad about not coming clean about Jeremy with her own brother the day of that meeting. She wasn't sure she could keep it from Mindy, too, especially when they were becoming so close. "I have to tell you something. But you have to promise not to breathe a word of it to Sam. At least not until the case is settled." She bit down on her lip, waiting for Mindy's response, hoping like hell that she could truly be trusted.

"I don't like the idea of secrets. But I also don't like the idea of you feeling like you can't tell me anything. Because you can." Mindy nodded eagerly. "So, yes. My lips are zipped. I won't say a peep to Sam."

Isabel took in a deep breath for confidence. "I slept with Jeremy."

Mindy slugged her in the arm playfully. "Shut up. Are you serious?" Her eyes bugged out. "Wait. When?"

"It was actually a few days before the first meeting. I had no idea who he was, and he had no idea who I was. It was pure coincidence." Isabel went on to share the most general of details from their night together, sparing Mindy the part about Jeremy's quick departure.

"So, how was it?"

"It was fantastic, but it was a one-night thing. You don't have anything to worry about. There will be no conflict of interest there. Jeremy's all business and he's devoted to his client. That goes much further than you might imagine."

"I trust your judgment, Isabel. Completely. I know you're an amazing lawyer and I'm sure you won't have a problem keeping it all aboveboard. So, how do you like our odds of saving the store?"

Isabel didn't want to sugarcoat anything, but she didn't want to set her future sister-in-law up for disappointment, either. "The optimist in me is thinking fifty-fifty."

"Really?" Mindy asked. "That bad?"

Isabel reached out and caressed Mindy's arm, wanting to be at least a little reassuring. "I'm going to do everything I can to keep you from losing."

"Everything?" Mindy asked with two perfectly arched eyebrows.

Isabel was now second-guessing the decision to spill the beans about Jeremy. She really hoped she didn't end up regretting it. "Nearly everything."

Mindy and Isabel put away the letters, tidied up the office, and went their separate ways. It was a chilly day, but the sun had come out, so Isabel decided to walk back to the Bacharach. When she arrived, there was a sign on the door: *All guests: Please see the front desk*

for information regarding your stay. There will be no
new check-ins until further notice.

Isabel strode inside to investigate, but there was a
sizable line of seemingly upset guests at the front desk.
"What's going on?" she asked a woman who was waiting for the elevator.

"The fire department has ordered the hotel to re-
place the alarm system. They start the work on Friday.
Everyone has to be out by then." The elevator dinged.
"It doesn't affect me, so I'm not too worried about it."

Isabel decided she wasn't going to wait with the
angry mob in the lobby and instead took the elevator
up with the woman. "Did they happen to say if they're
sending guests to another hotel?"

"It's Christmas in Manhattan. There are no other
hotel rooms. That's why everyone is so mad."

Isabel wasn't sure how things could get much worse.
She'd just have to move in with Sam and Mindy for a
few days until she could find something more permanent. If nothing else, she needed to get back to looking
for an apartment in earnest.

The woman got off on her floor and Isabel rode up
another two to her own. She'd hardly keyed her way into
her room when her phone rang. It was Jeremy.

"Hello?" she asked, plopping down on the bed.

"Did I catch you at a bad time?"

Isabel disliked the way her body reacted to his voice,
like a puppy that's just been told it's time for a treat.
"No. It's fine. What's up?"

"We got the authentication of the note. I just wanted
to tell you as soon as I knew."

Isabel reclined back on the bed and stared up at the
ceiling. This was not surprising news, but it was certainly not what they wanted. "Okay, then. I'll notify my

client. And I guess we need to get together to hammer out these negotiations."

"Yeah. About that. I talked to Mr. Summers and in light of the authentication, he has changed his terms. He wants an even billion or the store. By January 1."

She shot straight up in bed, her heart hammering. She could hardly believe what he had just said. "It's Christmas. Is he really that cold and heartless? I'm sorry, but your client is behaving like Ebenezer Scrooge."

"From where I'm sitting, he has an ironclad case."

Isabel fought the grumble in her throat. She also tamped back her natural urge to launch into her side of the argument. There was no point in that right now. Isabel had seen the letters. She'd known that this was coming. Victoria Eden and Bradley Summers had absolutely had an affair. And by all accounts, it had been a doozy. Her heart sank at the thought of the call she had to make, to break this news to Mindy and Sam, then let them break it to Sophie and Emma. It would take the wind out of their sails, for sure, but Isabel would not let this be the end of the story. It would not be the final chapter of Eden's Department Store. Somehow, they would pull this off. She would. "I'll talk to my clients and see what we can do."

"You'll get back to me?"

"I don't see that I have a choice."

Seven

Since the moment the promissory note had been authenticated, Isabel had been doing nothing but playing cat and mouse with Jeremy. His client was refusing to budge. Mr. Summers wouldn't give an inch. Jeremy was holding fast. She knew from experience that she'd never be able to exercise any influence over him unless they could meet in person, but he was insisting on phone calls, much to her dismay. He was avoiding her, and it was starting to feel personal.

By Friday, things were becoming dire. Sam and Mindy had spent the entire week moving assets, trying to sell properties, but they were finding the task more difficult the closer they got to the holidays. It would be nearly impossible to liquidate anything between Christmas and New Year's. There were simply too many people who weren't working. With Christmas six days away, time was running out.

As if life couldn't possibly get more complicated,

Isabel had to vacate the Bacharach by noon that day. She'd originally planned to stay with Sam and Mindy, but they'd both been working so hard that they'd managed to come down with a dreadful cold. Isabel's back-up plan was to fly to DC and stay with a friend for the weekend. This close to Christmas, there wasn't a spare hotel room anywhere in the city.

Before she left for the airport, Isabel was set to meet with Sophie and Emma at Eden's and if all went okay, Sam or Mindy would call in. Isabel arrived at Eden's first thing that morning. Eight o'clock to be exact, right when the offices were first open. A burly but friendly security officer named Duane met her at one of the main entrances.

"Sophie and Emma are already here," he said, walking her through the cosmetics department and back to the executive elevators.

"Thank you. Have they been here long?"

"Most of the night."

Isabel had been afraid of that. Coming up with a cool billion to get Benjamin Summers to go away was no small job and they were all going to extraordinary measures to attempt the impossible.

The store was eerily quiet, with only a handful of lights on. It would open early at 9:00 a.m. for holiday shopping hours, but there was still a sense that she was taking part in a death march. Just like the entire Eden family, she desperately didn't want the store to slip into Mr. Summers's hands. There were no guarantees that he'd continue to run the store at all. Isabel could imagine him taking a wrecking ball to the whole thing out of spite. What would happen to the employees? Or the history contained in this beautiful old building? And what would happen to the Eden sisters if they lost their birthright, this very permanent fixture of this city, emblazoned with their name?

Duane pressed the elevator button for her. "Do you know your way upstairs? Lizzie, the receptionist, should be here soon, but not yet. She just texted me to say her train was delayed."

"Eden's really is like a family, isn't it?" Isabel asked. Where else did the receptionist check in with the security guard when she was running late?

"Yes, ma'am. Lizzie is like a little sister to me. She tells me everything." His eyebrows bounced and he smiled. "Even about her new beau."

"Ooh. Anyone I know?" Lizzie was a total sweetheart and Isabel had grown to adore her.

"I shouldn't say anything." Duane's face said that he was dying to tell someone.

Isabel reached out and touched his arm. "Look. I'm very good at keeping secrets. You can tell me. I won't say a peep."

"It's James, one of the salespeople in menswear," he blurted. "He's a Brit like Emma's husband, Daniel."

As if there hadn't been enough excitement about the Eden family, Emma and Daniel had decided to get married at city hall last week. With a baby on the way, Daniel was eager to start the process of becoming an American citizen, apparently much to his mother's disappointment.

"I'll have to find a reason to sneak down to menswear later and see if I can get an eyeful of James."

Duane laughed and the elevator dinged. "Have a good meeting."

"Thank you." A minute later, Isabel arrived on the executive floor.

Sophie was waiting right outside the elevator bank,

pacing. She lunged for Isabel the instant the door opened. "Thank God you're here. We have an emergency and it's bad."

Isabel could hardly keep up anymore. She'd dealt with plenty of panicked clients, but this was turning into an hourly thing with the Eden family. Fortunately, she had a great deal of experience in this arena. "Whatever it is, it's okay. Did something happen with one of the deals Sam and Mindy were working on? Or something you and your husband were setting up?"

Emma strode out of her office. Her baby bump was now visible. Small, but apparent. "I read the article, Sophie. I really don't think it's that bad. I mean, it's not great, but I've seen worse things."

Isabel was starting to put this all together. "Something in the tabloids, I take it?"

Sophie waved her ahead. "Come on. My office. I'll show you."

Isabel was starting to bristle at Sophie's cloak-and-dagger approach as she found herself marching with Sophie and Emma down the hall to Sophie's office. Inside, a stack of newspapers sat on her desk. Even upside down, Isabel saw the headline: Eden's Matriarch's Secret Affair Exposed. Of course, those words—*secret affair*—leaped off the page. Isabel wasn't much for prurient accounts, but anyone would have to be intrigued. "How did this happen?" Isabel took the liberty of taking a copy and began scanning the story.

"We have no idea. I guess the reporter called Mindy last night but she was so hopped up on cold medicine that she barely remembers the conversation."

Isabel had to hand it to Mindy. For someone on cold medicine, the quote she'd given the newspaper was remarkably smart and diplomatic. She'd said precisely what Isabel would have coached her to say. Mr. Summers, however, was a different case. Clearly Jeremy had *not* had a say in the formulation of his comment. No lawyer would have allowed their client to say such a thing.

"It's so horrible. The things he said about our grandmother." Sophie plopped down on the couch. "And right before Christmas, no less. I wouldn't be surprised if people start boycotting the store. We need to hire a PR person and start fighting this. We need to put our own version of this story out there. We can't let Gram's memory be tarnished like this."

Isabel very pointedly shook her head at Emma, who was the only one paying attention to her. Sophie was dead wrong. "Actually, ladies, this is amazing news. I believe we finally have a leg up in this negotiation."

Jeremy had reached a new low—he arrived at the office having had no more than ten minutes of sleep. Granted, it was Friday morning and it had been an incredibly long week, which usually left him stumbling into the weekend. With his grueling job, he already didn't sleep well. but that had gotten progressively worse since his night with Isabel. She was this beautiful dangling string in his life, unfinished business, both personally and professionally. Situations like that had always bothered him.

When Kelsey left him, it was yet another situation where he was left with far more questions than answers. She took off with no warning, leaving only a note that he'd made her deeply unhappy. He never had the chance to ask how or why—she went right to the press and smeared him, telling them their marriage was over. It wasn't until later that Jeremy learned she'd been unfaithful, but he couldn't prove it, and the court of public opinion was squarely against him. He'd been painted as heartless, and since it was clear to Jeremy that the situation would not get better if he spoke up, he put his head down and gave in to her demands. Just to get her out of his life. He simply hadn't had the fight.

If Jeremy had learned anything over the past five days, it was that the Eden family would go down swinging. Isabel had been incredible to work with, and they'd talked every day, but she was doing nothing but push, even from her disadvantaged position. He loved the fight in her. He loved it a little too much. Every conversation with her was a turn-on, precisely why he'd made excuses all week and kept their back-and-forth on the phone.

Of course, last night before he left the office, Isabel had called him on it. "I'm beginning to think you're avoiding me, Sharp." She referred to him by his last name when she really wanted to put on the pressure. It was playful and toying and sexy. On some level, she *had* to know what it was doing to him. "Why don't we meet for a drink? Or I'll come out to Brooklyn. I still haven't met your cat. Does she have a name yet?"

"I'm calling her Cat."

"You have got to be kidding me."

Jeremy had not appreciated the inference. "No. I am a kind soul who took in an animal. But she's not staying and I don't want to get attached. Hence, I put only enough time into giving her a name as absolutely necessary. Her next owner can give her a real name."

"Any sign of the kittens?"

"Soon, I guess."

"You guess?" Isabel then went on to read him a laundry list of the things he should be looking for in Cat's behavior. He had noticed nothing she mentioned.

Jeremy's only response had been to change the subject. "My client refuses to budge, so unless you have a check for me to collect, I guess I don't see the point in a face-to-face meeting."

"I think that what you're really saying is that it's harder to negotiate with me when you and I are in the same room."

She was *not* wrong. In fact, that had been his number one fear—Isabel would get him to do something he shouldn't if they had to meet in person. Sure, he *wanted* to see her. He'd be an idiot to not want that. But was it a good idea? No. "Goodbye, Ms. Blackwell. Have a good night."

Jeremy had called Mr. Summers immediately after, but got nowhere. "There is no wiggle room," Mr. Summers said. "From where I sit, we have them right where we want them. They will pay or they'll hand over the store. They're lying and stalling."

"Every day they continue to delay is another day you have to pay me. We could expedite the process and get it all wrapped up if you were willing to concede to a payment plan. You'll still get your money, just on a different timeline."

"No. Absolutely not. And please don't ask me again."

Jeremy had a duty to give Mr. Summers whatever he wanted, no matter how punitive he was being about the whole thing. "Very well then. Have a good night."

Now back at work, he couldn't get his head screwed on right. Maybe Isabel was right. Maybe they did need to meet. He couldn't concede with anything, but he could at least see her. Let her beat him up with her words. It would likely be the only fun to be had with this case.

"Knock, knock." Jeremy's father appeared at his office door. "Good morning."

Simply hearing his father's voice these days made him cringe, and this reaction was starting to get to him. He didn't enjoy having this negative relationship. In fact, he hated it. His only real hope was to keep plugging ahead so that he could convince his dad to retire or at least taper down to far fewer hours in the office. Once they could lessen the day-to-day professional grind that was ever-present between them, Jeremy hoped they could return to being what they should be—father and son. "Hey. Good morning."

His dad took a seat on the leather sofa just inside the door of Jeremy's office. "I need to steal you for a few minutes. I spoke with Benjamin Summers on my way in."

Jeremy didn't need to hear another word to know that this was likely bad. "Why did he call you? I always make myself available to him. Always."

"He didn't. I called him."

Jeremy instantly found his hands balling up into fists. His neck went tight. His jaw, too. "He's my client. Why would you do that?"

"I'm seeing no movement on this case, Jeremy. I had to know that he was happy."

"Then ask me directly. I would've gotten you up to speed without you making me look bad to a client." Jeremy leaned forward in his chair and planted his elbow on his desk, closing his eyes and attempting to knead away the tension in his forehead with his hand. But the more he thought about it, the angrier he became. Finally, he pushed back from his desk and stood, marching over to his dad with determination. He wanted him to know that this was serious. He would not let this stand. "In fact, I'd say that what you did was wholly unprofessional. You don't just make me look bad, you make the entire firm look bad. And there's absolutely no reason for it other than the fact that you don't trust me to do what I need to do."

"I trusted you with the Patterson case. We all know how that ended."

"I was in the middle of getting a divorce and my soon-to-be ex-wife, who I thought loved me, was dragging my name through the tabloids. If I wasn't on top of my game at the time, I think it's understandable."

"You can't allow your personal life to get in the way of your job."

"And I might have let that happen one time, but it's not the case right now. Summers isn't budging on anything, and Eden's simply doesn't have the capital to pay him off in a single lump-sum cash payment, as he's demanding."

"Sometimes, it's a lawyer's job to convince a client that it's in their best interest to move the goalposts."

"I understand that. And I have tried. It's only been a few weeks. The trouble is that what I really think he wants is revenge. And I don't think that's possible."

His dad drew a deep breath through his nose, looking right at Jeremy, although in many ways it felt as though he was looking through him. Jeremy never felt that his dad truly saw him. "I just want you to get this done. Get together with Ms. Blackwell and remind her in person that she has no choice but to acquiesce to Summers's demands. I'm not buying that they don't have the cash. The Edens' war chest has to run deep."

Jeremy nodded. "I'll get it done. But it's not because you decided to interfere. I have it under control. I wish you knew that."

His dad stood, which was a great relief to Jeremy. Hopefully this meant he was leaving. "I don't care what it takes. Lock yourselves up in a room until there's only one person left standing."

Jeremy fought back a grin, which at least helped the tightness in his neck go away. How he would love a negotiation with Isabel that involved them locked away. The tougher she proved herself to be, the more he wanted to show her that he could match her intensity. In every way. "I'll suggest it."

"And another thing, you need to be careful with this Blackwell woman. I looked into her history and she's worked with some very high-level but shady clients. There's no telling what she'll pull to make Summers go away. We should be ready to torpedo her in the press if necessary."

Jeremy took a step forward. "Dad. No." Even he was surprised at his protective response. He might not know Isabel very well, but he didn't want his dad to go after her. Not like that. As someone who'd been taken down by the tabloids, Jeremy knew firsthand exactly how brutal it was. He didn't want that for anyone. Jeremy wasn't going to fault Isabel for the things she'd had to do professionally. He knew very well how lawyers could get pushed into a corner by a client and have no real choice but to work their way out. It was how you got ahead. It was how you made a name for yourself. "We're not doing that. It's unseemly and unnecessary."

"You're too soft, Jeremy. Always have been. You let Kelsey walk all over you. You're letting Summers do it to you, too."

I loved Kelsey. And I'm trying to make my client happy. "I'll get it done without torpedoing anyone. I will get both sides to meet somewhere in the middle."

His dad pursed his lips, a sign that he remained un-convinced. "It'd better be a lot closer to what Summers wants than the middle."

"It will be."

His dad turned to leave. No handshake. No pat on the shoulder. Just one lawyer leaving another lawyer's office. But he stopped when he reached the doorway. "Have you and your mother talked about the tree-trim-ming party?"

Christmas. Jeremy was so knee-deep in this case, his mother was the only thing reminding him that the holiday was just around the corner. "We did. A few days ago. Although there's not much to talk about, is there? We've been doing this every year on December 23 for as long as I can remember."

"And it's my job as your father to make sure you're going to be there. You're the only child and your mom looks forward to that night all year long."

"I will not disappoint her."

Jeremy's dad had hardly been gone a minute before Jeremy's phone rang. His heart sped up when he saw the caller ID. It was Isabel. "Hey there. Calling to give me a hard time about the cat again?"

"Have you seen the papers?" Isabel's voice could sometimes be cutting, but her tone was particularly icy.

"I haven't. I never read them."

"I suggest you do it right now. You can look online. Do a search for Eden's Department Store. I'm sure it'll come right up."

Jeremy took a seat at his desk. "Can I call you back when I'm done?"

"I'd rather wait on the line and hear your reaction."

This couldn't be good. "Ten minutes. I'll call you back. I promise." He ended the call and did exactly what she suggested. When the headline popped up in the search results, Jeremy's stomach sank so low it felt like it was at his knees. The words "secret affair" jumped right out at him.

Jeremy only had time to scan the article. He wanted to call Mr. Summers before he spoke to Isabel and he knew she'd hold him to the promise of ten minutes. The story laid out the facts as the two parties generally understood them. The bad of it was that these details had now become public information. The worst of it was the comments from Mr. Summers as contrasted with those from Mindy Eden. Mindy's only comment was, "Mr. Summers has made a claim and we're doing everything we can to negotiate with him in good faith. My sisters and I loved our grandmother very much and want everyone to know that she was a generous and kind person with a big heart."

Mr. Summers's comment wasn't quite so delicate. "Victoria Eden barged into my parents' marriage and destroyed it. She was a vile money-hungry woman who handed her naive granddaughters a business wrongly built on my father's money. I will get restitution if it's the last thing I do."

Jeremy physically winced when he reread it. Then he picked up the phone and called his client. "Mr. Summers. I saw your quote in the newspaper today. You have painted us into a corner."

"That reporter misquoted me."

"You might have to prove that to me. Do you know who fed the story to the papers in the first place?"

"I don't."

Jeremy wasn't convinced, but he had no evidence that his client had started this. "Okay, then. I'm calling to let you know that the Eden's team has read the article and they are not happy about the things you said. They could easily countersue you for defamation of character."

"You can't defame the dead. I looked it up."

"Ah, but survivors can make a claim that the defamation of their dead relative reflects on their reputation. Knowing Ms. Blackwell's previous legal work, I have no doubt she will make exactly that argument." Jeremy took in a deep breath and kept going. "Also, the Eden sisters are immensely popular in the city of New York. They are in the tabloids all the time. People love them and their store. So if you think that you could somehow get somewhere by bad-mouthing them to the press, you were sorely mistaken. Public opinion is important, Ben. And you have officially hurt your own chances by trying to mess with the Eden heiresses."

Mr. Summers cleared his throat. "What do you suggest I do? Call the reporter?"

"What's done is done. Nobody reads retractions, anyway. I want you to give me permission to negotiate with Eden's. You're going to have to give a little."

A distinct grumble came from the other end of the line. "Promise me you'll give up as little as possible."

"I'll do my best." Jeremy said goodbye and hung up, wasting no time returning Isabel's call. "I'm sorry," he said when she answered. "I saw the article. He claims he was misquoted, but regardless, people are reading it and I'm sorry that it happened in the first place. We need to get this hashed out."

"I can't negotiate with you if you won't give in on anything, Sharp."

He caught himself smiling. How could she do that when he was as stressed as could be? "Will you please stop calling me that? You've seen me naked. Can we go with Jeremy?"

"Are we starting negotiations already? Because I think you know that you're now the one at a disadvantage. Which means that technically, I can probably call you whatever I want."

Jeremy sat back in his chair and glanced out the window. It was starting to snow. He was tired. He really just wanted to get home. "If you're going to call me something bad, I think you should say it to my face."

"Oh, so now you'll meet with me in person? Now that you're forced to do it? That doesn't say much about your good faith, Jeremy."

Good God, it made heat rush through him to hear her say his first name. Inviting her to his place was not a great idea. But he had to get this done, get his dad and Mr. Summers off his back, and well, there was the matter of Cat, too. Isabel seemed to know what she was talking about when it came to his feline houseguest. "I know. I know. You were right all along. I owed you this meeting days ago. You can come to Brooklyn and meet Cat and we'll get things worked out."

"Actually, I was about to get on a plane back to DC. I've been kicked out of my hotel for the weekend and there are no vacancies this close to Christmas. My brother and Mindy both have some dreadful cold, so I don't want to stay with them. I can't afford to get sick."

Jeremy's mind was racing. He had more than enough room for Isabel. But could he resist her for a night or two? "I could put you up. If it's just for the weekend. In your own room, of course."

"You have that kind of space at your place?"

Jeremy wanted to keep things simple. He wasn't about to explain to Isabel that he had a big empty house because he'd been stupid enough to hope that someday he and his wife would have children. "I do. Plenty of room."

"Okay, then. Text me the address and I'll be there a little after noon, suitcase in hand."

Eight

Isabel had no idea what to expect when she got out of the car in front of Jeremy's brownstone. Overhead, the early-afternoon sky had darkened with clouds and big, fat flakes were falling steadily. Ahead, an ornate wrought iron gate awaited, with a long flight of stairs up to a beautiful arched wood door. It was straight out of a movie, but Isabel couldn't help but notice that Jeremy's neighbors all had Christmas wreaths or holiday garland adorning their facade. Not Jeremy. Not the guy who couldn't be bothered to give a cat a proper name. Which was just fine with Isabel. It wasn't like she was doing much better with celebrating the holiday.

She rang the bell and waited for Jeremy to answer. When he unlatched the lock and opened the door, she was presented with an image she admired a little too much—Jeremy with his salt-and-pepper temples wearing a black sweater and dark jeans. "You weren't kidding about the suitcase." He gestured with a nod.

"I never joke about imposing on someone for a night or two. Are you sure this is okay? Are you sure you have enough room?"

Jeremy rolled his eyes and reached for her bag. "I wouldn't extend the invitation if I didn't have the space. I've put up plenty of clients at the house."

"But never opposing counsel, I'm guessing." Isabel followed him inside, where a square of beautifully restored ebony penny-tile floor marked the landing. From this first peek, his home was a showplace, every detail exceptional. Above, the ceiling soared with graceful moldings, lit up by vintage fixtures of seeded glass and rich bronze. To her left, a staircase with neat white treads and a scrolled black railing led to the floor above, then doubled back, climbing to yet another level. Ahead, a glossy dark wood floor stretched the full length of the house, past what appeared to be living room and kitchen, ending when it reached tall leaded windows through which she saw only snow-dusted trees. Taking this all in felt like more than a view of Jeremy's residence. It felt like a look into his soul. For the man who seemed to bristle at any personal burden, keeping this home had to be, on some level, a labor of love.

He closed the door behind her, set down her bag and came up beside her, giving her a whiff of his irresistible smell. It was like the finest bourbon, rich and warm without any trace of booziness. "Actually, you'd be wrong about that. I did a negotiation here when another lawyer had a long layover at JFK. His flight got canceled and he ended up spending the night."

Isabel felt a little better about the propriety of this

now. Although given her history with Jeremy, their situation wasn't *exactly* the same. "I see."

"No need to be jealous," Jeremy said. "He wasn't anywhere near as cute as you."

Isabel blushed and smiled, but then a spark in his eye caught her gaze and she was immobilized by the zap of electricity only Jeremy could deliver. Mere inches separated them, reminding her body of how blissful it was to be pressed against him, comb her fingers through his thick hair and kiss him. The fact that he was tossing around words like *cute* wasn't making him any easier to resist.

"I hate that it's this close to Christmas and we have to do this," he said, leaning against the stair railing.

"As far as I'm concerned, as long as the fire alarm doesn't go off, this is a vacation."

"Brooklyn *is* lovely this time of year." It was Jeremy's turn to smile, but that only made her want him more. She was going to have to learn to ignore the four or five hundred irresistible traits he seemed to have. Too bad she needed the negotiations ahead to go smoothly. A little jerkish behavior on his part might help stem her personal tide of desire.

Isabel laughed. "It's fine. I don't celebrate Christmas anyway."

"Jewish?"

She shook her head. "No. Just a habit I got into a long time ago."

He pressed his lips together and nodded. "Come on. I'll show you the place."

Jeremy provided a quick tour of the main floor—a comfortable living room with chocolate-brown leather furniture in front of a stately fireplace with a carved white stone surround that had to be an antique. The kitchen was a cook's delight with a generous center is-land topped with Carrara marble and custom cabinets of creamy gray. The sink overlooked a courtyard off the back of the house, with a patio shielded from the outside world by a row of snow-flocked Italian cypress trees, the kind you see growing alongside the roads of Tuscany.

Isabel went to the window to admire Jeremy's out-door retreat, an uncommon luxury, even in Brooklyn. "It's so lovely out there. It must be amazing to sit out there in the spring or summer with a book."

Jeremy came right up behind her and Isabel stayed impossibly still, keenly aware of her breaths as they filled her lungs. This house was a magical place, an oasis of calm and beauty in the middle of a bustling me-tropolis, and its owner a little too enticing. "Actually, it's even better in the fall, when there's a nip of cold in the air. I get the firepit going and can sit outside for hours."

That sounded like sheer heaven to Isabel. "The house is beautiful. Truly stunning." She dared to turn around and face him. In the natural light coming from the win-dow, he was somehow even more handsome. More kiss-able.

"Thank you. It was a big project. It did not look like this when we bought it."

We, meaning he and his wife. She really didn't want Jeremy to know that she'd gone digging into his private history, so she kept that detail to herself. "Oh?"

He stuffed his hands into his pockets and cast his sights down at the floor. "Yeah. I was married until a few years ago. She really wanted a fixer-upper. I wanted a lot of space, so this was the perfect choice."

Before Isabel had a chance to comment, in traipsed an adorable orange tabby, clearly taking her time with her sizable belly. "Oh my God. That must be Cat."

"Unless I somehow managed to get another one, yes."

Isabel rushed over to her, crouched down and offered her hand. Cat rubbed up against the kitchen island, then did the same to Isabel's fingers. She immediately began to purr, pacing back and forth and brushing Isabel's knees with her tail. "She's so sweet. And so friendly." Isabel went ahead and sat on the floor, Cat purring even more loudly now that Isabel was able to pet her with both hands.

"Yeah. She's been coming to my back door for a while now. I saw her the other morning and it was so cold out, I couldn't leave her out there. My housekeeper put up flyers in the neighborhood and the veterinarian said she isn't microchipped, so we don't know who she belongs to."

"Must just be a neighborhood cat. We had a few of those around when I was growing up. My mom was crazy about cats." Isabel looked up at Jeremy. "They all ended up living at our house in one form or another. Even the ones who were too skittish to come inside got taken to the vet and immunized and fixed. My mom bankrolled it all."

"Wow."

Isabel's heart felt heavy just thinking about her mom. In her mind, she could see her out on their back patio, dishing up wet food for any cat who cared to show up. She talked to them all, gave them all names. She was a woman who was so full of love that showering her kids and husband with it simply wasn't enough. It said a lot about her—Isabel and Sam had never gone a day without feeling truly loved by their mom. "I need to get a kitty when I find a place." She'd never taken the time to get one when she lived in DC, but now that she was shifting her life in a more meaningful direction, a cat or even a few were an obvious choice.

"I know where you can get a pretty cute orange one."

Isabel grinned and looked Cat in the face. "If I adopt you, you're getting a new and better name. No question about that."

"Go for it."

"Are you seriously not going to keep her?" Isabel asked, getting up from the floor. "She has such a wonderful personality and she seems to be comfortable here."

Cat meowed and rubbed up against Jeremy's leg.

"I'm just not a pet person. My life is so crazy with work, it's hard to imagine caring for another living thing."

Isabel nodded. She'd felt that way for a long time. Not anymore. "Right. Work. I guess you'd better show me to my room so we can get something accomplished today."

Having Isabel in his home—a woman he'd kissed, laughed with, made love to and even argued against—was leaving Jeremy off-balance. A different energy had tiptoed into his private world, and it was both confusing and exhilarating to experience. There was just enough inkling of his past to make him again question what in the world he was doing by allowing himself to be so drawn to her. He and Isabel might be opponents professionally, but there was no denying that they could effortlessly slip into comfortable conversation. They seemed to naturally fall in sync. There was a part of him, deep in his core, that craved that so badly he would do anything to have it. But a bigger part of him had hardened around his needs and desires. That shell was there to protect him, but it was exhausting to carry around all day. He could set it aside when he was at home, and with the snow coming down outside and the weekend stretched out before them, he was in no mood to put it back on again.

With her suitcase in tow, he led her upstairs to the guest room, carrying it inside and setting it down on a bench at the foot of the bed. "It's no Bacharach, but the mattress is incredibly comfortable."

"I'd say it's a big step up for me. I haven't heard a single fire alarm since I got here." Isabel took her handbag and laptop bag and placed them on the bed. She smoothed her hand over the butter-soft duvet. "Ooh. Nice."

Just like the night they met, Jeremy was having to remind himself to slow down. It would be way too easy to kiss her right now and show her exactly how nice that bedding was. "You have your own bath." He traipsed over to the door and flipped on the light for her. When he turned back, she was sitting on the edge of the bed, looking as perfect as he could imagine.

"Thank you. Seriously. This works out great for me, and not just because I needed a place to sleep. I'm eager to get this case squared away. It's of monumental importance."

"To the Eden family or to you?"

"Take your pick. Yes, it's a job, and I'm being paid well to do it, but over the course of the last few weeks, Mindy and her sisters have been amazing to me. They've even invited me to celebrate Christmas with them."

"I thought you didn't celebrate."

"I haven't made the effort, but that doesn't mean I won't take part. I love this time of year and I used to be the sort of person who lived for every minute of

Christmas. It's just been a while since I took much joy in it. Like a bad habit, which I suppose is possible for anyone to fall into. Something doesn't feel as good as it used to and so you turn your back on it."

That got the gears in his head going. It was an incredibly insightful thing to say. Jeremy didn't want to tread too heavily on Isabel's personal life, but he was curious. "Any particular reason it stopped feeling good? Work? Career?"

"Work definitely kept me away from it, but this started way before that. My mom. And my dad." She pulled in a breath through her nose, her shoulders rising up to her ears. "They both passed away the same year. It's just been Sam and me since then."

"Oh, wow. I'm so sorry. I didn't know."

She nodded and painted a smile on her face, like she felt a need to comfort him. "So that's why it's important to me to make the Eden sisters happy. You don't luck into a new family very often."

"That sounds nice. A tidy little package." Jeremy decided against giving in to his greatest inclination at the moment, which was to express the depths of his skepticism. In his experience, families like the Edens would turn their backs on you just as easily as they welcomed you in. "Your brother must be part of this for you, too."

"Absolutely. I love seeing him happy for once in his life, and he's so over the moon for Mindy. They are so in love, it's amazing. I doubt they'll ever get around to planning a real wedding. They just want to get the show on the road."

"I wish them the best of luck."

"Don't you mean happiness?"

"Personally? I think luck plays a much bigger role." Isabel reached out with her foot and knocked it against his calf. "Hey. That's not nice. They aren't even married yet and you're acting like they're getting ready for a divorce."

Funny, but he never fully appreciated just how pessimistic he'd become until someone took the time to pick apart his words. "You're right. You're absolutely right. Just because I got burned doesn't mean that some people don't have a happy ending."

Isabel reached into her purse and pulled out a lip balm, glossing it over her sumptuous lips. "Sorry. It's so dry out this time of year."

Jeremy cleared his throat, trying to keep from admiring her mouth.

"And it's okay that you're down on love," she continued. "I get it. I've been burned a few times, too."

"Oh yeah? Anybody I know?"

Isabel smirked. "Like I would actually tell you. And no, I'm guessing you don't know him. He was…" She pursed her lips and furrowed her brow. "Let's just say that he wasn't much for the idea of commitment."

He nodded, knowing all too well what it was like to be on the business end of someone who was willing to take promises and devotion and toss them in the trash. "That's a problem for a lot of guys." It didn't used to be an issue for Jeremy at all. He was once the guy who said "I love you" at the drop of a hat. He used to be the sort of man who made romantic gestures any day of the week, not just on Valentine's Day, Christmas and anniversaries. But when you're endlessly giving, and that generosity is labeled as "not enough," it's hard to see the point in making an effort. At his age, Jeremy wasn't convinced it would ever be worth it to try.

"I was probably asking too much of this guy. But it was just the situation we were in. I try not to harbor too many bad feelings about it. Holding on to that stuff will eat you alive."

"What was he like? The guy who couldn't commit?"

Surprise crossed Isabel's face. "Why do you want to know?"

Jeremy shrugged it off as trivial, but he was so interested in the answer he wasn't sure he could take it if she declined. Perhaps it was because he was still trying so damn hard to figure out what made her tick. "I don't know. Curious, I guess."

She got up from the bed, placed her hand on his shoulder and peered up into his eyes. "Don't worry. He wasn't nearly as cute as you."

Jeremy fought to hold back the full force of the smile that wanted to spread across his face. He loved their back-and-forth. He loved talking to her. For the first time in his entire career, he couldn't have been more excited about negotiations if he tried. "Honestly, I'm surprised you ever had a single man walk away from you. You seem like the type of woman who does the burning."

"I may run hot, but I know better than to set a good thing on fire."

Jeremy swallowed hard.

"And on that note," she said, pulling a legal pad out of her laptop bag, "I think we should get to work."

Nine

The snow kept falling, and Isabel and Jeremy kept working. In the moments when the negotiation grew particularly complicated or even contentious, both Isabel and Jeremy would stare out the window of his home office, watching the fat flakes drift to earth. They were hypnotic and calming, and they both seemed to need the escape, and what a perfect setting, tucked away in Jeremy's cozy office, the room lined with books and decorated with masculine furniture in dark wood and leather.

"It's really coming down out there." Jeremy tossed a pen onto the small conference table they were working at and leaned back in his office chair. He stretched his arms high over his head, causing the hem of his sweater to inch up, revealing a peek of his stomach.

Isabel was nothing if not incredibly distracted by this subtle reminder that her hands, and her mouth for that matter, had once been all over his incredible torso. "It is. The sky's getting dark, too."

Chair tilted back at an angle, Jeremy consulted his watch. "It's nearly five. Do you want to keep going? Or we could take a break."

Isabel flipped through her notes—they'd made so much progress on a compromise for the interest calculations on the loan repayment, along with a schedule for getting Mr. Summers his money. But there were other options she was hoping she'd convince Jeremy to run by his client. "Depends on how generous you're feeling about talking through the alternate forms of repayment I've proposed."

"We've been over this, Isabel. Do you really think that's a good idea? Give my client a chunk of Eden's in exchange for the loan? Right now, both parties despise each other."

"Ten percent is hardly a chunk. It's not like your client would have any control. Just enough to make him a tidy sum every year."

"I really don't see it. With the volatility in retail, I'd have a hard time advising him to take that."

"The store is doing great."

He was still sitting with his chair leaned all the way back, hands clasped and resting on top of his head. He raised both eyebrows and looked down his nose at her. It was inexplicably hot. "If it was truly doing great, you'd be able to fork over the money and we wouldn't be discussing this at all."

"What about a piece of the online business? Would you be happier with that?"

"I'd need to see the numbers."

"Okay, then. Let's get it done."

"Such a shark. Gotta keep swimming, huh?"

"We're so close to figuring this out."

An hour later, everything but the smallest of details had been ironed out. "Did we really just do that?" Jeremy asked, seeming incredulous.

"We did." Isabel surveyed the landscape of the meeting table, which was strewn with papers, files and notes. She couldn't help but feel at least a little jubilant, even though she knew from experience that things could fall apart any time. For now, she would be happy. She held up her hand and reached across the table. "High five?"

"Yes." Jeremy smiled and smacked his hand against hers. "Good job."

From the doorway, Cat meowed loudly, then padded her way to Jeremy. It was at least the fifth or sixth such interruption.

"She seems restless," Isabel said. "I wonder if it's close to kitten time. Has she nested anywhere in the house?"

Jeremy reached down to show Cat some affection. "I have no clue what you're talking about."

"Nesting. Finding herself a safe and cozy spot to have the kittens."

"The vet had me put a blanket in a cardboard box, but I can't get her to stay in it. She's been sleeping on the floor of my closet since she got here."

It was adorable how truly clueless Jeremy was about this. "My guess is she's planning on giving birth in there."

"Seriously?" His eyes went wide with horror. "In my closet?"

"Why don't you show me?"

"Yeah. Absolutely. No more reason to hang out in here today."

Jeremy got up from his chair and Isabel followed

him out of the room, down the hall to the last door on the left. Inside was a magnificent and sumptuous bedroom, tastefully decorated with a warm touch. The bed seemed to go on forever, with a charcoal-gray duvet and plump pillows. Overhead, a wrought iron chandelier gave the space a soft glow. The windows, overlooking the back patio, brought in the perfect amount of natural light.

"No wonder you've never needed a sleep mask. This room is so peaceful. I think I could sleep in here for days."

Jeremy smiled. "You don't need that thing at home, do you? I mean, if you aren't staying in a hotel?"

Isabel brushed her fingers on the silky soft bedding. "Depends on how worn out I am." She instantly regretted her choice of words, especially when Jeremy cocked an eyebrow.

Cat sauntered into the room and darted right into the closet.

"I'm telling you, you're about to have a bunch of kittens in with your designer suits and Italian leather shoes." Isabel nodded at the closet. "May I?"

"Please. Be my guest."

Isabel stepped inside and Jeremy was right behind her, flipping on the light. Either Jeremy was an incredibly smart man or his ex had been highly concerned with her appearance. His closet had the sort of lighting you find at a cosmetics counter, gentle enough to make anyone look amazing. Which of course meant that Jeremy appeared flawless, even with his stubble showing the effects of late day.

"She's been sleeping down here." Jeremy pulled back a row of dress shirts to reveal the back corner, where sure enough, Cat had made herself a bed. "Hey. Wait a minute. That's my favorite T-shirt." He crouched down. Isabel knelt next to him. "I wondered where that went. I took it off the other morning to take a shower after my workout and never saw it again."

Isabel was momentarily stuck on the mental image of Jeremy in the shower, with droplets of water on his chest. She'd never wanted so badly to have a bar of soap in her hands. "Did you think it just disappeared? She clearly stole it. Dragged it in here to make her bed."

He shook his head in disbelief. "I figured I must have tossed it in the hamper and didn't remember doing it. I have a lot on my mind these days."

She couldn't help but notice the weighty drag in his voice. Not putting much thought into it, she placed her hand on the center of his back to comfort him, but that caused him to look at her, his gray eyes showing mysterious flecks of blue in this light. If they were a window into his soul, she wished she could see some true happiness in there. She was desperate for a reason *not* to kiss him. Make him happy. She could do that, at least for a little while, with the snow falling heavily outside.

Jeremy cleared his throat and returned his sights to Cat's nest. "I can't believe she stole my stinky, sweaty T-shirt."

"It means she loves you. Pets love things that smell like their owners."

"I'm not her owner. This is temporary." He stood up and stepped away, as if that could somehow extricate him from the situation.

"Uh-huh. Tell that to Cat."

He turned back to her, kneading his forehead. "How do I get her to not have the kittens in here? Won't it make a big mess?"

"First off, you don't get her to do anything. If she's

happy and feels safe there, you should let her do her thing. You do not want to get into a battle of wills with a mama cat. Second, we can put down an old towel or two and you can toss them out once the kittens arrive."

"What about the T-shirt?"

She patted his shoulder in consolation. "I think that's pretty much a goner."

"I never should have let her in that morning."

"Oh, Jeremy, no. You had to do it. She could have died out there. Her and her kittens. You did the right thing."

He twisted his lips, which made her think he was considering the other side of the coin she'd just shown him. "You really are good at forming an argument."

She loved not only knowing that she could show him when he was wrong, but that he would actually listen. She found that a rare quality in a man, especially a lawyer. "Thanks. I appreciate that. Now what do I have to do to convince you to open a bottle of wine?"

"You don't. It's six on a Friday and there's cause for celebration. I can't believe it's taken us this long to get around to it."

"You're speaking my language. I'm just going to grab my purse from the guest room. I can't live this time of year without lip balm."

Down the hall they went, making a brief stop so Isabel could fetch her bag, then descending the stairs and back to the kitchen. Isabel perched on a barstool at the kitchen island and watched Jeremy go to work. "Red or white?" he asked.

She glanced out the patio windows. The snow was still pretty and fluffy, but the wind had started to whip. "Considering the weather? Definitely red."

"Perfect. I have a Spanish rioja that's absolutely delicious."

"Sounds amazing."

Jeremy opened a tall cabinet at the far end of the kitchen, which had a waist-high wine chiller below and diagonal bottle storage above, the entire setup going from floor to ceiling.

"It's like your own little cellar."

"There's a real cellar downstairs on the ground floor. I got really into wine about ten years ago. I was starting to wonder if I was going to be a bachelor forever, so I figured I might get a hobby." He brought the bottle to the island and expertly opened it, then pulled two glasses from an upper cabinet near the fridge.

"And then you met the woman you married and the bachelor was reformed?" Isabel was indeed curious about the notion of Jeremy seeing himself as never getting married, and that apparently changing at some point.

"It had nothing to do with being reformed. I was on board from the beginning."

"Head over heels?"

"I guess you could say that, but she also had a way of sweeping you up into her world. Or maybe sucking you into the eye of her personal hurricane is a more apt analogy."

"She sounds lovely."

Jeremy laughed. "It happened fast. That's all I can tell you. I think she liked the fact that I wasn't the typical Manhattan playboy. She'd dated a lot of guys like that." He filled their glasses and handed her one. "Cheers. To not talking about my ex-wife."

Isabel took a quick sip. "It's delicious. Thank you. But not so fast." She had questions. A lot of questions.

Things weren't entirely adding up. "Okay, confession time. I looked you up on the internet after the first meeting at your office."

"Of course you did."

"You did the same thing to me, did you not?"

He brought his glass around to the other side of the island, but didn't sit with her. "Come on. If we're going to talk about this, we're going in the living room. I'd rather be comfortable while discussing unpleasant subjects." He didn't wait for her reply, but instead wandered off.

Isabel followed in earnest, worried she'd hurt him. "I don't mean for it to be unpleasant. I'm just curious because what you're telling me isn't matching up with what I read."

He set his glass and the bottle on the coffee table and began building a fire in the fireplace, crumpling up newspaper, then stacking logs across it and striking a match. She stood and watched him work. "Isabel. As a former Washington, DC, lawyer with a bunch of very high-profile clients, I have to think that you would know better than anyone that what's in the paper isn't always the full story. A lot of it has to do with who gets there first."

"Well, sure. Things get twisted. But they don't usually take a one-eighty."

He stood and brushed his hands off on his pants, then pointed to the couch. "Please. Sit."

She felt like she was in trouble, and just like upstairs when he'd admonished her during negotiations, she found it incredibly sexy. "Yes, sir." She did as she was told, sinking down into the comfortable cushions. The fire began to crackle and blaze. Between the wine and Jeremy, she never wanted to leave the room.

"Actually, a one-eighty is the perfect way to spin something." He took a long draw of his wine and Isabel admired his profile in the golden glow of the fire. "It's a believable story since it's true, so you simply take whatever you're guilty of and accuse the other person of it."

"So if I'm a woman who wants out of my marriage, but I'm worried about how that will be perceived, I tell the press that my husband isn't the settling-down type, or that he isn't loving."

He turned to her, his eyes full of resignation. She'd seen this expression from him before, the look of someone who was hurt and sad, but who had learned to live with it. Isabel hated the idea that anyone would have to live that way, especially a man as extraordinary as Jeremy. "Precisely."

Isabel took another sip of her wine, her mind still churning. No wonder the things she'd read about Jeremy had seemed so off. "I almost hate to ask this…"

A corner of his mouth shot up in a wry smile. "You don't hate to ask anything."

She leaned forward and grasped his forearm. "No. I really don't want to upset you. Truly. I don't. You've been nothing but gracious in letting me stay here."

"Go for it. I have no secrets."

Isabel found herself hoping that was really true. Because every minute with Jeremy was starting to feel like the start of something.

I really don't want to upset you. Even though Isabel was capable of a good sneak attack, he was sure of what she was about to ask. He'd never spoken about it to anyone. His parents spent their time making themselves the victims by claiming their own embarrassment at the way their son had been dragged through the tabloids. His friends made themselves scarce after the divorce. Nobody wanted to go out to dinner with the guy who was getting snide comments from perfect strangers who'd sided with the socialite. So Jeremy kept it all bottled up inside, another attempt at holding on to his pride.

"I shouldn't ask," she said. "Let's talk about something else."

"No. Please. Just do it. Let's put the whole thing to rest. Honestly, it'll be a relief."

"Was it all a one-eighty? There was a suggestion that you'd been unfaithful." She held up a finger. "And before you answer, I want to make it clear that I will not judge you. Everyone has their reasons for doing things."

Jeremy had every reason in the world to keep a wall up with Isabel, both personal and professional. But the reality of their situation was that they were close to wrapping up negotiations. Their clients would come away happy. As for the personal side, she was so easy to talk to. It had been like that from the moment he'd met her. There was something almost therapeutic about baring his soul to her. "Everything she did to sabotage our marriage, or every unpleasant feeling she had, she put on me. The thing about not being made for commitment, the thing about not being the settling-down type. So yes, there was infidelity, and it was all hers."

"I'm so sorry. That's such a terrible betrayal."

She wasn't wrong. It had been. But now that it was years later and he couldn't imagine himself with Kelsey at all, the pain wasn't quite so persistent. "I didn't find out about the affair until after she left. I've somehow convinced myself that it wasn't that bad because I didn't know about it while it was going on. That might be some faulty logic at work."

"Those are the things we say when we're trying to protect ourselves. There's only so much hurt a person can endure."

"Is there really a maximum? Sometimes life keeps throwing stuff at you, whether you want it or not."

"I have to ask why you didn't stand up to her. You had no comment in the article I read. I have a hard time imagining you taking that lying down. A lawyer always fights back."

"But a lawyer also knows when to quit. Some battles just aren't worth it. Plus, who wants to get into a fight over love? In the newspapers? Either it's there between you or it isn't. You can't just pull it out of thin air. And it wasn't like I was going to convince her to come back."

He watched as she sank farther back against the cushions, wineglass in hand. What kind of pain had she endured? Was that why she sometimes seemed like such a mystery? "Now that I told you my sad story, I want to know if I can ask about the guy who burned you."

She looked down into the rioja in her glass, swirling it round and round. "Bad timing. It wasn't all his fault. It was an unfortunate situation."

"Those are an awful lot of vague details."

"Okay, then. Here are the specifics. I got pregnant and he panicked. He couldn't handle it. We'd only been going out about six months and it had been very casual." She breathed deeply and sighed. "So I did him a favor and I called it off. I already knew that I wanted to have a baby, so I decided I would just deal with it on my own, but then life decided to throw me the cruelest of curveballs when I lost the pregnancy." Her voice cracked when she uttered those last few words. The room fell impossibly quiet.

"I'm so sorry. That must have been awful."

"Nobody knows about it. I mean, he must have figured it out when I never had a baby, but it's not like he ever checked in on me or asked."

"You never told your brother what happened?"

A sad smile crossed her lips. "You know, I thought about it, but I don't think Sam would have dealt very well with it. I think it would have made him feel helpless, and I didn't see any good in that. So I dusted myself off and I went back to work and I tried to forget."

She was so tough. So resilient. No wonder she made such an excellent attorney. "Back to being a shark?"

"That's the last thing I am." Isabel waved it off.

"A beautiful shark, of course."

Her eyes flashed in the soft light from the fireplace. "Flattery will get you everywhere."

"I'm no dummy."

"And I'm serious when I say I'm not a shark. It's an act. Acting is how you win. You can't tell me you aren't the same way."

"I'm not acting right now."

Cocking her head to one side, a dark strand of her hair fell across her cheek. The way she narrowed her sights on him made him feel as vulnerable as he'd felt in a very long time. "I believe that. But when you're working, you have on your armor. You're ready for battle. And if I'm being completely honest, I think you were playing an act the night we met."

Jeremy reached for the wine bottle and poured more into her glass before topping off his own. "Isn't everyone on their best behavior when they first meet? Trying to impress the other person?"

"Yes, and that's why I didn't want to talk about work. I wanted us to just be a man and a woman having a conversation."

"And you think I was faking my way through it? I guarantee you, I didn't fake a damn thing up in your room. That was all legit."

Isabel grinned, her cheeks flushing pink. "I believe that. I do. It's the first part of the night when you were acting. Playing the part of the fun-loving guy."

"Hey. I love fun. I just don't have a lot of it."

"But you're not as cavalier as you try to make yourself seem. You act like nothing bothers you, but you aren't like that. You're thoughtful and serious." She took another sip of her wine, then scooted closer on the couch. "And now that you've told me the story about your marriage, I know why. You're trying to hide your pain from everyone."

Jeremy swallowed back the emotion of having her see right through him. "I just don't want to feel hurt anymore. That's all that is. So I pretend like it's not there and I figure it'll eventually go away."

Slowly and evenly, she nodded, gazing up at him with her sweet and tenderhearted eyes. He loved that she had so many sides, that she was a woman of many facets. She could be determined one minute and gentle the next. "I know. I just want you to know that you don't have to pretend with me." She ran her finger around the rim of her wineglass. "We're nearly off the clock."

"Just a man and a woman having a conversation."

"No hiding."

Two simple words from Isabel and a wave of heat rose in Jeremy, starting in his thighs and rolling upward, taking hold in his hips, stomach and chest. He fixed his gaze on her, on the rise and fall of her breaths, the flush in her cheeks, the brilliant flash of life in her eyes. Electricity was arcing between them. A current. A jolt. One minute they were talking work and life and pain and now...well, he would have had to be a complete idiot to not notice that this was all leading somewhere he hadn't quite planned on.

What was it about Isabel that didn't merely tug at his heartstrings, but unraveled them? It was more than attraction, although that was its own powerful force. There was a connection between them, one that went beyond working together.

"I was hiding from you this week." The words rolled out of his mouth as if he'd planned to say them all along, which he hadn't at all, but it still felt good to own up to it. So good that he wanted to keep going. "That night at dinner, all I wanted to do was kiss you. But the pressure is on with this case and I worried I would end up sabotaging myself if I spent any time with you."

"So you invited me here because you didn't have a choice."

He shook his head. "No. I invited you because I had a reason. I finally had a legitimate reason to do what I'd wanted to do all along."

"I have an admission of my own." She sat forward, angling her body toward his.

Jeremy's pulse picked up, running along at a clip. "I'm listening."

"I thought about kissing you way before dinner. I thought about it that day in your office."

All he wanted was for her to bend at the waist and plant her soft lips on his. He wanted to feel her body pressed against his. He wanted to get lost in her and never be found. "And since then?"

"There's been a lot of inner conflict over it." She licked her lower lip and placed her wineglass on the coffee table, which felt like an ultimatum—kiss me, or don't.

Jeremy didn't want to leave any challenge from Isabel unaccepted.

Ten

Isabel was tired of waiting. She had to have Jeremy. The trouble was, the fragile parts of her ego really wanted him to make the first move. And he was being the perfect gentleman. Apparently setting aside her wineglass and biting down on her lower lip were not enough of an invitation.

She scooted closer to him on the couch, pulling her leg up all the way onto the cushion and facing him. Looking at him was both the easiest thing in the world and the most difficult—he was so handsome, it made the center of her chest burn. The fire popped and crackled, the heat warming one side of her face. He tossed back the last of his wine, as if needing liquid encouragement, and there was a very big part of her that wanted to just come out and say it—*I want you, Jeremy. Now.*

He finally placed his own glass on the table and turned to her, his eyes beautifully dark with desire. She'd wanted plenty of men in her lifetime, but none as bad as Jeremy. None so bad that it made it hard to breathe. Whether it was unfinished business or the notion of false starts, they both deserved this.

"I don't want you to feel as though I'm taking advantage," he said, reaching for her hand, caressing her fingers softly. "It's my house and you're vulnerable here."

Isabel's heart *and* body were aching for his touch. "I don't know that I've ever felt more comfortable. Anywhere." She inched herself closer until their knees were touching, then she took his other hand and raised it to her lips. Even that one touch of skin against skin left her nearly gasping for more. She had to be closer. She had to be next to him. And it had to happen now.

Isabel shifted up onto her knees and straddled Jeremy's lap. The pleased look on his face was her reward for bravery. She let her weight settle, pressing her hips into his, already the heat and need pooling between her legs. Her hands went to the hem of her sweater and she pulled it up over her head, her hair collapsing around her shoulders when she cast the garment aside. She loved falling under his appraisal, his dark eyes scanning her body. She didn't need him to tell her she was beautiful. She saw it all in his expression.

The first kiss was the softest, as if they were marking the moment. The beginning. His lips were just as firm and perfect as she remembered. Possibly more so. She set her elbows on his shoulders and dug her fingers into his thick hair, rocking her center against his. She could already feel how hard he was, even through the layers of denim between them. Their tongues wound together. He ran his across her lower lip. His warm hands roved the landscape of her back, then he finally had the good sense to remove her shirt and unhook her bra, pulling the straps forward to be rid of it. He took her breasts in his hands, cupping them completely and rolling her nipples between his fingers. Her skin gathered and grew hard beneath his touch, the perfect contrast to the softness of the kiss. But she wanted his lips and tongue everywhere, so she wrenched her mouth from his.

He took the invitation, licking and sucking one nipple, then the other, his hands squeezing her breasts firmly. Electricity zapped from her chest straight to her center, as if there were a line connecting the two. It felt so good that she wanted to close her eyes and simply languish in the sensation, but it was so hot to watch his face as he flicked his tongue against the tight buds of sensitive skin. Isabel curled her fingers into his shoulders, letting her nails dig into his skin. Jeremy's eyes popped open and he looked up at her, their gazes connecting before he took a gentle bite of her nipple. It was the perfect amount of pain, just enough to show how much he wanted her. It took every bit of pent-up desire inside her and ratcheted it up another notch.

Isabel reached down and lifted his sweater up over his head, spreading her hands across his glorious chest, firm and muscled with the perfect amount of hair. She kissed one sculpted shoulder, then across his clavicle, nestling her face in his neck, letting the stubble scratch at her nose and cheek while she inhaled his warm smell. Jeremy's hands were at both of her hips, squeezing hard and pulling her against him even more tightly. White-hot liquid heat pooled between her legs as she felt his erection against her center.

Both of his hands traveled north to the middle of her back and the next thing she knew, he had shifted her until she was lying back on the couch, the leather cool against her overheated skin. Jeremy stood and shucked his jeans and boxers, never taking his eyes off her. He was everything she wanted, long and lean and so primed for her that it was impossible to not feel lucky. She wedged her mind in the moment and focused on the physical, like the way her need picked up when she watched him take his steely length into his own hand and give it a few careful strokes. She loved seeing his own hand on his body, but it also made her desperate to touch him.

Isabel unbuttoned her jeans and lifted her hips off the couch, shimmying them and her panties down her legs. Jeremy helped her pull them from her ankles and then she was completely bare to him, ready and dying to have him inside her. "Come here," she said, her voice sounding a bit desperate.

"I want to see you touch yourself," he replied.

Isabel wasn't much of an exhibitionist, but Jeremy had her so turned on right now, she would have done anything he wanted. She dropped one foot to the floor and eased her knee up, spreading her legs. She brushed her fingertips against her chest, down along the flat plane of skin between her breasts. The anticipation on Jeremy's face was priceless. He watched her, both enthralled and speechless, standing next to her and stroking his erection. She studied what he liked, even as she relished her own touch as her fingers rode down her belly and finally between her legs.

A gasp left her lips when she touched her apex, the skin warm and slick with desire. She began to move her fingers in delicate circles, feeling as though she could rocket into space in no time at all if she wasn't careful. Jeremy lowered himself to a kneeling position before her, kissing the knee of the leg that was still up on the couch. Isabel didn't stop with the ministrations, even when it was pushing her even closer to her peak. She wanted to see what he would do next. She was desperate for it.

He kissed his way along her inner thigh and she moved her hands out of the way to comb his thick hair as he moved lower. His mouth found her center and he used his fingers to gently spread her folds and give himself better access. As hot as it was, Isabel's eyes clamped shut as he drove her to her peak with his tongue, which traveled in circles hard against her. She did her best to hold off on the pressure, but it eventually became too much, and she felt the dam break, the way her body gave in to him completely. She knocked her head back and called out as she rode out wave after wave of warmth and pleasure. On the other side of the room, the fire continued to roar, but Isabel knew that the heat coming from it was only a fraction of what Jeremy was about to give to her.

Jeremy took one more taste of Isabel, wanting to be immersed in the sensory delights of her unbelievably gorgeous body. Everything about her was soft and sweet, yet hot and carnal. If things between them never went any further than tonight, at least he'd always have the mental image of her touching herself, of her fingers rolling over her most delicate places, while the heat of the room flushed her skin with a breathtaking shade of pink.

But right now, he had more pressing needs. He had to be inside her. Isabel pulled her legs back, then knelt down next to him on the floor and pushed the coffee table a good foot or so away from them. Jeremy stretched out on the plush area rug as Isabel positioned herself between his knees, taking his throbbing erection into her hands and stroking delicately. Everything in his body went tight—his abs, his hips and thighs. She took her time and he loved watching as her slender fingers rode his length, up and down. As good as it felt, he wanted more of her, and as if she knew what he was thinking, she lowered her head and took him between her plump lips.

Her tongue was hot and wet on his skin, which was already straining from the tension. He couldn't think of another time he'd been so hard or wanted a woman so badly. He gently rolled his fingers through her silky hair as she swirled her tongue and made it nearly impossible to think about anything other than pleasure and warmth. Just when he was starting to feel as though he couldn't take much more of the pressure, Isabel released him from her mouth, kissing his lower belly.

"Don't move. I'm going to get a condom from my purse." She flitted off to the kitchen and was back in seconds, tearing open the packet and kneeling next to him. She then climbed on top of him, taking his length in her hand and guiding him inside.

As she sank down on top of him, he marveled at how well they fit together, how this was even better than that first night together, when logic said that it could never be better because the excitement of everything new tends to eclipse the familiar. They moved together, perfectly in sync, and Isabel lowered her head to kiss him. Their tongues wound together as his fingers roamed down her back to the velvety skin of her bottom, his hands encouraging her to raise her hips as far as she could, only because it felt so damn good to have her ride his entire length.

The pressure was building in his hips, and everything was pulling tight again. Isabel's breaths were ragged, but he wanted her closer before he came, so he slipped one of his hands between their bodies and found her center with his thumb. She countered with pressure of her own, pressing her pelvis into his harder and harder, grinding her body in a circle with every pass.

Isabel rounded her back, using her hips to force him closer to his peak. He clamped his eyes shut and his body gave way, pleasure pulsing and slamming into him. Isabel followed mere seconds later, burying her face in his neck and rotating her hips, making the final waves longer and even more pleasurable. She collapsed on top of him, warm and a bit sweaty, resting her head against his chest. He wrapped his arms around her tightly and kissed the top of her head over and over again. There were no words between them and Jeremy felt that was only fitting. They had exchanged plenty of them in the few short weeks they'd known each other. It was nice to get back to a place where they could let actions speak louder than words.

She rolled to his side and curled into him. He wrapped his arm around her waist and for a moment, they both got lost in the warm flicker of the fire. This was not how he'd imagined tonight going, but if he was being honest, it was everything he ever could have hoped for.

Eleven

Jeremy woke with a feeling he hadn't had in a long time—hope. He was also drunk on infatuation. Isabel was simply amazing, and last night had been unbelievable. Everything he'd thought about their sexual chemistry had been on the money. He hadn't made it up.

"Good morning, beautiful," he said, kissing her bare shoulder.

She smiled, eyes still closed, lying on her stomach. The early light of day filtered in through the windows, bathing her in a bright and beautiful glow. "Good morning."

He cozied up next to her, their naked bodies pressed together. It was so good to not wake up alone. "What do you want to do today?"

In response, Isabel's stomach rumbled loudly. "Food might be a good idea."

"We never ate last night, did we?"

She opened an eye and popped up onto her elbow.

"We did not. I feel like I should file a complaint, except you're still way ahead of the Bacharach. Not a single siren went off in the middle of the night."

"We never would've met if it weren't for that silly alarm."

She rolled to her back and clutched the covers to her chest. "We still would have met. It just would've been under far different circumstances."

Their first rendezvous had set the stage for last night, so he was immensely thankful that things had played out the way they had. "I'm glad the first time we encountered each other wasn't at the negotiating table."

"Me, too." She leaned forward and kissed him. "Now let's get some food. I'm starving."

Downstairs in the kitchen, Jeremy put some bacon in a skillet and began cracking eggs for breakfast. Cat had come downstairs for her own morning meal, which Isabel dished up for her before taking a seat at the center island. "I like watching a man cook."

"Lots of years as a bachelor," he said. "And my ex didn't cook anyway, so it was all up to me." Looking back, he should have known it was never going to last. Kelsey spent too little time in this house. She was always out, desperate for her next adventure. It had taken a long time for him to figure out that her absence wasn't about him. It was about the bottomless hole in her psyche that would always need filling.

"What did you and your wife plan to do with all of this space anyway?"

Jeremy dished up the bacon and eggs and grabbed slices of buttered toast, then ferried the plates to the island. "Madam, your breakfast is served."

Her entire face lit up when she smiled. "Thank you, sir."

He took the seat next to her. "I assumed we would have kids, and if we were going to create our dream house, it only seemed logical to me that we would have space for a growing family. That never happened, obviously. I wanted kids and she did not."

Isabel sipped her coffee, hands wrapped around the mug. "Did you guys not talk about it ahead of time? That's a pretty important topic before marriage."

"We did discuss it. I told her that I wanted a family and she said she did, too. But when it came time to try to get pregnant, she kept secretly taking her birth control pills. I guess she just never had the guts to tell me she'd changed her mind. Or she'd been lying to me all along." He was proud of himself for saying all of that without losing his cool. Something about Isabel made it so easy to confide in her. "Maybe I'm not cut out for parenthood, anyway. My own parents did not embrace their role."

"I wouldn't call your dad warm and fuzzy. At least what I saw of him."

Jeremy had to laugh, even if it was a sound born of sadness. "He's not. Neither is my mom, unfortunately. Although she has a softer edge to her. I'll give her that much. They've both always been more interested in what a person accomplishes than what kind of person they are."

"That's terrible."

"They've always been like that and I fed into it. I learned from an early age that if I did exactly what they wanted, and especially if I excelled at it, I was showered with praise. That was as close as they came to expressing affection."

"Is that why you became a lawyer?"

"Actually, it isn't. My dad wanted me to follow in

his footsteps, but it was my grandfather who inspired me to do it. He was all about the subtleties of the law and he loved the interpretation of it. He loved forming an argument." Jeremy turned to Isabel. "Very much like you, actually."

"He sounds like an awesome guy."

"He was. Those are all his law books in my office upstairs."

"So that's why you like to work here. Stay away from your dad and be surrounded by reminders of the real reason you got into this crazy business in the first place."

"Absolutely." Jeremy nodded, perhaps a little too eagerly. Isabel was an angel who'd dropped out of the sky. She understood him so naturally. "So, I was thinking, since it's Saturday and there are only a few days until Christmas, maybe we could do something holiday-related today."

"What did you have in mind? I hope not caroling. I'm a terrible singer."

"You and me both." He took another bite of his toast. "Shopping? I've already done mine. I get the same thing for my parents every year." A year's supply of monogrammed golf balls for his dad, who not only hit the links regularly, he was apt to lose them in the water hazards. For his mom, Jeremy went to Tiffany & Co. and bought the most recent offerings of earrings or a bracelet.

"I'm done, too. I got everything at Eden's. It was the first time in years that I've done that." She slid him a glance. "What about decorating? A Christmas tree?"

"I don't have an artificial one. There's a tree lot about seven or eight blocks away. Even with the snow, it's probably open. We could drag it back?"

Isabel turned and looked out the patio doors. "We don't need to buy one. You already have plenty."

"Out there?" This option had never occurred to him. Not once.

"Do you have any lights? Ornaments?"

"Well, yeah. I haven't used them since my divorce, but they're definitely still there."

"Let's decorate one of the trees out on your patio. It'll be so pretty at night. Plus you won't have to worry about Cat climbing it or messing around with it."

"You want to go out there in the cold? And decorate one of the cypress trees?"

"It's not snowing anymore. The sun is shining. It'll be nice. Plus, it'll be good to get some fresh air."

This was about the craziest idea Jeremy had ever heard. And he loved it. "We'll go hunting for everything in the attic in a little bit."

"We have all day, don't we?"

After breakfast was done and the kitchen cleaned, they trekked upstairs to the top floor of the house, where the attic was. It wasn't difficult to find the boxes of Christmas decor. They were some of the only things up there—thus was the life of the single guy with too much space. Jeremy certainly hesitated before he opened the first box. He and Kelsey had bought these decorations together, back when he believed they were building a life and would use them for years to come. Back when he'd thought that they might have kids and those children would eventually hang these ornaments on the tree. He didn't want to think about it too much as a reflection of the life he no longer had. Here with Isabel, his heart was nothing but light. If she'd never come along, these Christmas baubles might have spent many more years tucked away in an attic, collecting dust and going unused and unappreciated. It wasn't difficult to see the parallel between the boxes of ornaments and his own existence.

"I think four strands of lights will be enough. And I think these red and silver ball ornaments will stand up to the elements." Isabel tapped a fingernail against the shiny orbs. "They don't seem particularly breakable."

"Perfect."

They carried the boxes down a floor, then each went and changed into more suitable clothes for outdoors— jeans and sweaters. Back downstairs, they bundled up in boots, coats and gloves. "Do you have an extra hat I can wear?" she asked. "I don't have one with me and it looks really cold out there."

"I'm sure I have something."

Jeremy rummaged through his front coat closet, where he pulled out a red hat he'd had for years. "I haven't worn this one since college." He tugged it on her head, which pulled much of her hair over her face. With his fingers, he gently brushed it aside, tucking it neatly under the cap. She looked up at him while he did it, eyes big and bright, leaving him with only one logical thing to say. "You're so beautiful, Isabel. Truly." He was so deep in her orbit right now, it would be difficult to ever pull himself out. He wasn't sure he'd ever want to.

"You aren't half bad yourself, you know." Leaning into him, she slowly rose up onto her tiptoes and placed a soft kiss on his lips.

All he wanted to do was melt into her. Stay like this forever. *You're perfect. You're the best thing that's happened to me in recent history.* The words were right there, zipping around in his head, desperately wanting to be set free. But Jeremy knew his worst tendencies, the way he wanted to jump many steps ahead and profess his affection. It didn't matter how amazing she was. It was too soon. "Ready for our Christmas tree adventure?"

"I was born ready."

Isabel was beginning to think she'd gravely misjudged Jeremy that first night they met. Normally, she was an exceptional judge of character from the get-go. She was good at picking up on signals—the little things people do that tell you what drives them or makes them tick. The talent was part and parcel of being a lawyer and it'd been honed over the years. If anything, she should be getting better at it, not worse.

So where did she go wrong with Jeremy? Or was it simply that he was putting on an act, the one that kept him from sharing his pain with the rest of the world? She couldn't decide which it was, but also decided that it didn't truly matter. For the first time in years, she was actually enjoying herself. And she wasn't about to let her overthinking ways come between herself and a good time.

Trudging out onto the snow-covered patio with Jeremy, Isabel realized this suggestion of hers had been a bit unorthodox. "Thanks for indulging my peculiar idea."

"Are you kidding?" Jeremy asked, swiping snow from a patio table to give them a spot to put the boxes. "This is far less work than dragging a Christmas tree seven or eight blocks."

"It's more eco-friendly if you think about it, too. This tree's already here."

Jeremy trekked over to the back door and plugged in an extension cord, then returned to Isabel so they could begin stringing the lights. They worked in tandem, with her uncoiling the strands around her arm and Jeremy climbing up on a patio chair to loop them around the tree. It was a bright and sunny day, the air perfectly crisp and cold. Despite the temperature, Jeremy had opted for no hat, which gave her the perfect view of his adorable forehead wrinkles as he concentrated so intently on the task before him.

"I know it's probably my job to tell you where you missed a spot, but you're doing an amazing job," she said. "Not surprising. You're pretty much perfect at everything you do."

Jeremy looked down at her so abruptly that his sunglasses slid to the end of his nose. "You have got to be kidding."

"Um. No. I'm not."

Shaking his head in disbelief, he placed the remainder of the final strand of lights. "We'll have to wait until it's dark to see how it turned out." He then climbed down from the chair and opened one of the ornament boxes.

"I was serious about what I said. You're an amazing lawyer. Negotiating with you was one of the highlights of my entire career."

That stopped him dead in his tracks. "You're the one who's amazing." He swiped off his sunglasses and before Isabel really knew what was happening, he had his arms around her. His mouth was on hers, passionate and giving. It sent ripples of excitement through her entire body. She couldn't wait to go back inside with him.

"Wow," she muttered, sounding and feeling drunk.

"You make me want to do things like that, Isabel. You make me feel good. In every way imaginable."

Funny how making someone else happy could be such a lift to your own spirits. Not that Isabel needed a lift—she was already floating on air. "You make me feel good, too."

They finished the tree and headed back inside, stomping the snow from their boots and peeling off the winter layers. The moment clothes of any sort started to come off, it all had to go. Jeremy approached Isabel like a man on the hunt, lifting her sweater up over her head, peeling her bra strap from her shoulder and kissing her bare skin.

She shuddered, in part from his touch and in part from the ambient temperature in the room. "There's too much cold air from outside down here. Let's go upstairs to your bedroom."

He took her hand and led her through the house, zeroing in on his bed, sitting on the edge of the mattress and encouraging her to stand between his knees. He kissed her stomach, kneaded her breasts, and then pulled her down on top of him. She felt like a goddess, so admired and adored. That alone was nearly enough to send her into oblivion. The rest of their clothes were gone in a flash and they became a frantic tangle of limbs, mouths roaming and craving caresses. Isabel gasped when Jeremy drove inside her, relishing every delicious inch of him. He took deep strokes and kissed her neck, scratching at her tender skin with the stubble on his face. She wrapped her legs around his waist and used her feet to hold him tighter. It didn't take long until he left her unraveling, calling his name and breathless.

Jeremy climbed out of bed and pulled back the covers, Isabel quickly ducking under them to get warm. With the postorgasmic glow taking over, and after their eventful morning, she craved sleep. Her eyelids were heavy, her mind fuzzy. "You wore me out, Sharp. I guess all of that fresh air and sex did me in."

"Take a nap. You work like crazy and this week-end should be for relaxing. Plus, I remember that you told me the night we met that it's one of your favorite things."

Isabel grinned at the memory of them sharing their three universal truths that night. "It's the truth. I absolutely love it."

Jeremy reached over onto his nightstand for a book. "Perfect. You nap. I'll read."

When Isabel woke, she was nothing if not disoriented. Jeremy was gone, the room dark. She squinted at his clock: 5:12 p.m. She'd taken a three-hour nap, so much longer than she would normally sleep during the day. As she slowly woke, delicious smells filtered to her nose—garlic, herbs and possibly wine. Jeremy must have started dinner.

She padded down the hall to the guest room to grab a cardigan, popping into her bathroom to freshen her makeup while she was at it. Still not quite awake, she knocked one of her toiletry bags from the counter, sending the contents flying. She crouched down to pick up the mess, but her hand froze on a small box of tampons. For a moment, she stared at the blue-and-yellow swirl pattern on the package. It was as if she was standing on the edge of a realization, and reality was about to push her over the edge. *I'm late.*

Frantically, she fished her phone out of her pocket and pulled up the app she used to track her cycle. She was remarkably calm despite what the notification on her screen was telling her—she was six days late. Maybe this was the upside of having been a high-powered attorney for so long. Most panic-laden situations did not make Isabel freak out. Even when she could potentially have a very big reason for going into a tizzy.

Could she have gotten pregnant the night of the broken condom? It was the only possible explanation. Jeremy was the only man she'd been with in the last year. And if that was the case, what was she supposed to do about it? What would it mean? They were getting along amazingly and had an unbelievable chemistry, but this was going to throw everything on a fast track that Jeremy couldn't possibly be prepared for. If he'd gone into a panic over the broken condom, she couldn't imagine him reacting well to news of an actual baby.

She sucked in a deep breath. She had to get her act together. Phone still in hand, she flicked over to a different app and placed an order from the chain drugstore nearby. They could deliver her a pregnancy test tomorrow, along with a few other things to help hide the contents of the order, and she could take it Monday morning if she hadn't started her period by then. It was the responsible thing to do, most likely completely unnecessary. She typed in Jeremy's address, clicked Place Order and shoved her phone back into her pocket. It was probably nothing. Just her cycle being wonky.

When she reached the main floor and rounded the staircase to walk to the back of the house, she saw the tree lit up out on the patio. She ambled along the main corridor, her pulse thumping in her chest, while the aromas from the kitchen enticed her to move a little more quickly. She *was* hungry. And she'd been incredibly tired.

"Hey there, sleepyhead," Jeremy said, turning away from the stove.

Isabel's heart did a full cartwheel at the sight of him. "Are you making me dinner?"

"I'm making up for last night and the noticeable lack

of food." He wrapped his arm around her shoulders and gave her a soft kiss.

"It smells amazing. Although I hope that doesn't mean we don't get to revisit the events of last night. Or this morning. Or this afternoon."

Jeremy slipped his hand under her jaw and brought her lips to his. The kiss was enough to make her lose all sense of time and place, which was perfect. She couldn't stack another worry inside her head. "I can't wait to do everything we did last night."

"Neither can I." Goose bumps raced over the surface of her skin and she focused on the thrill of being with him.

"Did you see the tree?" He took her hand and led her to the patio doors. "It's so beautiful. You're a genius. I'm going to do this every year from now on."

"How wonderful. A new tradition." Isabel leaned into him and put her arm around his waist. The lights twinkled in the inky darkness outside and the wind blew enough to send snow from the tree boughs in puffs of white.

Jeremy wrapped his arm around Isabel. "Can I tell you a secret?"

Truly, the question could have easily been her own. "You can tell me anything."

"I'm so happy right now."

A heavy sigh left her lips, equal parts contentment and worry. "Me, too," she replied, hoping against hope that this happiness would last.

Twelve

Isabel's worries about being pregnant had manifested themselves in some very specific dreams. The truly odd part was that they were still lingering, at least in her head. Half-awake with her eyes still shut, she heard tiny cries—baby wails so peculiar they didn't sound human.

"The kittens." She bolted upright, blinking in the early light of Jeremy's bedroom. She reached over and shook his arm. "Jeremy. I think Cat had her babies."

"What?" He managed to make disorientation adorable, lifting his head off the pillow, then plopping it back down. "We don't have to do anything, right? You told me she can take care of them on her own."

Typical guy. "We don't have to do anything, but don't you want to make sure she's okay? That the babies are okay?" She tore back the comforter and tiptoed over to the closet door, turning on the light. She wasn't too worried about scaring Cat or the babies—it was plenty dark in their little corner. "Don't you want to see how many there are? Or what they look like?"

"Oh. Uh. Sure." He sat up in bed and flipped on the light on his bedside table, pushing his sexy bedhead hair off his face. "I'm coming."

Isabel tiptoed into the closet and pulled back Jeremy's shirts, peeking down into the box. Suckling Cat's belly were two tiny kittens; both appeared to be orange, although their fur was still matted. A third, with orange, gray and white patches, was blindly wandering around the box, crawling on its belly and mewing. Cat looked completely spent, asleep on her side.

"I thought they would be cuter," Jeremy said, peering over Isabel's shoulder. "Kittens are supposed to be cute."

Isabel shook her head and looked back at him. "Not at first. Not really. They'll be plenty cute in a few days."

"I'll have to trust you on that one."

He consulted his Apple watch. "It's nearly seven thirty, which seems way too early a time to be up on a Sunday morning, but I guess we're up, huh? Should I go make coffee?"

"That would be great. Bring me a cup?" She made herself at home on the floor, right next to the box.

"Are we spending our whole day in the closet?"

"I just want to sit here a little while. Make sure they're doing okay before we leave Cat to it."

He leaned down and pecked the top of her head. "I will not begrudge you your kitten time."

Isabel turned her attention to the box, watching as the stray kitten finally found her way to Cat's belly. It had been a long time since she'd been around this scene. She'd been a teenager the last time their family had newborn kittens in the house. Even all these years later, witnessing this made her feel connected to her mom. She pressed her hand to her lower belly, wondering what her body would ultimately tell her. She'd have been lying if she said she didn't desperately want a baby and to become a mom. But she wanted it all— true love and a partner. She would do this on her own, but it wasn't what her heart desired.

Jeremy returned and handed her a cup of coffee. "Good?" he asked, distracted by his iPad.

"Yes. Perfect." It was prepared exactly the way she liked it, with a splash of cream and one sugar.

"Good. Because here's where I have to ruin your day. There's a story in the paper this morning. Apparently somebody found love letters written to Victoria Eden by Mr. Summers's father. And the papers decided to publish them."

Isabel felt all of the blood drain from her face. *No no no.* She scrambled to standing and took the tablet from Jeremy when he offered it to her. There in black and white were the letters she and Mindy had discovered that afternoon in her grandmother's apartment. They had agreed to hide them away. They had agreed that no good came of anyone seeing them.

"How did you find out about this?" She felt her entire body go tight, fearing the answer.

"Summers, of course. Nothing gets past that guy. He texted me a link and asked me to call him, but I wanted to talk to you first. What the hell, Isabel? I thought we had a deal. I thought we were putting this whole thing to rest."

"We *do* have a deal." She hated seeing the expression on his face—the sheer disappointment was excruciating. Meanwhile, her mind was racing, wondering how this could have possibly happened. "Why are you looking at me like that? I didn't do this."

"Your clients must have done it. There's no other explanation." He took the tablet from her hand and stalked out of the closet.

She followed him back into his room. "But that doesn't make any sense. Why would they do this? Especially when I specifically asked Mindy not to?"

The look on Jeremy's face when he turned around told her what a grave error she'd made. She'd grown so comfortable with him that she'd let down her guard. He didn't know about the letters. She'd never said a peep about them, not even after he'd called to let her know that the promissory note had been authenticated. "Please tell me you didn't plan this. Please tell me this isn't a trademark Isabel Blackwell move."

That stung like no other thing he could have said. "Jeremy, no. I didn't plan this. I don't know what to tell you, but I didn't have anything to do with this story."

"Did you know about the letters?"

A sigh left her lips involuntarily and he stormed out of the room. "Jeremy, wait!" She ran out into the hall after him, grabbing his arm just as he reached the top of the landing. "Please let me explain. Yes, I knew about the letters. Mindy and I found them right before the promissory note was authenticated."

"But you still waited for me to call you and tell you about the authentication. Even when you knew at that point that it was all real? The affair between Mr. Summers's father and Victoria Eden was real?"

"Of course I waited. You would have done the same thing in my situation."

He closed his eyes and pinched the bridge of his nose, not saying a thing.

"You would have. You know it."

"Of course I would have, Isabel. My first duty is to my client. Which only illustrates how far you and I have crossed the line together. And now I have feelings for you and what in the hell am I supposed to do about that?"

She sharply sucked in a breath. "Feelings?" She had feelings for him, too, but she didn't have the nerve to express them now. The thought of sitting down and examining them, or daring to put a label on them, was too terrifying an idea. Meanwhile, there was no sign of her period and the drugstore was scheduled to deliver a pregnancy test at any time.

"Please don't throw my word back at me like I've said something horrible. We've had a great weekend together and now we're right back where we started except that it's quite possibly worse. I don't see any way that Summers is going to agree to a single term you and I so carefully worked out. The entire deal is off as far as I'm concerned."

Isabel's stomach sank. She'd not only disappointed Jeremy, she was about to crush the entire Eden family and her brother, for that matter. Best-case scenario, Eden's would end up embroiled in a legal battle for months, one that would cost them untold sums of money. Mr. Summers had been headed for the warpath from the very beginning and it was only understandable that this story in the papers would convince him it was the only course. Mindy and Isabel had found the letters extremely romantic when they read them, but there was no doubt that they were the flowery ramblings of a man smitten with a woman who was not his wife. They were a chronicle of lust, passion, obsession and ultimately, infidelity. They told the story of two people casting aside the sanctity of marriage.

"Please. Let me talk to Mindy and Sophie. Let me get to the bottom of this."

"I don't see what good it's going to do, but I'm not going to prevent you from doing whatever you need to do to take care of your client."

"Gee, thanks. That's so generous of you." Isabel retreated to the guest room, fuming and upset and uncharacteristically on the brink of tears. Normally when things went wrong with a case, she immediately went on the offensive. Right now, she wanted to crumple into a ball and hide. She got out her phone and called her brother.

"Hey. What's up?" he asked, sounding as though he was still recovering from his cold.

"Have you seen the papers?"

"No. Why?"

Isabel gave Sam a quick recap. "So I need to know if Mindy fed this story to the newspapers."

"I don't see how she possibly could have. At least not in the last few days. She's been completely out of it on cold medicine. The only person she's talked to has been Sophie."

Isabel felt like a light bulb had been flicked on above her head. Sophie was the most likely person to do something like this. When Isabel had tried to calm her down the other morning, she was all ready to hire a PR person and take Mr. Summers down. "Okay. Thanks. I need to call her and talk to her."

"Are we in hot water because of this?" Sam asked.

Isabel wasn't about to couch it. "I'd say we're about to boil."

Unfortunately, when Isabel called Sophie's cell, all

she got was voice mail. She left a message, asking—no, begging—for Sophie to call her back. Then she flopped back on the bed and stared up at the ceiling, wondering how she was possibly ever going to get herself out of this.

Jeremy had sought the solitude of his office, closing the door behind him. He wasn't interested in Isabel's excuses or reasoning. All he could think about were the things he'd learned about her the first time he'd looked into her career trajectory and discovered what she'd done in Washington, DC. This was straight out of the Isabel Blackwell playbook—when one party can destroy you, you destroy them first. Although he didn't want to make this situation about him, this was far too much like the things Kelsey had done to him. His heart legitimately went out to Mr. Summers. Who wants to read a newspaper article where their father, in his own words, professes his love for someone who isn't his wife?

He couldn't believe he'd fallen back into bed with Isabel. He couldn't believe he'd let himself get so carried away again. Even five minutes ago out in the hall with her—why had he uttered that word? *Feelings?* For someone who was supposed to be exceptionally good with words, he'd sure chosen a terrible one. Right now, he had a few too many feelings coursing through his system, anger being pretty high on the list. Everyone was pissing him off—the Eden sisters, the situation and honestly, even Isabel.

Jeremy's phone, which was facedown on his desk, beeped with a text. Then another. He flipped over the device and scanned the screen.

The first message was from his father. Summers case

is no longer under your control. We need to take down Blackwell.

The second was from a reporter, and just because today seemed to be hell-bent on destroying him, it was the same one who'd sought Jeremy's comment after Kelsey ran her smear piece. Can we talk re: the Benjamin Summers lawsuit?

Before he spoke to either of those people, he needed to call Ben. He didn't want to risk him talking to his father first. "Ben. Good morning. I got your text," Jeremy said, wanting to be as upbeat and diplomatic as possible, even though it felt like the world was crumbling around him.

"It appears that the shoe is on the other foot, doesn't it? I'm embarrassed beyond words at the atrocity in the papers this morning, but I suppose I should be thankful that the Eden's team has finally shown their true colors."

"I don't know about that. We're still trying to get to the bottom of exactly what happened." Why was it his inclination to try to walk any of this back? Logic said that he should be going for the jugular right now, but the truth was that he just wanted this done. He couldn't spend more time with Isabel. She'd shown that she was just as capable of inflicting damage as any woman he'd ever allowed himself to get close to. He needed this case to be over. "I have to tell you that Ms. Blackwell and I worked out some extremely favorable terms for you on Friday. It's an attractive offer, and yes, today might give us additional leverage for perhaps a few more concessions, but I don't think we should throw the whole thing out the window because of one story in a tabloid."

"And I'd think you would be happy about this. Don't lawyers love leverage?"

"Not when it means that we needlessly drag something out for longer than it needs to go." He could see this going on for months and months, during which he would have to battle Isabel. He didn't want that. Frankly, he wanted this whole thing to go away so he could decide for himself, without any outside intrusion, whether he could trust her. Whether they could be something.

"Do you have these supposed favorable terms for me to look at?" Mr. Summers asked.

"I'm in the process of drawing them up. We can meet tomorrow morning if that works for you."

"Fine. Nine o'clock. My office."

"Absolutely. I will be there."

"And if I'm not happy, I'm prepared to drop the gloves and go to war." The line went dead before Jeremy had a chance to respond. Not that he had anything to say. He'd wait until tomorrow to do battle with Mr. Summers.

Of course, now he had no choice but to call his dad and explain what was going on. As the phone rang, dread began to build in his system, and all Jeremy could think was that this entire situation was wrong, starting with the fact that he couldn't stand to speak to a man he should have been able to trust and confide in—his own father.

"I just got off the phone with Mr. Summers," Jeremy started. "We're meeting tomorrow morning. I'm presenting the terms of the negotiation to him. I'm hoping he can put aside what happened in the papers today and agree to everything. He'll get his money. He'll get that and more."

"That's not even my worry anymore, Jeremy. My concern is that you have caused irreparable damage to our firm's reputation. You're making us look like a bunch of hacks."

"Dad. I'm not a public relations guy. I have no control over what runs in the newspaper."

"But if you had put this case to bed at that first meeting, if you had the nerve to be ruthless with Ms. Blackwell, we wouldn't be having this discussion."

"It wouldn't have changed the tabloid story. That still could have run."

"And Summers would have had his settlement by then. At that point, Sharp and Sharp would only be bandied about as the firm who had come out on top. Instead, we're flopping around like a fish out of water." His father cleared his throat. "I think I need to level the playing field."

"By doing what exactly?"

"We need to get rid of Ms. Blackwell. Get Eden's to fire her."

"They won't fire her. Her brother is engaged to Mindy Eden. He's a special adviser to the store." Jeremy couldn't explain further, about how Isabel felt like she was part of the Eden family and how it all meant a great deal to her. He couldn't divulge his personal involvement with her. It would infuriate his father to no end, and Jeremy had to admit, he would be justified in being angry.

"Trust me, they'll get rid of her when she's a liability, and I know exactly how to make that happen. Then they'll hand it over to their in-house counsel. You can steamroller those guys in your sleep."

"Dad. Please don't do anything reckless. Just let me meet with Summers tomorrow morning and see where we get. Just give me this one last chance."

Thirteen

Monday morning had arrived, which meant it was do-or-die time. Jeremy would be leaving the house in a half hour to meet with Mr. Summers. He hoped that Ben had taken some time to cool off. He hoped that he could see that there was no point in letting pride get in the way. It was time for an agreement. An armistice. That was the best-case scenario for Jeremy and he wanted it so badly he could taste it.

Sunday had been horrible—Jeremy stewing in his office and Isabel in the guest room, tucked away. Their only real interaction came when she got a delivery and he brought it to her room.

"This came from the drugstore." He handed her the paper shopping bag, hating that he felt as though he had to stay out of a room in his own house.

"Thank you," she said, clutching it to her chest. "I got a call from the Bacharach and I can move back in on Tuesday morning. If you want, I can see if Mindy and

Sam can take me in. Or maybe I could stay in Mindy's grandmother's old apartment."

"Don't do that. Just stay. It's fine." He desperately wanted that to be true. It was killing him to not be where they'd been mere hours before that, enjoying each other's company, touching each other, kissing.

"I know this story just made everything worse. And I'm really sorry for that. I still don't know what happened, but I will get to the bottom of it. I wish I had something you could tell Mr. Summers, but I don't."

"Okay. I still plan to meet with him tomorrow morning. No telling what he's going to say, but I will present our agreement to him if you still want me to."

Isabel had picked at her fingernail, seeming to want any reason to not look at him. "I'll do the same and I guess we'll just see where we end up?"

He nodded in agreement. "Do you want something to eat?"

She shook her head. "Not right now. Maybe later. I'm tired and I have work to do."

"Okay then. Let me know if you need anything." He'd been about to walk away when she said one more thing.

"I checked on the kittens while you were in your office. I made sure Cat got some food and water. They seem like they're doing well."

"Good. Thank you."

"Of course."

With that, she'd shut the door, and Jeremy was left much like he'd been before Isabel had arrived on his doorstep—alone. It stayed like that for the rest of the day. And the night. And for all of that morning.

In his closet, he was choosing a suit to wear for his meeting with Mr. Summers when he heard one of the kittens mewing. In all of the commotion of yesterday, he'd frankly forgotten that they were there. The two orange kittens were nursing, but the other one was wandering around the box, bumping into the sides. Cat would nudge at her with her nose occasionally, but the kitten, quite frankly, seemed lost. Jeremy was unsure of what to do, but something told him he had to help the poor thing, so he reached in, picked it up and placed her next to her siblings, mouth near Cat's belly. He watched as she rooted around and latched on to nurse. There was some consolation in that one silly achievement—today wouldn't have to be a total loss.

After dressing, he went into his office to gather his things. That was when Isabel appeared at his door. She was just as beautiful as always, but he could tell that there was something on her mind. She wasn't her normal lively self, and the dread that prompted in him made him sick to his stomach.

"Do you have a minute?" she asked. "I have two things I need to talk to you about."

"Sure. I have to leave soon, but I'll always make time for you."

"First off, you should know that your dad tried to get one of the tabloids to run a smear piece on me. The reporter called me late last night for comment and after I spoke to the editor, they agreed not to run it."

Jeremy looked up at the ceiling, furious with his father for attempting to sabotage her while also relieved that he hadn't been successful. "I'm so sorry. I don't know what to say."

She waved it off. "Don't worry. I've had worse things happen to me. And I'm sure that whatever they wanted to print would probably be true. I've represented some people who aren't great. But I've always acted in accordance with the law. I don't have anything I'm ashamed of."

"Well, good. I'm glad."

"I simply don't want to be a part of any of this anymore. I can't deal with the mudslinging and the backstabbing and everyone trying so hard to disparage each other. I'm hoping we can wrap up the case, but if we can't, I think I will likely step away from it. I've had my fill of it. I love the Eden sisters and care about them deeply, but I also need my sanity."

"I can't say that I blame you. If my dad wasn't in the middle of it, I might be tempted to bail on Summers. None of this has been very fun, has it?"

She shrugged and a slight smile crossed her lips. It was like stepping into the sunlight for the first time— that small glimmer of happiness from her made everything better. "I don't know about that. I had fun with you. I had more than fun."

A grin that he was sure was quite goofy broke out on his face. "Me, too. I don't regret that part."

"Me, either. Which brings me to the other thing I have to tell you. There's no easy way to say this, so I'm just going to come out with it. I'm pregnant and you're the father."

Of the many things Jeremy had thought Isabel might tell him, that one piece of information had never occurred to him. Not even for a second. "The night we met?"

"Yes."

"But you…"

"I know. I thought there was no chance. I was wrong."

"I, uh… I don't even know what to say."

"I know. It's okay. You don't need to say anything.

This is all very sudden and it's a lot to deal with, especially given everything else that's going on." Now that she was talking, she was picking up speed, as if she had a long list of things she'd been dying to say. "I realize that the timing couldn't possibly be any worse. And we don't really know each other that well, so I understand that you would be wanting to distance yourself from me, and I can appreciate why. It's okay. I will be completely fine on my own. I don't want you to worry."

He got up from his desk and went to her, taking her hands. "Hey. Hey. Slow down a minute. Take a breath."

She dropped her head for a moment and when she looked up at him, there were tears rolling down her cheeks. "I've wanted a baby for so long, Jeremy. I've always wanted to be a mom. But this isn't the way I wanted it to happen. And I hate putting you on the spot. You're a good man. I know that. You're sweet and generous and you don't deserve to be in this situation."

Jeremy wasn't sure what to think about any of this. He'd wanted a family for a long time. He'd wanted a woman like Isabel for a long time. But this was traveling on a preposterous timeline. He wanted to put the entire world on pause, if only for a day so he could have time and space to think. A baby? With Isabel? How would this work? Would it be yet another negotiation? That was the last thing he wanted. And what if things didn't work out? He didn't want to be an absentee father, around every other weekend and select holidays. That wasn't what he wanted for himself at all. It wasn't what he wanted for Isabel, either.

His phone beeped—the reminder that he had to leave for his meeting. "Shoot. I'm going to be late to meet with Summers. He's such a stickler for punctuality. I can't afford to make him angry."

"I understand. It's okay. Just forget what I said. We can talk about it after everything with the case is over."

Jeremy grabbed his briefcase from his desk, then returned to her. "Hey. Will you stop trying to let me off the hook? I'm not like that guy who burned you. I don't turn my back on people who need me, okay? So just give me a chance to meet with Summers, and talk to my dad, and, and..." He looked at her, certain he couldn't possibly be in a bigger state of disbelief. "Then we'll talk about the baby."

That fresh start Isabel had wanted so badly? It felt like she was watching it crumble to dust in her hands. How could she possibly save Eden's now? How could Jeremy salvage this situation for Mr. Summers? Even more important, how could the two of them reach an understanding about impending parenthood? They'd hardly had enough time to fall in love.

The scene in the guest bath at Jeremy's house was still rolling around in her mind. She'd paced back and forth across the white marble floor, arms wrapped around her middle like she was giving herself a hug. She'd been unable to escape how lonely it felt to be doing that on her own, for the second time. It had played out like that when she found out she was pregnant with Garrett's baby all those years ago—Isabel enduring the painfully slow ticks of the clock while she waited for news that could change her whole life.

The timer on Isabel's phone had gone off, echoing in the bathroom. She'd closed her eyes for a moment to steel herself for the news, unable to decide what result she hoped for, although she'd known that there was no reason to reach a solid conclusion. Her heart would tell her with its own reaction.

She'd opened her eyes and grabbed the test from the counter. *Two blue lines. Positive.* She'd stumbled back into the bathroom wall, steadying herself with her hand. *Positive. A baby.* Her heart did the inexplicable, even when her stomach wobbled—it began to flutter in her chest. However imperfect her situation, a baby was something she wanted more than anything. She'd been waiting years for another chance.

She had to admit to herself that Jeremy had handled the news far better than expected. She'd been prepared for the absolute worst, and he'd kept everything on an even keel. He'd been a rock. She hoped and prayed that this wasn't another of his acting jobs. She didn't think she could take it if he wasn't at least going to play some role in this baby's life. She couldn't handle it if he was going to turn his back on her as Garrett had done.

In the car on the way to Eden's to meet with Sam, Mindy, Sophie and Emma, her heart was heavy. Perhaps her first mistake had been taking this job—she'd only agreed out of loyalty to Sam. But now she was so much closer to Mindy, Sophie and Emma than she'd ever imagined she could be, and it was all on her that they could lose the store. Isabel the fixer had not only failed to fix anything, she'd allowed it to get worse. She should have had the sense to take the letters into her possession that day at Victoria Eden's apartment. She never should have trusted her clients to keep them out of public view.

Arriving at Eden's, she waved to Duane the security guard and marched right back to the elevator, prepared to unleash a few unpleasant things on the Eden sisters if necessary. If they'd gotten themselves into this mess, she wasn't sure she could get them out. She strode into the lobby feeling determined, but the instant she saw

Sam, she burst into tears. He rushed over to her and gathered her up in his arms.

"What's wrong?" he asked. "Are you that upset about the case?"

She sank against his chest, unable to speak. As much as Eden's had weighed on her as recently as a few minutes ago, that was definitely not what was on her mind.

Mindy appeared in the reception area. "Is everything okay?" She stepped closer, but kept her distance. "Sorry. I'd hug you, but I'm still getting over this cold."

"Is Summers going to go after the store?" Sam asked.

"I still haven't talked to Sophie, but it has to be her," Mindy said. "I don't completely remember our conversation over the weekend, but I'm pretty sure I told her about the letters. Leave it to her to go to our grandmother's apartment, find them and leak them to the press."

Mindy's explanation was of little consolation. Isabel still felt as though she had let down her new friends. She'd let down their entire family. She'd let down Sam's wife-to-be. She'd failed in every way imaginable, at least when it came to her legal responsibilities. "I'm so sorry. I really wish I had better news. Summers is just out for revenge. I'm not sure we ever had a chance."

Sam placed his hands on Isabel's shoulders. "I know you did your best. Some of this has to be his lawyer. I didn't like Sharp from the very first meeting. He seems like a real weasel."

Isabel froze, looking up into her brother's eyes. Sam's opinion mattered. It mattered a lot. And she couldn't allow him to think of Jeremy that way. She also couldn't keep him in the dark any longer about the full scope of her relationship with him, especially now that it had become infinitely more complicated. "Jeremy's a good man. He's caught in an impossible situation. Summers is unreasonable."

"You have Stockholm syndrome. You were stuck negotiating with that guy. You've convinced yourself he's not that bad."

"I don't know about that," Mindy said.

Sam turned to her. "Don't you agree?" he asked.

"For Isabel's sake, I can't. If she says he's a good guy, I believe her."

"Why? This guy is about to destroy your entire family."

"He's not going to destroy our family. He might end up being part and parcel of ending our business, but it's not the same."

"Wait a minute. Why do I have the feeling you two have talked about him before?" Sam asked. "Am I missing something?"

"We did talk about him. The day we rummaged around in Gram's apartment."

Isabel had fond memories of that day, despite the things they'd discovered. She felt closer to Mindy afterward. She felt as though she was becoming part of the Eden family. "We talked about a lot that day." Isabel loved her brother deeply, and it was time to tell him and Mindy everything. "I need to tell you both something. There's more going on than just the negotiations breaking down. Jeremy and I are involved," Isabel whispered.

It wasn't easy to take Sam by surprise, but he noticeably reared back his head. "Are you serious? Why would you do that? That's so unprofessional."

Mindy grabbed both of their arms. "You two. In my office. We can't have this conversation out here."

As soon as they were behind a closed door, Isabel confronted Sam. "You're going to lecture me about professionalism? Seriously? I didn't even want this job to begin with."

"Wait. You didn't?" Mindy asked, incredulous. "I thought you did. Sam, you told me she wanted to help us."

"She took the job. That was all you needed to know."

Mindy let out a frustrated grumble. "You can't keep things like this from me. Isabel is going to be my sister-in-law. We've been getting along great and now I find out that the foundation of that is all a lie."

Isabel reached for Mindy's arm. "It's not a lie. As soon as we spent that afternoon together, I knew I was doing the right thing. I wanted to help you and your sisters. I wanted us to be close. That's why I told you about my thing with Jer..." Isabel stopped herself, but it was too late.

"Whoa. Hold on a minute. You were involved with Jeremy before? I'm so confused. And Min, you knew about this?"

Isabel couldn't allow Mindy to take heat for this, so she explained that she and Jeremy had a one-night stand before they were involved in the case. Then she told him about the broken condom.

Sam shook his head, holding up both hands. "Enough. I don't need to hear about that." He closed his eyes and pinched the bridge of his nose. "So when we met him in his office that day, you guys had already slept together? And you didn't say a thing to any of us."

"What was I supposed to do? He had his client and I had mine and none of that was going to change the fact that there was this case standing between us."

"And now what? Where do you two stand?" Sam asked.

Isabel knew she had to come clean. About everything. "I got pregnant that first night. With Jeremy's baby. I found out this morning."

Sam walked over and sat on the couch, but Mindy went straight to Isabel.

"Oh my God. Are you okay?" she asked.

Isabel had to take a moment to reflect. Was she okay? "I am. I mean, I've wanted to have a baby for a long time now. Ever since…" There were far too many details of her life she had kept from Sam. Perhaps it had been Isabel's way of protecting him. With both of their parents gone and Isabel being two years older, she certainly felt responsible for him.

"Ever since what?" Sam asked, seeming desperate. "Just tell me what's going on, Isabel. I feel like I am completely in the dark, which is not a good feeling when it comes to my own sister."

Apparently that day was for nothing but revelations and admissions. So she finally told Sam about the heartache of losing her first pregnancy, and how she so desperately wanted this child.

"What are you going to do?" he asked when she'd told him everything.

"Right now, all I can do is my best for me and the baby. I have absolutely no idea what's going to happen with any of it. The deal or Jeremy."

Fourteen

Jeremy left his meeting with Mr. Summers feeling as though he'd been hit by a truck. The man's ability to hold on to a grudge and to allow every perceived slight to fester…well, it was unparalleled.

Nothing had been resolved, but Mr. Summers promised him a phone call in an hour with an answer. Either he would accept the terms from the Eden's team or it would be all-out war. Which left Jeremy with one more thing to deal with—his dad. No matter what happened with the case, he was done.

He headed straight to the office and didn't even stop to drop off his things. "I need to speak to my father," he said to his dad's admin, striding right past her desk and opening the door. "I heard that your plan to smear Ms. Blackwell didn't work. I guess I should be thankful you failed."

Jeremy's dad was on a call. "I'm gong to have to call

you back," he said into the receiver before hanging up. "I can still make it happen. I just need to dig up more dirt on her."

"Just don't. Just stop all of this. You're as bad as Mr. Summers. There is no winning when you play the game like this. It's just a race to the bottom and I'm tired of it."

"You're complaining about your boss and your biggest client. Apparently you don't know who signs your paychecks."

"Don't posture with me, Dad. You know that the other lawyers and I are the ones who keep the lights on. You're just the head of the dragon, spitting fire and still trying to prove yourself because you know that no matter how hard you try, you will never be as good as your own dad."

"That's not true. The success of this firm begins and ends with me. It's my legacy."

That word didn't sit right with Jeremy. "I'm your son. Am I not your real legacy? The firm could go under tomorrow and I would still be here, trying to find a way to make you happy. Trying to find a way to get through to you."

Just then, the door to his father's office opened and in walked the last person he expected to see—his mother. "Jeremy. I thought it was strange that you weren't at your desk."

"Mom. What are you doing here?"

"Trying to get your father to go Christmas shopping with me."

"I'm in the middle of something," his dad said. "I can't drop everything and go shopping."

"Why not?" Jeremy asked. "Everything is under control here. The other lawyers and I have everything in hand."

"The Summers case isn't resolved."

"No, it isn't. But it will be. And I'll see it through."

"Then what?" his dad asked. "You'll get another client I have to bother you about?"

"You never had to bother me about this one. If you trusted me to do my job, it would get done. Grandpa trusted you. I don't know why you can't place that same faith in me." Jeremy stuffed his hands into his pants pockets, frustrated.

His mother turned to him. "Your grandfather never trusted him. Your dad was proving himself until the day his father died. He never had a chance to win his confidence."

Jeremy was frozen for a moment, letting that bit of information tumble around in his head. "What? Seriously?"

His dad drew in a deep breath, staring off into space as if he couldn't possibly handle the admission. "He never made things easy on me. That's for sure."

Jeremy's mom stepped closer to him. "As the person who had to listen to your father complain every night when he came home from work, I can tell you that it was far worse than that."

"Dad? Why didn't you ever tell me this? And why are you doing the same thing to me?"

"Because it made me stronger to be tested like that," his dad snapped. "It made me a better lawyer."

Jeremy wanted to laugh, but this was all striking him as incredibly sad. If only they'd had this conversation ten or fifteen years ago. He might be in a very different place. "You don't have to be miserable to be strong. That all comes from within as far as I'm concerned."

"It's the only way I know, Jeremy. I don't know what you want me to tell you."

Jeremy approached his dad's desk. "Dad. I love you. I hope you know that. I love you even though you make it very difficult some days. But I can't work with you anymore. Either you step aside or I do. I'll leave it up to you."

His mom came up behind him. "Son. Do you really want to do that? Close this door on your career?"

He turned to her and placed his hand on her arm. He really did love her. "My career isn't going anywhere. But at the rate we're going, the three of us aren't going to be much of a family. The situation at work has been bad enough, but we need to talk about how things went south after Kelsey left me. I didn't feel supported. And I never took the time to think about how unhappy it made me until I talked to a friend about it." Isabel had shown him so much in such a short amount of time. How had she done that?

"You never told us you felt that way. I thought we were supportive."

"I should have said something. I know that now. I shouldn't have kept it bottled in. But you were not supportive. You were embarrassed."

"Embarrassed for you. The things Kelsey said about you were horrible. No mother wants her son to go through that. To experience that kind of betrayal."

"But you never really said those things to me. All I heard were the things your friends were telling you."

Jeremy's mom frowned and her eyes grew misty. "I didn't?"

He shook his head. "You didn't."

She wrapped her arms around him. "I'm so sorry. I never, ever wanted to hurt you. You and your father are the most important things to me in the entire world. I love you. I love you both."

Jeremy returned his mom's hug. "I love you guys, too. Hopefully that can save us." As soon as the words left his lips, he realized that they weren't really his. They were Isabel's. From the night they met. *I believe that love is the only thing that saves anyone.*

The thought of Isabel sent goose bumps racing over the surface of his skin and that was when he realized it—he loved her. As improbable as it was, he'd fallen in love with her. Could love save him? Was it as simple as that? Was it meant for him? He'd spent the last few years so unhappy, convinced that his empty existence was something he must learn to accept. A fact of life. But did it really have to be that way? He wanted to believe that it didn't.

"Are we going to see you for the tree-trimming party?" his mom asked. "I look forward to it all year."

Jeremy was determined to keep building bridges, not tearing them down. He wanted to be the sort of man who made connections, not destroyed them. "My only problem is that I'd like to bring a date. Isabel Blackwell."

His dad's eyes became as large as dinner plates. "Excuse me?"

Jeremy wasn't about to go into a long, drawn-out explanation. He wasn't even certain Isabel would accept the invitation. "Yes, Dad. We actually had a brief romantic relationship before the case started. I never said anything because I thought it wouldn't be a problem. And honestly, it wasn't, until you decided to try to drag her through the mud today."

Jeremy's mother's face was full of horror. "Oh. Well, that's awkward, isn't it?"

Honestly, it couldn't be any more uncomfortable for

Jeremy than anything else he'd endured with his parents. "It doesn't have to be if Dad apologizes."

"You have to apologize," his mother blurted. "Otherwise, it'll ruin Christmas."

"You can't ruin Christmas, Dad."

Full of resignation, his father nodded. "I will apologize. First thing."

Jeremy could be content with that. "Then I will do my best to convince her to come."

Jeremy said his goodbyes to his parents, then marched down the hall, feeling as though a weight had been lifted. He'd finally said his piece with his family and the world hadn't ended. In fact, it had gone quite well.

Just then, his phone rang. He plucked it from his pocket and answered, striding down the hall.

"Yes?"

"Jeremy. It's Ben."

At this point, Jeremy was prepared for anything. "Do you have news for me?"

"I do."

"Am I going to be happy about it?"

"Depends on what you were hoping for."

Was Jeremy ready for the answer? He had to be. Because the truth was that he wanted to put this whole thing to bed and turn his attention to Isabel and the baby.

Isabel arrived back at Jeremy's place, and of course, it just *had* to be snowing. Again. As if the sight of his beautiful brownstone, with the grand steps and stunning front door, didn't hold enough vibrant reminders of what had happened between them. They'd not only fallen into bed, she'd fallen into the Christmas spirit for the first time in years.

Funnily enough, the most pressing thing she could think of as she looked at the facade of Jeremy's house was that it needed a wreath with a big fat red bow. She needed to rein herself in. There was no telling what that afternoon might hold. Jeremy was having a showdown with his father and Mr. Summers. There were too many things that could go wrong.

As she climbed out of the car and zipped up her coat, she had to admit to herself that despite her predicament, she wasn't feeling truly pessimistic right now. She accepted the reality of her situation. Jeremy had never asked for this—an undeniable tie to her, forever. And that was fine. She was strong and independent. She could care for a child on her own. And she'd wanted this more than anything for so long. Nothing was going to keep her from building her own little family. Life was once again proving to be quite unlike what she had hoped for, but she wouldn't put herself or her future on hold. She'd done that after Garrett left, and the pain of losing her first pregnancy had made her tread water for years.

But as she ascended his front steps, she was overcome with another wave of melancholy. She and Jeremy could be good together if they had a chance. They could be great. She cared for him deeply, and was holding on to feelings that sure felt an awful lot like love. Such was the case with bad timing. Only some things in life lined up perfectly. Not everything. At least not for Isabel.

She unlocked the door with the key Jeremy had given her and flipped on the light in the foyer. After taking off her coat, she made her way upstairs to check on Cat and the kittens.

"Hey there, Mama," she said when she carefully pulled back Jeremy's dress shirts to reveal the cardboard box. Cat was half-asleep with her eyes part open, the kittens nursing and kneading at her belly. Cat looked up at Isabel and blinked—such a simple thing, and yet Isabel was so taken by the beauty of the moment. There was this sweet and beautiful creature caring for her babies, at utter peace with the world. Isabel hoped that her future could be like that.

She hoped more than was probably reasonable.

"Hello? Isabel?" Jeremy's voice came from downstairs. "Are you home?"

Home. She was home. She wanted to believe she was. "I'm up here. With the cats."

She heard his steady footfalls on the stairs and moments later, he appeared at the closet doorway. "Of course you're up here."

"I had to get my kitten time."

"I'm wondering if I can steal a minute with you. Or maybe more." From behind his back, he produced a huge bouquet of red roses. "I'm hoping these will convince you."

Isabel popped up from the floor, planted her face in the flowers and drew in the heavenly smell. "I don't need convincing to talk to you. Although I appreciate the effort. They're beautiful." She then worried there might be a specific reason for the kind gesture. "Mr. Summers. Did you talk to him? Is he throwing down the gauntlet?"

"I did talk to him. For quite a while, actually. Turns out that when he got so mad about the story yesterday, he hadn't actually read the letters. After I talked to him this morning, he finally did."

"And that made things better or worse?"

"Better. Much better. He called and told me that he realized just how much his father loved Victoria Eden. Truly loved her. I guess that in the end, he stopped seeing it as this salacious affair and more as a love story between two people who met at the wrong time."

Isabel blinked several times, struggling to catch up. "So what does that mean?"

"He's agreed to the terms. A lump sum of the original loan amount by January 1 and 10 percent of the Eden's online business in perpetuity." Jeremy shrugged his way out of his suit jacket and hung it on a hanger. "So I guess what I need to know from you is whether the Eden family is definitely on board."

"They are. I heard from Mindy on my way back here and it was Sophie who leaked the letters to the press. I told her that they had to agree to the terms if we had any chance of wrapping this up."

"See? What a shark you are."

"I'm not. I'm just like you, Jeremy. I wanted this to be over so we could deal with the real-life stuff that's sitting in front of us. I know that I unloaded a lot on you today, and I'm not trying to let you off the hook, but I do want you to know that there is no pressure from me. You can take all the time you want to think about this and decide what you want."

"I already know what I want."

Isabel was surprised by his quick response. She only hoped that he wasn't going to say that he'd decided he didn't want her. "You do?"

"Yes. And it all came to me when I had it out with my dad this morning." He reached for Isabel's hand. "Come on. Let's go sit on the bed so I can tell you the whole story."

They traced into the bedroom and sat on the edge of

the mattress. He held her hand the whole time he was recounting what had happened with his parents and how relieved he was to finally clear the air.

"I'm so glad it all worked out. But I'm still not sure how that helped you figure out what you want."

"I ended up telling my mom something you said the night we met."

Isabel narrowed her eyes in confusion. "Good Lord, Jeremy. What in the heck were you talking to your mom about?"

He laughed so hard that she could see his body relax. "Love. We were talking about love."

"I don't remember us discussing that. At all."

"When you were telling me your universal truths. You said that you believe that love is the only thing that ever saves anyone. And as soon as the words came out of my mouth, I realized that you saved me. You brought me back to life."

He reached out and smoothed her hair back and she peered up into his eyes, which were full of tenderness and love, the things she most craved. "If I did that, Jeremy, it was only because you make it easy. You're so pure of heart. It's impossible to not get caught up in that. To admire it."

"If that's the case, it's because I'm better when I'm with you. That's all there is to it. And I don't want to walk away from what's already between us."

Isabel's mind raced. She felt the same way. Exactly. And it was only leaving her with one conclusion.

He sucked in a deep breath and blew it out. "It might sound crazy..."

Oh my God.

"I know we've only known each other for a little while..." he continued.

"But I love you." They both said it. At the exact same time.

For a moment, they sat there, staring at each other in disbelief. Then the laughter came and an embrace and finally a kiss that made every bad thing that had ever happened fade into nothingness. Isabel had waited her whole life for this moment, and she knew Jeremy had, too.

"The baby," she said. "I know it's a lot."

"Of course it's a lot. But I'm forty years old. I don't want to let life pass me by. I don't want to let you or this moment pass me by. We have to take everything life has given us here, Isabel."

"We have to take each other."

"Yes. Absolutely."

"And never let go."

Epilogue

"Do you think it's cheesy to get married on Valentine's Day?" Mindy posed the question to Isabel as they stood in the grand master bedroom of Sam and Mindy's splendid new home.

Isabel shook her head, helping her future sister-in-law adjust the bustle of her wedding gown. It was a jaw-dropping bias-cut silk charmeuse that hugged every curve. Isabel was guessing Sam might pass out the minute he saw her. "No. I think it's sweet."

"It was Sam's idea, you know. Who knew he could be such a sap?"

"I knew. I knew it all along." Isabel already found herself blinking away tears. It would be a miracle if she could get through the ceremony without sobbing. Pregnancy hormones were definitely getting the best of her, but she relished every frantic and slightly chaotic moment of it. She'd be twelve weeks along in six days, then she and Jeremy would finally tell his parents. It'd been a bit of a rocky road to start with them, but they were making strides, especially since Jeremy's dad had apologized for trying to drag Isabel through the mud.

"How are we doing in here?" Sophie ducked into the room with Emma at her side.

Emma, who was showing all five months of her pregnancy, clasped her hand over her mouth when she saw Mindy. "You look so gorgeous. Sam is going to freak."

"You do look amazing. But I figured you already knew that," Sophie said, wandering farther into the room.

Mindy shot her a look. "A bride still wants to hear it, you know."

Sophie sat on the edge of the bed, watching Mindy adjust her hair. "I'm still surprised you didn't opt for a big wedding, but I suppose you've always been a bit contrary."

"After Emma and Daniel got married at city hall, I started to see the wisdom of it," Mindy said. "Having something low-key means way less drama. Plus, Sam didn't want to wait any longer, and honestly, I didn't want to, either."

The question of not waiting for life to start was certainly on Isabel's mind. She and Jeremy hadn't discussed marriage aside from agreeing it was best for the baby if it happened eventually. It wasn't that she was expecting a grand proclamation of love, more that she just wanted that certainty in her life. If he didn't pop the question soon, she planned to do it herself.

Of course, Jeremy had a lot on his plate now that he'd convinced his father to retire and step aside. There were lots of changes afoot at Sharp and Sharp as a result, including Jeremy bringing Isabel on board to start a new family law division. It was not only a good move forward for the firm, it was a way to save on office space, and they agreed that it would make things much easier when the baby arrived. They would likely get a nanny, but they also wanted to be as hands-on as possible.

A knock came at the bedroom door. Reginald, Eden's creative director and by all accounts, the sisters' de facto uncle, poked his head inside. "Everybody decent?" He didn't wait for a response, waltzing into the room in a pink suit and black bowtie festooned with pink hearts.

"Reginald, Gram would have loved that outfit," Sophie said.

He took it for a spin. "You think?"

"Definitely."

Mindy glanced at the clock on the bedside table. "You guys should head out there and get your seats."

Sophie, Emma and Isabel descended on Mindy, giving hugs and the gentlest of kisses on the cheek so as not to mess up her makeup. Sophie in particular was getting extremely choked up by the moment. "I love you all so much. Emma, you're the light and joy of this family. You make everything better. Mindy, you're the one who manages to keep us all moving forward." She then turned to Isabel. "And Isabel, at this point, you're pretty much our sister. We love you, too, and not just for saving Eden's. You helped us preserve our grandmother's legacy."

Isabel was so overwhelmed with emotion as the four of them joined in a group hug. "This means a lot to me. I've always wanted sisters."

Reginald cleared his throat loudly. "What about the stand-in for the father of the bride?"

"Get over here." Mindy waved him into the fray, but he only stayed for a beat or two before getting them all on schedule.

"Ladies, I need you to clear out. I have a bride to escort to the altar."

Isabel, Sophie and Emma hurried down the hall and descended the grand staircase into the foyer where the chairs were assembled. It was a small gathering—a few people from Eden's, like Lizzie and her new boyfriend, and Duane, the security guard. There were some people from Sam's office and Mindy's company, as well.

Isabel ducked into the seat next to Jeremy. "Hi," she whispered, pecking him on the cheek.

He took her hand and smiled, but otherwise kept quiet. Honestly, he'd been a little on edge all day, but she tried not to read anything into it. They were happy together, but he was under a lot of pressure to keep Sharp and Sharp firing on all cylinders.

Soft music began to play and everyone's attention was drawn to the top of the staircase, where Mindy stood with Reginald. As they began to descend, step by step, Isabel couldn't help but turn to a different sight, that of her brother waiting for his bride. She and Sam had been through so much together, and it felt like both a miracle and a blessing that they'd each found love, that they'd both found professional fulfillment and that they were now living in the same city. Her heart swelled at the thought of him having the happiness he so richly deserved.

The ceremony was short and sweet, officiated by one of Sam's friends from college, who'd recently moved to New York from Boston to work with him. He'd been ordained online for exactly this occasion. As her brother took Mindy into his arms, she couldn't have kept the tears at bay if she'd wanted to. It was too beautiful a moment to believe. Jeremy held her hand tightly, not letting go, and she hoped that it meant that no matter life's ups and downs, he would stay by her side.

As soon as Mindy and Sam walked down the very short aisle, the music got louder and decidedly more up-beat. "Now we get to have a party," Mindy announced, grabbing a glass of champagne from a waiter who had appeared from the kitchen. "Let's get these chairs out of here for dancing."

Sam pulled Isabel aside and gave her a warm hug. "It means the world to me that you could be here for this."

"Are you kidding? I wouldn't miss it for the world."

He looked down at the platinum band now circling the ring finger on his left hand. "Did you ever think I'd get married? Be honest."

"I always knew it would happen. It just took finding the right woman."

He pulled her into another bear hug. "So, at some point, Mindy and I want to talk to you about a legal matter."

Isabel reared back her head. "Not something to do with Eden's again. I barely survived the last one."

"Not that. The store is just fine. It's the question of children. Mindy and I were talking and we're consid-ering adoption."

This surprised Isabel. "Is something wrong?"

"No. We haven't even started trying yet. I just…" He looked around the room at this massive home he and Mindy now owned. "There's a lot of room here and there are a lot of children in the world who need a good home. I think we'd like to do both. Have our own kids and adopt."

"Yes. Of course, yes. I would love to help."

"So you'll take our case?"

"Don't be silly. Just try to keep me away."

Jeremy came up by her side and shook Sam's hand. "Congratulations. It's a big day."

"The best big day ever." Sam unleashed a toothy grin, then winked at Jeremy, which Isabel found odd but decided it was because he was goofy with love. "Now if you'll excuse me, I need to hunt down the bride."

Isabel and Jeremy held hands as they watched him disappear into the other room. "How long do you want to stay?" Jeremy asked.

"I guess I feel like we should stay for the whole thing. Is everything okay? You seem preoccupied." She didn't want to let paranoia get the best of her, but she couldn't escape the feeling that something was wrong.

"Everything is absolutely perfect. You know me. I always want to get you home."

Isabel fought a smile. "Well, if that's what you're getting after, I'm thinking we stay an hour, tops."

They ended up staying fifty minutes. Isabel was tired and they had quite a ride back to Brooklyn. Jeremy was quiet as they sat in the back seat of the town car.

"You sure everything's okay?" she asked for what felt like the one hundredth time.

"Yeah. I spoke to my dad today. You know how that goes. It's getting better, but I still feel like I'm feeling my way around in the dark."

"Talk about work stuff?"

He nodded. "And just trying to get to a point where I have a better relationship with him. I went ahead and asked them about dinner next week. So we can tell them about the baby."

"And?"

He smiled. "Obviously I didn't tell them that part. But yes, they said that they would love to have dinner. My mom really adores you. She says you're good for me."

Isabel squeezed his hand tight. "Somebody needs to tell her that you're good for me."

They arrived back at Jeremy's and performed their new coming-home ritual, which was checking on the kittens. Jeremy, never the big cat fan, conceded that he had "warmed" to them. Of course, Isabel was over the moon for them, and the thought of them being adopted out soon weighed heavy on her heart. They wouldn't have this fun to look forward to much longer.

Isabel sat on the floor of the guest room and played with the three kittens, who still didn't have names. For now, they were Things 1, 2 and 3—the orange male, the orange female and the calico respectively. Jeremy, however, excused himself and said he needed to get something. That only left Isabel to worry about what his dad had said and how that played into the future of their relationship.

"What do you think, Thing 1?" Isabel scooped up the kitten and kissed him on the nose. The cat squirmed to get down and frolic with his littermates. In the corner, Cat was watching over everything. "Is Jeremy acting strangely?" Isabel asked Cat.

"I don't know. Am I?" Behind her, Jeremy had walked into the room.

Isabel turned quickly. "Whoa. You are stealthy. I didn't even hear you open the door."

"I think that's only because you're so wrapped up in the kittens."

She returned her attention to them as they wrestled on the carpet. "I do adore them. I love them."

Just then Jeremy knelt down next to her. "Do you know who I adore and love?"

She eyed him with great suspicion. "Okay, now you are definitely acting weird."

"You, Isabel. I love and adore you." He reached into the pocket of his pants and pulled out a small velvet bag. "And the reason I've been quiet all night is because I have a big question on my mind."

Isabel sat perfectly still, her heart beating unevenly in her chest. She didn't want to miss a moment or a single word of what she hoped was about to happen.

He reached for her hand and held on to it tightly. His gaze met hers, and she saw exactly how sincere he was. The hurt that she'd once seen in his eyes was gone. And now, she saw hope. "I love you, Isabel Blackwell, and it's not just because you're brilliant or beautiful. And it's not merely because you're having my baby, although that's part of it. I love you because you make my whole life better. I want you to be my wife." With that, he let go of her hand and opened the velvet bag, presenting a beautiful gold-and-diamond solitaire. "This is why I talked to my dad. It's the ring my grandfather gave to my grandmother. He gave it to my dad, but my dad gave a different ring to my mom. He always felt bad about it, and I can't help but feel like this is all coming full circle now. As long as you'll say yes."

She had to laugh, at least a little bit, even as the tears streamed down her cheeks. "Of course the answer is yes. I love you, Jeremy. I love you for being strong and sensitive. I love you for not giving up on people. I love you for the way you make me feel like I'm the most important woman in the entire world."

"You *are* the most important woman in the world. No doubt about that." He leaned forward and kissed her, softly and sweetly, with just enough of that sexy Jeremy edge. She combed her fingers into his hair, wanting more.

Unfortunately, the kittens had different plans, tumbling around on the floor between them. In the excitement, Jeremy had dropped the velvet bag on the floor and they were fighting over it. "Bunch of hooligans," Isabel muttered, taking the pouch and pretending to scold them. "I can just see one of you choking on the string."

Jeremy laughed. "Can I make another crazy suggestion?"

"On top of marriage?"

"Yes. Let's keep the kittens. And Cat. Let's not give them up for adoption."

Isabel could hardly believe the words that had just come from Jeremy's mouth, which was saying a lot given that he'd just proposed. "But you don't really like cats."

"Like a lot of things, you managed to show me what I was missing out on."

"It'll be a ton of work. Four cats running around here."

Jeremy shrugged and pulled her closer. "So? I have spent years walking around this big house, hardly using it or enjoying it for that matter. And then I met you and the whole place sprang back to life. I don't want to hold back on that. So we have four cats and a baby. Bring it on."

Isabel smiled harder than she'd ever smiled, even more than she had while watching her brother say "I do" mere hours ago. "Oh, you know what I just realized? If I change my name to Isabel Blackwell-Sharp after we get married, you can still keep the firm's name as Sharp and Sharp."

"First off, I'm not doing the same thing to you that

my dad did to me. We will change the firm's name to whatever you want it to be. To whatever you want your last name to be."

She then realized what a pushover she was being. "You've got me into way too much of a charitable mood, Sharp. I should be negotiating with you, not offering concessions from the word go."

"I don't want to talk work, Isabel." He threaded his fingers through her hair, then rubbed his thumb along her lower lip. "I don't want to talk about who we know or what we do."

Isabel smiled at the echo of the magical night they'd met, when she'd dared to take a chance on Jeremy. How lucky was she that he ended up being the one? "Yeah? Then what do you want to talk about?"

"How do you feel about good views? Because there's a spectacular one in our bedroom."

* * * * *

THE CHRISTMAS
BABY BONUS

YVONNE LINDSAY

To my wonderful friends, who often know me better than I know myself. In particular to Nalini, Nicky and Peta for prompting (aka pestering) me to write this book while I stared with loathing (yes, I'm a Grinch) at a Christmas tree, and to Shar, who couldn't make it that night but who would have been pestering, ahem, prompting me right along with them.

One

There, let that be the last tartan bow to be tied, Faye begged silently as she stood back and eyed the turned-wood balustrade that led to the upstairs gallery of the lodge. Swags of Christmas ribbon looped up the stairs, with a large tartan bow at each peak.

Not for the first time, she cursed the bad luck that had seen her boss's usual decorator fall off a ladder and dislocate her shoulder a week before Piers was due to arrive at his holiday home here in Wyoming for his annual Christmas retreat and weeklong house party.

Faye had suggested he go with a minimalistic look for the festive season this year, but, no, he'd been adamant. Tradition, he'd called it. A pain in the butt, she'd called it. Either way, she'd been forced out of her warm sunny home in Santa Monica and onto an airplane, only to arrive in Jackson Hole to discover weather better suited to a polar bear than a person. So, here she was. Six days away from Christmas, decorating a house for a bunch of people who probably wouldn't appreciate it. Except for her boss, of course. He loved this time of year with a childlike passion, right down to the snow.

She hated snow, but not as much as she hated Christmas.

She turned slowly and surveyed the main hall of the lodge. Even her late mother would have been proud, Faye thought with a sharp pang in her chest, before she pushed that thought very firmly away. The entire house looked disgustingly festive. It was enough to make a sane person want to hurl, she told herself firmly, clinging to her hatred of the season of goodwill. There was no reason to be sad about being alone for the holidays when she hated the holidays with a passion, right?

At least her task was over and she could head back to the sun, where she could hide in her perfectly climate-controlled apartment and lose herself in her annual tradition of binge-watching every *Predator* movie made, followed by every *Alien* DVD in her collection, followed by any other sci-fi horror flick that was as disassociated from Christmas as it was from reality.

She moved toward the front door where her compact carry-on bag was already packed and waiting for her retreat to normality and a world without decorations or Christmas carols or—

The front door swung open and swirl of frigid air preceded the arrival of her boss, Piers Luckman. Lucky by name and luckier by nature, they said. Only she knew what a hard worker he was beneath that handsome playboy exterior. She'd worked for him for the past three years and had the utmost respect for him as a businessman. And as a man...? A tiny curl of something unfurled deep inside her. Something forbidden. Something that in another person could resemble a hint of longing, of desire. Something she clamped down on with her usual resolute ferocity. No. She didn't go there.

Piers stomped the snow off his feet on the porch outside then stepped into the lobby and unslung his battered leather computer satchel from one shoulder.

"Good flight?" she asked, knowing he'd probably piloted the company jet himself for the journey from LA to Jackson Hole.

He had no luggage because he always kept a full wardrobe at each of his homes peppered around the world.

"Merry Christmas!" Piers greeted her as he saw her standing there and unzipped his down-filled puffer jacket.

Oh, dear mother of God, what on earth was he wearing underneath it?

"Weren't you supposed arrive on Saturday, the day before your party? You're four days early," she commented, ignoring his festive greeting. "And what, by all that's holy, is *that*?"

She pointed at the gaudy hand-knitted sweater he wore. The reindeer's eyes were lopsided, his antlers crooked and…his nose? Well, suffice to say the red woolen pompom was very…bright.

A breathtaking grin spread across Piers's face.

Faye focused her gaze slightly off center so she wouldn't be tempted to stare or smile in return. The man was far too good-looking, and she only remained immune to his charms because of her personal vow to remain single and childless. That aside, she loved her job and getting a crush on her boss would be a surefire way to the unemployment office.

After all, wasn't that what had happened to a long line

of her predecessors? It wasn't like he could help it if personal assistants, who had an excuse to spend so much time with him, often found him incredibly appealing. He was charming, intelligent, handsome and, even though he'd been born with a silver spoon lodged very firmly in that beautiful mouth, he wasn't averse to working hard, overseeing his empire with confidence and charisma. The only time Faye had ever seen him shaken had been last January, when his twin brother had died in a sky-diving accident. Since then he'd been somewhat quieter, more reflective than usual.

While Faye had often felt Piers had been a little on the cavalier side in his treatment of others—particularly his revolving door of girlfriends—he'd become more considerate over this past year. As if Quin's death had reminded him just how fleeting life could be. Even Lydia, his latest girlfriend, had been on the scene far longer than was usual. Faye had even begun to wonder if Piers was contemplating making the relationship a permanent one, but then she'd received the memo to send his usual parting gift of an exquisite piece of jewelry in a signature pale blue box along with his handwritten card.

It was purely for reasons of self-preservation that she didn't find him irresistible, and she was nothing if not good at self-preservation. Besides, if you didn't have ridiculous dreams of happy-ever-after then you didn't see them dashed, and you didn't get hurt—and without all of that, you existed quite nicely, thank you.

"This?" he said, stroking a hand across the breadth of his chest and down over what she knew, from working with him at his place on the Côte D'Azur where swimwear replaced office wear, was a tautly ripped abdomen. "It's my great-aunt Florence's gift to me this year. I have a collection of them. Like it?"

"It's hideous," she said firmly. "Now you're here, I can go. Is there anything else you need me to attend to when I get back to LA?"

Piers looked at his erstwhile PA. He'd never met anyone like Faye Darby, which was exactly why he kept her around. She intrigued him, and in his jaded world there weren't many who still had that ability. Plus, she was ruthlessly capable, in a way he couldn't help but admire. It might have been cruel to have sent her to decorate the house for him for the holidays—especially knowing she had such a deep dislike of the festive season—but it needed doing and, quite frankly, he didn't trust anyone else to do it for him.

And as to the sweater, although his late great-aunt Florence had knitted him several equally jaw-droppingly hideous garments in the past, the truth was that he'd seen this one in the window of the thrift store during his morning run and he'd fallen in love with it instantly, knowing exactly how much Faye would hate it. The donation he'd made to the store in exchange for the sweater was well worth the look on Faye's face when he'd revealed the masterpiece.

But now she was standing there, having asked him a question, and waiting for a response.

"I can't think of anything at the moment. Did you send the thank-you gift to Lydia?" he asked.

Another thing he probably should have dealt with himself, but why not delegate when the person you delegated to was so incredibly competent? Besides, extricating himself from liaisons that showed every sign of getting complicated was something best left to an expert. And, goodness knew, Faye had gained more than sufficient experience in fare-welling his lady friends on his behalf.

To his delight, Faye rolled her eyes. Ah, she was so easy to tease—so very serious. Which only made him work that much harder to get a reaction out of her one way or another.

"Of course I did," Faye responded icily. "She returned it, by the way. Do you want to know what she said?"

Piers had no doubt his latest love interest—make that ex-love interest—had been less than impressed to be dusted off with diamonds and had sent the bracelet and matching earrings back to the office with a very tersely worded note. Lydia had a knack for telling people exactly what she thought of them with very few words, and he would put money on her having told him exactly where he could put said items of jewelry.

He also had every belief that Faye agreed with Lydia's stance. The two women had gotten on well. Perhaps a little too well. He cringed at the thought of the two of them ganging up on him. He wouldn't have stood a chance. Either way, he would stick firm to his decision to cut her out of his life, although he'd had the sneaking suspicion that Lydia would not give up as easily as those who'd gone before her.

"No, it's okay, I can guess," he answered with a slight grimace.

"She isn't going to give up," Faye continued as though he hadn't spoken. "She said she understands you'd be getting cold feet, given how much you mean to one another and your inability to commit."

"My what?"

"She also said you can give the jewelry to her in person and suggested dinner at her favorite restaurant in the New Year. I've put it in your calendar."

Piers groaned. "Fine, I'll tell her to her face."

"Good. Now, if there's nothing else, I'll be on my way."

She was in an all-fired hurry to leave, wasn't she? He'd told her she was welcome to stay for his annual holiday house party, but Faye had looked at him as if she'd rather gargle with shards of glass.

"No, nothing else. Take care on the road. The forecasted storm looks as if it's blowing in early. It's pretty gnarly out there. Will you be okay to drive?"

"Of course," she said with an air of supreme confidence.

Beneath it, though, he got the impression that her attitude was one of bravado rather than self-assurance. He'd gotten to understand Faye's little nuances pretty well in the time she'd worked for him. He wondered if she knew she had those little "tells."

Faye continued, "The rental company assured me I have snow tires on the car and that it will handle the weather. They even supplied me with chains for the tires, which I fitted this morning."

"You know how to fit chains?" he asked and then mentally rolled his eyes. Of course she knew how to fit chains. She pretty much could do everything, couldn't she?

"You don't need to worry about me."

While she didn't ever seem to think *anyone* should worry about her, Piers was pretty certain he was the only person looking out for her. She had nobody else. Her background check had revealed her to be an orphan from the age of fifteen. Not even any extended family hidden in the nooks and crannies of the world.

What would it be like to be so completely alone? he wondered. Even though his twin brother had died suddenly last January, both his parents were still living and he had aunts and uncles and cousins too numerous to count—even if they weren't the kinds of people he wanted to necessarily be around. He couldn't imagine what it would be like to be so completely on your own.

She reached for her coat and Piers moved behind her to help her shrug it on, then Faye bent to lift her overnight case at the same time he did.

"I'll take it," she said firmly. "No point in you having to go back out in the cold."

Her words made sense but grated on his sense of chivalry. In his world, no woman should ever have to lift a finger let alone her own case. But then again, Faye wasn't of his world, was she? And she went to great pains to remind him of that. "Thanks for stepping into the breach and doing the house for me," he said as they hesitated by the door.

Faye gave one last look at the fully decorated great hall—her eyes lingered on the stockings for Piers's expected guests pinned over the fireplace, at the tree glittering with softly glowing lights and spun-glass ornaments—and actually shuddered.

"I'll leave you to it, then," she said with obvious relief.

It was patently clear she couldn't wait to get out of there.

"Thanks, Faye. I do appreciate it."

"You'd better," she warned direly. "I've directed the payroll office to give me a large bonus for this one."

"Double it, you're worth it," he countered with another one of his grins that usually turned women to putty in his hands no matter their age—women except for his PA, that was.

"Thank you," Faye said tightly as she zipped up the front of her coat and pulled up her hood.

He watched as she lifted her overnight case and hoisted the strap of her purse higher on her shoulder.

Piers held the door open for her. "Take care on the

driveway and watch out for the drop-off on the side. I know the surface has been graded recently but you can't be too careful in this weather."

"Trust me, careful is my middle name."

"Why is that, Faye?"

She pretended she didn't hear the question the same way he'd noticed she ignored all his questions that veered into personal territory.

"Enjoy yourself, see you next year," she said and headed for the main stairs.

Piers watched her trudge down the stairs and across the driveway toward the garage, and closed the front door against the bitter-cold air that swirled around him. He turned and faced the interior of the house. Soon it would be filled with people—friends he'd invited for the holidays. But right now, with Faye gone, the place felt echoingly empty.

The wind had picked up outside in the past couple of hours and Faye bent over a little as she made her way toward the converted stables where she'd parked her rental SUV. Piers hadn't seen fit to garage the Range Rover she'd had waiting for him at the airport, she noted with a frown, but had left the vehicle at the bottom of the stairs to the front door. *Serve him right if he has to dig it out come morning*, she thought.

It would especially serve him right for delivering that blasted megawatt smile in her direction not once but twice in a short space of time. She knew he used it like the weapon it truly was. No, it didn't make her heart sing and, no, it didn't do strange things to her downstairs, either. But it could, if she let it.

Faye blinked firmly, as if to rid herself of the mental image of him standing there looking far more tempting than any man should in such a truly awful sweater—good grief, was one sleeve really longer than the other?

Well, none of that mattered now. She was on her way to the airport and then to normality. A flurry of snow whipped against her, sticking wetly to any exposed patches of skin. Had she mentioned how much she hated snow? Faye gritted her teeth and pressed the remote in her pocket that opened the garage door. She scurried into the building that, despite being renovated into a six-stall garage, was still redolent with the lingering scents of hay and horses and a time when things around here were vastly different.

Across the garage she thought she saw a movement and stared into the dark recesses of the far bay before dismissing the notion as a figment of her imagination. Faye opened the trunk of the SUV and hefted her overnight bag into the voluminous space. A bit of a sad analogy for her life when she thought about it—a small, compact, cram-filled object inside an echoing, empty void. But she didn't think about it. Well, hardly ever. Except at this time of year. Which was exactly why she hated it so much. No matter where she turned she couldn't escape the pain she kept so conscientiously at bay the rest of the year.

An odd sound from inside the SUV made her stop in her tracks. The hair on the back of her neck prickled and Faye looked around carefully. She could see nothing out of order. No mass murderers loitering in the shadows. No extraterrestrial creatures poised to hunt her down and rip her spine out. Nothing. Correction, nothing but the sudden howl of a massive squall of wind and snow. She really needed to get going before the weather got too rough for her to reach the airport and the subsequent sanity her flight home promised.

Stepping around the SUV to the driver's door, Faye

realized something was perched on her seat. Strange. She didn't remember leaving anything there when she'd pulled in two days ago, nor had she noticed anything amiss this morning when she'd come out to fit the chains on the tires in readiness to leave. Was this Piers's idea of a joke? His joy in the festive season saw him insist every year on giving her a gift, which every year she refused to open.

She moved a little closer and realized there were, in fact, two objects. One on her passenger seat, which looked like a large tote of some kind, the other a blanket-covered something-or-other shaped suspiciously like a baby's car seat. A trickle of foreboding sent a shiver down Faye's spine.

At the end of the garage, a door to the outside opened and then slammed shut, making her jump. What was going on? Then, from the back of the building, she heard a vehicle start up and drive away. Fast. She raced to the doorway in time to see a flicker of taillights as a small hatchback gunned it down the driveway. What? Who?

From her SUV she heard another sound. One she had no difficulty recognizing. If there was anything that made her more antsy than the festive season, it was miniature people. The sound came again, this time louder and with a great deal more distress.

Even though she'd seen the hatchback leaving, she still looked around, waiting for whomever it was who'd thought it funny to leave a child here to spring out and yell, "Surprise!" But she, and the baby, were alone. "This isn't funny anymore," she muttered.

It wasn't funny to start with, she reminded herself. The blanket covering the car seat began to move as if tiny fists and feet were waving beneath it. A slip of paper pinned to the blanket crackled with the movement. With her heart hammering in her chest, Faye gently tugged the blanket down.

The baby—a boy, she guessed by the blue knitted-woolen hat he wore and the tiny, puffy blue jacket that enveloped him—looked at her with startled eyes. He was completely silent for the length of about a split second before his little face scrunched up and he let loose a giant wail.

Nausea threatened to swamp her. No, no, no! This couldn't be happening. Every natural instinct in her body urged her to comfort the child, but fear held her back. The very thought of holding that small body to hers, of cupping that small head with the palm of her hand, of inhaling that sweet baby scent—no, she couldn't do that again.

Faye thought quickly. She had to get the baby inside where it was warm. Babysitting might not be the holiday break Piers had been looking forward to, but he would just have to cope with it. She reached out to jiggle the car seat, hoping the movement might calm the baby down, but he wasn't having it.

"Sorry, little man," she said, flipping the blanket back over him to protect him from the elements outside. "But you're going to have to go undercover until I can get you to the house."

The paper on the blanket rustled and Faye took a second to rip it free and shove it in her pocket. She could read it later. Right now she had to get the baby where the temperature was not approaching subzero.

Again she wondered who had left the baby there. What kind of homicidal idiot did something like that? In these temperatures, he'd have died all too quickly. Another futile loss in a world full of losses, she thought bleakly. Whoever it was had waited until she'd showed, though, hadn't they? What would they have done if she'd chosen to stay an extra night? Leave the child at the door and ring the doorbell before hightailing it down the driveway? Who would do something like that?

Whoever it was didn't matter right now, she reminded herself. She had to get the baby to the house.

Swallowing back the queasiness that assailed her, Faye hooked the tote bag over one shoulder and then hugged the car seat close to her body, her arms wrapped firmly around the edges of the blanket so it wouldn't fly away in the wind. She scurried across to the house, slipping a little on the driveway in shoes that were better suited to strolling the Santa Monica pier than battling winter in Wyoming, and staggered up the front stairs.

The baby didn't let up his screaming for one darn second. She didn't blame him. By the time she reached the front door, she felt like weeping herself. She dropped the tote at her feet and hammered on the thick wooden surface, relieved when the door swung open almost immediately.

"Car trouble?" Piers asked, filling the doorway before stepping aside and gesturing for her to enter.

"No," she answered. "Baby trouble."

Two

"Baby trouble?" he repeated, looked stunned.

"That's what I said. Someone left this in the garage. Here, take it."

Faye thrust the car seat into his arms and pulled the door closed behind them. Damn his eyes, he'd already started the Christmas carols collection. One thousand, two hundred and forty-seven versions of every carol known to modern man and in six different languages. She knew because she'd had the torturous task of creating the compilation for him. Seriously, could her day get any worse?

Piers looked in horror at the screaming object in his arms. "What is it?"

Faye sighed and rolled her eyes. "I told you. A baby. A boy, I'd guess."

She reached over and flipped down the blanket, exposing the baby's red, unhappy face.

Piers looked from the baby to her in bewilderment. "But who…? What…?"

"My thoughts exactly," Faye replied. "I don't know who, or what, left him behind. Although I suspect it was possibly the person I caught a glimpse of speeding away in a car down the driveway. For the record, no, I did not get the license plate number. Look, I have to leave him with you, I'm running late. Oh, by the way, he came with a note." She reached into her jacket pocket, pulled out the crumpled paper and squinted at the handwriting before putting the note on top of the blanket. "Looks like it's addressed to you. Have fun," she said firmly and turned to leave.

"You can't leave me with this," Piers protested.

"I can and I will. I'm off the clock, remember. Seriously, if you can't cope, just call up someone from Jackson Hole. I'm sure there'll be any number of people willing to assist you. I can't miss my flight. I have to go."

"I'll double your salary. Triple it!"

Faye shook her head and resolutely turned to the door. There wasn't enough money in the world to make her stay. With the baby's wails ringing in her ears and a look of abject horror on her playboy boss's face firmly embedded in her mind, she went outside.

Faye hadn't realized she was shaking until the door closed at her back. The baby's cries even made it through the heavy wood. Faye blinked away her own tears. She. Would. Not. Cry. Ignoring her need to provide comfort might rank up there with the hardest things she'd ever done, but at least this way no one would get hurt—especially not her. Piers had resources at his disposal; there were people constantly ready to jump at his beck and call. And if all else failed, there was always Google.

Stiffening her spine, she headed to the garage, got into her SUV and started down the drive. It might only be four in the afternoon, but with the storm it was already gloomy out. Despite the snow tires and the chains, nothing could get her used to the sensation of driving on a snow-and-ice-covered road. Nothing quite overcame that sickening, all-encompassing sense of dread that struck her every time the tires began to lose purchase—nothing quite managed to hold off the memories that came flooding back in that moment. Nothing, except perhaps the overpowering sense of reprieve when the all-wheel-drive kicked in and she knew she wasn't going to suffer a repeat of that night.

And then, as always, came the guilt. Survivor's guilt they called it. Thirteen years later and it still felt a lot more like punishment. It was part of why she'd chosen to live in Southern California rather than her hometown in Michigan or anyplace that got snow and ice in winter. It didn't make the memories go away, but sunshine had a way of blurring them over time.

The sturdy SUV rocked under the onslaught of the wind and Faye's fingers wrapped tight around the steering wheel. She should have left ages ago. Waiting a couple extra hours at the airport would have been infinitely preferable to this.

"Relax," she told herself. "You've got this."

Another gust rocked the vehicle and it slid a little in the icy conditions. Faye's heart rate picked up a few notches and beneath her coat she felt perspiration begin to form in her armpits and under her breasts. Damn snow. Damn Piers. Damn Christmas.

And then it happened. A pine tree on the side of the road just ahead toppled across the road in front of her. Faye jammed on the brakes and tried to steer to the side, but it was too late—there was no way she could avoid the impact. The airbag deployed in her face with a shotgun-like boom, shoving her back into her seat. The air around her filled with fine dust that almost looked like smoke, making her cough, and an acrid scent like gunpowder filled her nostrils.

Memories flooded into her mind. Of screams, of the scent of blood and gasoline, of the heat and flare of flames and then of pain and loss and the end of everything she'd ever known. Faye shook uncontrollably and struggled to get out of the SUV. It took her a while to realize she still had her seat belt on.

"I'm okay," she said shakily, willing it to be true. "I'm okay."

She took a swift inventory of her limbs, her face. A quick glance in the rearview mirror confirmed she had what looked like gravel rash on her face from the airbag. It was minor in the grand scheme of things, she told herself. It could have been so much worse. At least this time she was alone.

Faye searched the foot well for her handbag and pulled out her cell phone. She needed to call for help, but the lack of bars on her screen made it clear there was no reception—not even enough for an emergency call.

With a groan of frustration, she hitched her bag crosswise over her body and pushed the door open. It took some effort as one of the front panels had jammed up against the door frame, but eventually she got it open wide enough to squeeze through.

She surveyed the damage. There was no way this vehicle was going anywhere anytime soon, and unless she could climb over the fallen tree and make it down the rest of the driveway and somehow hail a cab at the bottom of the mountain, she was very definitely going to miss her flight.

She weighed her options and looked toward the house, not so terribly far away, where light blazed from the downstairs' windows and the trees outside twinkled with Christmas lights. Then she looked back down—over the tree with its massive girth, the snowdrifts on one side of the driveway and the sheer drop on the other.

She had only one choice.

Piers stared incredulously at the closed front door. She'd actually done it. She'd left him with a screaming baby and no idea of what to do. He'd fire her on the spot, if he didn't need her so damn much. Faye basically ran his life with Swiss precision. On the rare occasions something went off the rails, she was always there to right things. Except for now.

Piers looked at the squalling baby in the car seat and set it on the floor. Darn kid was loud.

He figured out how to extricate the little human from his bindings and picked him up, instinctively resting the baby against his chest and patting him on the bottom. To his amazement, the little tyke began to settle. And nuzzle, as if he was seeking something Piers was pretty sure he was incapable of providing.

Before the little guy could work himself up to more tears, Piers bent, lifted the tote his traitorous PA had dropped on the floor and carried it and the baby through to the kitchen.

Sure enough, when he managed to one-handedly wrangle the thing open, he found a premixed baby bottle in a cooler sleeve.

"Right, now what?" he asked the infant in his arms. "You guys like this stuff warm, don't you?"

He vaguely remembered hearing somewhere that heating formula in a microwave was a no-no and right now he knew that standing the bottle in a pot of warm water and waiting for it to heat wouldn't be quick enough for him or for the baby. On cue, the baby began to fret. His little hands curled into tight fists that clutched at Piers's sweater impatiently and he banged his little face against Piers' neck.

"Okay, okay. I'm new at this. You're just going to have to be patient a while longer."

With an air of desperation, Piers continued to check the voluminous tote—taking everything out and laying it on the broad slab of granite that was his kitchen counter.

The tote reminded him of Mary Poppins's magical bag with the amount of stuff it held—a tin of formula along with a massive stash of disposable diapers and a couple of sets of clothing. In the bottom of the bag he found a contraption that looked like it would hold a baby bottle. He checked the side and huffed a massive sigh of relief on discovering it was a bottle warmer. Four to six minutes, according to the directions, and the demanding tyrant in his arms could be fed.

"Okay, buddy, here we go. Let's get this warmed up for you," Piers muttered to his ungrateful audience, who'd had enough of waiting and screwed up his face again before letting out a massive wail.

Piers frantically jiggled the baby while following the directions to warm the bottle. It was undoubtedly the longest four minutes of his life. The baby banged his forehead against Piers's neck again. Oh, hell, he was hot. Did he have a fever? Piers felt the child's forehead with one of his big hands. A bit too warm, yes, but not feverish. He hoped. Maybe he just needed to get out of that jacket. But how on earth was Piers going to manage that? Feeling about as clumsy as if attempting to disrobe the baby while wearing oven gloves, Piers carefully wrestled the baby out of the jacket.

"There we go, buddy. Mission accomplished."

The baby rewarded him with a demanding bellow of frustration, reminding Piers that the time had to be up for warming the bottle. He lifted the bottle, gave it a good shake, tested it on his wrist and then offered it to the baby. Poor mite must have been starving; he took to the bottle as if his life depended on it. And it did, Piers realized. And right now this little life depended on him, too.

So where on earth had he come from?

Remembering the note Faye had left with him, Piers walked to the entrance of the house and shifted the blanket until he found the crumpled piece of paper. Carefully balancing the baby and bottle with one hand, he went to sit in the main room and read the note.

Dear Mr. Luckman,
It's time you took responsibility for your actions. You've ignored all my attempts to contact you so far. Maybe this will make you sit up and take notice. His name is Casey, he was born on September 10 and he's your son. I relinquish all rights to him. I never wanted him in the first place, but he deserves to know his father. Do not try to find me.

There was an indecipherable signature scrawled along the bottom. Piers read the note again and flipped the single sheet over to see if the author had left a name on the other side. There was nothing.

His son? Impossible. Well, perhaps not completely impossible, but about as highly unlikely as growing a market garden on the moon. He was meticulous about protection in all his relationships. Accidents like this did not happen to him. Or at least they hadn't, until now.

Piers did the mental math and figured, if he was the child's father, he had to have met the baby's mother around the New Year. He was always in Jackson Hole from before Christmas until early January and hosted his usual festivities around the twenty-fourth and on the thirty-first. But he'd been between girlfriends at the time and he certainly didn't remember sleeping with anyone.

The baby had slowed down on the bottle and he stared up at Piers with very solemn brown eyes. Eyes that were very much like Piers's own. His son? Could it somehow be true? Even as he mentally rejected the idea, he began to feel a connection to the infant in his arms. A connection that was surely as unfeasible as the idea that he was responsible for this tiny life.

The bottle was empty and Piers removed it from the baby's mouth. So now what?

Casey looked blissed out on the formula, the expression on his face making Piers smile as the baby blew a milky bubble. In seconds the infant was asleep. Piers laid the kid down on the couch and packed some pillows around him like a soft fortress. Then he got to his feet and reached for his phone. Someone in town had to know where the baby belonged. Because as cute as Casey was, he surely didn't belong to him.

He dialed the number for one of the café and bar joints in town, a place where the locals gathered to gossip by day and party and occasionally fight by night. If anyone knew anything about a new baby in town, it would be these guys. Except the call didn't go through. He checked the screen—no reception. He reached for the landline only to discover it was out of action, too.

"Damn," Piers cursed on a heavy sigh.

The storm had clearly grown a lot worse while he was occupied with his unexpected guest. Maybe he should go and check on the backup generator. He was just about to do so when he heard a knocking at the front door. Puzzled, as he wasn't expecting any of his guests for a few more days yet, he went across to open it.

"Faye? What happened to you?"

His eyes roamed her face as he took her arm and led her inside toward the warmth of the fireplace. She was pale and she had a large red mark on her face, like a mild gravel rash or something, and she shivered uncontrollably. Her jacket, which was fine for show but obviously useless in actual snowy conditions, was sodden, as were the jeans she wore, and her sneakers made a squelching sound on the floor tiles.

"A t-t-tree came d-d-down on the driveway," she managed through chattering teeth.

"You're going to have to get out of these wet clothes before you get hypothermic," he said.

"T-too late," she said with a wry grin. "I think I'm already th-there."

"Come on," he said leading the way to a downstairs bathroom. "Get in a hot shower and I'll get you something dry to put on. Where's your suitcase?"

"St-still in the b-b-back of the SUV," she said through lips tinged with blue.

"And the SUV?"

"It's stuck against the tree that came down across the drive about halfway down."

"Are you hurt anywhere other than your face?"

"A f-few bruises, maybe, b-but mostly just c-cold."

No wonder she looked so shocky. A crash and then walking back up the drive in this weather? It was a miracle she'd made it.

"Let's get you out of these wet things."

He reached for her jacket and tugged the zipper down. Chilled fingers closed around his hands.

"I-I can m-manage," she said weakly.

"You can barely speak," he answered firmly, brushing her hands away and tugging the jacket off her. "I'll help you get out of your clothes, that's all. Okay?"

Faye nodded, her hair dripping. Beneath her jacket, Faye's fine wool sweater was also soaked through and her nipples peaked against the fabric through her bra. He bent to undo the laces on her sneakers and yanked them off, then peeled away her wet socks. She had pretty feet, even though they were currently blue with cold and, to his surprise, she had tiny daisies painted on each of her big toes. Cute and whimsical, he thought, and nothing like the automaton he was used to in the office. Near her ankle he caught sight of some scar tissue that appeared to be snaking out from beneath her sodden jeans.

"We've got two options," Piers said as he reached for the button fly of her jeans. "The best way to warm you up is skin-to-skin contact, or a nice hot shower."

"S-shower," Faye said emphatically.

Piers smiled a little. So, she wasn't so far gone she couldn't make a decision. For that he could be thankful, even if the prospect of skin-to-skin contact with her held greater appeal than it ought to. At least the under-floor heating would help to restore some warmth to her frigid feet. He peeled the wet denim down her legs. He always knew she was slightly built but there was lean muscle there, too. As if she did distance running or something like that.

He'd always been a leg man and a twitch in his groin inconveniently reminded him of that fact. Now wasn't the time for those kinds of thoughts, he reminded himself firmly. But then he noticed her lower legs and the ropey scar tissue. Faye's hands had been on his shoulder, to help her keep her balance as he removed her jeans. Her fingers tightened against his muscles when he exposed her damaged skin.

"I can take it from h-here," she said, her voice still shaking with the effect of the cold.

"No, don't worry, I've got it," he insisted and finished pulling her jeans off for her.

No wonder she always wore trousers in the office. Those were some serious scars and she was obviously self-conscious about them. Still, they were the least of their worries right now. First priority was getting her warm again.

"Okay." He stepped away. "Can you manage the sweater and your underwear on your own? I'll get the shower running."

Faye nodded and began to pull her sweater up and over her head. For all that she lived in Los Angeles, she had the fairest skin of anyone he'd ever seen. And were those freckles scattering down her chest and over the swell of her perfect breasts? Suddenly disgusted with himself for sneaking a peek, Piers snapped his attention back to his task before she caught him staring, but he knew he'd never be able to see her in her usual buttoned-up office wear without seeing those freckles in the back of his mind.

The bathroom soon began to fill with steam and he turned to see Faye had wrapped a towel around herself, protecting her modesty. Even so, he couldn't quite rid himself of the vision of her as she'd pulled her sweater off. Of the slenderness of her hips and thighs and how very tiny her waist was. Of the scar across her abdomen that had told of a major surgery at some time. Of that intriguing dusting of freckles that invited closer exploration—

No, stop it! he castigated himself. *She's your PA, not your plaything.*

"Shower's all ready. Stay in there as long as you need. I'll be back with some clothes, then I'll warm up something to eat."

For a second he considered trekking down the drive to retrieve her suitcase, but that wasn't a practical consideration with both her and the baby needing his supervision. Which left him with the task of finding her something out of his wardrobe. An imp of mischief tugged his lips into a grin. Oh, yes, he knew exactly what he'd get her.

"You can't be serious!" Faye exclaimed as she came through the bathroom door. "Surely you could have found me something better than this to wear!"

Now that she was warm again she was well and truly back to her usual self.

Piers fought the urge to laugh out loud. She was swamped in the Christmas sweater he'd chosen for her out of his collection and the track pants ballooned around her slender legs. At least the knitted socks he favored while he stayed here didn't look too ridiculous, even if the heel part was probably up around her ankles. It was a relief to see her with some natural color back in her cheeks, though.

"You needed something warm." He shrugged. "I didn't have time to be picky. Besides, you look adorable."

Faye snorted. "I don't do adorable."

"Not normally, no," he agreed amicably. "But you have to admit you're warmer in those clothes than you would be in your own."

"Speaking of my own… Where are they?"

"In the dryer—except for your coat, which is hanging up in the mudroom."

Faye nodded in approval and looked around. "What have you done with the baby?"

As if on cue, a squawk arose from the sofa. A squawk that soon rose to a high-pitched scream that was enough to raise the hairs on the back of Piers's neck. He groaned inwardly. One problem solved and another just popped right back up. It was like playing Whac-A-Mole except a whole lot less satisfying.

"Well, aren't you going to do something?" Faye asked with a pained expression on her face.

"I was going to get you something to eat. Perhaps you could see to Casey."

"That's his name?"

Piers winced as the baby screamed again and he rushed over to the sofa to pick him up. The little tyke's knees were pulled up against his chest and his fists flailed angrily in the air. For a wee thing, he sure had bushels full of temper.

"According to the note, yes." He held the baby up against him, but Casey wouldn't be consoled. "What do I do now?"

"Why would you expect me to know?" his currently very unhelpful PA responded.

"Because..." His voice trailed off. He'd been about to say "because you're a woman," but saved himself in time. It was an unfair assumption to make. "Because you seem to know everything else," he hastily blurted.

"You deal with him. I'll go find us something to eat."

"Faye, please. What should I do?" he implored, jiggling Casey up and down and swaying on the spot. All things he'd seen other people do with babies with far greater success than he was currently experiencing. If he didn't know better, he'd think the child was in pain, but how could that be so?

Faye gestured to the empty bottle he'd left on the coffee table. "Did you burp him after you fed him?"

"Burp him?"

"You know, keep him upright, rub his back, encourage him to burp."

"No."

"Then he's probably just got gas in his stomach. Put a cloth or a towel on your shoulder and rub his back firmly. He'll come around."

"Like this?" Piers said, rubbing the baby's tiny little back for all he was worth.

"Yes, but you'll need a towel—"

Casey let out an almighty belch and Piers felt something warm and wet congeal on his shoulder and against the side of his neck. He fought a shudder, almost too afraid to look.

"—in case he spits up on you," Faye finished with a smug expression on her face.

If he didn't know better he'd have accused her of enjoying his discomfort, but, never one to let the little things get him down, Piers merely went through to the kitchen and grabbed a handful of paper towels to wipe off his neck and shoulder. His nostrils flared at the scent of slightly soured milk.

"Try not to let it get on his clothes if you can help it. Unless you want to bathe and change him, that is."

Yes, there was no mistaking the humor in her tone. Piers turned on her, the now silent baby cradled in one arm as he continued to dab at the moisture on his shoulder.

"You do know about babies," he accused her.

She shrugged in much the same way he had when she'd protested the clothing he'd given her. "Maybe I just know everything, like you said."

"Can you hold him for me while I go and change?"

"You could just get me something decent to wear and I can give you this abominable snowman back," she answered, tugging at the front of the sweater he'd given her. "Seriously, do you have an entire collection of these things?"

"Actually, I do. So, back to my question, can you hold him for me?"

"No."

She turned and walked away.

"Then what am I supposed to do with him?"

"Put him on a blanket on the floor or lay him on your bed while you get changed. Although, if you've fed him you might want to check his diaper before you put him on the bed. You wouldn't want anything to leak out on that silk comforter of yours."

Piers shuddered in horror. "Check his diaper? How does one do that?"

Faye sighed heavily and turned to face him. "You really don't know?"

"It doesn't fall under the category of running a Fortune 500 company and keeping thousands of staff in employment. Nor does it come under the banner of relaxing and enjoying the spoils of my labors," he answered tightly. "Seriously, Faye. I need your help."

A look of reluctant resignation crossed her dainty features. "Fine," she said with all the enthusiasm of a pirate about to walk the plank into shark-infested waters. "Give him to me, go get changed and come straight back. I'll give you a lesson when you're ready."

Faye reluctantly accepted the infant as Piers handed him over and was instantly forced to quell the instinctive urge to hold him close and to nuzzle the fuzz on the top of his head. Instead she walked swiftly over to the Christmas tree, where there were more than enough ornaments and sparkling lights to hold his attention until Piers returned.

She could do this, she told herself firmly. It was just a baby. And she was just a woman, whose every instinct compelled her to nurture, to protect, to care. Okay, so that might have been the old Faye, she admitted. But the reinvented Faye was self-sufficient and completely independent. She did not need other people to find her joy in life, and she was happier with everyone at a firm distance. She did what she could on a day-to-day basis to ensure Piers's life ran smoothly, both in business and personally, and that was where her human interactions began and ended. She did not need people. Period. Especially little people, who in return needed you so much more.

"You look comfortable with him. Has he been okay?"

Faye hoped Piers hadn't seen her flinch at the unexpected sound of his voice. Give the man an inch and he took a mile. No wonder it had become her personal mission to stay on top of their professional relationship every single day.

"What? Did you expect me to have carved him up and cooked him for dinner?"

Piers cocked his head and looked at her. "Maybe. You don't seem too thrilled to be around him."

Faye pushed the child back into his arms. "I'm not a baby person."

"And yet you seemed to know what was wrong with him before."

Faye ignored his comment.

Of course she knew what was likely wrong with little Casey. Hadn't she helped her mom from the day she'd brought little Henry home from the hospital? Then, after the accident, hadn't she spent three years in foster care, assisting her foster mom as often as humanly possible with the little ones as some way to assuage the guilt she felt over the deaths of her baby brother, her mom and her stepdad? Deaths she'd been responsible for. Hadn't her heart been riven in two as every baby and toddler had been adopted or returned to their families, taking a piece of her with them every time? And still the guilt remained.

"Knowing what to do and actually wanting to do it are two completely different things," she said brusquely. "Now, you need to learn to change his diaper. By the way, did that note explain who he belongs to?" She switched subjects rather than risk revealing a glimmer of her feelings.

"Me, apparently. Although I have my doubts. Quin was here at the time he was likely conceived. Casey could just as easily be his."

More likely be his, Faye thought privately. While Piers was a wealthy man who enjoyed a playboy lifestyle when he wasn't working his butt off, his identical twin brother had made a habit of taking his privileged lifestyle to even greater heights—and greater irresponsibility—always leaving a scattering of broken hearts wherever he went. Faye could easily imagine that he might have been casual enough to have left a piece of himself here and moved on to his next conquest with not even a thought to the chaos he may have left behind. Still, it didn't do to think ill of the dead. She knew Piers missed his brother. With Quin's death, it had been as though he'd lost a piece of himself.

"What do you plan to do?" she asked.

"Keep him if he is my son or Quin's."

"What if he's not?"

"Why would his mother have any reason to bring him here if he wasn't?"

She had to admit he had a good point, but she noticed he'd dodged her question quite neatly. Almost as neatly as she might have done in similar circumstances.

"How long do you think it'll be before the phones are back up and we can get some help to clear the driveway?"

"A day. Maybe more. Depends on how long before the storm blows over, I guess."

"A few days! Don't you have a satellite phone or a backup radio or *something*?"

Faye began to feel a little panicked. Being here alone with her boss wasn't the problem. They had a working relationship only and she would never presume to believe she came even close to his "type" for anything romantic, not that she wanted that, anyway. But alone with him and a baby? A baby that even now was cooing and smiling in her direction while Piers held it? That was akin to sheer torture.

Three

"No, no radio."

"Well, I plan to get right on that as soon as I get home. You can't be stranded here like this. In fact, I'm not sure how an event like this is even covered under your protection insurance for the firm."

"Faye, relax," Piers instructed her with a wry grin. "We're hardly about to die."

"I am relaxed."

"No, you're not. You know, to be honest, I don't think I've ever seen you relaxed."

"Of course you have. I'm always relaxed at work."

His brows lifted in incredulity. "Seriously?"

"Seriously," she affirmed, averting her gaze from his perfectly symmetrical face with its quizzical expression and the similar expression on the infant so comfortable in his arms. For a man who had no experience with babies, he certainly looked very natural with this one.

Fay willed her heart rate back to normal. Right, so they had no external communication. It wasn't her worst nightmare, but with a baby on hand it came pretty darn close. What if something went wrong and they needed medical assistance? What if—

The lights flickered.

"What was that?" she demanded.

"Just a flicker, that's all. It's perfectly normal, considering the weather. How about you show me how to do this diaper thing?"

"Diaper. Yes. Okay. Fine." Faye looked around the room, searching for the tote bag. "Where's the bag with his things?"

"It's in the kitchen," Piers said.

"Great."

Faye marched in the direction of the kitchen and retrieved what she—correction, what Piers—would need, and detoured past the massive linen closet near the housekeeper's quarters for a thick towel to lay the baby on. She wondered what Meredith, Piers's housekeeper, would think of the situation when she arrived. When she actually could arrive, that was. Faye felt a flutter of panic in her chest again. She thought she'd overcome her anxiety issues years ago, but it was a little daunting to realize that all it took was being stranded with her boss and a baby and they all came flooding back.

"Okay," she said on her return to the main room. "Pick a nice, flat spot and lay the towel down, double thickness."

Piers took the towel from her and did as she instructed, spreading it with one hand on the sofa where he'd put Casey to sleep earlier.

"Good," Faye said from her safe distance at the end of the couch. "Open the wipes container and put it next to where you'll be working, then lay him down on the towel and undo the snaps that run along the inside of the legs of his onesie."

"Okay, that's not so bad so far," Piers said.

"Keep one hand on his tummy. It's a good habit to get into so when he starts to wriggle more, or roll over, he's less likely to fall and hurt himself."

"How *do* you know this stuff?" Piers asked, doing what he was told and looking up at her. "Jokes aside, I didn't see anything about baby wrangling in your résumé."

Faye ignored the question. Of course she did. She wasn't about to launch into the bleeding heart story of her tragic past. The last thing she wanted from Piers was pity.

The last thing? What about the first? a tiny voice tickled at the back of her mind.

There was no first, she told herself firmly.

"Now, do you see the tapes on the sides of his diaper? Undo them carefully and pull the front of the diaper down and check for—"

A string of expletives poured from Piers's lips. "What on earth? Is that normal?"

Faye couldn't help it. She laughed out loud. As if he knew exactly what she found so funny—and he probably did—Casey gurgled happily under Piers's hand.

"I'm sorry," she said, getting herself back under control. "I shouldn't laugh. Yes, it's entirely normal when a child is on a liquid-only diet. His gut is still very immature and doesn't process stuff like an older child begins to. Watch out, though, don't let his feet kick into it."

She continued with her instructions, stifling more laughter as Piers gagged when it came to wiping Casey's little bottom clean. But that was nothing compared to his reaction to the water fountain the baby spouted right before he got the clean diaper on.

Faye couldn't quite remember when she had last enjoyed herself so much. Her usually suave and capable boss—the lady slayer, as they called him in the office—was all fingers and thumbs when it came to changing a baby.

Eventually the job was done and Piers sat back on his heels with a look of accomplishment on his face.

"You do realize you're probably going to have to do this about eight to ten times a day, don't you?" Faye said with a wicked sense of glee. "Including at night if he doesn't sleep through yet."

"You're kidding me, aren't you? That took me, how long?"

"Fifteen minutes. But then, you're a newbie at this. You'll get faster as you get used to it."

"No way. There aren't enough hours in a day."

"What else were you planning to do with your time? It's not like you were planning to work this week."

"Entertain my guests, maybe?"

"If we can't get out, they can't get in," Faye reminded him, ignoring the little clench in her gut at the thought.

She hated the idea of being trapped anywhere, even if it was in a luxury ten-bedroom lodge in the mountains.

"True, but I expect once the storm blows through we'll have the phones back, mobiles if not the landline, and we can call someone to come and clear the road and retrieve your car."

"And then I can head back home," she said with a heartfelt sigh.

"And then you can head home," Piers agreed. He balanced Casey standing on his thighs, smiling at him as Casey locked his knees and bore his weight for a few seconds before his legs buckled and he sagged back down again.

"Why do you hate Christmas so much, Faye?"

"I don't hate it," she said defensively.

"Oh, you do."

Piers looked her square in the eye and Faye shifted a little under his penetrating gaze. Against the well-washed wool of the snowman sweater her bare nipples tightened and she felt her breath hitch in her chest.

No, she wasn't attracted to him. He wasn't at all appealing as he sat there wearing a mutant Rudolph sweater and cuddling a tiny baby on his lap as if it was the most natural thing in the world. The lights flickered again.

"I'd better find some flashlights. Where do you keep them?"

"In the kitchen, I suppose. Usually, Meredith takes care of all that," he answered, referring to the housekeeper who'd been due to arrive this evening.

Overhead, the lights dimmed again before going right out. Faye shot to her feet.

"It's dark!" she blurted unnecessarily.

"Let your eyes adjust. With the fire going we'll be able to see okay in a minute," Piers soothed her.

Faye felt inexplicably helpless and that was something she generally avoided at all cost. Not being in control or being able to direct the outcome of what was going on around her was the tenth circle of hell as far as she was concerned. Where was her mobile? She had a flashlight app she could use. Better yet, she could use Piers's. His was undoubtedly closer.

"Give me your phone," she demanded.

"No reception, remember?" he drawled.

She could just make out that he was still playing with the baby, who remained completely unfazed by this new development. Mind you, after being abandoned by your mother, facing a power outage was nothing by comparison in his little world.

"It has a flashlight function, remember?" she sniped in return.

Piers stood, reached into his pocket and handed her the phone.

It held the warmth of his body and she felt that warmth seep into the palm of her hand, almost as intensely as if he'd touched her. She swapped the phone into her other hand and rubbed her palm over the soft cotton of the track pants, but it did little to alleviate the little tingle that warmth had left behind. The realization made her exhale impatiently.

"Faye, they'll get the power back on soon, don't worry. Besides, I have a backup generator. I'll get that going in a moment or two. In the meantime, relax—enjoy the ambience."

Ambience? On the bright side, at least the Christmas lights were also out and the carols were no longer playing. Okay, she could do ambience if she had to.

"I'm not worrying, I'm making contingency plans. It's what I do," she replied.

After selecting the right app on his phone, she made her way into the kitchen and searched the drawers for flashlights. Uttering a small prayer of thanks that Meredith was such an organized soul that she not only had several bright flashlights but spare bulbs and batteries, as well, Faye returned to the main room. Piers was right, with the firelight it didn't take long for her eyes to adjust to the cozy glow that limned the furnishings. But the flickering light reminded her all too quickly of another time, another night, another fire—and the screams that had come with it.

Forcing down the quiver juddering through her, Faye methodically lined up the flashlights on the coffee table, then sat.

"I guess you're not a fan of the dark, either, then?" Piers commented casually, as if they'd been discussing her likes and dislikes already.

"I never said that. I just like to be prepared for all eventualities."

In the gloom she saw Piers shrug a little. "Sometimes it pays to live dangerously. To roll with the unexpected."

"Not on my watch," she said firmly.

The unexpected had always delivered the worst stages of her life, and she'd made it her goal to never be that vulnerable to circumstances again. So far, she'd aced it.

Across from her, Piers chuckled and the baby made a similar sound in response.

"He seems happy enough," Faye observed. What would it be to have a life so simple? A full tummy, a nap and clean diaper, and all was well with the world. But the helplessness? Faye cringed internally. No, she was better off the way she was. An island. "What are you going to do with him?" she asked.

"Aside from keep him?" Piers asked with a laconic grin. "Raise him to be a Luckman, I guess. According to the note, he's mine."

Faye shot to her feet again. "We both know that's impossible. You weren't even going out with anyone around the time he was conceived. You'd broken up with Adele and hadn't met Lydia yet. Unless you had a casual hookup over the Christmas break?"

Piers snorted. "I can't believe you know exactly who and when I was going out with someone."

"Of course I keep track of those details. For the most

part I've had a closer relationship with any of those women than you have, remember?"

"I do remember, and you're right. I wasn't with anyone, in any sense, that holiday."

"Then why would his mother say he's yours? Surely she knew who she slept with that holiday?"

Or had she known?

Piers's twin had been at the lodge since before that New Year's Eve when Piers had flown to LA for two days to countersign a new deal he'd been waiting on. While Quin had always been charming enough, he'd very clearly lacked the moral fiber and work ethic of his slightly older twin. Faye privately thought part of Quin's problem was that everything in his life had come too easily to him—especially women—and that had left him jaded and often cynical. Not for the first time she wondered if he'd masqueraded as his brother sometimes, purely for the nuisance factor. And this baby development was nothing if not a nuisance.

"If we ever track her down, I'll make sure to ask her," Piers said with a wry twist to his mouth. "We don't have much to go on, do we?"

No, they didn't. Faye made a mental note to add speaking to their private investigators to her to-do list the moment she returned to civilization.

Piers shifted Casey into the crook of his arm and the baby snuggled against him, his little eyes drifting closed again. The picture of the two of them was so poignantly sweet it made Faye want to head straight out into the nearest snowdrift and freeze away any sense of longing that dared spark deep inside her.

She moved toward the fireplace and put her hands out to the flames.

"Still cold?" Piers asked.

"Not really."

"I should get that food I promised you."

"No, it's okay. I'll get it. You hold the baby," she said firmly and grabbed a flashlight from the table. "I'll be back in a few minutes."

Piers watched her scurry away as if the hounds of hell were after her. Why was his super-efficient PA so afraid of babies? It was more than fear, though, he mused. On the surface, it appeared as if she couldn't bear to be around the child, but Piers wasn't fooled by that. He hadn't doubled the family's billion-dollar empire by being deceived by what lay on the surface. His ability to delve into the heart of matters was one of his greatest strengths, and the idea of delving into Faye's closely held secrets definitely held a great deal of appeal.

Casey was now fast asleep in his arms. He settled the baby down inside the cushion fort he'd created earlier and covered him with his blanket. As Piers fingered the covering—hand-knitted in the softest of yarns—he wondered if the baby had other family who cared about him. Family who might be wondering where he was and who was caring for him.

While Piers projected the image of a lazy playboy, beneath the surface he had a quick mind that never stopped working. It frustrated him that there was nothing further he could do to solve the question of how Casey had come to be delivered to his door.

But he could certainly delve a little deeper into Faye's apparent phobia when it came to infants. She intrigued him on many levels. Always had. He'd always sensed she bore scars, emotional if not physical, because she was so locked down. But now he knew she had scars on her body, too, and suddenly he wanted to know why. Were the two linked? And how did she know her way around a diaper bag so well?

Satisfied the baby was safe where he was placed, Piers rose and made his way through to the kitchen, where he could hear Faye clattering around. From the scent that tweaked his nostrils, she'd found one of Meredith's signature rich tomato soups in the freezer and was reheating it on the stove top, tiny blue flames dancing merrily beneath the pot. Ever resourceful, she'd lit some candles and placed them in mason jars to give more light.

Faye was in the middle of slicing a loaf of ciabatta and sprinkling grated cheese onto the slices when she became aware of his presence.

"Bored with the baby already?"

"He's asleep, so I thought I'd come and annoy you instead."

"It takes a lot to annoy me."

"Casey seemed to manage it," Piers said succinctly, determined to get to the root of her aversion to the infant.

"He doesn't annoy me. I'm just not a baby person," she said lightly, turning her attention back to putting the tray of sliced bread and cheese under the broiler. "Not every woman is, you know."

"Most have a reason," he pressed. "What's yours?"

Sometimes it was best to go directly to the issue, he'd found. With Faye, it was fifty-fifty that he'd get a response. Tonight, it seemed, he was out of luck.

"Did you want a glass of wine with the meal?" she asked, moving to the tall wine fridge against the wall.

"No, thanks, but go ahead if you want one."

She shook her head. Piers watched her move around the kitchen, finding everything she needed to set up trays for them to eat from. He'd always appreciated her competence and reliability, but right now he wished there was a little less polished professionalism and little more about her that was forthcoming. Like, who was she really? How did she get to be so competent around babies and yet seem to detest them at the same time? No, *detest* was too strong a word. It had been fear in her eyes, together with a genuine need to create distance between her and little Casey.

"Are you scared of him?" Piers asked conversationally. "I can understand if you are. I was always terrified that I'd drop a baby if I ever had to hold one."

"You? Terrified?" she asked, raising a skeptical brow at him as she turned from checking the bread under the broiler.

Under the candle glow, he could see the hot air had flushed her cheeks and was reminded again that Faye was a very attractive woman. Not that he was into her or anything. *Liar*, said the small voice at the back of his head. Half of her appeal had always been her looks, the other half had been her apparent immunity to his charms. It didn't matter what he said, did or wore—or didn't wear—she remained impervious to him. She also wasn't in the least sycophantic—and not at all hesitant to bluntly tell him when his ideas or demands were outrageous or unreasonable.

He realized she'd managed to deflect the question away from herself again.

"You're very good at that, you know," he commented with a wry grin.

"What, cheese on toast?" she answered flippantly, presenting her back to him as she bent to lift the tray of toasted golden goodness from the oven. Faye began piling the cheese toast slices onto a plate on his tray, taking only two small bits for herself.

No wonder she was so slender. She barely ate enough to keep a bird alive.

"I meant your ability to avoid answering my questions."

"Did you want cream in your soup?"

And there she went again. She was so much better at this than him, but he was nothing if not tenacious.

"Faye, tell me. Are you scared of babies?"

She sighed heavily and looked up from ladling out the steaming, hot soup into bowls.

"No. Did you want cream or not?"

He acceded. "Fine, whatever."

As with everything Faye did, she paid meticulous attention to presentation, and he watched with amusement as she swirled cream into his bowl and then, using a skewer like some kind of soup barista, created a snowflake pattern in the cream before sprinkling a little chopped parsley on top and setting the bowl on his tray.

"That's cute. Where did you learn to do that?"

"Nowhere special," she said softly. But then a stricken expression crossed her face and she seemed to draw herself together even tighter. Her voice, when she spoke, held a slight tremor. "Actually, that's not true. I learned it as a kid."

She bit her lower lip, as if she'd realized she'd suddenly said too much.

Piers pressed home with another more pointed question. "From your mom?"

She gave a brief, jerky nod of her head.

Piers sensed the memory had pained her and regretted having pushed her for a response. But he knew, better than most people realized, that sometimes you had to endure the pain before you could reap the rewards. Oh, sure, he'd been born into a life of entitlement and with more money at his disposal while he was growing up than any child should ever have. Most people thought he had no idea as to the meaning of suffering or being without—and maybe, on their scale, he didn't. Yet, despite all of the advantages his life had afforded him, he knew what emptiness felt like, and right now he could see a yawning emptiness in his PA's eyes that urged him to do something to fill it.

But how could a man who had everything, and yet nothing at the same time, offer help to someone who kept everyone beyond arms' length?

Something hanging from the light fitting above Faye's head caught his eye. Mistletoe. Before he knew it, Piers was rising and taking her in his arms. Then he did the one thing he knew he did better than any man on earth. He kissed her.

Four

Shock rippled through her mind, followed very closely by something else. Something that offered a thrill of enticement, a promise of pleasure. Piers's lips were warm and firm, and the pressure of them against hers was gentle, coaxing.

Even though her mind argued that this was wrong on so many levels, a piece of her—deep down inside—unfurled in the unexpected warmth and comfort his kiss offered. Comfort, yes, and another promise layered beneath it. One that told her that *she* decided what happened next. That she could take this wherever she wanted to.

In her bid to protect herself from further emotional pain, she'd always kept her distance from people. She knew how much it hurt to lose the ones you loved—how it had torn her apart and left her a devastated shell. How her attempts to fill that emptiness had only left her hurting all over again. How she'd shored up her personal walls until nothing and no one could get back inside into the deepest recesses of her heart ever again. And yet, here she was, being kissed by the man she worked for and *feeling* emotions she'd been hiding from for years. Wanting more. It was exhilarating and terrifying in equal proportions.

Even as Faye's mind protested, her body reacted. Her heart rate kicked up a beat. An ember of desire flickered to molten life at her core. Oh, sure, she'd been kissed before, but nothing in her limited experience had prepared her for this onslaught of need and heat and confusion.

Finally her mind overruled her body, reminding her that this was not just any man in any situation. This was her boss. In his house. With a baby in the next room.

Faye put a hand against Piers's chest, her palm tingling at the heat that radiated from behind his shirt—at the firmly muscled contours that lay beneath the finely woven linen. Her fingers curled into the fabric, ever so briefly, before she flattened her palm and pushed against him.

To his credit, he reacted immediately—stepping back with a slightly stunned expression in his eyes for a moment before it was masked. If she hadn't seen that brief glimpse in his eyes, seen the shock that had briefly mirrored her own reflected there, she would have believed the good-guy smile that now curved those wicked lips and seemed to say that the kiss had been no big deal.

Faye fought to calm her rapidly beating heart—to not betray even an inkling of the chaos that rattled through her mind over what had just happened. She bent her head to avoid looking at him, to avoid betraying just how much she'd enjoyed that kiss. She took in a deep breath and chose her words very deliberately.

"If you want me to continue to work for you, that had better be the last time you ever do something like that to me," she said in a voice that was surprisingly even. "Here, your tray is ready."

She picked up the tray with his supper and handed it to him, then turned away to finish preparing her own.

"Faye, I—"

"Really, there's no need to rehash it. Or apologize, if that's what you were thinking. Let's just drop it, hmm?"

"For the record, I do want you to keep working for me."

"Good, then there won't be a repeat of that, then."

"Was it so awful?" he asked, a glimmer of uncertainty flickering briefly in his dark brown eyes.

"I thought we agreed not to rehash it."

"Actually *we* didn't agree on anything. But, fine, if you don't want to talk about it, we won't talk about it."

Had she offended him? That hadn't been her intention…but if it meant he wouldn't do something as insane as try to kiss her again, that was a very good thing. Wasn't it? Of course it was. And he wasn't the kind of guy to carry a grudge. It was one of things she'd always admired about him.

Faye finished fussing over her tray and checked that the stove was turned off.

"Let me take that for you," Piers said, easily balancing his tray on one hand while sliding hers off the countertop with his other. "You can lead the way with the flashlight."

He was laughing at her. Oh, not in any obvious way, but she sensed the humor that hovered beneath the surface of his smooth demeanor. What she'd said had actually amused him rather than offended him, she was certain.

Determined to avoid too much further interaction, she decided the best course of action was to do as he'd suggested rather than fight over her tray. It wasn't as if they had far to walk, and if she chose one of the deep armchairs to sit in by the fire she wouldn't have to sit next to him.

By the time she was settled in the chair, with her tray on her lap, she was back to thinking about that kiss and the man who'd chosen the seat opposite her.

The glow of the fireplace cast golden flickers of light and contrasting shadows across his face, highlighting the hollows beneath his cheekbones and the set of his firm jaw. He'd lost some weight this past year, since the death of his twin. She was shocked to realize she hadn't noticed until now. She'd been too busy avoiding letting her eyes linger on any part of him. In simply taking instructions, preempting others and basically just doing her job to the best of her ability. For a personal assistant, though, she'd hadn't paid much attention to the actual personal side of Piers Luckman.

Oh, sure, she'd organized his social calendar, ensured none of his engagements clashed, seen off unwelcome interest from women who saw him as a short road to a comfortable future and, more recently, forwarded his farewell gift to the girlfriend who'd stuck longer than so many others.

But even though she'd done most of the coordination for Quin Luckman's funeral, she hadn't offered more than the usual cursory expression of sympathy to his twin. How had it felt for him, losing that half of himself that had been there from conception? She'd been so locked under her own carapace of protection that she'd rendered herself immune to his grief once the initial shock of Quin's death had blunted.

And why on earth was she even worrying about it? It wasn't as if he was about to lay his sorrow at her feet now that he'd kissed her. Without thinking, she pressed her lips together, catching her lower lip between her teeth in an unconscious effort to relive the pressure of his lips on hers. The clatter of a spoon on an empty bowl dragged her attention back to the man sitting opposite and a flush of embarrassment swept across her cheeks.

"That was good. Remind me to thank Meredith for having the foresight to lay in such tasty supplies."

"I'll do that," Faye said, reaching automatically for the small tablet that she kept in her bag to note his command immediately.

"Faye, I'm kidding. You're off the clock, remember?"

His voice held that note of humor again and it made the back of her neck prickle. She looked him squarely in the eye.

"You don't pay me to be off the clock. Besides, I'll just call this overtime."

Piers sighed, a thread of frustration clear in the huff of air he expelled. "You can relax, Faye. On or off the clock, I'm glad you're here."

He cast a glance at the sleeping baby and even with the shadows she could see the concern that played across his features. She felt compelled to reassure him.

"He'll be fine, you know. You're doing a good job with him so far."

"I can't help feeling sorry for him. His mother abandoning him. His father gone." Piers's voice broke on the last word. "I miss Quin so much, you know? I kind of feel that having Casey here is giving me another chance."

"Another chance?" Faye asked gently when he lapsed into silence.

"At a real family."

"You have your parents," she pointed out pragmatically, "and I know you have extended family, as well. They're all quite real."

"And yet, for as long as I can remember, I always felt like Quin and I only had each other."

Faye shifted uncomfortably on her chair. This was getting altogether too personal for comfort. Piers had never really talked about his family at great length. She'd always privately envied him that they, until Quin's sudden death, were all still there for him. But were they really?

When she thought back, her dealings with his parents and other relatives had hinged around what Piers could do for them, never the other way around. Even thinking about his annual house party here, Piers had always instructed her on what gifts to ensure were under the tree for whom. But, aside from his great-aunt Florence's questionable Christmas sweaters, had Faye ever heard of anyone bringing him a gift in return?

"I'm sorry," she said for lack of anything else to say to fill the sudden silence that fell between them.

"This little one isn't going to grow up alone. I will always be there for him."

"You don't even know for sure he's your brother's child," Faye protested.

"It fits. You know what Quin was like. I'm only sorry I didn't know about Casey sooner—then I could have helped his mom more."

Faye saw his shoulders rise and fall on a deep sigh. There was a resoluteness to his voice when he spoke again.

"She needed help and Quin couldn't be there for her. I'll find her, Faye. I'll make sure she's okay before going any further with Casey but I want to offer him the kind of life he deserves."

Piers's words made something twist deep in Faye's chest. Made her see another side of him that was all too appealing. It was the baby, it had to be. After her infant brother's death thirteen years ago she'd spent some time subconsciously trying to fill that gaping hole in her life. Tried and failed and learned the hard way to inure herself to getting involved, to forming an emotional bond. And here she was, stranded with a man who appealed to her on so many levels—despite her best efforts to keep her reactions under control—and a helpless infant who called on those old instincts she thought she'd suppressed.

Faye rose to take their trays back to the kitchen.

"Here, let me do that. You cooked."

She swiftly maneuvered out of reach. "I hardly would call reheating soup and making grilled cheese on toast cooking. Besides, he's waking up. You'll need to check his diaper."

"Again?"

"Yup," she said and, with her flashlight balanced on a tray to light her way forward, she made her way to the kitchen.

Piers watched her go before turning his attention to his charge. He was determined to get to the root of why she was so unwavering about having nothing to do with the baby.

"I can't see the problem, can you?" he said softly to the little boy who was now looking up at him and kicking his legs under the blanket.

But maybe it wasn't the baby she was avoiding now. Maybe it was just him. At first, he could have sworn she was reacting favorably to that kiss he'd given her under the mistletoe. Hell, favorably? She'd been melting under his touch, but that had been nothing compared to how their brief embrace had made him feel. Even now, thinking about it, it still had the power to leave him feeling a little stunned.

He'd kissed a fair few women in his time but, so far, none had moved him the way that simple touch had. The sensations that had struck him from the minute his lips touched hers were electric—curious and demanding at the same time. He'd had to hold back, had to force himself not to pull her hard against the length of his body. Had to fight every instinct inside him to keep the kiss simple, light, when what she'd awakened in him demanded so much more.

"Who would have known?" he said under his breath and lifting Casey in his arms. "Just one kiss, eh? What do we do now?"

What had he unleashed in himself with that embrace? He'd been trying to distract her. Her face, always composed and serene even in the most trying circumstances in the office, had looked stricken. His instinct had been to divert her thoughts, perhaps even to provide comfort. Instead he'd ticked her off—probably just as effective at distracting her, even if it didn't quite lend itself to them repeating the exercise, as much as he wanted to.

Did he pursue it further when she'd made it categorically clear that she wanted no further intimacy between them? He wasn't the kind of man who gave up when he reached the first obstacle, but there was a lot riding on this. Faye was the best assistant he'd ever had. Her very aloofness had been instrumental in keeping his mind focused on the job and his busy workdays on an even keel. Her ability to anticipate his needs was second to none. In fact, sometimes he felt like she knew him better than he knew himself.

He'd found her attractive from the get-go. From the interview selection process right through to the day she'd started she'd intrigued him, but he'd respected the boundaries they'd had between them as boss and employee.

Boundaries he himself had insisted on after his last two assistants—one male and one female—had complicated things by declaring their love for him. He'd worked with Faye for three years now. He respected her, relied on her and trusted her. But now that he'd kissed her... Well, it had opened the door on something else entirely.

For all her cool and inscrutable manner at work, she'd been different here from the moment he'd arrived. Maybe it was because it was the first time he'd seen her in anything other than her usual neatly practical and understated office attire. He had to admit, despite the horrible sweater he'd forced on her, the sight of her in his clothing appealed to him on an instinctive level, as if by her being dressed in something of his she'd become more accessible to him. As if, somehow, she belonged to him.

And she had, for that brief moment. They'd connected both physically and, he liked to think, on some emotional plane, as well. He'd felt the curiosity in her response, the interest. Right up until that moment she'd pushed him away, she'd been as invested in their kiss as he had been.

"I'm not dreaming, am I?" he said to the baby in his arms.

Casey looked at him with solemn dark eyes and then his little mouth curled into a gummy grin.

"Maybe, just maybe, it's time to see if dreams really can come true," Piers said with an answering smile of his own.

He'd have to approach this carefully. The last thing he wanted was for Faye to actually turn around and quit. But surely he could push things forward without pushing her to that extreme. He was a resourceful kind of guy. He'd think of something. He wasn't afraid of hard work. Not when something was important, and he had the strongest feeling that Faye had the potential to be far more important to him than she already was. And, he realized with a sense of recognition that felt as if it came from deep at his center, he wanted to be equally as important to her, too. If only she'd let him.

When Faye returned to the main room he stood with Casey and held him out to her. She looked as if she was going to instinctively put her hands out to take him, but then she took a step back.

"What are you doing?" she asked warily.

"Handing him to you. He doesn't bite. He hasn't even got teeth. It's not like he'll gum you to death."

Faye rolled her eyes in obvious exasperation. "I know he doesn't bite, but why would I hold him?"

"I need to check on the generator, see if we can get some power running."

"Perhaps I can do that for you," she said, still avoiding taking the baby.

"It's easier if I do it. I know exactly where it is and how to operate it. I'll be quick, I promise."

"Fine," she said, her irritation clear in her tone. "Be quick."

Piers watched as she nestled the baby against her, her movements sure and hinting of a physical memory that intrigued him. He liked seeing this side of her, even though she was so reluctant to display it.

It didn't take long to check the generator, which was housed in a small shed at the back of the house. Getting it going, however, took a little longer. In the end he'd had to pull his gloves off to get the job done. His fingers were turning white in reaction to the cold by the time he wrestled the shed door closed and reentered the house.

He'd expected the house to be blazing with light and sound when he got back in but instead all he could hear was a gentle humming coming from the kitchen. He followed the sound and discovered Faye in the kitchen with the baby, one-handedly making up a bottle of formula for Casey while humming a little tune that seemed to hold the baby transfixed. The humming stopped the instant she saw him.

"I thought you were going to be quick. Problems?"

"Nothing I couldn't handle." He glanced out into the main room. "No tree lights?"

"I thought it best not to draw too much on the generator if we could avoid it," Faye replied, ducking her head.

He suspected her decision may have more to do with her unexplained and very obvious disdain of the festive season than with any need to conserve power. His backup generator could keep a small factory running, but he wasn't about to argue.

"Where were you planning to have Casey sleep tonight?" she asked, her back turned to him.

"I hadn't actually thought that far. I guess in the bed with me. He'll be warmer that way, won't he?"

"There's a lot of data against co-sleeping with a baby. To be honest, I think you'd do better to make him up a type of crib out of one of your dresser drawers or even a large cardboard box. You'll need to fold up a blanket or several towels to make a firm mattress base and he'll probably be okay with his knitted baby blanket over him. Your room should be warm enough with the central heat."

Piers couldn't help it, his eyebrows shot up in surprise. She could have been quoting a baby care manual. How did she know this stuff?

"Okay, I'll get on it right away, but before I go I have to ask. How do you know these things?"

She shrugged her slender shoulders beneath the overlarge sweater he'd given her. "It's just common sense, really. By the way, I'll make up an extra bottle for Casey in case he needs a night feeding. It'll be in the fridge here."

"A night feeding?"

She sighed and shook her head. "You really know absolutely nothing about babies, do you?"

"Guilty as charged. They haven't really been on my radar until now. Do you think it's safe for me to look after him on my own tonight? Don't you think it would be better if you—"

"Oh, no, don't involve me. I'm already doing more than I wanted to. Here." She passed him the baby. "You feed him. I'll go make up a bed for him in your room."

And before he could stop her, she did just that. Piers looked down at the solemn little boy in his arms.

"We're going to get to the bottom of it eventually, Casey, my boy. One way or another, I'm going to get through those layers she's got built up around her."

Five

The sun was barely up when Faye gave up all pretense of trying to sleep. All night her mind had raced over ways she could get out of this situation. By 3:00 a.m. she'd decided that, no matter the dent in her savings, she'd call a helicopter to come rescue her if necessary. Anything to get out of there. In the literally cold light of day that didn't appear to be such a rational solution to her dilemma. After all, it wasn't as if she was in an emergency situation.

At least the storm had passed, she noted as she shoved her heavy drapes aside to expose a clear sky and a landscape blanketed in white. There was a tranquil stillness about it that had a calming effect on her weary nerves, right up until she heard the excited squawk of an infant followed by the low rumble that was Piers's response.

She had to admit that he'd stepped up to the plate pretty well last night. By the time she'd made up the makeshift crib in Piers's room and returned downstairs, he'd competently fed and changed the baby. And later, when she'd instructed him on how to bathe Casey, he'd handled the slippery wee man with confidence and ease and no small amount of laughter. For the briefest moment she'd forgotten why she was even at the lodge and had caught herself on the verge of laughing with them. But she didn't deserve that kind of happiness. Not after what she'd done to her own family.

It was true, people said the crash hadn't been her fault. But she had to live every day with her choices, which included pestering her beloved stepdad to let her drive home that Christmas Eve. Her mom had expressed her concern but Ellis had agreed with Faye, telling her mother the girl needed the experience on the icy roads. And now they were all gone. Her mom. Ellis. And her adorable baby brother.

Tears burned at the backs of Faye's eyes and she looked up at the ceiling, refusing to allow them to fall. She'd grieved. Oh, how she'd grieved. And she'd borne her punishment stoically these past years. Rising with each new dawn, putting one foot in front of the other. Doing what had to be done. And never letting anyone close.

She turned from the window and her memories and went to the bathroom to get ready for the day. Thankfully, she'd be able to wear her own clothing today, but as she passed Piers's neatly folded sweater on top of her dresser she couldn't help but wistfully stroke the outline of the crooked snowman on its front.

"What's the matter with you, woman?" she said out loud. "You hate Christmas and you're not in the least bit interested in Piers that way."

Liar.

Her fingertips automatically rose to her lips as she remembered that kiss, but then she rubbed her fingers hard across them, as if by doing so she could somehow wipe away the physical recall her body seemed determined to hold on to. She turned on the shower and stripped off the T-shirt Piers had given her to sleep in. Hoping against hope that the symbolic action of peeling the last thing of his off her body would also remove any lingering ideas said body had about her boss at the same time.

Now that the storm was gone, with any luck she'd be able to get away from there, and Piers and Casey, before she fell any deeper under their spell. But even the best laid plans seemed fated to go awry.

As she crunched down the snow-covered private road to her car she was forced to accept that even in broad daylight the road remained impassable. In fact, she was darn lucky she'd escaped without serious injury, or worse.

The tree could have struck her vehicle. She could have swerved off the driveway and down into the steep gully on the other side. The realization was sobering and left her shivering with more than just the cold as she opened the trunk of the SUV and pulled out her suitcase before trekking back up to the house.

"I was beginning to think you'd decided to hike cross-country to get away from us," Piers remarked laconically when she returned.

"I thought about it," she admitted. "I see we have cell phone reception now."

"Yes, I've called the authorities and requested assistance in removing the tree and getting your car towed. There are a few others in more extreme circumstances needing attention before us."

"And the police? Did you call them about Casey?"

"I did. Again, not much anyone can do until they can

get up to the house. I also called my lawyer to see where I stand legally with custody of Casey. Under the circumstances of his abandonment, they're drawing up temporary guardianship papers."

"You're not wasting any time," Faye commented, not entirely sure how she felt about this version of her boss. "What if his mom changes her mind? It's only been a day."

"I'll cross that bridge if that happens."

Over the next couple of days, if she wanted to get away from Piers's interminable holiday spirit, she had to tuck herself away in her room to read or watch movies. Otherwise she'd find herself sticking around downstairs and watching Piers interact with the baby. It was enough to soften the hardest shell and, shred by shred, her carefully wrapped emotions were beginning to be exposed and she could feel herself actually wanting to spend time with the two males.

Watching Piers fall in love with the baby was a wonder in itself. Sometimes she found it hard to believe that this was the same man who usually wore bespoke suits and steered a multibillion-dollar corporation to new successes and achievements each and every year. It was as if the world had shrunk and closed in around them—putting them in a cocoon where nothing and no one could interrupt.

Piers's comment a few days ago about heading away cross-country should be beginning to hold appeal. She'd kept her feelings wrapped up so tight for so long that the thought of being vulnerable to anyone was enough to make her hunt out a pair of snowshoes and find her way down the mountain. Except as each day passed, she found her desperation to get away growing less and less.

One night, three days after the storm, Faye was preparing dinner when Piers joined her in the kitchen.

"A glass of wine while you work?" he asked.

"Sure, that would be nice," she admitted.

She'd avoided having anything to drink these past few days because she didn't trust herself not to lower her barriers, or her inhibitions, should Piers try to kiss her again, but since that first night he hadn't so much as laid a hand on her shoulder again.

Piers poured them each a glass of red wine in tall, stemmed glasses and put hers next to her on the countertop.

"Thank you," she acknowledged and reached for the glass to take a sip.

"What can I do to help you?"

Piers leaned one hip against the counter and raised his glass to his lips. Faye found herself mesmerized by the action, his nearness making her feel as though she ought to back away. And yet she didn't. Instead her eyes fixed on his mouth, on the faint glisten of moisture on his lips. That darn mistletoe was just to the right of him. All she had to do was to rise up on her toes and kiss him and that would be—

Absolutely insanely stupid, she silently growled at herself as she reached for a knife to chop the vegetables she'd taken from the refrigerator earlier.

"Nothing," she snapped. "I've got this."

Piers's eyebrows rose slightly. "You okay?"

"Just cabin fever, I guess. Looking forward to getting out of here."

Even as she said the words she knew she was lying. Truth was, she had begun to enjoy this enforced idyll just a little too much. She had to get away before she lost all reason.

"Look, why don't you sit down? Let me finish making dinner. You sound a bit stressed."

"Stressed? You think I'm stressed? It's all this doing nothing that's driving me crazy," Faye said on a strangled laugh. "Seriously, I don't need you to pander to me."

"Everyone needs someone to pander to them from time to time."

"Not me," she said resolutely and started to chop a carrot with more vigor than finesse.

She stiffened as gentle hands closed over hers, as the warmth of Piers's body surrounded her from behind.

"Everyone," he said firmly. "Now, go. Sit. Tell me what needs to be done and just watch me to make sure I don't mess anything up, okay?"

He picked up her wine, pushed the glass into her hand and steered her to a stool on the other side of the kitchen island.

"So I'm guessing these need to be diced?" he asked, gesturing with the knife to the irregularly sized chunks of carrot.

She nodded in surrender and took another sip of her wine.

He followed her instructions to the letter and soon their meal was simmering on the stove top. Piers topped up their glasses, took a seat beside her and swiveled to face her.

"Now, tell me what's really bothering you. Why do you hate it here so much? Most people would give their right arm to be stranded with two gorgeous males for a few days."

"I'm not most people," she said bluntly.

"I noticed. Is there someone waiting for you at home? Is that what it is?"

"No, there's no one waiting for me at home."

No one. Not a pet. Not even a plant since she'd managed to kill off the maidenhair fern and the ficus she'd been given by one of her colleagues who'd jokingly said she needed something less inanimate than four walls to come home to each day.

"Then what is it?"

"This." She gestured widely with one hand. "It just isn't me, okay? I like California. I like sunshine. The beach. Dry roads."

"It's always good to have some contrast in your life," he commented, his face suddenly serious. "But it's more than that, isn't it? It's Casey."

Faye let her shoulders slump. "I don't hate him," she said defensively.

"But you don't want anything to do with him."

"Look, even you, if you had the chance, would have run a mile from a baby a few days ago."

"True." Piers nodded. "But I'm enjoying this time with him and with you more than I ever would have expected. C'mon, you have to admit it. Even you've enjoyed some of our time together."

She felt as if he'd backed her up against a corner and she had nowhere to go. "Look, this is an unusual situation for us both. Once you're back in Santa Monica you'll be back to your usual whirl of work, travel and women— no doubt in that order—and Casey will be tucked away to be someone else's problem."

"Wow, why don't you tell me how you really feel?" Piers said, feeling a wave of defensiveness swell through his whole body.

Her blunt assessment of his priorities angered him, he admitted, but he couldn't deny she'd hit the nail very squarely on the head.

"So you don't think I'll be a suitable parent to Casey?" he pressed, fighting to hold on to his temper.

"To be honest, I think it would be a huge leap for you to learn to balance your existing lifestyle with caring for a child. Of course, it all seems so easy when you're here. There's nothing else for you to do all day other than look after him. But what about when you're in negotiations in your next takeover and you're working eighteen-hour days and he's had his immunizations and he's running a low fever and he wants you? What about when you're attending a theater premiere in New York and he wakes with colic or he's teething and grumpy and inconsolable? What about—"

"Okay, okay, you've made your point. I'm going to need help."

"You really haven't thought this through, Piers. It's going to take more than help," Faye argued, putting air quotes around the last word. "There's more to raising a child than feeding it and changing a diaper, and you can't just expect to be there when it suits you and leave him to others when it doesn't. It's just not right or fair."

Piers wanted to argue with her, to shout her accusations down. But there was a ring of truth in her words that pricked his conscience and reminded him that the very upbringing he'd endured was likely the kind of up- bringing he'd end up giving to Casey.

For all that he wanted to raise Quin's son as his own, and give him all the love that he and his brother had missed out on growing up, how could he continue to do what he did—live the life he led—and still give Casey the nurturing he would need? The little boy was only three and a half months old. There was a lifetime of commitment ahead. Could he really do that? Be the person Casey needed? Be everything his own parents had never been?

His mom and dad had loved the attention that being parents of twins had brought them, but they'd left the basics of child rearing to a team of nannies and staff, and as soon as he and his brother were old enough they'd been shipped to boarding school. At least they'd always had each other. Who would Casey have?

Piers felt a massive leaden weight of responsibility settle heavily on his shoulders. "You're right."

"I beg your pardon?"

"I said, you're right." He turned the stem of his wineglass between his fingers and watched the ruby liquid inside the bowl spin around the sides of the glass. "I haven't thought this through."

"What will you do then? Surrender Casey to child services?"

"Absolutely not. He's my responsibility. I will make sure he doesn't want for anything and if I make a few mistakes along the way then I'm sure you'll be there to remind me how things should be done."

"Me?" she squeaked.

"Yes, you. You're not planning to leave my employ anytime soon are you?"

The question hung on the air between them.

"Leave? No, why should I? But I'm not a nanny. I'm your assistant."

"And as such you can guide me in making sure I don't work longer than I ought to and you can help me ensure that I employ the right people to help me care for Casey."

He looked into Faye's blue-gray eyes, noticing for the first time the tiny silver striations that marked her irises. Realizing, too, that the thick black fringe of her eyelashes were her own and not the product of artifice created by some cosmetic manufacturer.

Tension built in his gut. He needed her and it was daunting to admit it. She'd become such an integral part of his working life that he now found it difficult to imagine his days without her keeping his course running smooth. She did such an incredible job in the office, the idea of having her extend her reach even deeper into his personal sphere, as well, was enticing. But could he convince her to do it? Could he show her that he was serious about being a suitable parent for Casey and that he was equally serious about her, too?

She got up from her chair, walked over to where she'd left her trusty tablet on the countertop and made a notation.

"I'll get on it when I get back. If I ever get out of here, that is."

Piers surprised himself by laughing at her hangdog expression and bleak tone.

"It's no laughing matter," she stressed.

"Hey, we're hardly suffering, are we? We're warm and dry. We have food and my wine cellar at our disposal—"

"And we're running out of diapers, or hadn't you noticed? I took the liberty of checking Meredith's linen supply. If we can't get out of here by late tomorrow, we're going to have to start using cloth napkins. It's going to create a lot of laundry."

"We'll manage," he said grimly, irked by her not so subtle reminder that he really didn't have the first idea of what was needed to care for Casey.

But he had her and she very obviously did.

Again he wondered where she'd gotten her knowledge from. Her CV had said she was from Michigan but she'd attended college in California and had worked in and around Santa Monica since graduation. She had no family that he knew of, and had never worked in child care. All the dots had connected. There were no significant gaps in between her education and work histories. So where had she learned so much about babies?

Six

The following evening, Piers was playing with the baby on a blanket on the floor when he took a call on his cell phone. It was a contractor with very good news. The road up the mountain would be cleared in the morning and a crew would remove the fallen tree. Piers had taken a walk to look at it a couple of days ago, while Casey had slept back at the house under Faye's supervision. Seeing her SUV crunched up against the solid tree trunk had made him sick to his stomach. The outcome could have been so very different for her and the thought of losing her sent a spear of dread right through him.

"Good news," he said as Faye came through to the main room with a basket of laundry tucked under one arm.

The sheer domesticity of the picture she made brought a smile to his face.

"Oh? What is it? By the way, here's your laundry,"

she said, dumping the contents of the basket on the sofa. "You do know how to fold it, don't you?"

The domestic picture blurred a little.

"How hard can it be, right?" Piers said, reaching for one of his Christmas sweaters and holding it up.

Was it his imagination or had the thing shrunk? Santa looked a lot shorter than he'd been before. He wouldn't put it past Faye to have shrunk it deliberately, but then he'd been the one to put the load into the dryer.

"What news?" Faye prompted, tapping her foot impatiently.

"The road will be cleared tomorrow morning."

"Oh, thank goodness."

The relief in her voice was palpable. Piers fought back the pang of disappointment. He'd known all along she couldn't wait to leave and realistically he knew they couldn't stay snowbound together forever, even if the idea was tempting. Baby logistics alone meant they had to venture out into the real world.

He dropped the sweater back onto the pile of clothing.

"We should celebrate tonight."

"Celebrate?" She frowned slightly then nodded. "I could celebrate but I'll be more inclined to do so when my plane takes off and heads toward the West Coast."

"Skeptic."

"Realist."

He smiled at her and felt a surge of elation when she reluctantly smiled in return.

"Well, I plan to celebrate," he said firmly. "Champagne, I think, after Casey is down, and dancing."

"I hope you have fun. I'm going to pack," Faye said, turning and heading for the stairs.

"Oh, come on," Piers coaxed. "Let yourself relax for once, Faye. It won't hurt. I promise."

"I know how to relax," she answered with a scowl.

Casey squealed from his position on the blanket.

"Even Casey thinks you need to lighten up."

"Casey is focused on the stockings you've got hanging over the fireplace," she pointed out drily.

"Yeah, about those. I know it's only a day's notice but I think we should cancel the Christmas Eve party—in fact, cancel the whole house party. I don't think a lodge full of guests will be a good environment for the little guy here and, to be honest, I think I'd rather just keep things low-key this year."

Faye looked at him in surprise. He'd been adamant that, despite the fact that the last time he'd been here with his friends it had been the last time Quin had partied with them all, he wanted to keep with his usual tradition.

"Are you certain?" she asked.

"Yeah. Somehow it doesn't feel right. I know it's short notice and people will be annoyed but, to be honest, if they can't understand that my change in circumstances makes me want to change my routine then I don't really want to be around them."

"Okay, I'll get right on it."

"Thank you, Faye. I know I don't say it often enough, but I couldn't function properly without you."

"Oh, I'm sure you'd do just fine."

"No," he answered seriously. "I don't think I would. You're important to me, Faye. More than you realize."

The flip response she'd been about to deliver froze on the tip of her tongue. The expression in Piers's eyes was serious, his brows drawn lightly together. Her heart gave a little flip. Important to him. What did he mean by that? She'd sensed a shift in their relationship in the time they'd been stranded but she'd put it down to the bizarreness of their situation. That pesky flicker of desire shimmered low in her body and she felt her skin tighten, her breathing become a little short, her mouth dry. She swallowed and forced her gaze away from his face.

What could she say? The atmosphere between them stretched out like a fog rich with innuendo. If he took a step toward her now, what would she do? Would she take a step back or would she hold her ground and let him come to her? And kiss her again, perhaps?

The flicker burned a little brighter and her nipples grew taut and achy. This was crazy, she thought with an edge of panic. He'd just been thanking her for her dedication to her job. That was all she had to offer him. And yet there was heat in his dark brown gaze. This wasn't just a boss expressing his gratitude to his employee; there was so much more subtext to what he'd uttered with such feeling.

Faye fought to find some words that would bring things back to her kind of normal. One where you didn't suddenly feel an overwhelming desire to run your fingers along the waistband of your boss's sweater and lift it up to see if the skin of his ridged abdomen was like heated silk. Her fingers curled into tight fists at her sides.

As if he could sense the strain in the air, Casey had fallen silent. Faye forced herself to look away from Piers and her gaze fell on the baby.

"Oh, look," she cried. "He's found his thumb."

It took Piers a moment or two to move but when he did a smile spread across his face.

"Hey, clever guy. I guess that means no more pacifier?"

"I guess. It may help him to self-settle better at night."

"I'm all for that."

"But it can lead to other issues. You can always throw

a pacifier away but it's not so easy when a kid gets attached to sucking their thumb."

"Hey, I'm prepared not to overthink it at this stage."

She watched as Piers settled back down on the floor beside the baby and started talking to him as if he was the cleverest kid in the world. This time when her heart strings pulled, it was a different kind of feeling. One that made her realize all that she'd forsaken in her life with her choice not to have a family. Faye made herself turn away and take the basket back to the laundry room. She couldn't stay here another second and allow herself to—

She cut off that train of thought but a persistent voice at the back of her mind asked, *Allow yourself to what? To fall in love with them?* That would be stupid. Stupid and self-destructive.

Faye made herself scarce during Casey's bath time and final feeding, leaving Piers to settle him for the night. Now that she knew she'd be leaving at some stage tomorrow, she didn't trust herself not to indulge in little Casey's nearness just that bit too much. It would be all too easy to nuzzle that dark fuzz of hair on his head, to pepper his chubby little cheeks with kisses, to coax just one more smile from him before bedtime, to feel the weight of his solid little body lying so trustingly in her arms. Just thinking about it made her ache to hold him, but she held firm on her decision to keep a safe distance between them. Piers was perfectly capable of seeing to Casey's immediate needs right now. The baby didn't need her any more than she wanted to be needed.

But you do *want to be needed*, came that insidious inner voice again. The voice that, no matter how resolute she determined to be, continued to wear at her psyche. It had been easy enough for her to keep away from situations where interaction with babies was inevitable, but in this enforced, close atmosphere here at the lodge, all her hard-fought-for internal barricades had begun to crumble.

She needed some distance. Right now.

Faye turned on her heel and left the room, checking the laundry to ensure she hadn't left anything behind before taking the back stairs up to the next floor. She closed the door behind her when she reached her bedroom, leaned against it and let out the pent-up sigh she'd been holding.

Tomorrow, she told herself. She'd have her life back tomorrow. Just a few more hours. She could do this. How hard could it be to continue to resist one exceptionally adorable baby and a man who made her breath hitch and her heart hammer a rapid beat in her chest? For now, though, she had work to do and she had a whole lot of people to contact on Piers's behalf to cancel the house party.

When that task was done, she decided to get the ball rolling with the private investigation firm Piers used on occasion to collate data on a prospective property development. They were discreet and detailed. Everything you needed an investigator to be.

She explained the situation with Casey and what little information they had about his mother, and asked if they could look into things. After hitting Send on the email, she lay back on her bed and wondered if she could simply hide out there for the rest of the night. But a knock at her bedroom door drew her up on her feet again.

Piers leaned against the doorjamb with a sardonic smile on his face.

"It's safe to come out now," he said. "Casey's down for the night."

"I wasn't hiding from Casey."

"Oh, you were hiding from me, then?"

"No, of course not. I was working," she protested, earning another devastating smile from her boss.

She detailed what she'd done and he nodded with approval.

"Thanks for taking care of all that. I'd have gotten onto the investigators myself, but I got busy with Casey."

"That's why you have me, remember."

The words tripped glibly off her tongue but her job truly meant the world to her. She actively enjoyed the sense of order she could restore when things went awry and, for her, the skill she'd developed for anticipating Piers's needs—whether professionally or personally—was something to take pride in. Doing her job well was important to her. Basically, when it came down to it, it was all she had.

Sure, she had a handful of friends, but they were more acquaintances really. She tended to keep people at arm's length because it was so much easier that way. She'd even lost touch with Brenda, her best friend from high school. Brenda had tried so hard to be there for Faye after the crash, but no one could truly understand what she'd been through, or how she'd felt, and eventually Brenda, too, had drifted out of her sphere. Now they occasionally exchanged birthday cards, but it was the sum total of their contact with one another.

"Yes, that's why I have you," he answered with a note of solemnity in his voice she couldn't quite understand. He held out a hand. "Come on downstairs. The fire's going, the music's playing and I have a very special bottle of champagne on ice."

"Champagne?" she asked, reluctantly giving him her hand and allowing him to tug her along the hallway.

"Yeah, we're celebrating, remember?"

"Ah, yes. Freedom."

"Is that all it is to you? A chance to run away?"

Was it?

"I had other plans, too, you know," she said defensively.

So what if those plans included allowing herself to go into deep mourning for her family the way she did every year. It was how she coped—how she kept herself together for the balance of the year. It was the only time of year she ever allowed herself to look through the old family albums that ended abruptly thirteen years ago. It hurt—oh, how it hurt—but they were snapshots of happier times and that one night was all she'd allow herself—it was all she deserved.

They reached the bottom of the stairs and Faye noticed he'd put lighted candles around the main room and turned the Christmas tree lights off. Piers spun her to face him, his expression serious.

"I'm really sorry you ended up stuck here. I mean it. I should have realized you'd have plans of your own. It's just that you're always there at the end of the phone or in the office working right next to me. I guess I'm guilty of taking you for granted."

"It's okay. I love my work, Piers. I wouldn't change it for the world."

"But there's more to life than work, right?"

She smiled in response and watched as he reached down and pulled a bottle of French champagne from the ice bucket that stood sweating on a place mat on the coffee table.

"The good stuff tonight, hmm?" she commented as he deftly popped the cork.

"Only the best. We've earned it, don't you think? Besides, we're celebrating the road being cleared."

Faye accepted a crystal flute filled with the golden, bubbling liquid. "It's not clear yet," she reminded him.

"Always so pedantic," he teased. "Then let's just say we're celebrating the *prospect* of the road being cleared, and of Casey not needing to use my good linen as diapers."

"To both of those things." Faye smiled and clinked her glass to his.

She cocked her head and listened to the music playing softly in the background.

"What? No Christmas carols?" she said over the rim of her glass.

"I know you don't like them. I thought tonight I'd cut you some slack," he said with a wink.

"Thank you, I appreciate it."

She sipped her champagne, enjoying the sensation of the bubbles dancing on her tongue before she swallowed. The sparkling wine was so much better than anything she allowed herself to indulge in at home. Piers turned to put another log on the fire and she found herself swaying gently to the music as she watched him. When he straightened from the fireplace, she realized she'd already drunk half her glass and it was already beginning to mess with her head. She was such a lightweight when it came to drinking, which was part of the reason she so rarely indulged.

"Enjoying that?" he asked. Without waiting for her answer, he reached for the bottle and topped off her glass.

"I am," she answered simply.

"Good, you deserve nothing but the best. Take a seat, I'll be right back."

He was as good as his word, returning from the kitchen a moment later with plate laden with cheese and crackers.

"Sorry there's not much of a selection," he said with a wink. "I haven't had a chance to get out to the grocery store."

Faye laughed out loud. "As if you ever go to the grocery store yourself."

"True." He nodded. "I've led an exceptionally privileged life, haven't I?"

But he'd known loneliness and loss, too, despite all that privilege. And, while he hid it well, she knew that he missed his brother more than words could ever say.

"On the other hand, you also provide employment to hundreds of people, with benefits, so I guess you can be forgiven for not ever doing your own shopping."

Faye put her glass down and helped herself to some cheese and crackers. It was probably better to put some food in her stomach before she had any more champagne. She had a fast metabolism and the light lunch she'd prepared hours ago had most certainly been burned up by now. A delicious aroma slowly began to filter through from the kitchen.

"Have you been cooking?" she asked.

"Just a little thing Casey and I threw together." He chuckled at her surprised expression. "No, to be honest, it's one of Meredith's stews that I found in the freezer. I thought we could eat here, in front of the fire. It's kind of nice to just chill out for a bit, don't you think?"

Faye nodded. It wasn't often that she chilled out completely. Maybe it was the champagne, or maybe the knowledge that she'd be leaving soon, but she felt deeply relaxed this evening. The plate with cheese and crackers seemed to empty itself rather quickly, she thought as she reached for her glass again. Or maybe she'd just been hungrier than she'd realized. When she apologized to Piers for having more than her share, he was magnanimous.

"Don't worry. You have no idea how many of them I had to sample before I got the combination of relish and cheese right on the crackers," he assured her.

He poured her another glass of champagne and she looked at the flute in her hand in surprise. Had the thing sprung a leak? Surely she hadn't drunk all that herself?

As if he could read her mind, Piers hastened to reassure her. "I won't let you drink too much. Responsible host and all that. Besides, I know how much you like to remain in control."

"I'm not worried," she protested.

In fact, she'd rarely felt less worried than she did right now. A delicious lassitude had spread through her limbs and there was a glowing warmth radiating from the pit of her belly. She curled her legs up beside her on the sofa and watched the flames dance and lick along the logs in the fireplace. She'd hated fire since the accident—hated how consuming it could be, how uncontrolled. But being here at the lodge these past few days had desensitized her from those fears somewhat. The curtain grille that Piers always pulled across the grate created both a physical and mental barrier to the potential harm that could be wrought. Of course, he'd have to put stronger barriers in place once Casey became mobile, she thought. If he stuck with his plans to keep the baby, she reminded herself.

But that was a problem for another time. And not hers to worry about, either, she told herself firmly. Tonight's goal was to chill out, so that's what she most definitely was going to do.

The latter part of Piers's remark, about her liking to remain in control, echoed in her mind. Was that how she portrayed herself to him? In control at all times? It was certainly the demeanor she strived to create. It was her protection. If she had everything under control, nothing could surprise her. Nothing could hurt her.

Being totally helpless in the face of the gas tanker skidding toward their car on the icy road that night had left scars that went far deeper than purely physical. Her whole life had imploded. By the time she'd recovered from the worst of her physical injuries, the emotional injuries had taken over her every waking thought.

Faye's transition into foster care had been a blur and, as a salve to her wounded, broken heart, she'd poured herself into the care of the younger children in the home. The babies had caught at her the most, each one feeling like a substitute for the baby brother she'd lost. The baby brother who may have still been alive today if she hadn't begged her stepdad to let her drive that night. For the longest time she'd wished she'd died along with her family. That the tanker driver hadn't been able to pull her free from the burning wreckage of their family sedan.

Subconsciously she rubbed her legs. The scar tissue wasn't as tight as it used to be, but it remained a constant reminder that she'd survived when her family hadn't.

"You okay? Your legs sore?" Piers asked.

It was the first time he'd said anything about her injuries since he'd seen her undress the night he'd arrived.

"They're fine. It's just a habit, I guess."

She waited for him to ask the inevitable questions, like how she'd gotten the scars, had it hurt and all the other things people asked.

"Would you like me to rub them for you? I guess massage helps, right?"

She looked at him, completely startled. "Well, yes, it has helped when I've tried it before—but I'm okay, truly."

A flutter of fear, intermingled with something else—

desire, maybe—flickered on the edges of her mind. What would it be like to feel his hands on her legs, to feel those long, supple fingers stroking her damaged skin? She slammed the door on that thought before it could gain purchase and swung her legs down to the floor again.

"Shall I go and check on dinner?" she asked, rising to her feet.

"Not at all, sit down. Tonight, let me wait on you, okay?"

Reluctantly, Faye sat again. "I'm not used to being waited upon."

"Then this will be an experience for you, won't it?" Piers said with a quick grin. "Now, relax. Boss's orders."

He went to the kitchen and she caught herself watching his every step. She couldn't help herself. From the broad sweep of his shoulders to the way his jeans cupped his backside, he appealed to her on so many forbidden levels it wasn't even funny. It was easy in the office to ignore his physical appeal. After all, at work she was too busy ensuring everything ran smoothly and that potential disasters were averted at all times to notice just how good Piers looked. So exactly when had her perception of him changed? When had he stopped simply being her boss and become a man she now desired?

Seven

As Piers sliced a loaf of bread he'd defrosted earlier, he wondered if Faye had any idea of how much she revealed in her expression. These past few days it was as if the careful mask she wore in her professional life had been destroyed and he was finally getting to see the woman who lived behind the facade. He put the slices in the basket he'd put on a large tray earlier and turned to lift the lid from the pot simmering on the stove.

The scent of the gently bubbling beef-and-red-wine stew made his mouth water. It was funny how living in isolation like this made you appreciate things so much more. He'd never take any of his staff for granted again. Not that he'd made a habit of it up to now, but it was time to show additional gratitude for the foresight the people around him displayed. Of course, that's why he employed those very people in the first place—without them he could hardly do his job properly, either.

Which brought him very firmly back to the woman

waiting for him in the main room. Tonight he'd seen a window into her vulnerability that he hadn't noticed before. It kind of made him feel as though it left a gap for him to fill. Some way to be of use to her, for a change, instead of being the one being shepherded and looked after all the time. It made him feel a little on edge. As if this was his one shot to make things change between them. If he screwed it up, that would be it. He'd not only lose any chance they had of genuinely forming a relationship together, but she'd no doubt hightail it out of the workplace, as well. Nothing had ever felt quite so vital to him before.

He couldn't understand why things had changed between them, but he wasn't about to question it. He already knew he trusted Faye with everything that was important to him. She'd been his absolute rock when his brother had died, ensuring everything continued to run while he was away dealing with tying up Quin's estate. Over the three years they'd worked together they'd formed a synchronicity he'd never experienced with anyone else. Did he dare hope that same synchronicity could spread into the personal side of their lives, too? And this snowstorm, their being stranded together—albeit with a miniature chaperone—it all conspired to open his eyes to what they really could be.

Realizing he was allowing himself to get thoroughly lost in his thoughts, he quickly ladled two large servings of the stew into bowls. After a final check of the tray to ensure he had sufficient cutlery and napkins, et cetera, he took the tray through to the main room.

Faye was staring vacantly into the flames. What was she thinking? She didn't hear him until he put the tray down on the coffee table and sat beside her on the sofa.

She straightened and moved a fraction away from him,

which only made him spread himself out a little more, closing the distance between them. He leaned forward, picked up one of the bowls and passed it to her with a fork.

"Dinner is served," he said.

"Thank you."

"Bread?"

He offered the bread basket and was relieved when she took a slice. She hardly ate a thing that he could tell, certainly far less than he did. Clearly she needed better looking after. It was a good thing he was just the man to do it. The thought made him feel a rising sense of anticipation build inside.

Some things were best savored slowly, he reminded himself, and together they ate their meal in companionable silence. It was later, when he'd cleared their plates away and tidied the kitchen, that he made his suggestion.

"Come on, let's dance some of that dinner off," he coaxed as he rose and held out one hand.

Faye eyed him dubiously. "Dance?"

"Oh, come on, Faye. Relax. I won't bite."

Even as he said the words he felt an almost overwhelming urge to lower his mouth to the curve of her neck and do just that, gently bite her fair skin, then pepper it with kisses to soothe away any hurt. The very idea sent a surge of something else coursing through his veins. Desire. Slick and hot and demanding. He clenched his jaw tight on the wave of need that overtook him. And waited.

It felt like forever but, eventually, she placed one small, pale hand in his and allowed him to tug her to her feet. Piers led her to an open area of the main room and pulled her into his arms. It came as no surprise to him that she fit as though she belonged there. He caught a faint whiff of her fragrance as he held her close. Her choice held a subtle suggestion as to the potential sensuality that lay beneath her carefully neutral surface. The sandalwood base note was warm and heady, and totally at odds with the woman he thought he knew. He'd have thought she'd wear something more astringent, sharper. Something more in keeping with her persona in the office—not that he'd ever had that many opportunities to get close enough to her to smell her perfume, he noted silently.

But right now, right here, on what he fervently hoped would not be their last evening together, they were *very* close. Piers began to move to the music, enjoying the way she moved with him and relishing the brush of their hips, the sensation of her hand in his and the feel of the subtle movement of her back muscles beneath his other hand. And all the while, those delicate hints of her scent teased and tantalized his senses.

The initial resistance he'd felt in her body began to soften. Her steps became more instinctive, losing the stiffness that showed she was overthinking every move. It was hardly as if they were in a dance competition, but to him it felt as though there was a unity to their movements that led his mind to temptingly explore how well they could move together under other circumstances.

He bent his head and kissed the top of hers. Faye pulled back and looked up at him with wide eyes. Did he dare follow through on what he truly wanted—what he suspected that deep down she wanted, too? Of course he did.

When he took Faye's lips with his, he felt the shock of recognition pulse through his body. As if this woman in his arms was the one he'd been looking for all his adult life. The need that had been simmering under his carefully controlled behavior ever since their first kiss flamed to demanding life as her lips parted beneath his and she began to return his kiss with equal fervor.

This was more than that incident under the mistletoe the night he'd arrived at the lodge. This was incendiary. Consuming. He wanted her so much he had begun to tremble. He raised his hands to her hair and tugged at the pins that confined it into a knot at the back of her head. The pins dropped unheeded to the floor and her hair fell in thick, wavy tresses past her shoulders. He pushed his fingers through the silken length until he cupped the back of her head and angled her ever so slightly so he could deepen their embrace.

That she let him was more speaking than any words they'd ever shared. That her hands had knotted in his sweater at his waist, as if she had to somehow anchor herself to something solid, told him she was as invested in what was happening as he was.

Relief coursed through his veins. He didn't know how he'd have coped if she'd pulled away from him completely or if she had asked him to stop. Of course he'd stop, but it would probably strip years off his life to have to do so.

She felt so dainty in his arms, so fragile, and yet he knew she had a core of steel that many people never developed. She was tough and strong, yet vulnerable and incredibly precious at the same time.

Her hands released their grip on his sweater and he felt her tug at the garment before sliding her hands underneath it. Then he felt the incredible sensation of her warm palms against his skin. He groaned ever so slightly and lifted his mouth from hers so he could look again in her eyes—to receive confirmation once again that he wasn't demanding anything from her that she wasn't willing to give.

The sheen of desire that reflected back in her blue-gray

gaze was almost his undoing. The semi-arousal he'd been hoping wouldn't terrify her into running away stepped up a notch. He couldn't help it. He flexed his hips against her. Her cheeks flushed in response and her eyelids fluttered as if she were riding her own wave of sensation.

Piers lowered his mouth and kissed her again, this time sweeping her lips with his tongue and teasing past the soft inner flesh to titillate. She was making soft sounds of pleasure and when he pressed his hips against her again, he immediately felt the hitch in her breath. Her fingers tightened on the muscles of his back, her short, practical nails digging into him ever so lightly. His skin, already sensitive to her touch, became even more so, and a thrill tingled through him.

He gently pulled one hand free of her hair and stroked it down her back to the taut globes of her butt. She was so perfect and she felt so right against him. His hand drifted over her hip and up under her sweater. He felt tiny goose bumps rise on the smooth skin of her belly. Felt each indentation between her ribs, then felt the slippery-smooth satin of her bra. His hand slid around to her back and he deftly unfastened the hooks that bound her.

"I want to see you," he groaned against the side of her throat. "I want to touch you. All of you."

"Yes," she whispered shakily.

It was all the encouragement he needed. He moved away from her only enough to tug her sweater up over her head and to slide the straps of her unfastened bra down her arms, freeing her breasts to his hungry gaze. And there they were—those freckles that had so inappropriately tantalized him only a few nights ago.

Piers reached out with the tip of his forefinger to trace a line from her collarbone, connecting the dots until they disappeared and her flesh turned creamy white. Creamy white tipped with deliciously tantalizing pink nipples that were currently tight buds begging for his touch, his mouth. Action immediately followed thought. One hand went to her tiny waist, the other supported her back, as he lowered his mouth to her and teased one nipple and then the other with the tip of his tongue. He felt her shudder from head to foot and saw the blush of desire that bloomed across her skin.

Knowing he did this to her gave him a sense of joy he'd never experienced before with another woman. She was so responsive, so honest in her reactions. It was as refreshing as it was enticing and it made him want to make this evening even more special for her, more memorable.

Maybe there was a stroke of selfishness in his purpose. If he got this right, then maybe she wouldn't hightail it out of there when the road was open. Maybe she'd want to linger, to explore just how great they could be together in every way possible.

She deserved the best of everything and he would see to it that she got it. It was as simple as that.

It was one thing to touch her, but he wanted to *feel* her, as well. He moved away slightly so he could tug his sweater off. The instant he was free of it he pulled her to him, skin to skin. The delicious shock of it made him feel giddy in a way he hadn't experienced since he was a crazy teenager with too many advantages and a whole lot of testosterone. He savored the sensation and stroked the top of Faye's slender shoulders.

Her arms closed around him and she pressed her breasts against his diaphragm.

"Your skin, it's so hot. It's like you're on fire," she said so softly he had to bend his head to hear her.

"I'm on fire, all right. For you."

* * *

Faye ran her fingers up the bumps in Piers's spine then let her nails trace down his arms. She'd seen him topless before. When she'd worked with him while he'd been closing a business deal in France, on the Côte d'Azur, it wasn't unusual for him to declare his poolside patio his office for the day. She'd marveled at the chiseled lines of his body but she'd never imagined they would feel like this to the touch. That beneath the golden tan of his heated skin his muscles would feel both hard and supple at the same time.

It was thrilling to caress him. Forbidden and yet not at the same time. Faye pushed away the confusion that clouded the back of her mind. The voice of reason that told her this was a very stupid idea. That she was merely a temporary amusement for him. But there was something about the way he looked at her, and the way his hands touched her with such reverence, that made her feel as though even if she only got to have him this one time, this interlude could still be an experience that would chase away the darkness and the loneliness that dwelled inside her.

Was it wrong to want, to need, this physical contact with another person? To want to feel cherished? Under normal circumstances the logical side of her brain—the one that had endured years of guilt, grief and recovery—would say that, of course, it was wrong. She didn't deserve that kind of happiness.

But these were not normal circumstances and tonight that inner voice had been silenced. Wooed by champagne, dinner by firelight and dancing in the arms of a man whose breathtaking physical beauty was only transcended by the care he'd showed her tonight. Tonight? No, at all times. He might tease her and try to wheedle her secrets out of her, but he'd never been unkind or unreasonable. In the office, while he was very firmly the boss, he'd always treated her as a valued equal. Considering her ideas and suggestions and giving credit where credit was due when he followed through on something that had been her brainchild.

Maybe she hadn't simply been wooed by tonight. Maybe she'd been wooed by Piers for the whole three years she'd known him and been working by his side, becoming more a part of his life than his parents and extended family. Certainly more a part of his life than the women he'd paraded in and out of his bed. For a brief moment she wondered, *If this went any further, would I be categorized as one of those women?* Okay, so maybe the inner voice wasn't completely silenced—she smiled gently to herself—but it was about to be.

Faye traced her fingertips up to the broad sweep of Piers's shoulders and back down over his biceps and forearms before shifting to his ridged abdomen. She heard his sharp intake of breath as she let her fingers slide lower, to the waistband of his trousers. One of his hands closed over hers as she started to tug at his belt.

"Let's take this slow." He practically ground out the words.

"Okay," she said in a small voice.

But she wanted him so much. She was almost afraid to acknowledge to herself just how deeply she was affected by him. How the heat of his body penetrated through her to warm her where she'd believed she'd never feel warm again. How that heat infiltrated to the depths of her very soul. How the strength of his arms made her feel protected and how his very presence made her feel so much less alone in the world.

His hips began to sway and she followed his lead as

they started again to dance. It felt so incredibly wicked to be dancing topless like this, but as his chest brushed against her breasts, as their bellies touched, as she felt his arousal press against her, it became less wicked and more and more right by the second.

When Piers tilted her face up to his and kissed her again, she felt as if she was melting from the inside out. His touch was magical, sending feathers of promise and delight singing along her veins. When he slowed their steps and reached for the fastener on her jeans to slowly slide her zipper down, she felt as though her entire body was humming like a tuning fork. She helped him push the denim to the floor and stepped out of the pool of fabric.

For a second she felt self-conscious about the burn scars that snaked over her lower legs, but then he kissed her and all thoughts of scars and the past fled.

His touch was so gentle, so reverent, she wanted to beg him to go further, harder, faster. But she was new at this. While she'd certainly been out with other men, even kissed a few, she'd never gone this far before. And what Piers was doing to her was making her insides quiver with a building tension that ached and demanded release.

Piers's fingers skimmed her mound through her panties and she pressed against him.

"Eager, hmm?"

"You make me feel so much," she acknowledged shyly. "But I… I want to feel more."

"I promise I will make you feel everything you can imagine and that you will enjoy every moment of it."

She chuckled softly, feeling a little self-conscious again. "Every moment?" she asked.

He pressed against her, his fingers cupping firmly between her thighs, leaving her quivering as an intense spear of longing pierced her.

"Every. Moment." He kissed the side of her neck to punctuate each word.

The sensation of his lips on her skin sent a sizzling tingle through her body. Who knew you could feel this much from something as simple as a caress?

"I will hold you to that, then," she said with all the solemnity she could muster.

"You know me. I love a challenge."

She shivered a little as she felt his lips pull into a smile against her sensitive skin. And, yes, she did know him. So why was she letting him touch her like this? His relationships in the past three years had been many—more than enough for her to recognize the similarities. The women all beautiful. Statuesque. Worldly. Experienced. Nothing like her. Her mind started ticking overtime. Was he simply amusing himself with her? Looking for someone to scratch an itch with and she was "it" purely by proximity and lack of other options?

And then his hands skimmed her rib cage and cupped her breasts, his fingers gently kneading the softness while his lips and tongue traced a line from the curve of her neck down to the tips of her tightly budded nipples. His teeth grazed one nipple as he drew it into the heated cavern of his mouth and all thought fled her mind as his tongue rasped her flesh. A moan escaped her and she clung to his broad shoulders as if her very ability to stand depended on him. And maybe it did. Maybe he was all that anchored her to this reality, these feelings, the need that pulsed an insistent demand through her body.

When Piers lifted her and laid her on the large sofa, she felt a ripple of anticipation undulate through her. She watched as he undid his trousers and pushed them down with his underwear, kicking off his shoes and socks with the grace that was inherent in everything he did. When he straightened, she found her gaze riveted to his arousal, the hard length of him jutting proudly from a nest of curls. A primal tug pulled through her body. An ancient answer to an equally ancient unspoken question. Piers bent and slid her panties down her legs, tossing them to the floor before lowering himself over her.

She reached for him, her fingers closing around the length of him, sliding gently up and down. His skin was so very hot and silky smooth. He groaned as she reached the tip and her fingertip met the drop of moisture that had gathered there.

"Damn it," he muttered. "Protection. I'll be right back."

He pulled away swiftly and she heard him leave the main room and head to one of the guest rooms. He was back in a moment, the rustle of foil barely audible over the crackle of the fire behind them. She watched, intrigued, as he rolled the sheath over his penis—her eyes flickering to the concentrated expression on his handsome face. His cheeks were flushed, his eyes shining with a fervor she'd never seen before. It took a moment to realize it was his desire for her that put that expression there.

The knowledge gave her strength. She knew that what came next could be uncomfortable, but she also knew that beyond the discomfort would come delight and gratification such as she'd never known. Her body already told her so. She knew she was ready.

When Piers settled over her, he looked her straight in the eye.

"Tell me if I'm taking this too fast," he urged as he nestled his hips between her open thighs.

Faye was aware of the blunt tip of his shaft nudging the soft folds of her skin, aware of his hand as he expertly guided himself to her entrance. A tiny sliver of apprehension pierced the veil of desire that gripped her, but it was soothed in the moment his fingers touched her just above that point where their bodies met.

He circled her clitoris, pressing gently against the nub and making her squirm against him. She moaned again as a fresh spiral of bliss began to radiate from her core. A spiral that grew in force commensurate with the pressure he applied until she felt her entire body become consumed with the strength of it. She surged against him and beneath the pleasure that racked her she was aware of a searing sensation as he entered her and filled her completely.

The pain was instantly forgotten as aftershocks of satisfaction rippled through her, making her inner muscles clench against him and, in turn, sending continued jolts of delight that spread from her core.

Piers didn't move and Faye slowly became aware of the strain that scored his face.

"What is it?" she said softly, her hands reaching up to cup his face. "Did I do something wrong?"

To her shock and surprise Piers withdrew from her body. He shook his head. "No, you did nothing wrong. Nothing except neglect to tell me you were still a virgin."

Eight

A virgin!

Piers's mind was in turmoil even as his body screamed at him to seek the release he'd been so close to attaining.

"Does it make a difference?" Faye asked beneath him in a small voice.

Her skin was still flushed with the aftermath of her orgasm, her eyes still glowed with the confirmation of the satisfaction he'd made it his mission to give her. But it wasn't enough. It had been her first time and if he'd known... Well, suffice it to say he wouldn't have taken her on a sofa the way he had.

"Piers?"

"Yes, it makes a difference."

He was disgusted with himself.

She was his employee. She should have been completely out of bounds. But these past few days he'd allowed himself to push all of his scruples out the door and to focus only on what he'd wanted. And he'd decided he'd wanted her. He still did. His blood still beat hot and fast through his veins with ferocious desire for her, every throb a painful reminder that he hadn't reached completion. But this wasn't about him anymore. It should never have been about him. The only person who mattered right here and now was the precious woman who'd trusted him with her virginity. Now it was up to him to make it right.

Without saying anything he rose, scooped her into his arms and began to head up the stairs.

"What are you doing?" she asked as she automatically hooked her arms around his neck.

Her room was just off the gallery. He toed the door open and walked through the darkened room toward the bed. Piers set her on her feet and swept the covers down.

"What am I doing? Well, I'm going to make love to you the way you deserve."

"But…but…" She sounded confused. "I know you didn't finish downstairs but you made me—"

Her voice broke as if she couldn't quite find the words to describe what she'd felt.

He'd have smiled at this—the first time he'd ever seen her at a complete loss for words—if he hadn't felt so damned serious.

"Lie down on the bed," he instructed her and reached over to switch on a bedside lamp. "That was nothing."

"Well, it felt like a whole lot more than nothing to me."

This time he couldn't help it. A twinge of male pride tugged his lips into a smile.

"Then you're really going to enjoy what I have planned for you this time."

"Oh?" she said with an arch to her brow that made her look a great deal more coquettish and experienced than he'd ever seen from her. "Well, it'll have to be something else to beat the last time."

He couldn't help it. He laughed and then realized this was first time he'd ever actually laughed in a situation like this.

"You know what I said about a challenge," he murmured as he settled on the mattress and began to stroke her body. "Nothing gives me more satisfaction than beating it—nothing except maybe this."

He moved to the base of the bed and began to run his fingertips from her feet up her legs. He felt her stiffen as he skimmed over the ropey scars on her feet and lower legs. Understanding her reluctance for him to focus too much attention on them, he moved upward, to her thighs, taking his time as he touched her. He chased each caress with a brush of his lips, a lick of his tongue or a nip of his teeth. Beneath his touch Faye began to quiver again, her thighs becoming rigid beneath his touch.

Yes, she thought he'd showed her pleasure, but that would pale in significance now.

His fingertips brushed the neatly trimmed patch of curls on her mound. He liked that she kept herself natural when so many went hairless these days. He tugged gently before letting his touch soothe again.

Faye squirmed against the sheets. He was drawing closer to the object of his goal and let his fingers drift across her clit.

She went still beneath him, as if trying to anticipate where he'd touch and what he'd do next. Piers smiled to himself as he bent his head lower. He could smell her scent, that wonderful musk of woman—a scent rich with promise that made his erection ache with a pleasure-pain that demanded he hurry this up. But he wouldn't be hurried. He was a man on a mission.

He touched her again with a fingertip, then let his hand trail to the top of her thighs. Her skin shivered with goose bumps and she clenched her hands in the sheets beside her. It was time. Piers lowered his mouth to her bud, flicking it with his tongue and relishing the taste of her. Faye uttered a startled gasp as he flicked his tongue across her again before blowing a cool stream of air on her heated flesh.

Again she gasped, her hands letting go of the sheets and tangling in his hair instead. He nuzzled her and traced his fingers higher, to the moist folds of skin that hid her entrance and beyond until he gently penetrated her. He felt her muscles tighten around his fingers, felt the shudder that racked her body. Yes, it was definitely time. He closed his mouth around her bud, swirling his tongue around the tiny nub and sucking gently until she was pressing against his mouth with abandon. He withdrew his fingers and then entered them into her body again, mimicking the action his arousal craved.

He tracked every indication of the escalating sensations that grew within her. Knew the exact moment she broke apart into a million pieces of pleasure. She looked so beautiful in her utter abandon that he had to fight to stay under control. He gentled the movement of his tongue, his fingers, until he felt her body begin to relax.

Faye's legs eased farther apart as she sank deeper into the mattress, and Piers moved between them, positioned himself and slowly slid into her molten heat. There was no resistance this time. No reminder that she had chosen to give herself to him and only him. Even so, he would eternally treasure that gift, treasure her, and make sure she realized just how incredibly special she was to him.

This time he coaxed her slowly to her peak, holding on to his control with every last thread of concentration and only letting himself go as he felt the deep, slow ripple of her climax undulate through her body. And then he let go, allowing his own pleasure to roll like thunder through him.

Spent, he finally collapsed on top of her, his heart pounding in his chest. He wrapped his arms around her slender form and rolled onto his side so that she was nestled up against him.

He pressed his lips to her forehead, feeling closer to her than he'd ever felt to anyone in his life. And he knew he wanted this new closeness between them to continue. He couldn't imagine his life without her in every aspect of it now.

"Are you okay?" he asked gently, nuzzling her hair and relishing the scent of it.

"Okay? I don't think I've ever felt more okay in my entire life." Faye's voice sounded thick and heavy, as though she was drugged with a combination of satisfaction and exhaustion. A soft chuckle escaped her. "I always knew you were a man of your word, but I didn't expect you to take things quite so literally. I think you can safely say your challenge has been met."

He smiled in response. "Well, you know what that means, don't you?"

She stiffened slightly in his arms, and though he wasn't sure what had triggered that response, Piers stroked the skin of her back to soothe her again.

"What does it mean?" she asked, fighting back a yawn.

"It means I have to do better next time."

"If there is a next time," she answered.

"Oh, there'll be a next time. And a time after that. But for now I think we should rest."

"Yeah, rest. That's a good idea. I don't think my body could handle all of that again too soon."

"Did I hurt you?" Piers asked, suddenly concerned.

He'd done his best to be gentle. To ensure her body was completely ready for him before he'd entered her.

"No, not at all. You were...you were amazing. Thank you."

He reached for the bedcovers and drew them over her, leaving the bed only long enough to dispense with the protection he'd worn before diving back under the covers and pulling her to him again. He felt that if he let her go she'd simply slip away like an ephemeral creature—there one minute, gone the next.

"Are you comfortable?" he asked.

"Very. I didn't know it could be like this, sharing a bed with someone else. It's cozy, isn't it?"

He laughed softly. "Very cozy." He fell silent a minute before asking the question that kept echoing in the back of his mind. "Why me, Faye? Why did you let me be your first?"

The minute he allowed the words to fall on the air he knew he'd made a mistake. He could feel her retreat, mentally if not physically.

"Why not?" she answered. "You did seem to be very good at it."

Now she was using humor to shield herself from revealing the truth. He'd have to tread carefully if he was to work his way past her protective shields without damaging the fragile link they now shared.

"For what it's worth, I'm honored I was your first. I—" He took a deep breath. Was it too soon? "I care about you, Faye."

She remained silent for what felt like forever but then he heard her indrawn breath and her voice softly filtered through the darkness around them.

"I care about you, too."

As admissions went, it was hard-won, and he allowed

a swell of relief dosed with a liberal coating of satisfaction to ride through him. It was a good start.

She snuggled right into his chest and he could feel the puffs of her breath against his skin.

"I haven't had many boyfriends," she admitted. "After my family died in a car wreck, I just wasn't interested in much of anything anymore. I was fostered in the same district where I'd grown up, so there was as little disruption to my routine as possible once I was released from hospital. Some of my friends at school…they tried to include me, but as we all got older we drifted apart."

"I'm sorry about your family, Faye. That must have been tough."

The words sounded so inane. Not nearly enough to describe his sorrow at the thought of what she must have been through. What would it have been like to suddenly be alone at fifteen? To be without the anchors that kept you feeling safe and loved. Growing up, his parents had been uninvolved, but he'd always had Quin by his side. The grief he'd felt at the loss of his brother had sent him to a dark, lonely place in his mind and it had forced him to reevaluate a lot of things in his life. But at least he'd been an adult while learning to cope with his loss. For Faye, just a teenager, how could she make decisions about her future when everything she'd ever known, every parameter she'd lived her life by, had been gone in a flash?

"Tough, yeah. That's one word for it. I had lovely foster parents, though. And my mom and stepdad had established a college fund for me so when I aged out of foster care I could choose where I went from there. I didn't want for anything."

Anything except for a family. Piers thought about the little boy sleeping down the hall in his bedroom, considered the ready-made family that he and Casey could offer

Faye. But he weighed that up with her obvious reluctance to have anything to do with the baby. Did that stem from the losses she'd suffered when she was still a teenager? How on earth did a man wade past that?

Encircled in Piers's arms, Faye didn't feel the usual searing pain that scored her when she thought about her family. Instead it was kind of a dull ache. Still there, still hurting, but muted, as if the edges had softened somehow. The realization made her feel disloyal to their memory. She didn't deserve this. Didn't deserve to let any aspect of the memory of their loss slide away. Guilt hammered at her with all the subtlety of a sledgehammer.

This was why she hadn't encouraged any relationships beyond friendship in the past. And it was why she should never have allowed things between her and Piers to go as far as they'd gone—no matter how fantastic it had been.

She'd made a mistake tonight—several mistakes. From the minute she'd accepted the glass of champagne from Piers to the second she'd allowed him to touch her. What had she been thinking?

Maybe that, for once in her life, she should reach out and sample what others took for granted?

No. She mentally shook her head. She had no right to do that. It was best that she get back on her path alone and leave in the morning as she'd planned. Leave before her heart became too heavily engaged with the man who had drifted to sleep beside her, not to mention the child he was determined to claim for his own.

Decision made, she closed her eyes, willing herself to drift to sleep. Goodness knew her body felt so sated and weary that sleep should have come easily. But for some reason her mind wouldn't let go, wouldn't allow her to find peace.

Instead she found herself concentrating on the smallest of things, like the way Piers's fingers continued to stroke her bare back every now and then, even though he was asleep. Like the deep, regular sound of his breathing and the scent of his skin. She would store these memories and lock them away, and maybe one day she'd be strong enough to think about them, about this magical night, again.

Faye woke to an empty bed and felt a rush of relief. At least the whole morning-after thing could be delayed until she was showered, dressed, packed and ready to leave. She shifted in the bedsheets, catching a drift of Piers's cologne. Just that tiny thing made her body tighten on a wave of longing so piercing that it almost brought tears to her eyes.

Instead of giving in to her emotions, Faye did what she'd always done. She focused on what needed to be accomplished first. That, at least, was something she could control.

Once dressed and packed, she double-checked the bathroom and bedroom to ensure she was leaving nothing behind and headed down the stairs to put her suitcase by the front door. She could hear Piers and Casey in the kitchen. With her stomach in knots, she walked toward the sound. Piers had his back to her and was talking a bunch of nonsense to the baby, who was staring up at him in rapt attention.

Faye would never have thought her heart could break any further than it already had, but the sight of those two was just about her undoing. Once again, tears sprang to her eyes. She blinked them back fiercely and turned to a cupboard to drag a mug out for her morning coffee.

"Good morning," Piers said. "Did you sleep well?"

"Better than I expected," she answered shortly.

"Me, too," he answered with a smile that sent a curl of lust winding through her.

This is impossible, she thought as she grabbed the carafe from the coffee machine and poured the steaming liquid into her mug. Just a look from him, a smile, and she was as pathetically eager for his attention as all his other women. Did that mean she was one of them now? She straightened her shoulders. No, it most certainly did not. One night did not change anything as far as she was concerned. If she could just get back to her apartment and back to a routine, everything would be okay.

She watched as Piers took the baby bottle from the warmer and gave it a little shake before testing a few drops on his wrist.

"Sir, your breakfast is served!" he said to the infant with a delightfully dramatically flourish.

Casey gave him a massive gummy grin in return. His little legs kicked wildly as Piers offered him the bottle.

"You're good with him," Faye observed. "Are you still going to keep him?"

"Yes."

The answer was simple and emphatic. No fluffing about responsibilities or honoring his brother's memory or anything like that. Just a simple yes.

She envied him his conviction.

Piers looked up at her and she saw something new in his gaze.

"Is it ridiculous to say that I love him already?" he asked.

She'd never known him to sound insecure about anything. Ever. That he should feel that way about Casey just made him even more human, more attractive. She shook her head.

"No, it's not."

Piers nodded in acceptance and turned his attention back to the little boy.

Faye took advantage of the shift in focus to start making breakfast. "Have you eaten?" she asked.

"Yeah, I ate when I got up. It was early, though. I could go a second round."

She busied herself making omelets with the last of the ingredients she could find in the refrigerator. It was a good thing the road would be cleared today and that Meredith, who'd been waiting at a motel in town, would be able to come through with supplies.

Faye was just plating up the food when the phone rang with the news that a crew had cleared the road up to the fallen tree and was now working to clear the log. The news made Faye feel as if every nerve in her body had coiled tight, ready to spring free the moment she could leave the building.

The next two hours were an exercise in torment as she tried to catch up on emails while Piers lay on the floor and played with the baby before putting him to bed for another nap. The moment she heard a sound near the front door she was up and all but running to let the newcomer inside.

"Ms. Darby! Are you all right? I saw your car. It's a miracle you're still alive!"

Piers's housekeeper bustled inside and grasped Faye by her upper arms, giving her a once-over as if checking for injuries. "Oh, Ms. Darby—your face!"

"It's okay, Meredith. It's what happened when the airbag went off. I wasn't hurt aside from that, and I'm almost all healed," Faye said as brightly as she could.

Satisfied Faye hadn't been seriously injured, Meredith gave her a nod and then drew her in for a quick hug, which Faye endured good-naturedly. She wasn't a hugger but she was used to Meredith's overwhelming need to mother everyone in her sphere.

"I'm fine, Meredith. I take it the road is clear now?"

"Yes, they've moved your wreck to the side and taken away most of the tree. Some of it will have to wait until they can get some heavier equipment up, but there's room to squeeze by."

Faye had expected to feel relieved at the news. Actually, she'd expected to feel jubilant. Instead there was a hollow sense of loss looming inside her. She shoved the thought away before it could take hold.

"Well, that's a relief!" she said with all the brightness she could muster. "I think I'm suffering a bit of cabin fever. I can't wait to get home."

"Mr. Luckman! I'm so glad to see you!" Meredith gushed effusively over Faye's shoulder.

Faye turned and saw the swiftly masked look of disappointment in Piers's eyes. Had he really thought that a spectacular night of sex would change her mind about leaving? She already knew there was a flight out early this afternoon. She had to be on it. She couldn't stay another minute or maybe she would change her mind and stay—and what then? More risk? More chance of loss? More joy and pleasure that she didn't deserve and couldn't allow herself to enjoy? No, it was far better that she left now.

"Meredith, good to see you, too."

"How have you been managing?" Meredith said, fussing over him.

"Just fine, thanks, Meredith. You left us so well stocked we could have stayed here a month on our own."

Faye suppressed a shudder. A month? She could never have lasted that long and still left with her sanity intact.

In a month Casey would have grown and changed and wound her completely around his pudgy little fingers. And a whole month confined here with Piers? She tried to think of the reasons why that was a bad idea but her newly awakened libido kept shouting them down. Every last one. Which in itself was exactly why she needed to put distance between her and Piers.

"We have run out of diapers, however," Piers continued. "I hope you got my text to add them and baby food to the groceries."

"I did. But why on earth…?" Meredith looked from Piers to Faye for an explanation.

Faye shrugged and looked at Piers. "You can explain it. I really need to get going. Meredith, after we've unloaded your car, can I borrow it to get to the airport? I'll organize for someone to return it for you."

Over Meredith's iron-gray curls, Faye saw Piers looking at her again. His expression appeared relaxed but she could see tiny lines of strain around his eyes.

"Do you really need to run away right now?" he asked.

"I can't stay. You know that. I have things to do. Places to go. People to see."

He knew she was lying, she could see it in the bleak expression that reflected back at her. Faye turned away. She couldn't bear to see his disappointment and it irritated her that it mattered to her so much.

She grabbed her coat, scurried down the front steps to where Meredith had left her station wagon and started to take bags of groceries from the rear. Piers was at her side before she could make her way back to the house.

"You know you're running away."

"I'm doing nothing of the kind. I wasn't supposed to be here in the first place, remember?"

"You're running away," he repeated emphatically. "But are you running away from me or from yourself?"

"Don't be ridiculous. I'm not running anywhere," she snapped and pushed past him to take the groceries to the house.

He was too astute. She'd always admired his perceptiveness in the workplace but she hated it when he applied it to her. Behind her she heard him grab the remaining sacks of supplies and follow her up the stairs.

She made her way swiftly to the kitchen, where Meredith was already taking inventory of what needed to be done.

He was close behind her, and as he brushed past he whispered in her ear, "Liar. I'd hoped you might change your plans and spend Christmas here with Casey and me. We don't have to worry about anyone else."

Words hovered on the edge of her lips—acceptance and denial warring with one another.

"Thanks, but no thanks," she eventually said, hoping she'd injected just the right amount of lightness into her tone.

"Faye, we need to talk. C'mon, stay. It's Christmas Eve."

The last three words were the reminder she needed. Christmas Eve. The anniversary of the death of her family. Shame filled her that she'd lost track of the days.

"I really need to go," she said, her voice hollow.

Meredith handed her the set of keys to the station wagon. "There you go, Ms. Darby. There's plenty of gas in the tank."

"Thanks, Meredith. I'll take good care of it, I promise. I'll leave Mr. Luckman to explain why he needs all these diapers," Faye answered, patting the bumper pack she'd carried in with the bags from the car.

Before Piers could stop her, she slipped out of the kitchen, through the main room and out the front door. The finality of pulling the heavy door closed behind her sent a shaft of anguish stinging through her, but she ignored it and kept going. It was the only way she could cope. She was used to loss. Used to pain. She'd honed her ability to survive, to get through every single day, on both those things. And, somehow, she'd get through this day exactly the same way.

Nine

Blue skies, sand and sunshine had never looked better, Faye decided as she opened the drapes of her sitting room on Christmas morning and stared out at the vista below. She'd paid a fine premium for this apartment with its tiny balcony overlooking the beach, but even though she'd chosen it because it was nothing like what she remembered of home, she never could quite shake off the memories.

Take last night. She'd started her movie marathon; the way she'd done every year since she'd lived alone. But for some reason the gory plotlines and the gripping action couldn't hold her attention and in the end she'd turned off the player. At a loss, she'd sought out the box of precious possessions among her parents' things. The entire household had been packed up and stored in a large locker after the accident and held for her until she turned eighteen—fees had been paid out of her parents' estate.

This particular box she saved for Christmas Eve alone.

Filled with photo albums of her throughout her child-hood, starting as a baby, with her mom, then with her stepdad and finally the unfinished album with the precious few photos she had of her baby brother. He'd have been just over thirteen years old by now. Maybe he'd have been an irritating teenager, pushing his boundaries—or a sports star in his favorite game. Or maybe he'd have been more bookish and quiet like she'd been as a child. She'd never know. The empty pages at the back of the album were an all-too-somber reminder of the lack of future for baby Henry.

Last night's visit to her past had reduced her to a shaking, sobbing mess, but when she'd woken this morning, instead of the yawning abyss of loss that had consumed her heart for so many years, she felt different. Yes, there was grief, and that would never completely go away. But overlaying that grief was a sense of closure, as if she'd finally been able to completely say goodbye.

She knew she'd never be able to stop thinking about her family, never stop loving them, but she felt less of a hostage to her grief than she'd been before. It was part of her. It had made her grow into the adult she was now and it had driven so many of her decisions, leading her to this point in her life. But maybe it was time for her to stop letting it direct her life. Maybe it was even time to let go of her grip on the guilt she felt for not having been able to avoid the crash that night. Perhaps she didn't deserve to be unhappy, after all. Maybe it was even time to take a risk on loving someone else again. Someone like Piers, perhaps, who now came with a ready-made family?

The thought struck terror into her heart, but before long she managed to push past it to examine the thought carefully.

The analytical side of her brain asked her if she thought she might genuinely be falling in love with Piers.

If she entered into a relationship with him, she'd be doing it with her eyes open. After all, she probably knew the man better than his own mother did. She'd been an integral part of his life for the past three years, managing both his work world and his private life in as much as he needed her to. And she admired him. He could so easily have been more like Quin. So easily have lived off the obscenely large trust fund that previous generations of Luckmans had provided for him, but he'd chosen to work and he worked hard. The business and residential property developments he'd undertaken since she'd worked with him had become among the most sought after anywhere in the world.

Yes, he had a playboy background and, yes, she'd seen how easily he discarded a lover when he'd felt a relationship had run its course. But he'd definitely been different since Quin had died. Quieter. More thoughtful. And, slowly, she'd begun to see yet another facet to him. One that had undoubtedly begun to unravel the bindings around her heart.

But was she actually falling in love with *him* or was she instead falling in love with the idea of being part of something bigger than just herself? A family? A new start? A chance to make amends for what she'd done?

Faye squeezed her eyes closed and growled out loud in frustration. So many questions. So few answers.

Piers returned from Wyoming in the second week of the new year. She heard his voice as he came down the corridor from the elevators and every nerve in her body stood to attention. She'd avoided all his calls since she'd left Jackson Hole, keeping their communications strictly to text messages and email. She'd sensed his frustration with her immediately but she hadn't been ready talk to him. To hear the timbre of his voice. To relive the intimacy they'd shared—the memory of which still took her by surprise every now and then and stole her breath away.

But there was no hiding now. Any second he'd round the corner and walk straight into the open-plan area they shared.

And then there he was.

The impact of seeing him was just as shocking as she'd anticipated. A flush of heat spread through her body as her eyes flew up to meet his. She swallowed hard against the sudden lump that formed in her throat when she realized he bore a baby car seat in one hand, with Casey sound asleep inside it, and his briefcase in the other.

"Good morning," she finally managed to squeeze the greeting past the constriction and stepped out from behind her desk. "Coffee?"

"Why wouldn't you answer my calls?"

"Coffee it is, then," she answered smoothly and turned her back on him.

"Faye, you can't keep avoiding me."

"I wasn't avoiding you. We spoke."

"Through the written word only. And, yes, before you remind me *again*, I have been in touch with Lydia and, not so surprisingly, she canceled dinner. It seems she wasn't quite ready for instant motherhood.

"But, back to you—after you left I was worried about you and until I was certain I could take Casey out of state with me, I couldn't exactly drop everything and come running to check on you, either."

She'd been aware of all that. She automatically went through the motions of making his coffee from the espresso machine in the corner. Once it was made to his preferred specifications, black and sweet, she carried his mug across to his desk.

"As you can see, you had nothing to worry about. I'm fine."

Piers put the carrier with the sleeping baby on his desk and turned to face her. His hand shot up and his fingers captured her chin lightly, tilting her face toward his. A shiver of anticipation ran through her. Was he planning to kiss her? Here, in the office?

"Still too many shadows, Faye. Too many secrets. I don't want there to be any secrets between us," he said gently. "Not anymore."

"Secrets? I'm sure I don't know what you're talking about. I'm an open book."

He laughed, a short, sharp sound that expressed his disbelief far more eloquently than any words could have done.

"Okay, so you want to play it that way for now. Fine. We'll get back to business, but you won't be able to hide from me forever."

Casey chose that moment to wake and squawk his disapproval with his new surroundings. Faye was riveted by the sight of Piers, in full corporate splendor, lifting the child from the car seat and holding him to him as if he'd been doing it from the day Casey had been born. The little guy settled immediately.

"You're spoiling him," Faye noted, settling behind her desk.

"According to Meredith, you can't spoil a baby. You can only love them. I'm inclined to agree."

Faye felt that all too familiar clench in her chest. She knew very well how it felt to love babies. And to lose them.

"Have you had any more news from your lawyers?"

"They tell me they're going to attempt a case based on abandonment. As Quin's next of kin, they believe I stand a strong chance of being able to adopt Casey outright. At the very least the emergency guardianship application has been approved."

"Are you sure that's what you want to do? Adoption? It's a big commitment. What if his mom changes her mind? What if even now she's looking for him?"

"She knew where to find me the first time, she can find me again. If she does reach out, then maybe we can get to the bottom of why she didn't see fit to contact us earlier about Casey."

Faye thought back to the note. "Do you think she knew that Quin had…?" Her voice trailed away.

"To be honest, no. I think she heard I was coming back to the house for Christmas and acted impulsively. Maybe she thought I was Quin. Who knows? From what we've been able to glean, she worked on a temporary basis for the company that catered for me. She's very young, only nineteen. She's from Australia and had been backpacking her way across the country and picking up casual work where she could. I don't even know if Casey was born in Wyoming. Whatever the case, his place is with me."

Piers's voice was emphatic on that last statement.

"Well, as long as you realize he's not like a toy you can pick up and put down at whim. He's a lifetime commitment. When you start a new relationship, I hope, whoever she is, she's on board with having a baby in her life."

Piers shot her a searing glance. She could see the banked irritation in his eyes.

"What are you implying, Faye? That I'll just ignore Casey when it suits me?"

"I'm not implying anything. But, let's face it, you've only had a few weeks with a baby, part of which you had with me and the rest with Meredith who probably hardly let you hold him once she got there. You didn't have any work or other priorities to deal with, so you could focus completely on him. It's not the real world. The reality involves dealing with fevers and colds, teething, colic, potty training, tantrums, sleepless nights on top of the busy schedule you usually keep. You seem to think it's going to be a walk in the park, but it's not like that. Raising a child is damn hard work."

"And you'd know because?" He pinned her under a hard stare, silently demanding she answer him.

"I know because I'm not some Pollyanna who thinks everything is always going to be all right. Bad things happen. Life doesn't always go the way you expect to."

As soon as she said the words she wished them back. It was almost the anniversary of Quin's death. Piers knew as well as anyone else who'd suffered great loss that life could deliver unexpected blows along with the highs.

She hastened to make amends. "Look, I'm sorry. I'm out of line. I'll get out of your way. I have a meeting with the new brand manager at ten so I'd better get down to marketing."

"Yeah, you do that," he said, his voice carrying a note of determination that made Faye's stomach lurch a little. "And while you're at it, ask yourself why you keep such strong emotional barriers up between you and everyone else. It's not just me, is it? It's everyone. Because while you're questioning my ability to commit to Casey, I think perhaps you ought to be asking yourself why you're not capable of committing to anything but your work."

She looked at him in shock. His acuity cut straight through everything and got immediately to the point. She took in a deep, steadying breath and met his gaze, but even as she did so she could feel the sting of tears burning at the backs of her eyes.

Piers saw the moisture begin to collect and his expression turned stricken. "Faye, I'm sorry, this time *I* overstepped."

"No, it's okay," she said, blinking fiercely and waving a hand between them. "I'd better go."

Piers watched her leave, feeling as if he was little more than a slug that had crawled out of a vegetable patch. What on earth had spurred him to be so cruel to Faye like that? Was it because she'd hit a nerve when questioning his commitment to Casey? Or had it been her comment about bad things happening to people? *Which she apologized for*, the voice at the back of his mind sternly reminded him. Either way, he knew he'd done wrong. He couldn't afford to lose her and it wasn't just because she knew his company almost as well as he knew it himself.

The last two weeks without her had been oddly empty. Sure, he'd been busy with the baby, who'd already grown and changed in that short time. Yes, Meredith had helped him, but he'd made sure he'd been Casey's primary caregiver. But Faye's absence had made him all the more aware of what she'd come to mean to him on a personal level. If only he could get past that barrier she kept so firmly between them. He sensed the only way that would happen would be if he learned what had occurred in her past to make her so closed off and wary.

Obviously his people had done a background check before she'd been offered the job here, but it had focused on her credentials and experience, and had been peripheral to what he needed to know about her now. Maybe he needed to delve a little deeper. A part of him cautioned him about digging into her past without her knowledge—warned him that if she wanted him to know that much about her, she'd tell him herself. But Piers didn't get things done by waiting for other people. Sometimes you just had to take control and steer the course yourself. This was one of those times.

By the time Faye returned from her meeting, Piers was satisfied that before long he'd get to the root of why she held herself so aloof. Of course, it didn't mean that he wouldn't keep trying to glean what he could from her in the meantime. As soon as she was back in the office, he rose from his desk and walked over to her.

"Everything go okay with the brand manager?"

"Yes, perfect in fact. You made an excellent choice there."

"I know people," he said without any smugness.

It was one of his greatest strengths and he wasn't afraid to admit it. It was also the reason why he knew Faye had unplumbed depths he needed to explore. She deserved more in her life than the shell of existence he knew she lived. She deserved to feel, to laugh—to love.

"You do seem to have a knack there," she admitted wryly.

"I'm glad you think so, but I'd like your help with the meetings I've scheduled for the afternoon. An agency is sending over some nannies for interviews. I want to establish a nursery for Casey on this floor. I was thinking of repurposing the archive room a couple of doors down, actually. Archives can be moved to another floor. I'll need someone who can be here with Casey during the day and at home when I have to make an overnight trip anywhere—although I plan to minimize travel where possible from now on."

Faye looked at him in surprise. "You want me to help you with interviews?"

"Of course, you're my right hand here."

She looked uncomfortable. "But choosing a nanny... Surely that's something you should do on your own."

"Why?"

She was running again, moving into classic avoidance mode, although perhaps not quite as literally as she had back at the lodge.

"Well... I..."

"I trust your judgment, Faye. Will you help me?"

He'd chosen his words carefully, knowing her pride in her work wouldn't allow her to say a flat-out no if he phrased it like that.

"Why me? Maybe you should ask someone else on staff who already has children and has hired nannies before."

"But you know what I need. You always do. First appointment is after lunch."

He saw her visibly sag. "Fine, I'll be ready. Is there anything in particular you want me to look out for?"

"No, just use your judgment like you always do. I know you won't be shy in telling me what you think. And, Faye," he continued just as she started to turn and walk away, "I want to apologize for my comment earlier about commitment. It was unkind of me to say that especially when you've always been there for me when I needed you."

"It's fine. Consider it forgotten."

"No, I can't forget it because I know I hurt you and it hurts me to know I did that. That said, things have changed between us and I'd like to see where we go from here."

"Changed?"

"You've forgotten our lovemaking already?" he teased. Even though he kept his tone light, deep down he felt a slight sting at the idea she'd put that incredible night to the back of her memory.

"Oh, that," she said, coloring again. "No. I haven't forgotten. Any of it."

"And it doesn't make you curious about maybe exploring that side of our relationship further?"

She shook her head firmly. "No. To be honest, I've thought about little else since I came home and, frankly, I think we should forget it."

"I can't forget it. I can't forget *you*." He stepped closer to her and took her hands in his. "I want to know you better, Faye. Sure, I know how great you are here at work. I also know how you sound when we make love. I know how to bring you pleasure, but…" He let go of one hand to tap gently at her forehead. "In here, I don't think I know you at all—and I really, really want to. Will you let me in, Faye? Will you let me know you?"

She looked shaken, uncertain…but he believed he was having an impact, that she was at least considering the idea.

A phone on her desk began to ring and Piers bit back a curse. Faye pulled loose from his hold.

"I'd better get that," she said, her voice sounding choked.

"Sure, but we will finish this discussion, Faye. I promise you. I won't give up. You mean too much to me."

And leaving that statement ringing in her ears, he left the room.

Ten

The nanny interviews went extremely well. So well, in fact, that Faye couldn't fault any of the women or the highly qualified male pediatric nurse who'd applied. When Piers suggested they discuss the applicants over dinner at his house, Faye sensed a rat, but she knew he wouldn't back down and decided the easiest thing would be to face him and get it over with.

She went home after work, showered and changed into a loose pair of pants and a long-sleeved silk blouse that drifted over her skin like a lover's touch. Huh? Where had that thought come from?

She frowned as she checked her reflection in the mirror. The cornflower blue of the silk with its darker navy print in a tribal pattern here and there made her eyes look more blue than gray. Was this too dressy? she wondered. Maybe she should just put on something she'd wear at work.

A glance at the time scotched that idea. Piers was expecting her in twenty minutes and it would take her all of that to get to his place in the Palisades. She slid her feet into low-heeled sandals, grabbed her bag and headed out the door. She took the Pacific Coast Highway to the turnoff, letting the view of the sea calm her—a comfort she badly needed when the prospect of spending the evening with Piers, and likely Casey, was the least relaxing thing she could think of.

Piers answered the door himself when she arrived, his cell phone stuck to his ear. He gestured for her to come in and take a seat in the living room off the main entrance. Rather than sit, Faye strolled over to the large French doors that opened to the gardens and looked out toward the pool. Despite the elegance and expense he'd put into furnishing the house, it looked and felt very much like a home. Although she'd been there many times for work, somehow this visit felt different. A tiny shiver ran down her back and she rubbed her arms before wrapping them around herself.

"Cold?" Piers asked from behind her, making her jump a little.

"No, it's nothing."

"You're nervous then."

"I am not," she protested. "I have nothing to be nervous about."

He studied her for a few seconds before quirking his mouth a little, as if he'd accepted what she said on face value and nothing more. It made her instinctively bristle, but she was prepared to let it drop if he was.

"Sorry I was on the phone when you arrived. It was my lawyer's office. They've tracked down Casey's mom. Turns out she's back in Australia."

"And? Is she okay?"

"That was the first thing I asked them. Apparently she's doing fine and she remains adamant that she wants nothing to do with Casey."

Faye felt a strong tug of sympathy for the little guy. "Why did she have him then, if she didn't want him? What was she thinking?"

"I get the impression she wasn't thinking much at all. She came to the US after ditching her boyfriend in Australia. She fell into a relationship with a new guy here, but he left her when they found out she was expecting. He said it couldn't be his baby because he was infertile, which, according to her, left Quin as the only other possible father.

"She says she tried to get ahold of Quin but never got an answer when she called his phone, which would make sense, of course." Piers's eyes grew bleak and he drew in another breath before continuing. "According to what she told the lawyer, she stayed in Wyoming, drifting from casual job to casual job until she had the baby. By then she'd saved enough to go home again. She'd originally believed Casey to be her boyfriend's child but when he told her he was infertile and their relationship broke down *and* she couldn't get ahold of Quin, she honestly didn't know where to turn. She hadn't wanted to call on her family back in Australia and, living a transient lifestyle here, had no idea of how to seek help. Now, she only sees Casey as a hindrance and, also according to my lawyer, is willing to sign off all her rights to access."

"She is getting legal counsel about her decision, isn't she?"

"I've insisted on it and agreed to pay all her expenses. I've also requested she have a psychological assessment. I would hate for her decision to be based on any possible psychosis as a result of having Casey."

Faye nodded in agreement. "That's a good idea. I'm glad you've done that."

"She insisted it wasn't necessary and that she simply wants to close the door on this episode of her life, but when we said we'd cover all costs, she reluctantly agreed."

"Did she know Quin had passed away?"

"Apparently not. She heard that I was coming up to the house and assumed I was the guy she'd had a relationship with. Although 'relationship' is a bit of a misnomer. It seems they were nothing more than a few brief liaisons during and after New Year's Eve.

"Anyway," Piers continued, "I'm leaving everything I can in the hands of my lawyers and my most pressing concern right now is choosing who I trust the most to be able to help me provide the best care for Casey."

He poured them both a drink. A Scotch on the rocks for him and a mineral water for her. They sat side by side on the sofa and pored over the folders he'd brought home.

"I think you should go with these two," Faye said, putting her finger on the guy's CV and one of the slightly older women.

"Tell me why."

"Well, I think they both have some very strong experience. Jeremy's worked in pediatrics and needs more regular hours to support his wife while she completes her degree, and Laurie has excellent references from all of her past positions. In fact, she's only leaving her current role because the family is moving to the UK and Laurie doesn't want to go. They could rotate from week to week between the office and the house. One week, day shifts. The next, nights."

"Do I really need two nannies? I plan to be on hand in the evenings and if Casey needs me during the night."

"I know you plan to minimize travel, but what about when you do site visits and you're away for several days, or if you're called to troubleshoot a problem at short notice and can't get home at night? Not to mention business dinners and other events that you can't skip that could take you away for hours at a time. Getting a sitter for him every time would be a hassle, and it would be rough for Casey, too. He needs continuity—to feel familiar with the person caring for him. Babies respond better to routine."

Piers fell silent and angled his body to face her, one arm resting along the back of the sofa.

"I asked you this before but this time I want an answer. How come you know so much about babies? I know you act like you want nothing to do with them but your advice is always spot-on. You talk about child care like you really understand it."

Faye felt the all too familiar lump solidify in her throat. She swallowed to try to clear it but it barely made any difference.

"I've seen kids in the care system. Some of them abandoned, some of them taken from their families through hardship or abuse. It gave me an insight, that's all."

The half lie made her heart begin to race in her chest. An insight? That was far too mild a description for what it had been like in her foster home when a baby was brought to the house for care—and in her years there, there had been several. She vividly remembered the first one who'd come into the home after her placement. Remembered hurrying home from high school each day so she could help her foster mom with the little boy's care. She didn't understand then, but now she knew that she'd poured all of her love for her dead baby brother into that child. When he was eventually returned to his parents, she'd felt the aching loss of his departure as if it was a physical pain.

She'd promised herself she wouldn't get so involved the next time, but she'd been unable to help herself. Each child had called to her on one level or another—each one a substitute; a vessel open to receive all the love she had inside her. Her foster mom had seen it all, had talked with Faye's caseworker about it, but the woman had told her it was a good thing. That it was allowing Faye to work through her grief for her family. But it hadn't. In the end, when she'd aged out of the system at eighteen and gone to college, she was just as broken as she'd been when she'd arrived.

A touch on her cheek made her realize she'd fallen deep into her reveries—forgotten where she was, and why. To her horror she realized she was crying. She bolted up from the sofa and dashed her hands across her face, wiping all trace of tears from her cheeks.

"Faye? It's more than that, isn't it?" Piers probed gently. "How did you see those kids in the system? Was it when you were placed in foster care yourself?"

She stopped at the French doors. Maybe this would be easier if she couldn't see him. Couldn't feel his strong reassuring presence so close beside her.

"Yes."

A shudder shook her. Warm hands settled on her shoulders but he made no move to turn her around.

"It must have been hell for you."

She didn't want to go into details, so she did the only thing she knew would distract him. She spun and slipped her hands around the back of his neck and gently coaxed his face to hers.

He didn't pull away; he didn't protest. He simply closed

his arms around her waist, let her take his mouth and coax his lips open.

The second she did, she felt a jolt of need course through her. A need that demanded he fill all the dark, empty spaces inside. The spaces she barely even wanted to acknowledge existed. She wanted him so badly her entire body shook with it, and when his hands began to move, one cupping her buttocks and pulling her more firmly into the cradle of his hips, she let herself give over to sensation.

She couldn't get enough of him. His taste, his scent, the strong, hard feeling of his body against hers. Her mind blazed with heat and longing, remembering the intense gratification he'd wrung from her. The feeling of him reaching his own peak and knowing he'd found that delight in her.

"Dinner is served in the conservatory, Mr. Luckman. Oh!"

Faye ripped her lips from his and tried to pull away, but Piers wouldn't let her go. Instead he firmly rubbed her back, as one would when trying to settle a skittish animal.

"Thank you, Meredith. We'll be along in a moment."

Faye ducked her head, unable to meet the housekeeper's eyes. Ashamed of what she'd done.

Piers tipped her chin so she'd looked up at him again.

"As a distraction tactic, I have to say, I admire your strategy. Shall we go through to dinner?"

Faye pulled away again and Piers let her go this time.

"No. Look, I'd better go. Meredith—"

"No more running away. Meredith won't say a word. You should know as well as anyone that she's the soul of discretion. Besides, she likes you."

Like her or not, Faye felt horribly uncomfortable as she let Piers tug her down the hall to the family room and through to an informal dining area in the conservatory, where Meredith had arranged their meal. A succulent-looking tri-tip roast nestled in its juices on a carving plate and a roasted vegetable salad was piled in a serving dish beside it. The scents of balsamic and garlic made Faye's mouth water hungrily.

Meredith looked up from tweaking a napkin at one of the place settings. "I've left the roast for you to carve, Mr. Luckman. The baby is down for the night, so I'll be off now. The monitor is on the sideboard over there. *Bon appétit!*" And, with a warm and knowing smile in Faye's direction, she bustled her way back to the kitchen.

Faye felt herself begin to relax. Okay, so Meredith didn't judge her for what she'd seen back there in the living room. *And why should she?* a little voice asked. *She's probably seen Piers kissing women every day.*

Across the table, Piers picked up the carving knife and fork. "What's your pleasure?" he asked with a hooded look.

Her insides clenched on a wave of heat at his simple question. "I... I beg your pardon?"

"Do you prefer the crispy end or something from the middle?"

"Oh, the end bit, please."

"Your wish is my command."

Faye watched, mesmerized, as Piers deftly carved the tri-tip into slices and then served her. The evening sun caught the hairs on his arm and instantly she was thrown back to Wyoming. Remembering how his body hair had felt under her fingertips. More, how the silky heat of his skin had felt against hers. She pressed her thighs together as another surge of need billowed through her.

What on earth had she been thinking, kissing him before? It had awakened a monster within her. A demanding monster that plucked at her psyche, drawing on select memories that would eventually drive her mad.

Mad with lust, perhaps, that thoroughly inconvenient droll little voice said at the back of her mind.

In an effort to distract herself, Faye served a large helping of balsamic-roasted vegetables onto Piers's plate and a smaller helping for herself. She tried to direct the conversation toward a project nearing completion in San Francisco but Piers wasn't having any of it.

"Let's leave work at the office for today, hmm?" he said, spearing some food on his fork and lifting it to his mouth. "What do you think of the vegetables? Meredith uses a secret ingredient that she refuses to disclose to me. Maybe you can help me figure out what it is?"

Was he serious? Apparently so, judging by the expression on his face. She'd never really stopped to watch him eat before, but now, with a faint glisten on his lips and a rapt expression on his face, she was reminded all too much of how seriously he took other pleasures. Biting back a moan, Faye sampled some of the vegetables herself.

"Tell me," Piers insisted. "What do you taste?"

"Well, balsamic vinegar, of course. And garlic. And..." She let the flavors roll over her tongue. "Rosemary. Definitely rosemary."

"Yes, but there's something else in there. It's subtle but sweet. Meredith obviously uses it sparingly."

Faye concentrated a little longer, closing her eyes this time as she sampled another mouthful.

"Honey!" she exclaimed. "It's barely there, like you said, but I just get a hint of it before I swallow."

Across the table Piers beamed at her. "You know, I've been trying to figure that out for the better part of two years. It's been driving me crazy."

"Really? That's been the driving question behind everything you do?" Faye teased, laughing softly.

"You're beautiful when you laugh like that. Actually, you're beautiful all the time, but when you let go and laugh—" He paused, his face growing serious and his eyes deepening into dark pools.

"Stop it," Faye insisted. "You're making me uncomfortable."

"I can't help it, Faye. I have feelings for you. I want to talk about them. About you. About us."

"The only *us* is the *us* that works together," she said adamantly and carved a piece of meat to put in her mouth.

"I'd like there to be more than that. Wouldn't you? Don't you think we owe it to ourselves to explore what we shared back at the lodge?"

She chewed, swallowed and set her knife and fork down before looking at him. It took all her control to keep her response short and to the point.

"No."

"Don't you ever get tired of hiding from your feelings, Faye?"

"I'm just being pragmatic. Look, your track record with women speaks volumes to your inability to commit long-term, even if I was interested in anything long-term. Which I'm not. Ever."

Faye looked at the skillfully prepared food on her plate and felt all appetite flee. She hated having to talk like this to Piers and fervently wished they'd never gone and complicated everything by having sex.

"That's a shame. As to my track record, perhaps I've been searching for the one who has been under my nose all the time?"

"You're being ridiculous," she scoffed.

But deep inside a little piece of her began to wish she

could reach out and accept what he was offering. She wondered what it would be like to belong to someone. To be a part of more than just one.

The monitor on the sideboard near the entrance to the conservatory crackled into life and Casey's cry broke into the air.

"You'd better go and see to him," Faye said.

Piers looked as if he wanted to say more to her but he couldn't ignore the growing demands of the baby upstairs.

"Don't you dare leave," he said. "I'll be right back."

"I—"

"Don't. Leave."

And with that demand he rose and walked quickly to the doorway.

A few minutes later, through the monitor, Faye heard Piers enter the baby's room. He made soothing sounds as he obviously picked the little boy up and tried to settle him. She felt as though she was eavesdropping on something precious and wished like crazy she could get up and walk away. That she could forget the man upstairs and the child he cared for. But she knew that both of them had somehow inveigled their way into her heart. She shook her head at her own stupidity. How had she let that happen? Why?

Casey had obviously soiled his diaper, and she could hear Piers gagging in the background as he cleaned the little boy up. Obviously he was going to be a while. Faye gathered their plates and took them through to the kitchen where she put them in the oven, which she set on warm. No need for cold dinner, she thought.

She went back to the table and played with her water glass, trying not to listen as Piers struggled through the diaper change. There was something about hearing her handsome, capable boss being so completely out of his element that really appealed to her. Her hand to her mouth, she tried to hold back the chuckle that rose from deep inside.

Eventually, Piers resettled the child and returned to the conservatory.

"I hope you washed your hands," she teased.

"As if my life depended on it." Piers shook his head. "I still can't believe a baby can do that."

Faye felt a smile pull at her lips but fought to hide it. "Just wait till he projectile v—"

"Don't!" Piers barked, holding up a hand in protest. "Just don't."

Faye shrugged. "It's not all roses, is all I'm saying."

"I've discovered that," Piers replied ruefully.

"I'll get our plates," she said, rising. "That's if you're still hungry?"

Piers pulled a face. "I guess I could still eat. Especially after Meredith went to all that effort."

"Good choice." Faye tossed the words over her shoulder as she went through to the kitchen to retrieve their meals.

"Thanks for keeping it warm for me," Piers said as he picked up his knife and fork.

"It's nothing."

"You do that all the time. Did you know that?"

"Do what?"

"Diminish what you do."

"Do I?"

Faye stopped and thought for a bit. She had to concede he was probably right.

"Why is that? Don't you think that what you do is good enough? That *you're* good enough?"

Faye just looked at him in surprise. She'd never really stopped to consider it before.

Piers continued, "Because you are. You're better than good enough. You're the best assistant I've ever had and I know you apply yourself one hundred percent to everything you do."

She looked away, uncomfortable with the praise. Wasn't it enough that she just did her job? Did he have to talk about it?

"But what about your personal life, Faye?" He pressed on. "You have friends, don't you?"

"Of course I do," she answered automatically.

"You never talk about them."

"I thought I'd made it clear. My private life is private."

"Faye, I want to be a part of your private life. I want to be a part of your life altogether."

"I can't do that," she answered, shaking her head.

"So far you haven't given me a decent reason as to why not. And I won't back down without one. You know I don't give up when I want something."

She pushed her chair back from the table and stood. "I'm not just something to be wanted, Piers. And I don't have to give you a reason for anything. You're my boss. So far, you've been a good one, but I'm beginning to revise my opinion on that."

"Is that why you won't let anything develop between us?" he said, swiftly coming around the table to stand between her and the exit. "Because I'm your boss? Because if it is, then I'll fire you here and now so we can be together."

There was another sound from the monitor and Faye went rigid.

Piers looked at her with questions in his eyes. "Is it Casey? Or is it me?"

"No, it's neither of you," she lied, her voice a little more than a whisper. "I just don't want to get involved. With anyone. Look, thanks for dinner. I have to go."

She pushed past him and all but ran to the living room, where she grabbed her bag and headed for the front door. Piers was a second behind her. She spun around to face him.

"Yes, before you say it, I am running away. It's how I deal with stuff, okay? If I don't like a situation I'm in, I remove myself from it."

"But you do like me, don't you, Faye?" He stepped a little closer, his strong, warm hands clasping her upper arms and pulling her gently to him. "In fact, you more than like me. You're just fighting it. If it makes it any easier, I more than like you, too. In fact, I—"

"Don't!" Faye pressed her fingers to his mouth before he could say another word. "Don't say anything, please. I don't deserve it."

And with that she tugged loose from his grasp, pulled open the front door and hightailed it to her car.

Eleven

Piers watched her leave in a state of shock. He'd been on the verge of declaring he loved her. In fact, right now he was probably more stunned by that almost-admission than she was.

He closed the door and slowly walked back to the conservatory, automatically clearing the table and putting away the leftovers. Meredith had her own suite downstairs in the house, with its own entrance, but she was away at a community college course tonight. Something he'd offered to fund for her when he'd heard of her long-held dream to study English literature. It certainly didn't hurt him to look after himself for one night a week, especially if that only meant cleaning up his dinner dishes.

Helping people achieve their dreams made him feel good. Whether it was at work and assisting them to develop further in their role or whether it was through the generous donations he made to various charities in the area. But never had he wanted to help someone as badly as he wanted to help Faye. What would it take to make her feel good? Something held her back. He could sense she wanted more—just as he did—but every time she started to reach for it, she yanked herself away. Almost as if she felt she had to punish herself for wanting it in the first place. The why of it might elude him forever if she didn't open up, unless the private investigator he'd contacted came up with what he needed to know.

Thinking about what he'd done, requesting the investigation, made him question his morals. Faye had a right to privacy and if she didn't want him to know about her past then he ought to respect that. In any other instance he would. But this was Faye. This was the woman who'd let him be her first lover. This was the woman he'd fallen in love with. Not a sudden headlong lunge into love, but a long and growing respect that had evolved into so much more while they'd been snowbound at the lodge.

He couldn't just ignore what they could potentially have together. They both deserved to know exactly where they could go with the feelings she so determinedly kept shoving away.

Piers went up to his master suite and stood at the window, looking out at the night sky. Ethics could take a hike. He had to know what he was dealing with here. How could he fight it, overcome it, if he didn't know what *it* was? Knowing would at least allow him to metaphorically arm himself for what would be the most important battle of his life. The battle to win Faye's heart.

The next few days passed in a blur of activity. The archive room next to the office Piers and Faye shared had been emptied and converted into a nursery for Casey. Thankfully the two nannies that had been both his and

Faye's top picks had been free to start working immediately and the roster system seemed to be working well.

As to Faye, she appeared determined to spend as little time with him in the office as possible. She was constantly in another part of the building or out at meetings on his behalf for one thing and another. Normally he wouldn't have questioned it, but in light of how she'd left his house earlier in the week he saw this as exactly what it was. Avoidance. Well, it didn't matter. She had to come back to the office eventually and, when she did, he'd be waiting.

There was still no news from the investigator regarding Faye's past. Piers had begun to question whether he'd done the right thing—whether he shouldn't just cancel the whole inquiry—but a niggling need to know now wouldn't leave him.

Another question had also taken up residence in his thoughts. Something his lawyer had discussed with him when he'd relayed the information from Casey's mom. Greg, his lawyer, had asked what it could mean if the infertility angle from the woman's other lover had just been something he had said to avoid responsibility. Or what if she'd made the whole thing up? She'd worked at the lodge that night and no doubt had some idea of the wealth behind the Luckman family. Maybe claiming Quin was the father was just an attempt to get a share of that wealth in exchange for the child?

Piers rejected one of the questions immediately. If money had been Casey's mom's goal, she would have asked for it outright. She would hardly have left the baby with him the way she had. And while the fact that she'd had sex with Quin while apparently involved with someone else didn't exactly speak volumes as to her reliability or her integrity, he didn't believe her actions in abandoning Casey had been for her own financial gain.

While Piers was convinced that Casey was his brother's son, Greg had thrown another scenario at him. What if the boyfriend was the real father and decided to demand access to Casey? Greg had strongly recommended Piers have DNA testing done to ensure that there would be no future threats to Casey's stability and his position in Piers's life. If Piers could prove his biological link to the baby, there could be no questions asked, ever. Hell, with the fact that as identical twins he and Quin shared identical DNA, even Piers couldn't be ruled out as Casey's biological father.

When Greg had first thrown that into the conversation Piers hadn't been in a hurry to follow his recommendation for the DNA test. But his lawyer had sown a seed. Piers wanted to be certain that Casey's stability would never be threatened. That he'd never become involved in a tug-of-war between parents the way Piers and Quin so often had with their own parents. Even though they'd never separated, they'd spent most of their marriage living very separate lives and constantly battling over their assets. Their children, though uninteresting to them personally, were often pawns used in their bickering.

No, Casey would have the stability he deserved. There would be no question about who was responsible for him or who would raise him. Piers would get the testing done and settle any doubt once and for all.

"Faye, I need you to do something for me," he said the moment she returned to the office from a meeting.

She raised one brow in question.

He explained what he needed and, true to form, within fifteen minutes she'd gathered the information he'd requested and ordered the test kit to be couriered directly to their office.

"Are you sure you want to do this?" she asked after she hung up the phone.

"I don't want any nasty surprises in the future," he answered firmly.

"But what if Casey's not Quin's, after all? Isn't that why you're keeping him rather than relinquishing him to state care?"

"It won't make any difference."

"Won't it?"

"Of course not. He's mine now. Forever."

"If he's not Quin's child, you can change your mind."

Piers felt the weight of her statement as if it was placed directly over his heart. "What are you suggesting?" he demanded, his voice hard.

"It wouldn't be the first time someone decided parenthood wasn't for them. I saw it at least twice when adoptions failed while I was being fostered. It's heartbreaking for everyone concerned."

He looked at her in shock. Was that a measure of how she saw him? Was that why she showed no inclination to take a risk on him? Did she truly think he was incapable of commitment to anyone—a woman or a child?

"Wow. Why don't you just tell me what you really think of me, Faye?"

He couldn't hide the hurt in his voice. Her words had scored deep cuts, whether she'd intended them to or not.

"I'm sorry, but it happens. This is all very new for you now and you're deeply invested in the whole idea of raising Casey. I can see that."

"But?" he prompted when she fell silent.

"There is no but. Before you complete the adoption

process you need to be certain, for all your sakes, that you're in this for the right reasons."

"And they would be?"

"That Casey gets the best and most loving home and upbringing he possibly can."

There was a note in her voice that surprised him. A passion that spoke volumes as to why she was playing devil's advocate so persistently. Was it possible that she'd allowed herself to develop feelings for Casey, too? That it would distress her if the adoption didn't work out?

The very idea that it mightn't made Piers feel sick to his stomach, but he forced that feeling aside, focusing instead on Faye.

"Those are my very reasons for adopting him," he said finally. "It heartens me that you care so much for his welfare."

He watched as myriad expressions raced over her fine features and as those features finally settled into a frown. She was just about to speak when Piers's cell phone chimed in his pocket.

"You'd better get that," she said before turning back to her computer.

Whatever the call was, it must have been important because with just a short "I'll be back by lunch," Piers headed out of the office.

She sagged in her office chair, the tension she hadn't even realized she'd been carrying in her shoulders finally letting go.

Faye closed her eyes for a moment and bowed her head, then took in a deep breath before letting it go slowly. She'd overstepped when she'd talked to him like that but someone had to advocate for Casey. From where she sat, Piers had lived a golden life. Born into money, given the best education that money could buy, raised in luxurious indulgence—even his position here at work had fallen into his lap after his father had declared his retirement.

While he was more than capable of hard work, he'd always started each battle with every advantage on his side. He didn't know true hardship. Sure, yes, he knew grief. He knew that life could change in an instant, but she'd seen very little about his world that showed he truly understood personal commitment. Casey deserved that.

"Ms. Darby?"

Faye's eyes flew open and she looked up to see Casey's male nanny, Jeremy, standing in front of her.

"Hi, Jeremy. Sorry, I was away with the fairies," she said with a smile of welcome. "What can I help you with?"

"I'm really sorry, but I've just received a call to say my wife has been in a car accident and she's being taken to the hospital. I've called Laurie and she's coming in to cover for me, but she won't be here for another half hour, at least. I wouldn't ask normally, but my wife is in a lot of pain and she needs to be seen as soon as possible.

"Could you listen for Casey? He's sleeping and I don't expect he'll wake until after Laurie gets here but—"

"Leave me the monitor and go. Your wife needs you. There are plenty of us who can listen out for when Casey wakes. Don't worry, okay? And let me know how your wife is doing after you've seen a doctor."

"Thanks, Ms. Darby. I really appreciate it."

"Faye. Please, call me Faye."

Jeremy smiled in response and popped the baby monitor on her desk. "Thanks, Faye. I owe you one."

"No problem, just go and see to your wife."

He was gone almost before the words had left her mouth.

Faye stared at the monitor he'd left on her desk with a wary expression. Even though she'd made sure she had no direct contact with him since returning from the lodge, she knew Casey's schedule by heart. Usually a good little sleeper, he wasn't due to wake for at least another hour, and by then Laurie would definitely be here. She could cope with this, she told herself. All care and yet no responsibility.

She returned her attention to her computer screen and studied the building cost analysis figures for a proposed refit of a collection of old warehouses in North Carolina. Something was off, but she couldn't put her finger on it. She sighed and scrolled back to the beginning. She'd find the discrepancy and deal with it. Details were what she did best.

Faye had been lost in numbers and projections for the better part of fifteen minutes when she heard an enraged howl through the monitor. A chill washed through her and she looked at the time on her computer screen. No way. Casey shouldn't be waking now. Another scream bellowed through the speaker on her desk, forcing her to her feet and out of the office. A few yards down the hall she stopped at the door to the nursery. Her hand trembled as she reached for the doorknob.

This was ridiculous, she told herself. He was just a baby. Just a helpless, sweet thing needing comfort. And yet she could barely bring herself to turn the knob and let herself into the room. Another cry from inside pushed her into action.

She opened the door and stepped into the nursery and was instantly assailed with an array of scents. Soothing lavender in an electric oil burner in one corner was overlaid with the powdery scent of talcum powder. Over that again was something sharper, more sour.

She hurried across the room to discover Casey had been sick in his bed.

"Oh, you poor wee thing," she cooed to him in an attempt to soothe him with her voice.

At the sound of her voice, Casey's cries lessened. She lifted him from the crib and took him across to the change table, swiftly divesting him of his dirty clothing and wiping him clean. She checked his diaper, which was thankfully dry, and then redressed him in a clean onesie.

"There we go," she crooned, lifting him into her arms and resting her cheek on the top of his downy head. "All tidied up. Now we just have your bed to sort out, don't we?"

He didn't feel feverish, she noted with relief. Hopefully his throwing up wasn't a precursor to something serious. With one hand she stripped the dirty linens from the crib, balled them up with his soiled clothing and put them in a hamper in a corner of the room. All the while she kept talking softly to Casey, who'd grown quieter in her arms—just emitting a grumble every now and then. Faye put him in the stroller—in the room for when the nanny took him out for fresh air a couple of times a day—so she could remake the bed, but he wasn't having any of it.

"Silly boy," she chided gently, picking him up again. "I can't make your bed if you don't let me put you down for a couple of minutes."

Casey settled against her, his little body curling up against her chest and his head resting on her shoulder. A fierce wave of emotion swept over her. So much trust from one so small. For as long as she held him, his world was just as it ought to be. Secure. Safe. Loved.

Loved? Tears sprang to her eyes and she blinked them away fiercely. No, she didn't deserve to love or be loved.

Her baby brother had loved her, as had her mom and her stepdad. And she'd let them down. Living without love was her punishment for destroying their future together. And Casey's trust in her was obviously misplaced.

She rubbed his tiny back with one hand and closed her eyes—allowing herself to pretend for just a minute that it was her brother, Henry, she held. That it was his little snuffles she heard. His sweet baby scent that filled her nostrils. The weight of his chubby little body that felt so right in her arms.

"Oh, Henry," she whispered brokenly. "I'm so sorry. I'm so very sorry."

Tears began in earnest now, rolling down her cheeks as though the floodgates had truly been opened. Faye reached for a box of tissues and wiped at the moisture, but it was no good. The tears kept on coming.

She had no idea how long she stood there, rocking gently with the infant in her arms and tears streaming down her face. He'd fallen asleep again, she realized, but she couldn't put him in the bassinette because it wasn't ready. At least, that's what she told herself. It was the only reason why, now that she held him, she couldn't let him go.

A movement at the door caught her gaze and then Piers's strong, male presence was in the room with them.

"Faye?" he asked gently, reaching a hand to touch the tear tracks on her cheek. "I heard you on the monitor. Are you okay?"

His touch, his words, they were the reality check she needed. She shouldn't be there. Shouldn't be holding this child like this.

"He was upset. He'd been sick," she choked out even though her throat felt as though it was clogged with cotton wool. "Here, take him. He doesn't need me."

She deftly transferred the sleeping child to Piers's

arms and tried to ignore the aching sense of emptiness that overcame her the second she let him go. Faye turned to make up the crib, keeping her back firmly to Piers. The moment she was done she left the room, not even trusting herself to speak another word.

Instead of returning to her office she took refuge in the ladies' restroom on their floor. She turned on the faucet and dashed cold water over her wrists and then her face before straightening and looking at her reflection in the mirror. Her face was pale—her eyes shadowed, haunted. Somehow she had to pull herself together, go back to her desk and get on with her day, but she knew something had irrevocably changed for her back there in the nursery.

She couldn't stay at this job. She couldn't face every day watching Piers bond with Casey, watching Casey grow and develop from baby to toddler. It hurt too much. It was a constant, aching reminder of all she'd lost. Of the pain she'd endured for so long now. She'd thought she had it under control. She lived her life the way she wanted it, by creating distance between herself and others. There was no risk that way. No chance she'd lose her heart and face the hazards that loving someone else brought.

But now she was lost on a sea of change and swirling emotion that threatened to drown her. She had to go. Had to leave this place—leave Piers, the job she looked forward to every day. Leave the baby who'd stolen her heart despite her best efforts to remain aloof. She reached for a paper towel and wiped her face one last time before straightening her shoulders and setting her mouth into a grim line of determination.

She'd hand in her notice today. And she'd survive this. Somehow.

Twelve

"You're resigning?" Piers couldn't keep the shock from his voice. "But why? Are you unhappy here? I thought you loved your job."

"I'm sorry, Piers. I'm giving you the required four weeks' notice, effective from today, and I'll contact HR straight away to begin recruitment."

She was still pale and he could see she was holding on to her composure by the merest thread. Everything about her urged him to take her into his arms and to say that whatever it was that worried or frightened her so very much back there in the nursery, he would make it okay—if only she'd let him. And there was the rub. She wouldn't let him, would she? She'd made being an island an art form. Though she was cordial and worked well with everyone, she had no true friends among the staff and, to the best of his knowledge, few, if any, close friends outside of work, either. Certainly, she was respected here in the office, but she was always strictly business and didn't allow herself to be included in anything personal.

He'd returned to the office today much sooner than he'd expected. Halfway to meet his mother for an unexpected and apparently urgent meeting during a layover at LAX, she'd called and said she'd changed her mind and could they make it dinner on her way home from Tahiti in ten days' time instead. He'd rolled his eyes and told himself he wasn't disappointed. That he hadn't dropped everything to spend some time with the woman who'd borne him. But he'd suggested that on her return she come to the house to meet Casey at the same time. It was rare that she was on the West Coast and he hoped to encourage some form of relationship between her and her grandson.

Upon his return, he'd been surprised to hear Faye through the monitor—to hear the raw emotion in her voice as she'd made an apology to someone. What was that name again? Henry. That was it. Was he the reason why she held herself so separate from everyone? He tucked the name away, determined to pass it on to his investigator the moment he'd dealt with the situation right now.

"I don't want to lose you, Faye. You're the best PA I've ever had, but you're so much more to me than that. I'd hoped we could be—"

"I never asked for anything more than to be your assistant," she interrupted. "I never made you any promises."

"No, you didn't. Why is that, Faye? What has you so scared that you'll distance yourself from me like this? Seriously, resigning from your position here is ludicrous. You don't have another job to go to, do you?"

She shook her head. "I can't stay, Piers. I can't do this anymore."

"Why not? Why won't you open up to me and tell me what is holding you back? Until I know what I'm dealing with, I'm in the dark. I don't know how to fix things between us."

"That's half the issue. There can't be any *us*. I've told you over and over again. Why won't you listen to me?"

The note of sheer desperation in her voice made him take a step back and give her space. But hadn't he done enough of that since she'd left him in Wyoming? They'd made love, damn it. Love. It was so much more than just sex. They'd shared something special, something that should have drawn them closer than ever, not driven an insurmountable wedge between them.

He knew she was hurting. He could see it in every line of her beautiful features, in the shadows that lingered in her expressive eyes, not to mention in the rigid lines in which she held her body. Somehow he needed to take action, to help her face the fear that was holding her in its claws, so she could face up to the feelings he knew she had for him.

A woman like Faye didn't just give herself to a man on a whim. The fact that she'd been a virgin the night they'd made love had been irrefutable proof of that. Right now, he was terrified he was on the verge of losing the only woman he'd ever truly loved, but what could he do? He was working in the dark, grasping at straws. He hated that he couldn't just bark a command and have everything fall into place, but he was prepared to keep working at this. If Faye still wanted to leave Luckman Developments after this, that was fine, but he couldn't let her leave him.

He had four weeks to somehow change her mind and Piers knew without a single doubt that it would be the toughest negotiation of his entire life.

* * *

Six days later he had his answers. The wait had almost driven him crazy, especially loaded on top of the growing pile of recommended applicants for Faye's position. But now he knew and he hoped like hell that somewhere in this information delivered privately to his home tonight, he'd have the answer to why Faye was so determined to keep her distance from him.

The reading was sobering. Her background began like so many other people's. Solo, hardworking mom—no father on the scene. A lifestyle he would have considered underprivileged when he was a kid, but now realized was likely rich in nonmaterial things like love and consistency. Faye's mom married when Faye was about thirteen and, from all accounts, the little family was very happy together. A happiness that, according to the report, grew when Faye's baby brother was born. Piers flipped through the notes, looking for the baby's name. Ah, there it was. Henry. The name he'd heard her whisper through the baby monitor last week. Things were starting to fall into place now.

It appeared the family had been involved in a tragic wreck on Christmas Eve. Faye had been the only survivor. Details about the wreck were scarce and Piers had an instinct that there was a great deal more to the event than the brief description on the file. He could understand why losing her entire family in one night would make a person put up walls. But surely those walls couldn't hold forever.

Piers skimmed the rest of the report, reading the summary of her time in foster care and her subsequent acceptance into college. At least she hadn't suffered financial hardship. Her stepdad had been very astute with his finances and her mom had been putting savings aside in a college fund from the day Faye had been born. Following the crash, all the assets had been consolidated. By the time the family home had been sold and life insurances paid out, and after three years of sound management by the executor of her family's estate, Faye had had quite a healthy little nest egg to set her up for her adult life.

He closed the file with a snap. Words. That's all it was. Nothing in there gave him a true insight into why Faye was so hell-bent on leaving him. Yes, yes, he could see the similarities between Casey and her brother Henry. He understood Casey was the same age as her brother had been when he'd died. He could, partially at least, understand why she'd steered clear of involvement with his soon-to-be adopted son. But to keep herself aloof from love and from children for the rest of her life? It was living half a life. No, it was even less than that.

Piers locked the file in a drawer in his home office. Somehow he had to find a way to peel away the protective layers Faye had gathered around her to get her to show him what truly lay in her heart. His future happiness, and hers, depended on it.

It was the kind of day where logic went to hell in a handbasket. Pretty much everything that could go wrong, did. Two new projects being quoted by contractors had come in way over the estimated budgets and asbestos had been found on another site, which had shut the operation down until the material could be safely removed.

Faye and Piers had been juggling balls and spinning plates all day, and it was nearly 8:00 p.m. when their phones stopped ringing.

Faye leaned back in her office chair and sighed heavily. "Do you think that's it? Have we put out enough fires for one day?"

"Enough for a year, I'd say. I want an inquiry into how those estimates were so far off track—"

"Already started," she said succinctly.

It was one of the first things she'd requested when the issue had arisen at the start of the day.

"I love that about you," Piers said suddenly.

Faye looked at him in shock. "I beg your pardon?"

"Your ability to anticipate my needs."

"Hmm," she responded noncommittally.

She looked away and refreshed the email on her screen, hoping something new had arisen that might distract her from what she suspected would be another less than subtle attempt to get her to change her mind about leaving.

"Faye, what would it take to make you stay?"

And there it is. She closed her eyes and silently prayed for strength.

"Nothing."

"Would love make you stay?"

"Love? No, why?"

"I love you."

"You love what I can do for you. Don't confuse that with love," she said as witheringly as she could manage.

Inside, though, she was a mess. He loved her? No. He couldn't. He only thought he loved her because she was probably the first person ever to say a flat-out no to him, and he loved a challenge. Of course he wanted her. And once he had her he'd lose interest because that's the way things went. Either that or he'd realize he never loved her, anyway.

Would that be so bad? her inner voice asked.

Of course not, she scoffed. She wasn't interested in love. Ever.

Liar.

"You think I don't know what love is? That's interesting," Piers continued undeterred. "You know what I think, Faye?"

She sighed theatrically but continued staring at her computer screen. "Whether I want to know or not, I'm sure you're going to tell me, aren't you?"

She heard him get up from his chair and move across the office to stand right beside her. Strong, warm hands descended on her shoulders and turned her chair so she faced him.

"I think you're too scared to love again."

"Again?"

"Yes, *again.* I'm pretty certain you have loved, and loved deeply. I'm also pretty certain you've been incredibly hurt. Faye, not wanting to take a risk on love is a genuine shame. I never really knew what love felt like, aside from the brotherly bond Quin and I shared. But now I think I've finally learned what love is."

"You seem to think you know a lot about me," she said. Her words were stilted and a knot tightened deep in her chest. She had a feeling she really wasn't going to like what he was about to say next so she decided to go on the attack instead. "Piers, please don't kid yourself that you love me. You're just attempting to manipulate me into staying because that's what would make your life easier."

He genuinely looked shocked at her words. "That's the second time recently you've made your perception of me clear—and I haven't been happy with the picture you've painted either time. Tell me, Faye. Is that why you slept with me back at the lodge? Because it meant nothing to you and because you thought it would mean nothing to me?"

His words robbed all the breath from her lungs. Wow, when he wanted to strike a low blow he really knew how and where to strike, didn't he? That night had meant everything to her, but she wasn't about to tell him that. It would only give him more ammunition in this crazy war of his against her defenses.

Faye pushed against the floor and skidded her chair back a little. She stood. "I don't need to take this from you. I'm leaving, remember?"

"And you're still running."

"Oh, for goodness' sake! Will you stop it with the running comments? So I choose to remove myself from situations I'm uncomfortable with. That's not a crime."

"No, it's not a crime." He closed the distance between them. "Unless by doing so you continue to hurt yourself and anyone who cares about you every time you do it. Faye, you can't keep living half a life. Your family would never have wanted that for you."

An arctic chill ran through her veins, freezing her in place and stealing away every thought.

"M-my family? What do you know of my family?"

The sense of anxiety she'd felt before had nothing on the dark hole slowly consuming her from the inside right now. Aside from the police, she'd never spoken to anyone about exactly what had happened on the night of the wreck. How could he know? Why would he?

Piers's next words were everything she'd dreaded and more. "I know everything. I'm so sorry for your loss."

His beautiful dark eyes reflected his deep compassion but she didn't want to see it. Even so, she remained trapped in the moment. Ensnared by his words, by his caring.

"Everything, huh?" she asked bitterly. "Did you know I killed them? That I was the one behind the wheel that night? I killed them all." She threw the words at him harshly, the constriction of her throat leaving her voice raw.

Shock splintered across his handsome features.

"I thought as much," she continued bitterly. "That information wasn't in any report you could commission because it was sealed. So, how much do you love me now that you know I'm a murderer?"

Piers shoved a hand through his hair. His brows drew into a straight line, twin creases forming between them. "How can you say you're a murderer? You know you didn't deliberately kill anyone. It was an accident."

"Was it? I'm the one who pestered my stepdad to let me drive that night. Mom didn't want me to. She said it was too icy on the road, that I didn't have the experience. But my stepdad said experience was the only way I'd learn."

"Even so, from what I read, the gas tanker skidded on the road, not you. You didn't stand a chance."

Her mouth twisted as she remembered seeing the tanker coming toward them, relived the moment it jackknifed and began its uncontrollable slide toward their car. She'd been petrified. She'd had no idea what to do, how to avoid the inevitable.

"You're right, I didn't. But when it happened, I froze— I didn't know what to do. If my stepdad had driven instead… If I'd listened to my mom…" Faye's voice broke and she dragged in a ragged breath before continuing. "If I'd listened to my mom, we might all have been alive today."

"You don't know that."

"No, I'll never know that. The one thing I do know is

that my decisions that night killed my family. And that's something I can never forget or forgive myself for. My stepdad and my brother died instantly. Henry was only three and a half months old. Don't you think he deserved to grow up, to have a life? And my mom—I can still hear her screams when I try to sleep at night. The only reason I didn't burn to death right along with her was because people pulled me from the wreck before the flames took complete hold of the car."

"Your scars," Piers said softly. "They're from the fire?"

Faye nodded. "So you see, I'm not worth loving."

"Everyone deserves to be loved, Faye. You more than anyone, if only for what you've been through. Don't you think you've paid enough? You need to learn to forgive yourself and rid yourself of the guilt that is keeping you from living."

"I live. That's my punishment."

He shook his head emphatically. "You exist. That's not living. The night we shared at the lodge—*that* was living. That was reveling in life, not this empty shell of subsistence you endure every day. Take a risk, Faye. Accept my love for you. Learn to love me."

She'd begun to tremble under the force of emotion in his words.

"I can't. I can't care. I won't."

"Why?" He pressed her.

"If I love someone again, I'll lose them. Can't you see? I did try to love after the crash. I cared for every baby that came into the foster home as if every single one of them was my chance to redeem myself for what I did to Henry. I poured my love and care into each one and you know what happened? Each and every one of them was taken from me again. Either they were re-homed or they were returned to their parents. Every.

Single. Time—I lost my baby brother all over again."
Faye hesitated and drew on every last ounce of strength
she possessed. "So you'll forgive me if I don't *ever* want
to love again."

Thirteen

Piers watched as she retrieved her bag from her bottom drawer and slung the strap over her shoulder. She still shook and her face was so very pale that her freckles stood out in harsh relief against her skin.

"Now, if you don't need me for anything else tonight, I'd like to go home."

He looked at her, desperate to haul her into his arms, to hold her and to reassure her that she didn't need to be alone anymore. That if she could only let go of that cloak of protection she'd pulled around her emotions and let him inside, everything would be all right. But even he couldn't guarantee that, could he? Accepting that fact was a painful realization. But even so, he was willing to take that chance because surely the reward far outweighed the possibility it would all go wrong?

"Faye, please, hear me out."

"Again?"

"For the last time. Please. After this, I'll let you go, if that's what you truly want me to do."

He saw the muscles working in the slender column of her throat, saw the tension that gripped her body in the set of her shoulders and her rigid stance.

"Fine. Say your piece."

"Look, I know I've had a charmed life compared to yours. I never wanted for anything. But in all my years growing up, those people who professed to love me—my own mom and dad—never showed any hint that their emotions went below the surface. Quin and I had each other, but we were just trophies to our parents. Either something to show off or something for our parents to fight about.

"I thought I was okay with that. That I could live my life like that. But it wasn't until Quin died that I began to take a good, long, hard look at myself and I didn't like what I saw anymore. In fact, I think Quin's thrill-seeking lifestyle was a direct result of how he coped with our parents' inability to express or feel genuine love for us, as well.

"His whole life he pushed the envelope. He took extreme risks in everything he did. Someone would climb a tree—he'd climb a taller one. Someone would ski a black-diamond trail—he'd go off piste. Right up until he died, he was searching for something. Whether it was praise or acceptance or even, just simply, love or a sense that he was deserving of love—I'll never know. But I do know that his dying taught me a valuable lesson about life. It's worth living, Faye, and in living it you have to make room for love because, if you don't, what are we doing on this earth?"

Was he getting through to her? She made no move to leave. In fact, was that a shimmer of tears in those blue-gray eyes of hers? Sensing he might have created a crack in her armor, he decided to continue to drive whatever kind of wedge in that chink that he possibly could.

"Do you know why I'm so crazy about Christmas?" When she rolled her eyes and shook her head, he continued. "I've spent my whole adult life trying to create a sense of family and to experience what Christmas can be all about. My family may have been wealthy, but we were so fractured. Dad living most of his retirement playing golf around the gators in Florida, Mom in New York. While they remain married, they've lived separate lives ever since Quin and I were carted off to boarding school. For the longest time I thought that was normal! Can you imagine it? Six years old and thinking that was how everyone did it?"

"I'm sorry, Piers. So sorry you didn't know a parents' love." Faye spoke softly, and he could see her understanding, feel her sympathy as if it was a physical thing reaching out to fill the empty spaces inside him.

"Then you'll understand when I say this. I want more than what I had growing up. I want Casey to have that, too. Quin's son will never know another minute where he isn't loved. And that's what I want, too, and I want to have it with you, Faye. I love you. I want you in my life, my arms, my bed."

He drew in a breath and let it out in a shudder. "But it has to be all or nothing. I don't want you to come to me with any part of you locked away. I'm prepared to lay everything on the line for you because I want you to be a part of the family I'm trying to create, the future I want to have. I will help you and support you and love you every day for the rest of my life—if you'll let me.

"So, what's it to be? Are you going to take what's

freely and openly offered to you? Will you take a chance on me and on yourself, and let yourself be happy?"

Faye just stood there, staring at him. Piers willed her to respond, willed her to say something. Anything. Hope leaped like a bright flame in his chest when she took a step toward him. This was it. This was when she would accept the offer of his heart and hopes and his promises for their future. Then she hesitated. Her head dropped.

"I can't."

She walked away and, despite every instinct in his body screaming at him to stop her, he let her go. He had to. He'd understood what she was doing when she took that single step toward him. She'd wanted him to meet her halfway. But in this, he had to know she was totally committed. It wasn't just his happiness that was at stake here, nor just hers. It was Casey's, too, and if she couldn't commit wholeheartedly, then they were destined to fail.

He hadn't realized letting her go could hurt so much.

After a night fraught with lack of sleep and an irritable teething baby to boot, Piers wasn't surprised to arrive in the office to discover a message for him from HR saying that Faye had requested urgent personal leave in lieu of working out the rest of her notice. He hated to admit it, but her decision was probably for the best. It would be absolute torture to be around her every day knowing that she'd closed the door on any chance of them having a future together.

He set to dealing with the fallout from the problems that had arisen the day before and, with every call, every email, every decision, he missed her more and more. It wasn't just her ability to do her job as well as he did his, nor her intuition when it came to what he needed. It was, quite simply, her. All through the day he found himself staring at her empty desk, or starting to say something to her only to realize she wasn't there. Nor would she be, ever again.

Had he been wrong to push her? A part of him agreed that he most definitely was every kind of fool. Surely half having her was better than not having her at all? But the other part of him, the part that still remained after the poor little rich boy had grown up, knew that he deserved more than that. And so did she. By her own admission, she didn't want what he could offer her. She didn't want his love or his soon-to-be adopted son. She didn't want the security he could offer her. The prospect of more children. She didn't want him, period.

He was at the end of his tether by day's end and decided it was time to head home. There was no need to work late tonight. He'd dismiss Laurie, who was caring for Casey at the office this week, and take the baby home.

Piers was at the door of his office when his cell phone vibrated in his pocket. He slid it out and, not recognizing the number, debated diverting the call to voice mail. But something prompted him to accept it.

"Mr. Luckman? This is Bruce Duncan from the lab. We have the results of the DNA testing you requested."

"That was quick. I wasn't expecting them for another week at least."

"Your assistant requested we handle the testing as promptly as possible. I understand there is an adoption in process?"

"Yes, that's right. My brother's son."

"Ah," Bruce Duncan said on a long sigh. "The results are quite clear on that. I'm sorry to inform you that the infant being tested is not your brother's son."

Piers staggered under the shock of the man's words. Not Quin's son? At the back of his mind he'd known it was a possibility, but he'd convinced himself that Casey was Quin's flesh and blood.

"Mr. Luckman? Are you still there?"

"Yes, yes. I'm here. And you're absolutely certain about that?" His voice was raw but not as raw as his bleeding heart.

Duncan began to rattle on about markers and strands and all manner of technical data to support the bombshell he'd just dropped, but it all just washed over Piers until Duncan made one last statement.

"The results are conclusive. The infant has no biological link to your family."

"Thank you," Piers managed to say through a jaw clenched against the pain that washed over him. "Please send the final report to my office addressed to my attention."

After receiving an assurance that a copy was already on its way, Piers severed the call. He put one hand against the door frame and leaned heavily against it. He'd said it didn't matter, that he'd go ahead with the adoption anyway—and he would—but the knowledge that he now had nothing left of Quin scored across his heart like a tiger's claw.

Losing his brother had come as such a shock, and the hope that Quin had left something of himself behind had buoyed Piers along these past several weeks. He hadn't realized how much it had lifted the pall of grief he'd carried with him since Quin's death. Or how much it had eased the shock of realization that his carefree brother was not as bulletproof as they both had always thought. That Piers now was, for all intents and purposes, alone.

He would have to let his lawyer know, although it would not change his wishes about the adoption process. But Casey's real father, if he could be found, would need to be notified. The whole process could open up a whole new can of worms. The thought of making that call right now was a mountain too far for him. Piers pushed off from the frame, straightened his shoulders and headed down the hall toward Casey's nursery.

Laurie looked up from where she was playing with the baby on the floor.

"Look, here's your daddy!" she cooed to the squirming infant on the play mat on the floor. "Just in time to see what a clever boy you are."

Laurie looked up from the baby and smiled at Piers. "He's coming along so well, Mr. Luckman. You must be so proud. His hand/eye coordination is improving every day. He can strike the hanging toys and even grip them at will from time to time."

"That's wonderful, Laurie."

"Mr. Luckman, is everything okay? You sound different."

Piers forced a smile to his face. "Just a little tired, is all. This little tyke had me up a few times last night."

"Oh, was Jeremy not on duty?"

"His wife had an early appointment to follow up on her injury from last week. I gave him the night off."

"Well, you know if you need me, I'm more than happy to take an extra duty. I just adore this little man. He's such a joy to care for."

"Thank you, Laurie, but we'll be okay. Jeremy is back on duty tonight. I'm finishing early for the day. You can head on home now."

Laurie quickly finished straightening the nursery while Piers settled on the floor with Casey. The moment he sat beside the little boy, the baby turned his head toward him and began to babble and pump his legs in excitement.

"He knows you," Laurie said with an indulgent smile. "He's always so happy to see you."

Some of the pain that had cut him so viciously at the news from the lab, eased a little. He scooped his wee charge up into his arms and held him close. As if sensing Piers's need for comfort, Casey settled immediately, his little thumb finding its way into his mouth and his head nestling under Piers's chin.

Child of his blood or not, he loved this little boy so very much. No matter what, he would fight to keep him.

Faye sat in the rental car opposite the house that had been her home for most of her childhood. With the engine still running and the heater blasting hot air into the car's cabin, she should have been warm. Instead she felt as though a solid lump of ice had solidified deep inside her. Coming here had been a mistake. She wouldn't find any answers here. There was no resolution to be found. Her family was gone.

She let her eyes drift over the house that was obviously still very much a home. It was still well-kept. The walk had been shoveled clear of snow and the driveway looked as though a car had been on it recently. Lights burned at the downstairs windows, glowing welcomingly from inside. She looked up to the window that had once been hers and wondered who slept in that room now. Did they stare out that window at night and gaze at the stars, wondering where life would lead them?

Did they ever imagine that everything could be torn away from them in an instant? That they could lose everything they held dear?

A movement at the window caught her eye. A woman, with a small child on her hip, moved from room to room downstairs and tugged the drapes closed. Cutting the coziness of their world off from the harsh winter night outside.

Faye swallowed against the lump in her throat. There was nothing to see here. Nothing to gain.

Life moved on.

But you haven't.

That pesky small voice was back. She put the car in gear and eased away from the curb, not really knowing what she'd been looking for. The only thing she was sure of right now was that whatever it was, it wasn't here anymore.

She'd thought coming back to Michigan, to her hometown, would give her a sense of closure. She'd visited with her foster parents, who'd now retired, and they'd been glad to see her—proud of her achievements in the years since she'd left their care. She'd even caught up on the phone with her old friend, Brenda, from high school. The only one who hadn't awkwardly withdrawn from her and her grief when she'd finally returned to class.

At the time, Faye had felt as though she was being justifiably punished by the other children. No wonder they'd shunned her. After all, they hadn't killed their parents and siblings, had they? They still lived their lives. Went to sport or band practice. Went to one another's houses to do homework and eat junk food and watch movies together. But looking back now, she realized she'd been to blame for most of the distance that had widened between her and her friends. They'd had little to no experience with death and loss, especially on the scale Faye had endured. And, subsequently, they'd had no idea of what to say, or how to cope with her withdrawal from them. Only Brenda had tried to maintain their friendship up until they'd gone their separate ways to college.

She was due at Brenda's for dinner soon, Faye realized

as she got to the end of the street and came to a halt at a stop sign. She started to roll forward, only to slam on her brakes as a large tanker bore down the cross street toward her. Her tires slipped on the icy road. Her heart began to race in her chest. She slid to a halt, the tanker continuing past her completely oblivious to the turmoil that rolled and pitched inside her.

An impatient honk of a horn behind her made Faye force herself to concentrate, to continue through the intersection and to keep on driving. To overcome her fright and to keep on going. And wasn't that what she'd done every day since that night?

Be honest with yourself. You haven't kept going. You've been hiding. Running. Just like Piers said.

"Damn it!" she muttered out loud. "Stop that."

Refusing to listen anymore to her inner voice, Faye focused on the drive to Brenda's house. It wasn't far from where Brenda had grown up, the house where her parents still lived—a blessing since Brenda's mom and dad cared for her little ones while she worked in her role as a busy family medicine doctor at a local practice. Faye had been surprised to hear that her career-focused friend now had two small children and a husband who adored her. By the sounds of things, her life was chaotic and full, and everything she'd never known she always wanted. And most of all, from talking with Brenda on the phone yesterday, it had been obvious that despite the chaos, her life was filled with love.

Faye drew to a halt outside Brenda's house and got out of the car. The front door flung open, sending warmth and light flooding onto the front porch.

"Come on in!" Brenda urged. "It's freezing out there."

The moment Faye was on the porch she was enveloped in a huge hug.

"Oh, I've missed you! I'm so glad you called," her old friend sighed happily in her ear.

She led Faye inside and introduced her to her husband and eighteen-month-old identical twin boys.

Faye felt tears prick at her eyes as she looked at the dark-haired miniatures of their father. Was this what Piers and Quin had been like as kids? she wondered. She shoved the thought aside. Piers had been on her mind constantly since she'd walked away from him that night, even though she'd tried her hardest not to think about him.

Despite her attempts to remain aloof, Faye was quickly drawn into the chaos of the young family, and when Brenda's husband went to put the boys to bed after dinner, Brenda led her into the sitting room where they perched on the sofa together.

"So, tell me. What have you been doing with yourself? And this isn't a general inquiry. This is me with my doctor's hat on. Something's not right, is it?"

"I'm fine. I've been working hard lately. You know how it is."

Brenda reached out and squeezed Faye's hand. "It's more than just work, isn't it? How did you cope this last Christmas? Was it as awful for you as it used to be?"

Faye started to brush off Brenda's concern but then somewhere along the line the words began to fall from her mouth. She told her old friend all about the lodge and having to decorate it. Brenda had laughed, but in a sympathetic way and urged her to keep talking. When she got to the part where she'd found Casey, Brenda was incredulous.

"How could anyone do something like that? The risks were terrible. He could have died!"

"In her defense, she waited until I was there before she left. To be honest, I don't think she was in a rational state of mind."

Brenda shook her head. "I've seen a lot of sad cases but this really makes me wonder about people's choices. There are so many avenues for help available if people would only ask."

"But sometimes it's too hard to ask. Sometimes it's easier just to keep it all in and deal with it however you can."

Brenda looked at her carefully. "We're not talking about the abandoned baby anymore, are we?"

Faye tried to steer Brenda's interest in another direction but her friend wasn't having any of it.

"Did you ever have any counseling after the accident, Faye?"

"I didn't need counseling. I knew what I'd done. I learned to deal with it."

"Deal with it, yes. But accept it? Move on from it?"

"Of course," Faye insisted, but even as she spoke she knew the words were a lie.

"I'm worried about you," Brenda said softly. She moved closer and took both of Faye's hands in hers. "You can talk to me, Faye. I know we haven't been close in years but I know what you went through. I watched you withdraw from everyone more and more until no one could reach you. I should have said something then, but we were still so young and clueless. So busy with what we were doing."

"There's no shame in that. Everyone had their life to live," Faye said in defense.

"As did you." Brenda gently squeezed Faye's fingers. "Think about it. If you want to see someone while you're here, I know several really good grief counselors. It's time you took your life back, Faye. You can't remain a victim of that dreadful accident forever."

Faye wanted to protest. Wanted to insist that this was her cross to bear. But then she thought about the new family living in the house where she'd grown up. Thought about Brenda and her busy life and her growing family. Thought about Piers's comment about what her family would have wanted for her.

Suddenly it was too hard to hold on to the guilt and the responsibility she'd borne on her shoulders for all this time. She felt a tremor rack her body, then another, and then the tears began to fall.

Brenda gathered her into her arms and held her as she wept. At some stage Brenda's husband entered the room but a fierce look from his wife sent him straight back out again. Eventually, Faye regained some semblance of control of her wayward emotions.

"I'm sorry," she said, blowing her nose on a wad of tissues Brenda had thrust into her hand. "I didn't come here to cry on your shoulder."

"I'm glad you did. You've needed it for far too long."

Her friend looked at her with concern in her eyes and a small frown creasing her forehead. "So, about that counselor?"

Faye found herself nodding. "Okay, yes. I think it's time."

"You won't regret it," Brenda said firmly, giving her hand another squeeze. "Now, let's go have a coffee and rescue Adam from the kitchen."

"Thank you, Bren. I mean that. I've missed you."

Her friend smiled back. "I've missed you, too. I'm glad you're back."

And she was. For the first time in forever, Faye felt as though she really was fighting her way back.

Fourteen

Piers hung up the phone and felt his body sag in relief. The adoption petition had been reviewed by the judge and his lawyer had assured him that despite the DNA findings two months ago, the adoption should still proceed unhindered.

Casey's mom had signed the papers and there'd been no protest from her family. Her ex had been tracked down in prison in Montana and had given his written and notarized statement that he wanted nothing to do with the baby. In fact, he had gone to great lengths to insist Casey wasn't his child and had refused to allow his DNA to be compared. Everything remained on the fast track his lawyer had promised.

Except he didn't feel as though he was on track at all. He felt as though he'd been derailed completely and he didn't quite know how to fill the chasm of Faye's absence. He'd tried to call her, if only to check on her to ensure she was okay, but there'd been no answer at her apartment and his calls to her cell had gone straight to voice mail. If he didn't think she was simply avoiding him, he would have asked his people to track her down. But surely he'd have heard by now if something had happened to her.

He tried to tell himself it wasn't his problem, but he couldn't let go of the concern. You didn't just turn love off like a faucet.

A sound at the door to his office made him turn around. Relief flooded through him as Faye stepped through the doorway. He didn't know what to say or to do. All he could do was stare at her as if he was afraid to look away in case she disappeared again.

"Hello, Piers," she said, looking straight at him.

"Long time no see," he said stiffly.

His eyes raked over her. Something was different about her, but he couldn't put his finger on it. Sure, her hair was slightly longer than it had been two months ago, but that wasn't it. There was something about her face, her expression, that had changed. She looked less severe somehow and it wasn't just because she wore her hair in long, loose waves that cascaded over her shoulders.

The last time he'd seen her hair unbound like that had been when they'd been in bed together back in December last year. She'd still been asleep and he'd had to force himself from the bed to attend to Casey. The memory sent a shaft of longing through him. They'd been so good together. But she'd chosen to leave him. Which made him want to know—what was she doing here now?

"Have you got a minute?" she asked shyly.

There was a hitch to her voice, betraying her nervousness. He was unused to seeing her like this. Soft. Unsure. Unguarded even. It made every one of his protective urges rise to the fore, compelling him to close that distance between them and to hold her in his arms and kiss her until every uncertainty was soothed and they were both senseless with need. Instead he stood his ground. He'd meant what he said two months ago. Every last word. If she couldn't commit to him fully and freely, they had no future.

Was the fact that she was here an indication that she was ready? That she'd found a way to pull down the walls she'd kept around herself for almost half her life? Was she ready to give her all? He wanted to believe it but, despite the open expression on her face, he couldn't read her.

"I can make time," he answered. "For you."

"Thank you. Do you, um, want to talk here?"

He looked around his office. "It's as good a place as any, isn't it?"

She firmed her lips and nodded.

"Would you rather go somewhere else? A restaurant, maybe?"

"No, this is fine. Can we…can we sit down?"

He'd never seen her this unsure of herself before. Her calm confidence had been such a strong part of who she was that he found himself worrying for what had caused this change in her.

"Sure," he said, gesturing to the twin sofas set adjacent to the window that looked out over the city.

He waited for her to sit, then took the other end of the sofa. "Can I get you anything?"

She shook her head. "I'm fine, but grab something if you want it."

"No, I'm good."

He stretched one arm across the back of the sofa and angled his body to face hers while he waited for her to speak. Silence thickened in the air between them, coercing him into saying something, anything, to fill it. But this was her time to speak, not his. He'd said all he could say the last time he'd seen her. Now it was her turn.

Faye cleared her throat and her fingers tangled with the strap of her purse. "How's Casey doing?"

"He's home today. He has a cold and I didn't think he should come into the office."

A glow of concern filled her eyes. "Poor wee guy. His first cold?"

"As far as I'm aware," Piers conceded. "He's pretty miserable."

Miserable had been an understatement. All blocked up, Casey had woken, crying, four times last night, which in turn had only made things worse. Jeremy had been on duty and between him and Piers they'd taken turns to soothe Casey back to sleep. Even so, it had been a tough night for all of them.

Faye twisted the purse strap into a tight coil, then let it go again before threading her fingers through the leather to start all over again.

Frustration bubbled to the surface for Piers. She'd come here of her own volition. There must be a reason for that. So why the hell didn't she just come out with what she wanted to say?

"I guess you're wondering why I'm here," Faye said in a rush.

Piers simply nodded.

Faye scooted to the edge of the sofa and put her bag on the floor, then she stood and stepped over to the window. With the afternoon light streaming around her, he could see she'd lost weight. Another point of concern but not his problem, he reminded himself firmly. Not unless she was willing to allow it to be.

"I'm sorry for leaving the way I did. I see my old desk is unused. Don't you have a new assistant yet?"

"Faye, you didn't come here to talk about whether or not I have a new assistant, did you? Because if so, I have somewhere I need to be."

She spun around to face him, worry streaking her pale face. "I'm holding you up? You should have said."

"I told you I could make time for you and I can—but please, get to the point of why you're here."

It pained him to be so blunt but he couldn't bear to have her beat around the bush any longer. He'd left message after message for her. Worried about her welfare, where she was, what she was doing. And she hadn't responded to him. Not even so much as an email or a text. It had alternately concerned and then angered him before rolling back to concern all over again. He hoped that whatever she was here to say, it would let him off this crazy roller coaster of emotion.

She drew in another breath. "Like I said, I'm sorry for how I left you. You deserved better than that, but I didn't know how to give it to you. I just knew I needed to get away, so I did. Just like you always said, I ran. Except this time, instead of running away from my problems, I decided to run right to the root of them. To face them."

"You went back to Michigan?"

Faye nodded and clasped her fingers tightly together. "It wasn't easy but I knew I had to face everything I'd left behind. One of my old high school friends—she's a doctor now—put me in touch with a grief counselor who has helped me put a lot of things into perspective."

"I see. And now?" he prompted when she fell silent again.

"Now I think I'm ready. Ready to be honest with myself and with you about everything. You see, I've been carrying so much guilt since the night of the crash. What I'd never told anyone before was that I'd been an absolute bitch to my stepdad in the weeks leading up to Christmas. He'd always done his best by me and always allowed me to take the lead in how our father-daughter relationship developed. To be honest, he was too good, too kind, too patient. For some stupid reason that made me lash out. Teenagers, huh?" She gave Piers a wry smile. "Anyway, when I started pestering him about allowing me to drive home from the carol singing I could see he was torn. I almost wanted him to say no, just so I'd have something to complain about."

"But he said yes," Piers said heavily.

Faye nodded again, her eyes washing with sudden tears. She wiped at them and accepted a handkerchief from Piers when he dragged it from his pocket.

"Thanks. I'm sorry. It seems in the past two months I've cried a lifetime of tears and I don't seem to be able to stop."

"It's okay, Faye. Sometimes we just need to let go."

"Do we? Do you?"

He thought of the days and nights he'd endured since she'd walked out on him, of the pain of losing her and not knowing where she was. It had been a different kind of grief to that of losing his brother, but it had been grief nonetheless.

"Yes, it's only natural. We might not like it, we might not be able to always control it, but sometimes we have to give in to it."

"That's another thing I've had to learn. And here I thought I was all grown up." Faye gave a self-deprecating laugh. "Anyway, I was doing okay on the road that night. Maybe going a little too fast for the conditions, but Ellis, my stepdad, just cautioned me gently to be aware of where I was and what I was doing. Henry was fussing in his car seat and Mom said he needed to be fed.

Ellis had just turned around to say something to Mom when I saw the tanker take a curve in the road in front of our car. He lost traction and jackknifed—then he slid straight into us.

"If I had been going slower, we'd have been farther back, I'd have had a longer time to react... Or, if I'd only let Ellis drive, we'd probably have been past that spot already, instead of wasting time bickering in the parking lot about who'd drive, and the truck would have missed us altogether."

"Faye, you can't torture yourself with the what-ifs and maybes. You don't know that it would have made any difference at all."

She wiped her eyes with his handkerchief again and nodded. "I understand that now, but fifteen-year-old me certainly didn't and, unfortunately, it has been fifteen-year-old me—still fighting to make sense of what I did— that's been driving my life for most of the past thirteen years."

Faye came back to the sofa and sat again. "I was told later that Ellis and Henry died on impact, but Mom and I were both trapped. The car caught fire almost immediately." She shuddered. "I still see the flames licking up over the hood and coming from under the dash. I can still smell my legs starting to burn. Mom was screaming in the back, telling the people who arrived on the scene to save her babies. Someone managed to drag Henry out in his car seat, but by that point, there was nothing they could do. Another man wrenched my door open and pulled me free. The last thing I remember is begging him to save my mom and dad—then I passed out. When I woke up, they told me I was the only survivor."

"It sounds like a nightmare. I'm so sorry you had to go through that, Faye."

She stared unseeingly out the window, her mind obviously lost back in that awful, tragic night. "It's taken me a long time to realize that so much of what happened was out of my control. It seemed like I should be able to blame someone for me losing my family—even if the only target I found was myself.

"When I helped with the babies at my foster home, they were my substitutes for the brother I lost. In them I saw that chance again to love him, to make up for what I'd done—until they left, anyway."

"It's why you were so reluctant to let yourself near Casey, isn't it? Because you were afraid of loving him and possibly losing him all over again," Piers said with sudden insight.

Faye inclined her head and clenched the sodden handkerchief in her hand. "My counselor has helped me understand why I behaved the way I did. Helped me realize that I was still trying to protect my teenage heart—the one that had lost everything and everyone. But she also helped me understand that it's okay to try again—to trust in my feelings and give them a chance to blossom. To open my heart to others. To accept that while things won't always work out, not everyone will be taken from me. It…it hasn't been easy and I'm not all the way there yet, but I'm determined to win this time. Because, if I don't, I will lose the most important thing in my life for good, if I haven't already."

Piers felt a spark of hope flicker to life in his chest. "And that is?"

"You," she answered simply. "You offered me your love—heck, you offered me everything that's always been missing since that night—and I was too afraid to take it. Too afraid to trust you. It was easier to walk—" Faye made a choked sound in her throat that almost sounded like a laugh "—okay, *run* away, than it was to accept what you promised me."

"And now?" he prompted.

"Now I want to be selfish. I want you. I want Casey. I want it all." She hesitated, uncertainty pulling her brows together and clouding her blue-gray eyes to the color of the sky on a stormy day. "If you'll still have me, that is. I know I've had my walls up and I know you've done your level best to scale them or break them down. I just hope you're still prepared to help me—to continue to fill the missing pieces in my life like you've been trying to do all along. Will you, Piers? Will you have me back?"

Piers reached out his hand and traced the line of her cheek, staring deeply into her eyes. He'd waited for these words, hoped against hope that one day she'd be ready to say them. But there was one thing still missing.

"Like I told you before, Faye, I want it all, not just pieces of you. Like you, I want everything, too. Maybe it's selfish of me, but I need to know you're in this all the way. It's been hell with you gone. Not just in the office, but here, too." He pounded a fist on his chest. "Some nights I couldn't sleep for wondering where you were or what you were doing. And every time Casey passed another milestone, I wanted to share it with you, and you weren't there."

Faye swallowed, the muscles in her slender throat working hard as she accepted what he had to say.

"I can only say I'm so sorry I've hurt you, Piers. I love you and I never want to hurt you in any way ever again."

All the tension he'd been holding in his body released on those oh-so-important three little words. She loved him. It was enough. He knew Faye wasn't the kind of person to toss that simple phrase around lightly. If she said it, she meant it.

"I know you never will. As long as you love me, I will have everything I ever need," he murmured.

Piers pulled her into his arms, every nerve in his body leaping from the sheer joy of having her back where she belonged.

"You know I'm going to want to formalize this. You're going to have to marry me," he pressed. "And you're going to have to adopt Casey, too. We come as a package deal, you know."

"Marry you? Are you sure?"

She sounded hesitant but it only took a second for Piers to realize she wasn't stalling because of her own feelings, more that she was seeking confirmation of his.

"Completely and utterly certain," he said firmly. "It might surprise you to know, I've never told anyone that I loved them. Ever. Except for you. It was a leap of faith when I admitted to you how I felt. You'd become such an integral part of so many aspects of my life that I didn't blame you for accusing me of using the L-word to manipulate you into staying with me. But admitting I loved you came as a bolt out of the blue for me and, once I understood it, I knew that would never change. You're it, for me. The first, the last, the only."

"Oh, Piers!" Faye lifted a hand to cup his cheek and a sweet smile tugged at her lips. "You've given me so much already and now this? I'm so very lucky to have you in my life. I never want to spend a day without you by my side. So, I guess that means you forgive me for running out on you?"

"I will forgive you anything provided you never leave me again."

"I never will," she promised and pulled his face to hers.

* * * * *